A STEP TOWARDS FALLING

Cammie McGovern is the author of *Amy & Matthew: A Love Story* (US title. *Say What You Will*), as well as the adult novels *Neighborhood Watch*, *Eye Contact* and *The Art of Seeing*. She is one of the founders of Whole Children, a resource centre that runs after-school classes and programmes for children with special needs. She currently lives in the US with her husband and three sons, the oldest of whom is autistic. Cammie's sister is Elizabeth McGovern, one of

Also by Cammie McGovern

Amy & Matthew

A STEP TOWARDS FALLING

CAMMIE McGOVERN

MACMILLAN

For everyone who has ever worked at
Whole Children/Milestones, and for every family
who has come through the door and found a home.

And especially for Carrie,
who started it all. . . .

First published in the US 2015 by HarperTeen, an imprint of HarperCollins Publishers
First published in the UK 2015 by Macmillan Children's Books

This edition published 2016 by Macmillan Children's Books
an imprint of Pan Macmillan
20 New Wharf Road, London N1 9RR
Associated companies throughout the world
www.panmacmillan.com

ISBN 978-1-4472-8021-7

1 3 5 7 9 8 6 4 2

A CIP catalogue record for this book is available from the British Library.

Typography by Sarah Creech and Alicia Mikles
Printed and bound by CPI Group (UK) Ltd, Croydon CR0 4YY

CHAPTER ONE
EMILY

AT OUR FIRST MEETING with the director of the Lifelong Learning Center, Lucas doesn't speak to me once. Elaine, the director, thanks us for "volunteering our time" even though she knows we aren't here voluntarily. We all know this.

"You have a choice," she says. "You can come in Saturday mornings and do office work or you can come Wednesday evenings for a class called Boundaries and Relationships that goes over basic rules about socializing and dating for young adults with developmental disabilities. Even though you're a few years younger, you'll provide examples of a typical peer's approach to friendships and dating. They'll be interested in what you do on dates and how you go about making new friends, that kind of thing."

I can just imagine what my friend Richard will say when I tell him this: "Wait, they're looking at *you* as a dating role model?"

I turn and look at Lucas. I expect him to say, "I'll take the office work, please." All things considered, the idea of sitting with a group of young adults with disabilities looking for dates seems like—well, like more than either one of us bargained on. Except here's the surprise: I want to do the class. I'm terrible at office work. Plus, I'm curious.

Then, before I can say anything, Lucas announces: "Yeah, I'll do the class." He doesn't even look at me. He seems to be pretending I'm not in the room.

"I will, too," I say. I'm not going to do office work just because sitting in the same room with Lucas will be super awkward. Forget that.

The following Wednesday, we come in an hour before class starts to meet with Mary, who teaches the class, and go over what she expects from us. Apparently not too much, at least in the beginning. She says we'll mostly do the activities along with the group. "We do a few role-plays every class and I may ask you to join some of those. Do either one of you have acting experience?"

I glance at Lucas, who still refuses to look at me. "No," he says.

"Some," I say. "When I was younger. Not for a while."

Mary smiles at me like she can tell that I'll probably be better at this than Lucas. Lucas plays football at our school, meaning he's huge and—not to be mean—a little scary-looking.

"Wonderful, Emily," Mary says now. "Do you have any improv experience?"

"A little," I say. "I was in a comedy troupe once, except

we weren't very funny." In middle school, the drama club tried to start an improv group. We lasted one semester and then gave up.

Mary laughs. "Oh, I know all about that. Don't worry, we're not playing for laughs here, thank heavens."

We finish up with twenty minutes before class starts, so Mary tells us to wait in the lobby until the other students arrive. It's awkward, of course, as sitting in every waiting room with Lucas has been for the last two weeks. He pulls out his phone as he always does. I pull out a book as I always do. After five minutes, I can't stand it anymore and lean toward him.

"I'm Emily, by the way. I know you're Lucas, but maybe you don't know my name, so there you have it. Emily."

He looks up. "I know your name."

Richard always warns me not to get too sarcastic with people who have no visible sense of humor. "They don't take it well," he tells me. "They think you're making fun of them. Because usually you are." But I can't help it.

"Oh, okay. Well, as long as we're doing this together for the rest of the semester, I just thought I'd make sure. We don't need to be friends or anything, but maybe the odd hello wouldn't kill us."

"I don't know about that," Lucas says, twisting around in his chair. "This may kill us. We'll have to see."

I can hear Richard's voice in the back of my head: *You shouldn't go around telling stupid people what you think all the time. First of all, they won't understand what you're saying because they're stupid. Secondly, they'll hate you.*

I want to, though. I want to say, *Look, Lucas, why don't we try and do this thing right? Why don't we acknowledge the guilt we both feel about Belinda by doing a decent job here?* Maybe for Lucas I should say it differently: *Why don't you stop being such a jerk about this?*

Mary comes out before I can say anything more: "Hello again! This group usually comes in the back door so they're all here, ready to meet you guys."

We stand up and suddenly I'm more nervous than I expected to be. I don't know any people with disabilities. I'm not sure why I thought this would be a good idea.

Mary walks us up the hallway and opens the door to a brightly painted room with about a dozen people sitting in a circle. It's pretty obvious they're all disabled. Though no one's in a wheelchair, they all look a little different. One woman is wearing a bright lime-colored sweater, sweat pants, and flip-flops. Another man is wearing a wool hat and gloves on his hands though it isn't cold in the room, or outside for that matter.

"Okay, everyone, I want to introduce Emily and Lucas. They'll be our new volunteers for this session. They're both in high school, which means they're a little younger than you folks, so you remember what that means?" She smiles as if they have an inside joke about high schoolers.

Apparently they do, because a ripple of laughter travels through the group.

Mary keeps going: "It means you're not going to say anything too shocking, especially not on their first day, right, Simon? Right, Thomas?" Everyone laughs again.

4

"Okay, what do we do when new folks join our class?"

Two hands go up. The woman in the green sweater says, "Ast the kesah."

Lucas and I almost look at each other, then don't. It's impossible to understand what she's saying.

"That's right, Francine," Mary says. "Everyone gets to ask them one question each. Who would like to go first?"

Six hands shoot up. Mary laughs. "Remember, they have to be *appropriate* questions." Two hands go down. Mary laughs again. "Okay. Sheila, why don't you start?"

A tall woman with curly brown hair stands up and twirls around in a circle so her skirt flies out a little. "This is a question for the girl. Do you know my friend Susan?"

I look at Mary. *Am I supposed to know Susan?* "I don't think so. Is she in this class?"

"No, but I could introduce you! Do you want to meet Susan?"

"That's two questions, Sheila," a man with thick glasses seated beside her says. He looks like he probably has Down syndrome. "Mary said one question each."

Mary nods. "I *did* say that, Sheila. I'm sorry. You can ask Emily your second question at break. Thomas, do you have a question for Lucas or Emily?"

"Yes." The man sitting next to Sheila stands and looks at the ceiling as he speaks. "This is for the boy. Do you have any favorite movies or TV shows or activities?" He sits back down.

"Um, let me think—" Lucas says. His voice sounds strange, almost breathy. I wonder if Lucas is as nervous as I am. I don't know what I was expecting, but now that I'm here, these people suddenly seem—well, *really* disabled. One is blind, judging by the cane he has laid sideways across his lap. Another is paying more attention to picking his nose than to anything we're saying.

"I play football so I practice most afternoons," Lucas continues, and I'm surprised. He *is* nervous. I can tell by the way he's wiping the palms of his hands on his shirtfront. "So I don't get to watch a lot of movies or TV shows."

Another hand goes up. "What team do you play for?"

"Westchester High," he says. In any other crowd, hearing this would produce a few whistles, or some applause, because we are currently the undefeated leaders of our division, headed toward the first state championship our school has ever had. By "we" of course I mean the football team, which I have no friends on and no relationship to. Still, you can't walk down the same locker-lined halls and not know the stats. Everyone's a little starry-eyed around our football players this year.

Everyone except this crowd, apparently, because no one says anything.

After this, the questions get more random. Have we ever been to the Grand Canyon? Do we know how to make lasagna? Did we know that one person in the class won a gold medal in the Special Olympics?

At this, Lucas raises his eyebrows in surprise. *"Really?"* he says, sounding genuinely impressed. "Who?"

A short woman with a bowl haircut raises her hand. "It was *Winter* Olympics for *bowling*." She sighs heavily, as if she's a little tired of talking about it.

Lucas laughs. It's the first time I've ever him seen do this. I'm not sure if I'm imagining this, but it seems like talking about football, then getting *off* the topic of football, has put him in a better mood. "A gold medal!" he says. "That's really great."

After everyone has asked their question, Mary tells us there's a second tradition for new volunteers. While the rest of the class works on another activity, Lucas and I will each be paired with one class member who will interview us so we can be introduced in a fuller way at the end of class.

"Great!" I say too loudly because I don't want her to see how nervous this makes me. I don't know if Mary realizes about half these people are almost impossible to understand. We only got through their questions because she was here, translating. Luckily, I get paired with Harrison, the blind one, who is easy to understand.

Mary points to two desk chairs in the corner and says, "Emily will show you where you're going, Harrison." She puts his hand on my elbow and he stands up. I'm surprised at what a relief this feels like, leading him across the room. *I can do this,* I think. *I can be a decent helper.* Then we sit down in two desks facing each other and for a long time, neither one of us, it seems, can think of anything to say. After a fairly excruciating silence, he says, "Okay, so do you like Wiffle ball?"

"Um. I don't think I've ever played it."

He nods. "Okay."

There's another long silence, as if, as far as Harrison's

concerned, we're now done with the interview. Finally I lean forward and whisper, "Do you want to ask me something else?"

"No," he says. "It's your turn."

"Oh." I look over at Lucas and his partner and realize he's right. Apparently we're meant to be interviewing each other, because Lucas is asking his partner a question. "What do you like to do?"

Harrison shrugs. "I don't know. Eat, I guess."

"Okay. Do you have any hobbies?"

"It's my turn."

"Oh, right, sorry."

"Do you have any hobbies?"

Now that he's asking me, I realize it's a hard question. I'm a high school senior taking three AP courses with college applications hovering over me like a black cloud. I co-chair our school's Youth Action Coalition with my friend Richard, which I feel very committed to but don't think of as a hobby really. I start to explain all this, but Harrison stops me. "Okay, that's enough. Your turn to ask a question." Of course that's enough. He's blind and has no way to write anything down.

I look over at Lucas to see if he's faring better with his partner. It seems like he is, but he got Francine, the bowling gold medalist, who is friendly and easy to talk to.

"How long have you been taking this class?" I ask. Mary had told us most students have been in this class for at least a year, so they know one another pretty well.

"Six years," Harrison says. "Technically, six years and

fourteen weeks."

"So you like it?"

"I like some parts of it. Some parts I don't like. My turn to ask a question."

"Right. Sorry."

"How long have you been taking this class?"

"Well—" Now I'm desperate. I look over at Lucas, who seems to be sharing a great joke with Francine. He's laughing and pointing to her piece of paper. "Just write it," he's saying.

"This is my first day!" I say with a fake laugh so it will look like Harrison and I are having fun, too. "I'm new, remember?"

He pulls his earlobe. "That's right. I forgot."

I don't know if he's mad about me laughing but he falls silent as if he is. "Do you want to ask me anything else?" I finally say. I feel terrible. I thought I would be good at this—or better than Lucas Kessler, at least—but apparently I'm wrong. I'm awkward and self-conscious and I have terrible instincts. I wonder what Harrison will say when he introduces me. In this group, there seems to be a tendency toward honesty that worries me.

"I only have one more question."

"Okay!" I say hopefully. Maybe this will be a breakthrough—he'll ask about school or what I'd like to do in the future.

"Why are you volunteering in this class?"

My face goes red. I don't know why it didn't occur to me that someone might ask this. Obviously I should have an answer prepared, but I don't. I can't get any words to come out of my mouth.

Harrison nods as if he understands. He may be blind but he's seen all he needs to of me.

Mary waits until the end of class to have our partners introduce us. She asks Lucas's partner, Francine, to go first. "Lucas is eighteen years old and is pretty good-looking even though he's very, very humongous. He likes cats, some TV show I never heard of, and football. He also plays football, but not for the Patriots. He plays for some school but I can't remember the name. His favorite food is . . ." She squints down at the paper. "I don't know. I can't read what I wrote."

He leans across his chair-desk and whispers in her ear.

"Really?" she says. Everyone laughs. "Meatloaf, I guess. But I don't know why."

Everyone claps. Francine smiles and takes a bow.

"Thank you for doing a wonderful job with that, Francine," Mary says. "Harrison, your turn to introduce Emily." My heart races as he stands up. I wonder if he'll say, *Emily seems like she feels very uncomfortable being here.*

But he doesn't. Instead, he says, "The week Emily was born in 1996, the number-one hit song on the Billboard charts was 'Because You Loved Me,' by Celine Dion."

I'm stunned. As we finished our interview, he asked for my birthday with the year, but could this possibly be right? Everyone laughs and claps as if this is another inside joke. Harrison smiles, bows, and sits back down. Mary asks what my birthday is and goes over to her desk in the corner to check on an iPad. "You're right, Harrison! Well done, sir!"

Everyone claps again, this time with a few whistles.

I'm not sure what just happened. Apparently Harrison isn't just blind, he has a savant's ability to memorize the entire history of Billboard number-one songs and their dates. It wasn't about me, but it also wasn't terrible. We've gotten through it fine, or at least everyone has overlooked the awful job I just did my first day in this class.

BELINDA

LATELY I'VE BEEN WATCHING *Pride and Prejudice* a lot. Not the new version starring Keira Knightly, but the old one that takes longer to watch and stars Colin Firth. It's the only boxed DVD set that Nan owns but she says that's okay, it's the only DVD set she needs. Nan loves Mr. Darcy who is also Colin Firth and so do I.

Lately I've been watching it all day long instead of going to school.

I go to Westchester High School but this is my last year, which means I am supposed to be having a great time. My first day of school this year Mom played a song called "Anticipation," because she wanted to make me feel less nervous. The singer kept saying, "Stay right here 'cause these are the good old days," which made me think maybe I should stay right there at home and not get on the school bus because sometimes at school, I do *not* feel like these are the good old days.

I got on the bus, though. Then I sat where I always sit, in the first seat behind the driver. Some years the driver changes and instead of a man named Carl, we have a woman named Sue. Even if this happens, though, I never change where I sit, which is right behind the driver. Behind the driver means no bus jerks can make fun of me or do their jokes where they pretend to be my friend and then give me candy that's been on the dirty bus floor. Behind the driver means I usually sit near seventh graders who are scared, too.

I've been going to school so long it shouldn't scare me anymore but sometimes it does. Before the first day of school, Nan reminds me of the things I love about school, like my job in the main office, which is sorting paper for recycling and delivering mail. Nan also makes a list of all the teachers I love like Rhonda, Carla, and Ms. Culpepper. By then, I usually remember other things I love like the mandarin oranges from the cafeteria, the art display cases, and listening to band practice. Nan helps me remember those things better than Mom, who tries but sometimes forgets stuff.

Now everything is different. Now Nan is trying to help me forget. Instead of going to school, she lets me stay home every day and watch *Pride and Prejudice*. If Mom asks her when I'm going to go back to school, Nan says, "For God's sake, Lauren, let her be. At least we know she's safe here."

Usually Mom and Nan don't fight in front of me.

Usually they don't fight much because Mom has limitations and depression. Mom does what she can to help me but I don't need much anymore so she doesn't do a lot. For instance, I used to make my own lunch and pack it in my zipper lunch bag. But that was back when I went to school and took a lunch. Now I don't go to school anymore so I don't pack my lunch either.

I watch the screen, where Jane is trying not to cry after Mr. Bingley leaves town without saying so much as a word. Just watching her try not to cry makes me start to cry. Even in *Pride and Prejudice* people are mean. They don't think about other people's feelings. Usually I like imagining I am Elizabeth, but today I close my eyes and feel just like Jane, who thought she'd made a friend and turned out to be wrong.

Sometimes I do things that make other people have uncomfortable thoughts. If I talk too much about Colin Firth, for instance, it gives teachers uncomfortable thoughts. Once Rhonda, my speech therapist, told me her uncomfortable thought: "I'm bored with Colin Firth! I don't know him. He lives far away and I don't want to talk about him anymore!"

We both laughed even though I didn't think what she said was funny. I can't imagine being bored with Colin Firth. That's because I love him and sometimes when he looks out at me from inside the TV screen, I'm pretty sure he loves me, too.

I know I'm not supposed to say this out loud. Because then people will think many uncomfortable thoughts like

I'm crazy. They'll say I've never met Mr. Firth and that means he can't love me. And I'd have to say what my mom told me: that love is a *feeling*. And you don't always kiss people you love. "Sometimes you just love them," she said.

When I asked her, "Does that mean they love me, too?" she said, "Oh sure, Belinda. Everyone loves you."

I think she meant teachers at school mostly, but I think it could also mean Colin Firth. When he looks at me, I feel it. I just do. I know it in my heart.

Rhonda, my speech teacher, doesn't agree: "He's a character. He's not real. He's on TV but TV isn't real."

I'm not sure what to say to that. To me he's real. Doesn't that make him real?

I don't always watch *Pride and Prejudice*. Sometimes I watch different old movies. I like *Gone with the Wind* and *The Sound of Music* except I don't like it when Maria and the Captain kiss because he's too old and looks like her father. I like Liesl and Rolfe's song even though Rolfe turns out to be a Nazi which is a terrible thing to be. In my mind afterward, I make him not a Nazi and I let them get married and live happily after.

Same with Scarlett from *Gone with the Wind*. In the beginning she loves Ashley who has a girl's name but is a man. Ashley is very nice but doesn't love her back. Then she meets Rhett who is dangerous and handsome and loves her right away. In my imagination, I make Ashley change his mind and decide to love Scarlett. Then she'll have someone she knows she can count on. She can't count on Rhett. He is exciting but not dependable. Sometimes exciting is exactly what you *don't* want in a boy.

I learned this from other movies about exciting but undependable boys. You have to be careful with them because a lot of times they're handsome, too. So that's confusing.

"I get around some of those men—they're so handsome, I can't talk," Mom says. "I mean it. My tongue gets all dry. It's like someone put glue in my mouth."

I know this feeling. I have it every time I watch *Pride and Prejudice* starring Colin Firth. I can't talk at all. Sometimes I try to watch without blinking and I can't do that either. I get light-headed which my mom says happened to her once on a date. When she stood up to go to the ladies' room, she fell back into her chair and felt embarrassed.

"That's what happens when I like the man," Mom says. "I don't act very likeable."

I know how this is. I've had it in real life, too, not just watching Colin Firth. I felt it every time I was around Ron Moody. Sometimes, just being near him, I felt like I wanted to laugh and cry at the same time. Or my heart might explode.

I didn't feel like myself. I felt like someone having a heart attack. Except it happened every time I saw him so it wasn't a real heart attack. It was love. That's what Mom said when I told her about him. "You're in love, Belinda, and that's a wonderful, special feeling . . ."

She didn't say it was bad to feel that way, or wrong. She didn't even say, "Be careful, Belinda," which she probably should have. She said, "You deserve love as much as anyone else," which got me confused for a while. It made me think maybe Ron loved me, too.

EMILY

THE TRUTH ABOUT LUCAS—AND why we're being punished—is a little more complicated than I want to admit to anyone, especially Richard, who loves to hate what he calls "the heteronormative class structure embodied by the football team." I'm not sure exactly what he means by this, except for the obvious part. Football players have too much power at our school, especially this year with their winning record. I've seen lunch ladies wave them through the line without paying a dime for a full tray of food. I've seen kids they don't know buy them sodas and carry their backpacks; anything to win three seconds of a football player's approval.

Richard thinks our group of friends is different but we aren't really. We might not prostrate ourselves to win the football team's attention, but we still spend some amount of time every lunch period staring over at their table. Just because we can *see* the problem doesn't mean we aren't part of it.

Lucas and I have never talked about what happened with Belinda, so I have no idea if he feels guilty the way I do or if he feels like he's being unfairly punished. I assume it's the latter—that he thinks what happened was terrible, of course, but not his fault. At the very least, he probably thinks it's more my fault than his, which—though I don't admit this to anyone—might be true.

It's still hard for me to understand what happened.

On the surface, it's a simple story. Three weeks ago, I was at a home game with my four best friends: Richard, Barry, Weilin, and Candace. Ordinarily we aren't big football fans, but this year everyone goes to home games. Every week, with every victory, the crowds get bigger.

That night, I was in a terrible mood, though I feel stupid admitting it now. Toby Schulz, a boy I thought I'd been flirting with for the last two weeks with funny texts and Facebook messages, was sitting two rows down from us, on a clear and obvious date with Jenny Birdwell, a cute sophomore with a blond ponytail. Three days earlier he'd sent me a message saying, "We should do something some time," which I had stupidly thought meant *with each other.* Apparently it didn't. Apparently it meant *we should sit near each other at a football game and wave hi while I'm on a date with someone else.*

It wasn't that I was so in love with Toby. He'd seemed smart and a little more engaged than our typical new recruits to Youth Action Coalition, who usually show up angry about one issue and bored by all the others. At the first meeting Toby came to, he stayed after to say he was impressed by the range of our "actions" and all "the cool things we were up to." He had curly brown hair and slightly crooked teeth that for some reason made him even cuter. LGBT support wasn't his main issue, he told us, not looking at Richard, but he was certainly on board with that. His main issue was the environment. He loved backpacking and wanted the mountains to still be around for his children to enjoy. How could I *not* get a crush on him? And when he messaged me three times over the next week, how could I *not* think maybe he liked me back?

If I'm being honest, though, I'd have to admit: it wasn't Toby being there with a cute sophomore that bothered me as much as a long series of Toby-like misjudgments on my part. It felt like I kept making the same mistakes over and over—thinking classroom joking was flirtation, thinking guys who asked for my phone number to get a homework assignment wanted my phone number more than they wanted the assignment.

I partly blame Richard for this. He loves to pretend that everyone is at least a little bit gay and might have a crush on him. He'll sit beside Wayne Cartwright, our gorgeous quarterback, in the main office waiting for a late pass and claim their arm hairs were reaching out for each other. He knows nothing will happen but he still dwells on these moments. "Arm hairs don't lie. They can't, actually. They don't have individual brains. Just instincts."

For him it's funny. Nobody expects Wayne Cartwright to miraculously come out of the closet and mix arm hairs with Richard, but when I try to dream big and jokingly say, "I think Toby Schulz wants to ask me out, but he's too shy," it's sad the next week to sit behind the evidence of how unshy he is. Richard didn't say anything, which made me feel even more pathetic, if that was possible. Like suddenly I'd become someone people tiptoed around.

This is one of my explanations for what happened that night. Not an excuse or a justification. Just a way for me to understand how I could be such a disappointment to myself. Toward the end of half time, I slipped away from my group to buy a soda at the snack stand and on the way back to my seat, I started to cry. Ridiculous, embarrassing tears of self-pity. I never cry in public—ever—and I didn't want my friends to see, so I went around the back of the bleachers. I thought if I let myself cry for a minute, I'd get it out of my system and be fine for the second half.

Then I couldn't find my way back. I was near the field house where the players spend half time. It was late; the team had run onto the field to thunderous applause five minutes earlier. We were behind by seven points, which was different for us. We'd gotten so used to winning by comfortable margins that the crowd was anxious and screaming and stamping their feet.

Even with all the commotion, though, I heard a strange noise under the bleachers. It sounded like an animal. A dog maybe, who'd fallen and was stuck in the latticework below the bleachers. That made no sense, of course, but that's what it sounded like. It was dark under the bleachers, and striped with light, which meant my eyes took a minute to adjust. I couldn't see anything at first, so I moved closer. *It must be a dog,* I thought. I could hear a whimpering sound. Then gradually, in the darkness, two figures took shape. I recognized one. Belinda Montgomery, a girl I'd known years earlier in a children's theater program, was pressed against a fence with a boy standing in front of her. It looked like her hair was caught and her dress was torn. For a second I thought: *She's stuck on the fence and he's lifting her off.*

Nothing else made sense. The last time I saw her, she was playing Little Red Riding Hood.

Then I realized the boy was Mitchell Breski, someone who'd been arrested once at our school and taken away in a police car. We never knew for what, but there were plenty of rumors, mostly about drugs. Knowing that much made the whole scene more frightening and, somehow, less comprehensible. *Wait,* I kept thinking. *Wait a minute.*

I should have screamed that, I know now.

I should have screamed *anything* to make it clear this didn't seem right. I *knew* Belinda, but my brain couldn't process what it was seeing: her pressed against the fence like that, powerless behind him. They couldn't have been a couple, couldn't have even been friends. I should have said her name. I should have called out, "Belinda, is that you?" even if I hadn't said hello to her once in the last three years. I didn't do that, though. I was struck mute in that instant and I remember very little after that. I know that at some point, a football player ran out from the locker room, which must have jolted me momentarily out of my panic. Maybe I thought, *It's okay to leave because he's here now and will take care of this.* I honestly don't remember.

I know I staggered out from under the bleachers to a roar of noise and light from the crowd. I know I found a teacher, Mrs. Avery, wearing a scarf and pompom earrings, screaming "DEFENSE!" between cupped hands, and I touched her elbow. "There's something happening under the bleachers!" I said. The roar behind us got bigger.

"WHAT?" she yelled.

"There's something happening. To a girl. Under the bleachers." My heartbeat was louder than my voice at that point.

All at once, everyone in the stands was up on their feet screaming. Later I learned, we'd made an interception and carried the ball for a forty-five-yard run. We'd taken a losing game and turned it around. Everyone was ecstatic— screaming and hugging and pounding their feet.

Then I saw the football player from under the bleachers jog onto the field and felt a great flood of relief. *He took care of it,* I thought. *He stopped whatever was about to happen.*

I sat for a few minutes so my heart could slow down. When it did, I walked back to the far end of the bleachers where I'd just come from and saw the flashing lights of a police car pulsing red in the parking lot near the snack stand. I was surprised at first and then relieved by what it meant: *Yes, the football player called the police.*

I didn't sleep much that night, which meant my nerves were raw when I read the newspaper the next morning and saw a small article on the fourth page under the headline INCIDENT BRINGS POLICE TO HIGH SCHOOL FOOTBALL GAME. Neither student was named, nor were many details given, but seeing the headline made me break down on the spot and confess to my parents what had happened. "I saw this. I walked in on it and—I don't know what happened—I froze. I didn't do anything."

My parents were quick to reassure me. "You were frightened for your safety, sweetheart. You were following your instincts. No one can blame you for that."

"Yes, they can," I told my mother. The more I thought about it, the worse my actions seemed. "I didn't help her. I ran away and let the other guy take care of it. It was terrible."

My mother tried to argue with me, but what could she say? I *hadn't* done anything. Finally she squeezed my hand and said, "Well, thank heavens that other boy was there. It sounds like the girl is going to be fine and it's time for everyone to put this behind us. It's *okay*, Em. Next time will be different."

It was impossible to know if Belinda *was* okay. I didn't see her in school, but then our paths hardly ever crossed, so maybe that didn't mean much. That whole week afterward, I looked for her at school, wandering past the Life Skills classroom where I assumed she spent most of her day. I never saw her, but I saw some of her classmates, joking around with one another, wearing aprons one morning. When one of them looked up and saw me, I asked, "Is Belinda here?"

"No," he said. "We haven't seen Beminda in a while."

What else could I do to find out if she was okay? Instead of going to lunch that day, I stood outside the athletic office and studied the roster of football players. I wanted to figure out which player had saved her. I hadn't seen his face but I remembered his number, which meant it was Lucas Kessler, who I'd never had a class with and didn't know except for his size. I remembered someone once saying he wore size sixteen shoes that he had to special order because no one mass-produced shoes like that.

It wasn't until the end of that day, when a summons to the guidance counselor told me I would no longer wrestle with my guilt in private but would have to discuss it— extensively, with various authorities, as it turned out— that I also learned this: I wasn't alone. Lucas hadn't done anything either.

It took another week to get the whole story, but when I finally did, I could hardly believe it. It turned out Belinda had saved herself.

CHAPTER TWO
BELINDA

Pride and Prejudice has many parts that I love. My favorites aren't the same as Nan's favorites and sometimes she talks right straight through my favorite parts even though I'm careful and never do that to her. It especially bothers me when she makes me answer her questions because I don't want Mr. Firth to look out from the TV and see me not paying attention to his show.

Nan says he can't see me and I shouldn't be ridiculous, he doesn't even know who I am. Mom says you never know, he might have read one of the letters I've written to him. The first time I wrote him a letter, he sent me a typed note thanking me for my letter and saying if I want an autographed picture I should write him back and enclose a self-addressed stamped envelope.

I wanted to do that, but then I worried that if I got an autographed picture I might have a hard time thinking about anything else. I know I would stare at it all the time and worry about something happening to it. I'm not sure I could fall asleep in the same room with an autographed picture of Mr. Firth, but if I had one, I couldn't imagine sleeping in a *different* room. I'd want to frame it of course and Mom would probably say frames are too much money, just use a sheet of plastic, which would upset me. Nan would probably buy me a frame but not a very nice one. She'd get one from CVS where she goes once a week to get her prescriptions filled. It would have plastic instead of glass and price stickers on it and it would make me sad to put Mr. Firth in something like that. Then Nan would say she lives on Social Security and what do I expect?

I decided it was better not to get any picture at all than to get something so special that it would only create problems, so I never sent him a self-addressed stamped envelope but I have kept writing him letters, usually about once a month.

I've told him about my family situation and a little about my health. He's one of the few people who know that as a baby I had three operations on my heart. I don't talk about that with other people because I don't like to think about being in hospitals. After a year of writing to him, though, it was something I thought he should know about me.

I've also told him a few hard stories about my life. I always get the feeling he isn't bothered by hearing them. I told him the terrible things that happened on the school bus when I first started riding it in seventh grade. How people pretended to be my friend so they could take my milk money and food from my lunch. That went on for a long time before I could figure out how to stop it.

I couldn't tell anyone at school because the kids on the bus would say, "Don't tell anyone, okay?" Then I thought of something smart. They hadn't told me not to *write* anyone. I have always been a very good typist even though I have problems with my eyes and reading is hard for me. When I was in elementary school, I did a program called *Type to Learn* every day. My fingers memorized where the letters were and now if I have to, I can type with my eyes closed. Usually I don't do this, though. I keep my eyes open and put the font on very big so I can see if I've made any mistakes, which happens a lot. Still, I like keyboard practice and sometimes it's my reward at school for getting the rest of my work done. The computer knows when I start and stop. Afterward, it can tell me how fast I've typed a paragraph and how many mistakes I've made. Then once, right in the middle of my timed test, I thought: "My fingers can type what my mouth isn't allowed to say."

So they did. They typed: *Boys are stealing my lunch and my money every day on the bus.* For that timed test, I had 321 mistakes which made the teacher wonder what happened and read what I had typed. I was surprised. She understood right away what my fingers were saying. She hugged me and said she'd get to the bottom of this, which she did.

Later, she told me I could either ride a special van for other kids with disabilities or have my own reserved seat on the regular bus behind the driver with a monitor who would sometimes ride with me. I had never ridden on the special needs van because Nan says I'm not disabled like

26

those kids are. I'm just a little disabled. I'm slow at learning things like math which I can't do at all. I tried to learn addition and subtraction for a long time until I got to tenth grade and the teachers finally said, "That's enough. Let's quit trying to learn addition and subtraction." Instead I worked on life skills math like telling time and counting money which is also hard for me. Even though Nan doesn't like the van with all the disabled kids, she wanted me to ride it so I could be safe, but Mom said leaving the bus forever would be like letting mean boys win. So I kept riding the regular bus, in my new seat. I wrote Mr. Firth about all of this because I was proud of myself. And the next time I watched *Pride and Prejudice*, he looked at me in a new way. As if he was a little bit sad but also proud of me.

I haven't written him yet about what happened to me at the football game because I don't want to worry him. I also don't know what I would say. Even if I went back to school where the only computers I can use are, I don't think my fingers would know what to type.

Recently I'm starting to think Mr. Firth is looking at me different again. Like he's wondering why I'm spending so much time watching him and not going to school. Like maybe he already knows the real reason even though I haven't written a letter and told him.

Today I look down and realize that even though I'm watching *Pride and Prejudice*, I'm wearing a T-shirt and pajama bottoms. Also, my hair isn't brushed.

I don't know why I haven't realized this before.

I'm so embarrassed, I turn off the TV and start to cry. Nan rushes in and says, "Belinda! What is it? You've scared me to death!"

I can't tell her why I'm crying. That I can't keep watching *Pride and Prejudice* in my pajamas because I'm scared Mr. Firth will look out and see me and I don't want him to be disappointed.

Nan helps me sit down and brings me water. I don't remember how long it's been since I've gone to school. I don't remember if I've gotten dressed at all but I don't think I have. Which means it's been a few weeks at least that Mr. Firth has seen me watching him in my pajamas. My heart keeps beating fast but finally, after a long time, I calm down enough to speak. "I have to get dressed," I say.

The next day I do.

My clothes are loose and my hair is longer than the last time I looked in a mirror. I'm so surprised at this I almost don't recognize myself. I look in the mirror and talk to see if my lips move. They do. It *is* me. "Hello," I say to the mirror. "My name is Belinda."

Seeing myself talk makes me cry again. I don't know if I'll ever look like the old me. I wish we had more pictures of the old me so I could remember what I used to look like but Mom doesn't have a camera and Nan says cameras have gotten too complicated for her. We have my school pictures framed along the wall but they don't look like the real me. In most of those, my smile is nervous, which means I don't remember what the real old me looked like. Maybe when Mr. Firth squinted from the TV, he wasn't worried, he just didn't recognize me.

Because my old clothes don't fit, I wear Nan's clothes around the house. Nan mostly wears dresses with matching belts and skirts with white shirts that button up. "In my day," she always says, "ladies never wore pants except to work in the garden." Usually this makes Mom stick her finger down her throat and lie down on the sofa. Wearing dresses makes me feel different, but not bad. I like the flowered prints and the little matching belts. One morning I try wearing nylons and orthopedic shoes like Nan, too, but those don't feel right. I like wearing the dresses, though. They make me feel like someone in an old fashioned story. Not *Pride and Prejudice* but something else. A story I haven't seen yet.

Sometimes I'll wear one of Nan's dresses and imagine people calling my name again. I picture boys saying, "Belinda! Hello! Look at you in that dress!"

It makes me feel hopeful and then I remember about not leaving the house and not going back to school ever again. I don't know when I'll see people who might say hello or comment on my clothes.

Even though I'm getting dressed now, nothing changes much except I let myself watch *Pride and Prejudice* again.

It's hard to be sure, but I think Mr. Firth notices my dress. He squints in the middle of one of his lines and then he stops speaking. It makes me smile. I almost stand up to show him the whole dress, but he has to get on with the story and I don't want to waste time either.

The first time Nan walks in the room and sees *Pride and Prejudice* back on, she says, "Oh good," then turns around and walks back out. She's happy because it means she doesn't have to worry about me all day if I'm busy with this.

EMILY

IN MY FIRST MEETING with the guidance counselor, Ms. Sadiq, I told her that I didn't remember everything that happened at the game, but I did remember trying to tell Mrs. Avery. Apparently Mrs. Avery remembered this, but also remembers me walking away without repeating what I told her. "So why didn't you do *more?*" Ms. Sadiq asked. "There were three police officers at the game. Why didn't you tell one of them?"

"I only saw them later," I stammered. "I knew someone must have called them to help Belinda."

"That was how long afterward, though?" She eyed me suspiciously. "Fifteen minutes? Twenty?" I knew what she wasn't saying: *A lot can happen in fifteen minutes.*

I had no answer. I told her my heart had started to race so hard I couldn't breathe for a while. I told her I felt like I was choking and then I lost all track of time.

She looked down at her paper, where she had notes written and a timeline of the events. "You sat there that *whole time*, having a hard time breathing?"

"That's right," I whispered. I couldn't look at her. How could I explain that I thought if I held still, if I closed my eyes and held my breath, maybe I could erase what I'd just seen? Or make it something else: A game they were playing. Or maybe a joke. Maybe there was some way to explain that what I saw wasn't what it looked like.

Then I remembered Lucas. "I saw the other guy run onto the field. I knew he saw them, too, and I assumed that he had helped her."

She closed her eyes and shook her head. "He didn't, though. You know that, right? He didn't do anything either."

That was when I understood why her tone was so unrelenting. Belinda had been left entirely alone. She'd had to save herself by screaming loud enough to alert a custodian working near the snack stand. He came running; he called the police.

Ms. Sadiq continued: "What we're trying to determine here is how culpable you two are for what happened to Belinda. If you witness an assault, it's your responsibility to *tell someone.* We need to make that message clear to you and the rest of the student body."

She hardly needed to tell me this. Every year, Youth Action Coalition, the group I cofounded with Richard, sponsors an anti-violence ribbon campaign where we set up a table at lunch and hand out white ribbons to everyone who signs the pledge: *I promise to never commit an act of violence against another living being and I promise to report any acts of violence I witness to an appropriate authority.* Though Richard developed the campaign and wrote the pledge, I do most of the legwork for that one. In my drawer at home, I have three white ribbons for every year I've signed the pledge. It made me sick to think about it.

"I understand," I told her.

In the week before our meeting with the disciplinary committee, Lucas and I didn't speak at all. I wasn't sure what he would say in his own defense, but I could have guessed: hundreds of people had come to watch a team he was part of. If I missed the second half kickoff, no one would notice; if he missed it, they would. I held a soda; he held a starting position on the defensive line.

The morning of our meeting, I walked into the waiting room outside the principal's office and Lucas was already there. I was with my parents, dressed in an outfit that felt ridiculous: a fair-isle sweater and wool skirt. Both items belonged to my mother. We'd had a fight that morning because I came downstairs wearing a black denim skirt and a long-sleeve T-shirt. "Absolutely not," my mother had said. Sitting alone beside a potted plant, Lucas looked as if he'd given no thought to his clothes, which made me angry at my mother all over again.

"Why does it matter if I *look* innocent?" I'd screamed at her. "I'm *not* innocent. And they shouldn't base their decision on what I'm wearing today!"

This whole business had been especially hard on my parents, who felt bad about Belinda and also worried for my future. A few nights before the meeting, my mother came into my room and told me I should show the committee how sorry I was, but also tell them I was afraid for my safety. I didn't disagree with what she was saying, but I disagreed with the idea of walking into the meeting armed with an overly defensive list of excuses. What I did was inexcusable. I could have screamed NO! I could have rushed out to the crowd fifty feet away and yelled at the top of my lungs about what was happening. If I'd done any of those things, I would have changed the story. Belinda would still have been attacked, but instead of learning the brutal truth about violent people, she also would have learned that there are people in the world who will *help* her.

As my parents got more anxious, I grew more dubious about mounting any defense. My father was afraid I might get suspended the same year I was sending off college applications.

"Maybe I *should* be suspended," I said when he brought it up for the second time.

"Emily, please. I don't see why the school should create more victims from this one dreadful incident. This is your whole future here."

"But what about *Belinda's* future? Why should mine matter more than hers?"

"Belinda will have a different kind of future than you."

"What's *that* supposed to mean?"

"She'll have supports in place. She'll be taken care of. It's different for you. You'll be independent. You'll need a college education to get a job."

"What if that's what she wants too?" I knew Belinda well enough to know this wasn't very likely—she spent most of her school day in the Life Skills room with a dozen other students with disabilities. I had no idea what Belinda wanted, I was only making the argument because I didn't like the way my parents had spent three days thinking only about

33

me and my defense. I was guilty too. I *should* be punished.

Then we got to the office and I saw in the way Lucas looked at me and then looked away. He thought the same thing—that if anyone was guilty, *I* was. Certainly not him. Not a football player with the responsibility of being part of an undefeated team. Not a guy who had a job that night. He said all this without any words. He said it in the way his arms were folded across his chest. In the way his feet were stuck out and crossed. Like if we weren't called in soon, he might use this time to take a nap. That he had no parent with him only underscored his point: he'd done nothing wrong and had nothing to worry about.

Only someone worried about her own guilt would come to a DC meeting costumed in her mother's clothes, hauling her parents along with her. (It hadn't occurred to my parents not to come. With so much on the line? Did his not feel the same? Did he somehow reassure them, *No need to worry, I didn't do anything wrong. It was the girl's fault.*)

He didn't say anything when I said hello. He wouldn't even look at me.

It made me mad. Here I'd been lying awake every night for a week, measuring the magnitude of what had happened, composing ways to express my sense of responsibility and remorse to the committee, and here was this guy—dressed in jeans and a T-shirt, looking more resentful than anything else.

Thankfully we were interviewed separately by the committee. I went first and made one point clearly: Lucas and I were equally responsible for failing to act on Belinda's behalf. We saw the same thing; we both failed to act. I didn't want him to be treated differently because he was on the football team. We might have had different reasons, but our crime was the same. We panicked and failed to help. I told them it's something I'll have to live with forever and I don't know if I'll ever understand why my instincts failed to do what my brain knew was right. I shook my head and told them I'd be haunted by it forever.

My mother nodded the whole time I spoke, then squeezed my hand as if to say, *That's wonderful, sweetheart, but no need to go overboard. Make your point and move on.*

What *was* my point?

"I *am* guilty," I said to the committee. "But so is Lucas Kessler. We should get punished equally."

Beside me, my father leaned forward. "What she means here isn't an admission of guilt, it's a *feeling* she has. I hardly think when a minor witnesses a violent crime, they should be held liable for actions that took place under duress."

"Dad—" I stopped him. "It's better for me if I take responsibility for this. But Lucas should, too. That's all I'm saying."

My heart quickened a bit at my own insistence. I hardly knew Lucas at all. What if he found out what I'd just told the committee? Ms. Sadiq, the guidance counselor, said, "I'll reassure all three of you that we've given this a great deal of thought and it helps Emily's case to hear her speak about taking responsibility."

Lucas and I didn't learn our punishment until the end of the day, when we were both asked to return to the guidance counselor's office after school. By then I had changed out of what Richard called my 1980s librarian look. The wool skirt was balled up in the bottom of my backpack along with the sweater. I wore my usual school attire: long-sleeve T-shirt and a denim skirt.

This time around, Lucas looked more nervous. He sat alone, chewing a thumbnail. He stared at me for a long time. "What, did you *change*?" he finally said.

I felt stupid at first and then mad all over again. "It's not that weird to dress up for a meeting with the disciplinary committee. Most people do."

"So shouldn't you still be dressed up now? Isn't changing like admitting, I'm not really Ms. *Skirt*?"

What a jerk, I thought. "I don't think it matters now. They've decided our punishment." I sounded snappy and the words came out wrong. Like my outfit *had* been just for show and now the show was over.

He shook his head as the door opened behind him. Ms. Sadiq leaned out. "Emily and Lucas, why don't you come in together this time?"

As we got to the door, Lucas stepped back to make a *ladies first* gesture with his hand. *And he's accusing me of putting on a show for the committee,* I thought. Then I wondered why I'd spent so much time insisting that we were both equally guilty, which might set us up to get the same punishment. What if we got after-school detentions in the same empty classroom?

Ms. Sadiq started by saying that the committee was impressed by the sense of remorse both of us showed. "Their feeling is that you are both good, trustworthy kids who demonstrated a momentary but unfortunate lack of judgment. In ordinary circumstances, that wouldn't necessitate a punishment on our part, but as you both know, this was not, in any way, a normal circumstance. A young woman was brutally attacked on school grounds. A uniquely vulnerable young woman whose life—if she recovers—will never be the same."

We didn't dare look at each other. *If she recovers?* I knew Belinda hadn't come to school this week, but did that mean she was in the hospital? No one had told us this. She might not *survive?* I felt the contents of my stomach crawl into my throat. I couldn't speak for fear I might throw up in my lap. Instead I concentrated on swallowing.

"She might *die?*" Lucas said.

I turned and looked at him. This close, his face looked ashy and terrible. He'd shaved badly so there were patches of hair and a zit was blooming on the side of his nose. I wondered if maybe this had affected him more than I realized.

"No, Lucas, but she's been badly traumatized. Her grandmother says she's hardly spoken since it happened. She's also not eating much."

I kept swallowing. I breathed through my nose and concentrated on not throwing up.

"Since you had such trouble helping someone as vulnerable as Belinda, we've decided that your punishment should include some education in working with people like her. We're going to ask that both of you put in forty hours of community service at the Lifelong Learning Center, which runs classes for young adults with disabilities. I've contacted the program director there. I've told her you would both be in touch."

I nodded, relieved there was no suspension. Maybe this wouldn't go on my transcript. But then I thought about Belinda and felt terrible. Her transcript wouldn't show it either and she'd be living with it for the rest of her life.

"What about—" Lucas leaned forward. He looked as if he didn't want to ask this in front of me. "My place on the team?"

"Yes." Ms. Sadiq nodded. "We've met with Coach Anderson. You may continue practicing with the team on a regular schedule, but you'll be benched for the next three games."

I looked at Lucas. His eyes closed as he took this in. Three games was a lot for a senior, even I knew this. These were the games college recruiters were coming to see. Lucas wasn't one of the star players that everyone talked about and I didn't know if he had a shot at a scholarship, but if he did, he was probably out of contention now.

I wondered if he was fighting an urge to argue with her. Impossible to tell. Finally he opened his eyes. "Okay," he said. "That's fine."

I almost felt sorry for him. I *did* feel sorry for him. I thought: *I still have college applications this won't show up on. For him, it's different.*

After we walked out of her office, we stood for a minute in the waiting room outside, gathering up our jackets and backpacks. "I'm sorry," I finally said. "About the game suspension." I wanted to say more—that it wasn't really fair, he was getting punished more than me when he hadn't done anything worse than I had. I had wanted to make sure he didn't get special treatment because he was on the team, but I hadn't meant for this to happen. "I wish—"

He didn't let me finish. "You want to know what it is?" he said, stepping around me to get to the door. "It's really fucking unfair."

The next day I saw him in the cafeteria, eating with the rest of the team, including two of the biggest stars, Wayne Cartwright and Ron Moody. Wayne was the quarterback but Ron Moody was the division leader in pass rushing. A lot of people said he was the reason our team was undefeated, not Wayne, who was so cute everyone called him the next Tom Brady. Ron had red hair and wasn't as good-looking, so people didn't talk about him as much.

I watched Lucas for a while to see if he was talking about his game suspension. If anyone spoke to him, he smiled and nodded. Twice, he laughed hard. No one seemed to treat him differently, like someone who'd been suspended from three games. Maybe he hadn't said anything. It was hard to tell. Presumably, they were all one another's best friends. At least that's the impression the rest of us had. They took the same classes; they sat on the hoods of one another's cars; they wore the same letter jackets and sneakers. What else could they be besides best friends? But it was strange watching Lucas sitting among them, nodding and laughing.

I wondered if he'd told them anything at all.

CHAPTER THREE
BELINDA

Nan's house has three bedrooms which is perfect, one for each of us. It also has a room off Nan's bedroom that's supposed to be for babies but we don't have any babies, so now it has her sewing supplies and leftover bags of yarn and things from craft projects we've started and haven't finished.

We love doing craft projects. We used to go to Michaels Arts and Crafts all the time to buy supplies like plastic fruit or Styrofoam balls. If Nan had all the money in the world, she'd change her decorations with every season. But she doesn't, so we don't. Plus, a lot of things we make don't turn out the way we wanted, so we put them away in Nan's sewing room and don't think about them too much.

In our house, Mom and I have the upstairs bedrooms and Nan's is downstairs because even though she says she's fit as a fiddle, she doesn't love stairs all that much.

Nan's days are always pretty much the same. In the

morning she watches the Weather Channel and the news and she screams at the people who tell her things she doesn't want to hear, like snow likely or two to three inches of rain overnight.

"Oh, be quiet," she'll say. "Enough rain already."

Every Tuesday Nan goes to her meeting with the women's club where I think they're supposed to talk about doing volunteer work for hospitals but mostly they talk about how expensive groceries are getting. Sometimes they also talk about the price of gas.

The other place she goes every week is the hairdresser. She says nobody gets a set and a comb-out anymore, but she does because otherwise she doesn't feel right and she might as well wear a hat around all the time. Nan doesn't look good in hats so she goes to the beauty parlor every Thursday for a set and a comb-out.

With Mom every day is different. Some days she's awake in the morning before I go to school. She asks me what I want for lunch, even though I always eat the same thing, which is spaghetti noodles, butter, and Parmesan cheese. I used to think this was a healthy lunch because I used to think spaghetti was a vegetable but it turns out it's not. That's okay, though, I still eat it every day because I'm used to it now. On good days, Mom gets dressed and goes for a long walk before she starts her job at home which is data entry. I don't know what this means exactly but she does it on her computer in the corner of the living room. Sometimes she has a lot of work and sometimes she doesn't have any. She takes walks in the morning because that way she can be outside but won't run into anyone she knows from her past. Mom doesn't like having to talk to people she hasn't seen in a long time. She thinks everyone acts phony and pretends to be more successful than they are. Or else everyone wants to tell her they're married now with lots of perfect kids. "Everyone's got a ten-year-old playing soccer these days," she says.

Mom doesn't have a ten-year-old playing soccer. Mom did things out of order and had me when she was still in high school so even though her friends have ten-year-olds, she has me and I'm twenty-one. "That's fine with me, Bee. You're not the problem, they are," she says.

That makes me feel better. Sometimes I wish my mom wasn't so shy and scared about seeing people she used to know in high school. I think maybe there *were* mean people, but maybe there were also nice people, too. She doesn't talk to anyone except for Nan and me and the people on the phone who send her data entry work every week.

Some people feel sorry for us because we are three women in a house without any man. A boy in my class once told me it's not a family if there's no dad. I told him it is too a family. It's not our fault my grandfather died of a heart attack when my mom was seventeen.

Nan says we are better than a regular family because we're happy to be together. "Every single day I wake up, Belinda, I'm happy to have you here with me, helping out with your mom. I don't know what I would have done without you."

She still says this even though Mom is much better now

than she used to be. It used to be she didn't get dressed a lot of days. Now she comes out of her room most mornings dressed like she's ready to go. She still doesn't go anywhere mostly, but the important part is, she *could*.

Nan still gets nervous. She says things like, "Maybe your mom is better but we need to be careful. Upbeat but careful." Upbeat means thinking about happy things and not crying about little things like buying a carton of eggs and finding one broken when you get home. That happened one time to Mom and she couldn't even eat the dinner she got so sad. So Nan and I ate the dinner and said, "These eggs sure taste good and it doesn't matter that one of them broke."

Upbeat means not talking about what happened at the football game.

I'm not supposed to ever talk about that. Nan says I shouldn't think about it either. "What's done is done, sweetheart. The important thing is you're home now and you're safe. You never have to go back to that school or see those people again as far as I'm concerned."

Nan used to say that school has done a great job because even though I can't see very well, I can read and alphabetize and type twenty-three words a minute which is better than anyone else in my class. In our classroom, I'm considered one of the smartest and definitely the best typist. No one else comes close to me in typing.

I used to love my teachers at school like Cynthia and Clover and Rhonda who is my speech therapist even though I talk fine and everyone can understand what I say. A lot of other kids in my class need help with pronunciation. She makes them blow feathers across the table so their mouths will get stronger and work better. Supposedly that will help them talk better, but I'm not sure it works. It seems like they're all better at blowing things, but they talk the same as they always did.

With me, Rhonda says we can just talk which is what we mostly do. She says we're working on social skills which is what you need to have when you're talking to people who don't know you very well. You have to know things like: don't spend the whole time talking about yourself. I used to have a little problem with this because silence makes me nervous and I fill it with whatever is in my head which is sometimes lines from movies other people haven't seen. Rhonda explained that if someone hasn't seen the movie, they won't understand what I'm saying. She had a different suggestion: "Try asking the other person a question about their life."

It turns out people are mostly happy to fill nervous silences with answers to questions. Sometimes they even look relieved and they make a long list of their favorite foods or TV shows or whatever question they're answering.

Even though Rhonda was a big help on some things, she wasn't that much help on Ron. She kept saying I should be careful. I thought she was being sisterly the way Lizzy was with Jane in *Pride and Prejudice*. Like I should be careful with my heart which is what people tell someone before they fall in love.

I haven't talked to Rhonda since the football game

or told her what happened. "Oh, they know," Nan says. "Believe me, they know."

Rhonda sent me a letter that said, "I hope I see you soon."

Cynthia baked cupcakes with some of the students and sent those.

Actually, she brought them, but I was in my room. Mom came up and asked if I wanted to come down and say hi and I shook my head no. I wasn't sure what to say and I didn't want to have a nervous silence so I stayed in my room.

EMILY

OUR SECOND WEEK OF Boundaries and Relationships, there's a new volunteer in class. He's wearing shorts and flip-flops and a macrame necklace with a little wooden bead. He looks like Ryan Harding, a skater I had a crush on in middle school because he was both very smart and very laid-back. He got all As in our honors classes even though he never seemed to carry a backpack or any books, for that matter.

This guy has the same flop of curly brown hair and the same blue eyes as Ryan. It's an almost eerie similarity except for this big difference: in the two years I had a crush on Ryan, he never spoke to me once. When I walk past this guy's chair, he looks up and smiles. "Hi. You must be one of the new volunteers. I'm Chad."

Class hasn't started yet, so theoretically there's no need to whisper, but we do anyway. "I'm Emily," I say and hold out my hand, taking the chair next to him. Usually I don't do things like this. It's weird—with this group, I feel more confident than I do at school.

"How'd your first day go?" he says, turning to face me.

"Great!" I say, hoping no one sitting around us overhears this and contradicts me.

He leans closer and whispers. "I was really nervous the first day I volunteered, and then you get to know these guys and they really grow on you. I don't even *have* to volunteer anymore and I signed up anyway. I knew I'd miss it if I didn't."

I can't mask my surprise. "You *had* to volunteer?" It's hard to imagine admitting this so easily: *I'm here as a punishment for something terrible I did.* It's hard to imagine admitting this at all.

"For a leadership class in high school. Community service credit. Everyone had to."

Oh, right. "Where do you go to high school?"

"Did. Garvey High. I graduated last year. Now I'm at Fairfield Community."

"All right, let's get started, everyone!" Mary says, dragging a chair over so we're in a circle. "You all remember Chad," Mary says. "He volunteered with us last spring. He hasn't been here yet this fall because he's getting settled into his new college classes but he called me this week and asked if he could come back because he missed volunteering with you."

"Thas *nice*," Francine says loudly.

"It *is* nice," Mary says. "We're happy to have you back, Chad."

Just then the door opens and Lucas comes in. "Sorry I'm late," he mumbles as he sits down in the only empty seat left.

"We start class on time," Mary says, sounding surprisingly curt. "If you're more than ten minutes late, you shouldn't bother coming, Lucas. We'll just add a session at the end for whatever you miss."

I wonder if everyone understands what she means by *we'll add a session at the end*. That we might be called volunteers, but we aren't here voluntarily? Surely Chad hasn't missed it, but maybe he assumes we're here like he was, for class credit, nothing more.

Thankfully Mary moves quickly on to the activity, a game called "Relationship *Jeopardy!*," which apparently is played like the TV show. She pulls out a whiteboard with categories on it: Good Communication; Okay/Not Okay Touching; Hygiene; Classy/Not Classy.

Simon, who has thick glasses that make his eyes look bigger than they are, goes first. "Okay/Not Okay Touching for one hundred points, please," he says. He has his hands folded on the table in front of him, like a contestant on the show. Mary reads the question. "If a waitress is nice and brings you extra barbecue sauce, it's okay to touch her butt as you thank her. True or false."

Simon thinks for a while. Finally, he shakes his

head. "No, no. That's not right."

"You have to say true or false, Simon."

"Touch her butt? No. I don't think so."

"Do you want to say false?"

"Definitely false."

"That's correct!"

Francine is up next. Technically we're not supposed to know what our classmate's disabilities are because we should get to know them as people, not disabilities, Mary told us in our training session. With Francine, though, it's pretty obvious she has Down syndrome. Her face is round, her eyes narrow. She takes "good communication" for 400 points. Apparently, to win more points, she has to role-play a scene. "We'll need two volunteers to help Francine with this one," Mary says, reading her slip of paper. "How about Emily and . . ." She takes a moment to decide between Lucas and Chad. "Okay, Lucas, how about you?"

My hands start to sweat as we walk up to the front of the room. It's been years since I've stood in front of an audience and even longer since I've tried to improvise a scene. I can't help but think about Chad watching.

"Here's the scenario," Mary says. "Emily and Lucas are your parents and they have said you're not allowed to date, Francine. You've met a young man at work who seems nice and has asked you out. How do you get your parents to change their minds?"

Francine nods and closes her eyes as if she's a real actress, taking a moment to get into character. Lucas and I wait, not looking at each other. "Are you ready?" Mary says. Francine nods. "Okay. And—scene!"

Francine starts the scene by dropping to her knees. "PLEEEEEEEASE," she pleads. It's very funny and everyone laughs. Then she says something else that's impossible to understand.

I look at Lucas, who obviously isn't going to be much help. "We're sorry, honey," I say. "But your dad and I have to make rules."

"O-hay," Francine says. It's like her tongue is too big for her mouth. She says something else I don't get.

"Can you repeat that? We didn't understand," Lucas says. At the last minute, he adds, "Honey?" which gets a laugh from the group.

It sounds like she's saying something about Winnie the Pooh but that can't be right. Lucas looks at Mary for help. I have to admit, I'm stuck, too.

Mary says, "Francine is wondering when the rules will change, Dad? She's twenty-two years old now."

Lucas looks at me, stumped. Dimly I remember a rule I learned from my old acting class days: every scene builds on conflict. One character wants something, the other says no. "The answer is no, Francine," I say. "Your father and I agree on this."

Neither one of us is ready for what comes next. Francine turns and fixes me with a stare full of fury and resentment. For a second I wonder if she really hates me. Her teeth begin to grind and her lips move as if an explosion is building up inside. Finally she screams, "BAH WAH YUV EE OTHER!" She flounces over to a nearby table and bangs her fists into it.

Suddenly it's amazing—we understand her perfectly because her acting is so good. "You *love* each other?" Lucas says.

She looks over at him gratefully, as if there's a long history of Dad understanding her needs better than Mom. "Yes. Wary much." There are real tears in her eyes.

"Uh . . . maybe your mother and I should talk about this," Lucas finally says.

Mary claps once. "Great and scene!" Francine turns away from the table, straightens her glasses on her face, and takes a bow before returning to her seat.

Mary turns to the group. "So it looks like Francine went with an all-out emotional plea to get what she wanted. Was that a smart thing to do?"

Harrison raises his hand. "Yes!" he says. "Because she got what she wanted!"

"Okay, good point. But let's say you're working a job and the boss says no dating between employees. You've met someone you like there and you both want to go out. Is crying the best way to get your boss to change her mind?"

No one says anything.

"Harrison's got a good point, but I'm thinking in different situations, probably not. If you're trying to make sure people don't treat you like a child, one of the most important things you can do is not act like a child. Emotional pleas can be effective, but we want to be careful when we use them, right?"

On our way back to our seats, Chad catches my eye.

"*Great* job," he whispers. I feel a tingle in my armpits. The truth is, he's even cuter than Ryan Harding.

After the *Jeopardy!* game is over, Mary introduces a new topic: learning how to say no without hurting other people's feelings. When she asks for volunteers to do a role-play, Chad's hand goes up. He smiles gamely around the room as if he's surprised no one else is raising their hand. Frankly, so am I. Surely one of the women would like to do a scene with someone as handsome as Chad, I assume, but no.

"Anyone else?" Mary asks.

No one. I look around the room and I think I know what's happening. I'm not the only person who has noticed how cute he is. He has the aura of celebrity. Last week, Sheila announced that if she could date anyone, she would pick Justin Bieber. Now it's as if Justin Bieber has joined our group for the night. There is that sort of electricity in the air. They can't talk and gawk at the same time.

I don't know if it's okay for two volunteers to do an improv together without a student as well but I raise my hand. "I'll do it."

Apparently with a new topic, it is. "Great, Emily! Thank you!"

I assume our scene will involve me turning down his request for a date. I can already tell Chad has a sense of humor by the way he pats his stomach after he stands up, as if we're about to eat a big meal. "Ready to go?" He smiles at me. This time the soles of my feet tingle.

"Ready," I say, wondering if I can summon the wherewithal to say no to a pretend invitation from this guy.

Mary hands us our scenario written on a piece of paper: *Jane and Adam are friends from work. Jane keeps asking Adam on a date, but he doesn't want to go and doesn't know how to tell her.*

Oh, great, I think. *Of course I have to be the sad girl haranguing the boy for a date.*

Chad walks up to the front of the room and starts the scene by stirring a large, invisible pot in front of him. I pick up the cue and pretend to carry a heavy tray of plates back to the kitchen. "Hi, Adam!" I say, putting my load down on the invisible counter next to him. "So I'm glad to see you because there's something I wanted to ask . . ."

Chad tastes his invisible concoction and makes a face. "Okay," he says, salting.

"I was wondering if you'd like to go out with me this weekend."

He looks at me and smiles again, his "spoon" raised to his lips. He's supposed to say no but the role-play can't end too quickly. "Go where?" he says.

"Maybe you could come over to my house. I could show you my music collection. It's mostly One Direction, but you like them, right?" I'm trying to suggest something pretty unappealing. A few people get the joke and laugh. His "spoon" doesn't move but his eyebrows go up. "Love them," he says.

"Great. So how about seven on Saturday?"

"Wait! I can't!" He laughs and drops his invisible "spoon." "I'm sorry, Mary. I blew it. I'm supposed to say no, right?"

"That's right, Chad. Try again. Start the scene over

from One Direction, Emily—nice suggestion, by the way—and go—"

I start again. "So I have six of their CDs. What I like to do is start with the first one and listen to them all straight through. They kind of sound the same but then if you keep listening you think, wow, they're such great musicians." I've gotten into a groove now, channeling the girls I remember who talked this way in middle school.

Chad works hard not to laugh. "I'd like to, seriously. It's just hard cause I'm working a lot and I'm kinda busy these days."

"You've got Wednesday off." I surprise myself with how quickly improvisation comes back. One more trick that I remember: the more a character clearly wants something, the easier they are to play. "Why don't we do it then? Please, Adam?"

I get a few laughs with my overeager act. Chad looks down and then back up and smiles so sweetly, I stop speaking. He's having a hard time saying no. A really hard time.

"*Please*, Adam," I say. We are grinning at each other now, like we are not our characters. And the word won't come out of his mouth. We both have to laugh because he's *terrible* at this.

Mary claps her hands to pause the scene. "Good work, Chad and Emily. Chad's showing everyone how hard it can be to say no sometimes. What could Chad say, folks? Let's make some suggestions."

Now I wonder if maybe Chad's silence was intentional.

He's done this before and maybe he knows the rules—like if two volunteers are acting out a scene, they need one person to freeze and get suggestions from the group. Sheila raises her hand. "He could say, I don't like One Direction, I like Justin Bieber."

"He could say no," Harrison suggests.

"He should say, I don't want to go with you," Francine says. It's funny—now that we've been around her more, she's easier to understand.

Mary continues, "Chad, do you want to pick one of those?"

Chad turns to me, still smiling. "Hmm," he says.

"Chad, why don't you tell Jane here you're not interested in having a relationship outside of work," Mary suggests. "Then she'll know she should stop asking you out."

Chad's eyes never move from mine. "Okay," he says. "Can we start over?"

"Sure. From the top, Emily!" Mary claps again and this time I make more suggestions, opening up the possibility of doing something every night of the week. He watches me with a smile in the corner of his mouth, as if he's stretching this out intentionally because he's enjoying my performance.

"Wow," he finally says. "It all sounds great, but I can't. I'm busy this weekend."

"What about next weekend?" I know the goal Mary is trying to get us to. He's meant to say no not only to these invitations but to future ones as well.

"I don't know. Maybe I could do next weekend."

Mary claps for us to stop again. This isn't going right. We're smiling too much and enjoying ourselves. Instead of stopping the scene, Chad leans over and whispers in my ear, "I might be able to go out next weekend."

I can't help myself. I laugh even though I see Lucas in the corner with his arms folded over his chest, looking on disapprovingly. I wish he were a friend so I could explain what this feels like. We can't act out this scenario because we like each other! I've never flirted like this before!

We try it a few more times until finally Mary gets tired of it. "Chad, tell Emily you aren't interested in having a relationship with her at all. That if she asks you out next week, the answer will be the same."

He turns and fixes his blue eyes on mine. "If you ask me out next week, my answer will be the same," he says.

After class is over, Chad walks out beside me. "That was fun," he whispers. "I should get your number just in case I change my mind about One Direction." I can't stop smiling at how easy this seems. Usually a conversation like this requires a long dissection with Richard afterward to determine if any flirting was actually taking place. Now there's no question. What's harder to tell is if he's really asking for my number. Then I can't believe it—he digs in his pocket and pulls out his phone. "I have to run and meet someone from school, but I can walk and type at the same time."

I'm so surprised by his ease that I don't say anything right away.

"It's good for volunteers to have each other's numbers.

This way if I need a ride or something I'll call you. Or you can call me."

"Sure," I say, remembering too late that I'm the one who needs a ride tonight. My mom needed the car and dropped me off earlier.

I tell him my number, which he types in one-handed. When we get near the front door, he turns around and walks backward, grinning the way he did when we were doing our improv. "If you ask me again, my answer will be the same," he says, laughing and shaking his head. "God, I was bad at that."

A moment later he's gone and I turn to see Lucas sitting by himself in the lobby. Apparently he didn't drive himself either. I sit down a few seats away from him. I assume we'll sit here in silence, which we've done plenty of times before, but Lucas surprises me. After a minute, he says, "What do you think about this class?"

I have a feeling I know what he wants me to say. *These people dating? No, thanks.* Suddenly I can't help myself. It's like flirting with Chad has given me enough self-confidence to say what I really think. "I like it. Mary isn't telling anyone that they shouldn't think about dating. She's saying there are rules to doing it the right way and you probably shouldn't bother setting your sights on Justin Bieber." Maybe I'm saying too much. Maybe his point is only, *I don't want to picture these folks on dates or touching each other. I've seen enough of that.*

"It didn't freak you out a little today?" he says.

I'm not sure what he means. To me it was like the

class the week before except for Chad joining it. Then I remember something else. After break, Annabel and Ken, the only established couple in the class, announced that they'd broken up over the weekend. "Would you like to talk about that with the group, Annabel, or is it private between you and Ken?" Mary had asked.

Annabel thought for a minute, then turned to Ken, who looked miserable. "It was about having sex, so I guess it's private."

"That's probably right," Mary said. "Good decision, Annabel."

The subject got dropped, but that must be what Lucas is thinking about now. "I mean, I'm sorry, but should those two be talking about *having sex*?"

I don't know if he's thinking about Belinda when he says this. We've never mentioned her name with each other. "Well. It sounded like they talked about it and they didn't agree on what they wanted so they broke up."

"Yeah, but should *any of us* be sitting around talking about sex?"

I'm surprised at Lucas saying "us" like we're part of the same group. Lucas and I are both seventeen. Of my friends, only Barry and Weilin have had sex (with each other, after a year and a half of dating) but I'm part of the nerd brigade. I've always assumed everyone in Lucas's crowd has done it plenty.

"I don't know," I say. "We have that class at school, Real World Issues. People talk about it there, right?" I've never taken Real World Issues. I only know about it because all my friends make fun of the end-of-semester project where everyone carries an egg around for a week so they'll understand the constant demand of having a baby. The teacher marks the egg so you can't switch it or hard-boil it. You also go down a full letter grade on the final if you're ever caught at school or around town without it. Students are encouraged to respectfully police one another, which means, for a full week, everyone walks around saying, "May I see your egg?" Even if you aren't enrolled in the class, it's a funny thing to say. Or, "How's your egg, mine's a little fussy." Richard thinks these jokes are so funny he makes them for weeks after the project is over even though no one in our crowd has ever taken the class. None of us has room in our schedule for a blow-off like Real World Issues. We're all trying to get through our AP credits.

Lucas is—well, the type to take Real World Issues. It's just a guess, but it turns out I'm right. "We didn't talk about sex that much," he says. "I mean, a little, but not like this."

I thought the whole class was about sex. The teacher, Ms. Simon, is wildly popular. "Doesn't everyone love Ms. Simon because she talks about sex a lot?"

"Not at all. Mostly she talks about other stuff. She did this thing where you could anonymously suggest a topic to discuss. You have to say something compassionate but also honest. Like if the topic is cutting yourself, you have to say, 'It makes me feel scared for someone who's doing that, but it also makes me think it's a cry for help.'"

This is the longest I've ever heard Lucas talk. I can't help feeling surprised. Mostly that he's used the word "compassionate" in a sentence.

"I think we should do stuff like that in this class."

"Talk to these people about cutting themselves?"

He rolls his eyes. "Talk about something *besides* relationships and sex."

"We do," I start to say, and then it occurs to me: the only other regular topic for discussion besides relationships is hygiene, which always has the implied motivator of a date behind it. "Before you go on a date, what are three things you want to make sure you've done?" was a 500-point Jeopardy! question today. The choices were a) take a shower, b) put on deodorant, c) brush your teeth, d) all of the above. Lucas has a good point. In this class, these rituals aren't done for dental health or personal comfort. They're done for dates.

"It's like the message is, if you're not in a relationship, you'd better start working harder to get in one. But maybe some of these people don't *want* to date."

This whole conversation surprises me. I know for a fact that Lucas has a girlfriend. He's been dating Debbie Warren since sophomore year, when I first noticed her sitting on his lap at lunch. I registered it the way I register all the relationships in the popular crowd, usually with the same thought: *Oh, okay. That makes sense.* As far as I know, they're still going out. She sits next to him at the popular table. The only french fries she eats are off his plate. Generally that's how you know who's dating who in that crowd.

"The class is half-titled 'Relationships.' That's the reason everyone signed up, right?"

I think about one of the main points Mary made during our training session: that adults with developmental disabilities have happier lives if they're able to express their sexuality in healthy ways. "We encourage people to meet with us privately if they're ready for a detailed discussion of sex, so you don't have to worry about that part in class. But the point is, we don't discourage them from thinking about sex. In fact, that's sort of the point."

I remind Lucas of what Mary said. "These people are adults. If they want to have sex, they shouldn't be told they can't."

"No, I get that. I'm fine with that part. I just think there's other kinds of relationships, right? Like friendships, maybe? Why don't we ever talk about those?" As he says this, he looks around the lobby. "If you ask me, those can be even more complicated."

I have to admit, this is the first time I've heard someone admit that being part of the football/cheerleader crowd isn't all that it's cracked up to be. It shouldn't surprise me, I know, but this year—where football players walk like gods down our hallways surrounded by angels in identical short skirts—it does.

BELINDA

MY MOM SAYS IT'S good I was born now not a long time ago because back then they didn't know what to do with people like me. I think she means people who believe in romance and love, because I do. I believe somebody will fall in love with me someday and ask me to marry him. Getting married means one person goes to live at the other person's house. It also means you share everything including food. Even if it's your special treats, like Skittles or candied ginger, you give him half. That's called showing love.

He also has to give you half of his things, too. You share them. That's also love.

It doesn't mean you never fight. Sometimes people in love do fight because they love each other so much and have strong opinions. It's fine to have opinions as long as you don't cry when other people have different opinions. Then you have to yoga breathe, in through your nose, and count to ten to calm your body.

This is what I do when I am sad or frustrated at school.

I used to get frustrated a lot in school, especially when I kept trying out for plays and Mr. Bergman said he was sorry but I couldn't be in one. Then I got frustrated and mad and had to yoga breathe a lot because I am a very good actress and I would like to be in a play.

I've been in twelve plays if you count Children's Story Theater as eight separate short plays which I do. I was in eight stories, sometimes with a big part, sometimes with a smaller one, like a townsperson or a duck. I started acting when I was ten and acted every year until I was sixteen and the Children's Story Theater director said I was too old to be in their plays. Her name was Linda and she said she wished she could keep me on because I was so good but that wasn't fair to the younger kids who wanted to play the parts I usually got like Red Riding Hood and Bremen Town Musician Number One.

During my time with Children's Story Theater, I could memorize lines and act better than most of the other children. I could also speak loud enough that everyone could hear me. Sometimes I repeated other people's lines if I knew someone's grandma was sitting in the back and hadn't heard them. I can also follow stage directions, which a lot of kids can't. They think upstage means toward the audience, which it doesn't.

I also helped with props and costume changes. I lined shoes up and kept the props table backstage tidy. I like standing backstage where you have to be quiet or people in the audience will hear you. I like when people whisper, "Break a leg," which means good luck in the theater, not "I hope you break your leg."

Even though I am a good actress, it's been five years since I've acted in any plays.

In ninth grade I tried out for a play but Mr. Bergman, the director, said I couldn't be in it because there wasn't an aide who could stay after school with me for the rehearsals. Nan came in to school and told them I didn't need an aide. She told them I did very well in theater and I had been in four plays before. He said he was sorry but he still couldn't do it.

He couldn't do it again the next year and the year after that and every year that I've been in this school. This year when I went to audition, he asked me why I kept auditioning and I told him, "Because I'm a good actress. I've been in twelve shows."

He said, "I wish we could use you. I really do, but the school won't let me. Someone has to be responsible for you and we don't have the staff."

"Who is responsible for everyone else?" I asked.

"I am," he said. "But you're special. They want you to have your own person so nothing happens to you and we can't afford it. We don't have the budget to pay someone."

This used to make me feel sad and frustrated. Now I'm used to it so I don't feel that way anymore.

My mom says there are different kinds of love. She says you can't be in love with an actor in a movie who you've never met. That's not love, that's called a crush. She says you *can* be in love with the character they play because a character is a whole person who you feel like you know even though you have to remember they don't really exist. What you do if you fall in love with a character in a movie is decide what you like about that person and start looking for those qualities in a real person you know from life. That's what my mom says.

I have memorized all the qualities I love about Mr. Darcy. He is shy but polite. He compliments things, like Elizabeth's piano playing. He pays for things like Wickham to marry Lydia. He has a beautiful house that is different in every movie, but is always big with lots of marble and artwork and fountains, usually.

Another thing I love: he goes swimming in his clothes. He's hot and he doesn't know Elizabeth is in his house, so he swims in his pond and walks out all wet.

I would like to go to England someday and visit Pemberley which is Mr. Darcy's house. Nan thinks there probably is a real Pemberley somewhere but she doesn't know where. She has to admit, it looks different in every movie version to her, too.

I've only been to one wedding, and I thought it was beautiful and magical until the end when my mom got sad and told Nan she was scared I'd never get married.

I didn't say anything, but I wanted to say, "Of course I'll get married, Mom."

Nan always says that everyone deserves to have someone to love, and I believe that's true. She was happily married to Grandpa who died when Mom was seventeen which means I never met him, but she always says what a good man he was. He was bald and short so he was different than Mr. Darcy, but that was okay. "He was *mine*," Nan says. "That's what happens after a while. You belong to someone, that's all. You belong to each other. They've got flaws, you've got flaws. You work it out. You learn to live with each other. That's called love."

This is what I dream will happen when I meet my Mr. Darcy. That at first we don't see each other's flaws because we are blinded by love. Then the clouds will clear away and we will see them. No one is perfect. But we will focus on happiness because we know we are meant to be together.

That's how I felt the first time I met Ron. It was at a Best

Buddies homecoming social. I was wearing my prettiest pink shirt with pearl buttons and a lace collar and skirt but my tights were crooked. One heel was on the front of my ankle, so I was in the corner of the room with my shoe off trying to fix my tights when a new song started and I felt a tap on my shoulder. "Would you like to dance?" Ron said. I knew he was a football player because our teacher told us some football players were coming to the dance. That made us all a little more nervous.

Before that moment, I'd never had anyone ask me to dance. I'd never had anyone hold out their hand so I could stand up and put my foot back into my shoe. I'd never had anyone touch my back to walk me across the room. There were other people dancing, but I didn't know how to dance the way the other people were dancing. I only know how to dance from watching *Pride and Prejudice*. Those dances are called waltzes.

I was too nervous to tell Ron I didn't know how to waltz. Instead I put my hands on my own shoulders. I made a triangle with my feet and moved around it. I laughed because it was my first time dancing and I was great! I put my head back and closed my eyes and smiled. "Are you okay?" Ron said because even though the song ended, I hadn't stopped dancing. I wanted it to keep going on forever. "Maybe we should go sit down," he said. He took my elbow to walk me over to the side of the room.

That made two things I'd never done before: dance with a boy, and walk with one holding my elbow. My heart started to beat blood up to my face and my ears. I felt a little dizzy so I sat down. I couldn't look Ron in the face, so I stared at his shoes, then his belt buckle, then his hands.

I couldn't think of anything to say. I remembered the dance parties in *Pride and Prejudice* where people talk about the weather and ask about each other's health. Sometimes they get so nervous they faint. I didn't want that to happen to me.

I tried to sit the way Jane does in *Pride and Prejudice*, leaning forward a little bit in my chair. I've learned a lot about men and romance from watching *Pride and Prejudice*. Another thing Jane does is never look directly at the boy she's talking to. Instead she talks to the air around his shoulder which is what I do naturally when I'm nervous! It's lucky, I guess.

Ron looked around the room like he was nervous, too. He had come with a group of other boys who were all bigger than everyone else in our school. In a group, they seemed very handsome and exciting, even the ones who weren't so handsome.

In my opinion, though, Ron was the handsomest one of all. He had blue eyes and hair that was red and gold at the same time. It's hard for me to describe his face because it was hard for me to look at it for too long. I can describe his hands because I was looking at those mostly. His hands were beautiful. On one side, they were covered with freckles and blond-gold hair. On the other side they were tough with cracks and calluses. This is because he plays football and has to catch hard balls with his bare hands. Judging by his hands, I assume this must hurt.

I wanted to hold one of his hands, but not the way some couples do around school, with their fingers all mixed. I wanted to put the tips of my fingers onto the tips of his. If everything had been perfect, I would have been wearing gloves. But we were sitting after our dance and there wasn't any reason for him to touch my hand so we had to talk. For a long time we both felt shy and neither one of us could think of anything to say. Finally I told him I'd never danced with a boy before. When he didn't hear me, I touched his elbow and said it again. I didn't know if he'd danced with a girl before. He nodded when I said this as if maybe he hadn't. *We'll need to take this nice and slow,* I thought. *Both of us are new at this.*

I wanted to tell Ron that he didn't need to worry, we could learn this together. One good way to start, I thought, would be inviting him to my house to watch *Pride and Prejudice*. Of course he'd probably already seen it, I thought, but if he hadn't, I'd like to be there, looking at his face as he watched it for the very first time.

CHAPTER FOUR
EMILY

"WAIT, SO YOU ASKED him out and he said *no*?" Richard says the next morning before school when I tell him what happened with Chad in class.

"We were improvising and he was supposed to say no when I asked him out on a date, but he couldn't because we had this *connection*."

Richard smiles, a little unsure. "That's great, Em."

"Afterward he asked for my number. When was the last time a guy asked for my number, unrelated to classwork or getting a ride?"

"He sounds really great." His smile looks even more forced than it did a moment ago.

Suddenly it occurs to me how horrible I sound. For three years Richard and I have joked about our nonexistent love lives. We spend most weekends going to movies together and promising that our lives will be different when we get to college. There, the boys will be different: older, smarter, more appreciative of our charms. This class was meant to be my punishment and here I've made it sound like my fast track to the future we've both imagined, with cute college boys who are nice enough to like us *and* do volunteer work.

"He'll probably never call," I reassure Richard. "In fact, I'm sure he won't."

"No, I'll bet he likes you, Em. He'll call."

For the rest of the day, I wonder what I'll do if Chad actually *does* call me. Will I tell him the real reason I'm "volunteering" for this class? Could I go out with him and *not* tell him the truth? I try to imagine it and can only picture freezing up before any words come out of my mouth.

One of the awful truths about the football game is that it wasn't the first time I've panicked and frozen up like that. I have a history of almost-but-not-quite speaking up when I should have. In fact, my friendship with Richard began thanks to one noteworthy example. In the fall of ninth grade, Jackie, a semi-popular girl I had a few classes with, asked if I wanted to sign up for flag team with her. "Supposedly it's really fun. It's all about raising school spirit and bringing people together," she promised. "It's not elitist like cheerleading. They include everyone." After a month, I realized this wasn't true. We weren't on a mission to increase school spirit or promote inclusive socializing. We were fifty-two girls trying out to be cheerleaders. Practices were gossipy and competitive with a tone set by bitter senior girls who hated one another. It was awful and

I hated it, but I couldn't muster up the courage to quit. These were the girls I ate lunch with. If I quit, I thought, I'll have no friends.

Then, just before the Harvest Day Parade—our biggest event of the year—I overheard Darla and Sue, two senior flag-team girls, talking about a plan they had for getting on to the cheer squad. "If they find booze in cheerleaders' gym bags, they'll get suspended for the rest of the season. There are only two alternates, so they'll have to pick us." Darla opened her backpack and showed Sue the airplane-sized liquor bottles she had in there.

I should have said something right away—but I didn't. Two days later, as we readied for the parade, I heard the news that four cheerleaders had been kicked off the squad for drinking violations. I couldn't get over it. Those cheerleaders would now have a record. I could have stopped it and I hadn't because I was afraid. A half hour later as I marched along in the parade, distracted and preoccupied with my own cowardice, I accidentally walked my flag into the bass drum in front of me. Kenton, the drummer, fell awkwardly, dislocating his elbow. The parade came to a grinding halt while an ambulance was called.

That night, Shannon, the flag-team captain, called me at home and said that even though no one blamed me for what happened, I should probably quit the team. "Out of respect for Kenton," she said.

I wanted to tell her the truth—I know what I did was bad, but Darla and Sue did something even worse—but it was too late for that. Though Darla and Sue eventually got caught, it wasn't thanks to any bravery on my part. In fact, that whole episode left me the opposite of brave. I never returned to practice and or the flag-team lunch table. I never spoke to anyone on the flag team again. Instead I hid in the library before school and at lunch.

Richard appeared in December, after six lonely weeks of eating by myself. We had French together, with a teacher who walked up and down the aisle speaking French so quickly I sometimes thought she was intentionally trying not to be understood. Richard had a funny way of bending his head down, trying not to get called on. When she did call on him, he always spoke in the same high, frightened voice. *"Répétez, s'il vous plait?"*

At a time when nothing else made me laugh, his desperate stabs at French did.

One lunch period I found him, alone like me, in the library, and I told him, "You're pretty funny in French."

He smirked and said, "The sad part is, I'm not trying to be. I'm trying to do my mind control tactics where I *will* her not to call on me and it's never once worked. I have *no* ability to control anyone's mind."

Please, I thought, trying my own version of mind control on him. *Talk to me for the rest of this lunch period.*

He did. He wasn't in the library to study, he said. He came because his usual lunch crowd were all in orchestra and they were playing a lunch concert at the middle school. I nodded and thought, *He'll probably be my one-day friend.* Then he added, "Mostly they're geeks, so I don't mind taking a break and talking to you."

I laughed and the next day he invited me to join them. They weren't all geeks; they were people like Richard, academically smart but interested in spending their high school days doing more than just getting good grades.

As I look back on it now, I wonder if I loved Richard from the start because he was brave in ways that I'd never been. The third time we talked, he told me he was gay, which seemed like a daring thing for a ninth grader to say, mostly because it meant admitting he sometimes thought about sex. Because we were getting to be better friends, I asked if there was a gay-straight alliance we could join together. A few days later he told me he'd asked around and there actually *wasn't* a club like that, which shocked him. "There's no club at the school to support any youth activism, can you believe that?" He wanted to start one, he said, not just for gay students but to raise awareness of other issues, too. "Want to do it with me?" he asked. "Now that you've got your afternoons free?"

A week later, we filed papers to form the Youth Action Coalition. From the beginning, I loved being politically active, even though Richard has been the president for three years and does most of the speaking. I do the background, administrative work—xeroxing, poster-making, circulating petitions. Even so, I'm proud of our accomplishments, like convincing the cafeteria administration to use only compostable materials and then to create a compost pile to put the material in, which might have seemed self-evident, but apparently wasn't. When we're short on direct-action campaigns, we pick a different issue every month and raise awareness. Richard writes letters to the editor and school administration. I oversee a lunch table literature handout. The trick to this, I've learned, is keeping a bowl of Hershey's Kisses at your elbow, so people see what they'll get if they sign our petition. We've had awareness-raising ribbon campaigns for breast cancer research, Oxfam world hunger relief efforts, and domestic violence prevention. We've made a good team, I think.

But this year, I've also discovered it's possible that I still haven't learned what I'm trying to show other people how to do: to take action in the moment it's most needed. I've never told Richard or any of our other friends the whole truth about what happened with Belinda. How could I admit that I panicked in a way that I didn't understand? We've spent three years fighting this mentality in our apathetic student body. How could I tell them I embodied the worst of it?

Instead, I told my friends an altered version of the truth. I said that when I walked under the bleachers, Lucas was already there. "I assumed he'd already called someone, otherwise why would he have waved me away?" I said. Then I conceded, "I should have done more. My biggest mistake was trusting his judgment." With this story, I put about 70 percent of the blame on Lucas but, as I discovered, my crowd was more than happy to put all of it on him.

"Oh, please," Candace tutted. "Of course he should have stopped it! He's twice that guy's size and he was wearing pads!"

I didn't even realize how much my friends resented football players until I gave them a reason to resent them more. "It's terrible that he did that," Weilin said.

"I always thought he seemed like a nice guy," Richard sighed. "Obviously he's not."

By then, it was too late to confess the truth—that I was *more* responsible than Lucas since *I* saw them first. My only comfort was assuming Lucas wouldn't care about the bad opinion of four nerds he'd probably never noticed anyway.

After my conversation with Richard this morning, though, I think about what Lucas said in the lobby, about friendships being more complicated than romances. Richard knows more of my secrets than anyone else. He was with me the one time I got so drunk I threw up in my own lap. He helped me clean up and as we left the party, he told people that I'd stood too close to the sink while I was washing my hands. I was the person he called when he smoked pot for the first time and thought it might be laced with LSD. "I can't tell if my toes are covered in fur or just more toe hair than I ever realized," he said over the phone. He was with a group of friends from summer camp that he couldn't stand anymore, so I talked to him for most of the night. I knew he was crying. Crying and laughing. It made me cry, too. And laugh.

"I hate these people," he said. "They make me feel like such a loser. I take off my shoes and the first thing they do is make fun of my toes."

I thought about the flag team and how Richard helped

me get past it. I told him, "You're better than that. You *are*." Because he was stoned and we were both crying a little, I told him something I'd wanted to say for a while: "You're my best friend, Richard. You're not a loser and I love you."

He went silent for a while. We never talked this way. Ever. Finally he said, "You're trying to make me feel better because you know I'm going to have to start shaving my toes."

We didn't talk about that conversation later. He never said, "I love you," or "You're my best friend, too." He'd been friends with Barry long before I came along and maybe it was presumptuous of me to have said anything. Once, about a month afterward, Barry ordered a vanilla shake at Denny's and Richard said, "My best friend for eleven years and I've never seen you drink a vanilla shake. You don't think it tastes a little like snot?"

The others might have missed it but I didn't. He called Barry his best friend, which meant I wasn't

What Lucas said in the lobby last night has stuck with me because he's right: Friendships are complicated. Friends have power. Friends can break your heart. Not that Richard has broken mine exactly, but I'm more careful these days. I don't always laugh at his jokes or agree with everything he says. And with Lucas, the more I thought about it, the more I think Lucas was trying to say he doesn't always love his football player friends. That he knows some of them are jerks, and that he's not like them. I'm starting to suspect he might be an okay guy, which only makes me feel ten times worse for what I said about him to my friends. It's like maybe on a different planet, in a different universe, Lucas and I might have been friends, and now, obviously, we never will be.

BELINDA

WHEN I ASKED RON if he'd like to watch *Pride and Prejudice* at my house, he laughed, but I think that was only because my invitation made him feel nervous. I said, "It's okay. My mother said I could invite a friend over and my grandmother said okay, too."

"See, here's the thing," Ron said. "I'm not really in Best Buddies like that. They asked a bunch of us to go to the dance cause we're supposed to do community service stuff. But we aren't official Best Buddies or anything like that."

I laughed because *of course* I know he's not my assigned buddy. They would *never* match a girl with a boy buddy. That wouldn't make *sense*. Maybe I laughed for a little too long because I started to hiccup and get red in the face.

"I'd like to," he said. "You know. Be your buddy. I just don't have the time. I have practice every day after school."

He looked like he felt sorry about this. Like he really wanted to be my best buddy. I said, "It's okay. My buddies are always girls. I can't have a boy. It's against the rules."

I wanted him to know that if I *could* be assigned a boy,

I'd *definitely* pick him. Since the afternoon of our dance, I thought more about him than I did about Colin Firth which had never happened before. I'd never had a real person matter more than Mr. Firth. It felt scary in a way. And also nice.

"So—ahh, sorry," he said. "I have to plow. I have a meeting with Coach."

I laughed again because plowing was something people did on farms, not in schools.

Later that day, I saw him standing at the end of the hallway talking to a group of girls. That was okay, I thought. I talked to other boys sometimes, too. I shouldn't ask him not to have any other friends. I told him there was something I forgot to ask him earlier. He said, "What?" I could tell he felt funny talking to me with these other girls watching. I did, too.

I asked anyway because the question was important to me. "Have you ever seen *Pride and Prejudice*?"

Everyone laughed like I was trying to make a joke. I wasn't, though.

"Go on, Ron," one of the girls said. "Tell her. Have you seen it?"

"Ah, no. I don't think so."

This explained a lot to me. It explained why he didn't understand how to dance. Or what to do after our dance was over. Watching *Pride and Prejudice* has taught me those things. He didn't know them yet. "You should," I said. And then, because I didn't want to be impolite, I said, "All of you should."

Actually I didn't care what these girls watched. I only cared about Ron.

"O-KAY!" he said. He smiled big and clapped his hands. "I will!"

I felt happy. I felt too happy and shy right then to look directly at his face. I was scared if I did I might explode from happiness.

"I gotta go, Belinda, okay?" he said. "But I'll let you know when I've watched it."

Then I felt even happier because it was the first time he ever said my name out loud. I wasn't sure if he knew it, but now I was sure—he did! And he didn't make any of the mistakes people sometimes make, saying Melinda or Lucinda or some other rhyming name which happens a lot. He said it perfectly. Belinda.

Like he'd thought about it and was saving the first time he said it for a special occasion. Which this was. So I said his name which I knew because after our dance I stood behind him when he went back over to his friends to talk to them.

They said, "Ron, man, look out behind you."

They meant me. I'd followed him across the room after he walked away. I didn't want him to leave too quickly. At first I thought his name was Ronman but later, when I told the whole story to Rhonda, my speech therapist, she said no, if he was on the football team he was probably Ron Moody. "With red hair? And a big nose? That's Ron Moody."

She made a face like she was thinking something about him. "He's a wonderful dancer," I told her. "He asked me to dance at the Best Buddies social and he talked to me afterward."

"Okay," she said.

"He wanted to be my buddy but I said no. A boy can't be a girl's buddy."

"You know you have to be careful with someone like Ron," Rhonda said.

"I know," I said. I think she meant that I should be careful with my heart. She was being sisterly toward me, like Lizzie and Jane are sisterly to each other in *Pride and Prejudice*.

EMILY

BY THE FRIDAY OF homecoming weekend, football mania at our school has escalated to new heights. Everyone is dressed in blue and gold. Even in my AP classes, girls have painted stars on their faces or GO BLUE on their notebooks.

I haven't been to any of the last three games and I've already decided I won't go tonight, even though Lucas is done with his suspension and will be playing. In theory, if he's going back to a game, I could, too. Not that Lucas and I have talked about this. We still don't speak to each other at school. I only know he's playing because I overheard my calculus teacher say he was happy Lucas Kessler was coming back this week because our defense really needs him.

By the end of the day, I can't wait to leave the six-hour

pep rally school has just felt like. I head out to the parking lot to see which of my friends is waiting beside my car. I'm the only one in my group who regularly drives to school, which doesn't mean I'm a good driver; it means none of my friends has access to a car. Most days we have a litany of jokes about activating the airbags before we take off to make the drive more relaxing for everyone. Even so, I'm apparently better than the bus. Today the whole group is waiting for a ride.

Even this crowd—which includes Candace, a National Merit Scholar, and Barry and Weilin, first and second chair violin players in our orchestra—has fallen under the spell of football mania. As I pull out of the parking lot, they sit in the backseat debating their favorite players. Candace loves Ron Moody because he's a redhead and, according to her, "Redheads have the best sense of humor. It's been scientifically proven." Candace has short red hair herself. If she weren't so gifted academically, she told me once, she'd skip college altogether and be a stand-up comedian.

Barry says, "That is—literally—the stupidest thing I've ever heard," as he brushes an eyelash from Weilin's cheek. Barry and Weilin have been dating for two years. They're the most mature high school couple any of us knows, which sometimes gives me hope and sometimes makes me feel even worse about myself.

"No, it's true. I've heard that, too," Richard says, from the front seat beside me. Because I drop him off last, he always rides shotgun.

"What do you mean, you heard it?" Barry snaps. "It's

completely unscientific. How do you *measure* sense of humor? You can't. It's a retarded notion."

For years this has been a standard insult I've heard often, but I'm shocked at how wrong this suddenly sounds to me. I think about Simon and Sheila and Francine puzzling over their *Jeopardy!* questions and I feel like he's just insulted all of them. "You shouldn't use that word, 'retarded.' You know that, right, Barry?"

Barry looks at me in the rearview mirror. "I don't get why that word is so bad. What word are we supposed to say instead?"

"'Developmentally disabled.'"

"Candace saying redheaded people are scientifically proven to be funnier isn't retarded, it's developmentally disabled?"

"No, the idea is stupid. The people are developmentally disabled."

Barry nods like he's considering this and then shakes his head. "I still don't get it. It's a pretty useful word that means stupid. I'm not talking about any person. I'm saying it's a retarded idea. Why is that so bad?"

"Because it's insulting and for years it was how we defined a whole group of people." It's strange—I don't know why, but it's not hard for me to speak up on this topic. "It's no different than using gay to describe someone doing something weird. Except think about how it's usually used: *Don't be gay.*" I've gotten so caught up with my argument, I've almost driven the car onto a curb. Richard holds a nervous hand near the wheel to help me correct.

"So what should I say to an idea like redheads are scientifically proven to be funnier?"

"Say it's stupid."

"Fine. It's stupid."

"So, Em, I've been thinking about this punishment of yours," Candace says after I've dropped Weilin off. "I think there's a way you can get back at Freak the Mighty." I know who she means, of course. After I told my friends what happened under the bleachers, she coined this nickname for Lucas and uses it as often as she can.

"Get back at him for *what*?" I say.

"*Hello?* For not doing anything. For getting you in trouble. You should play mind games on him in class. Pass him notes like they're from another student."

I can't tell if this is one of her bad jokes. "Why would I do that?"

"To freak him out. Mess with his head. Those football guys and their cheerleaders have no capacity to deal with anyone outside their circle."

Richard rolls his eyes. Even Barry has to say, "The thing is, Candace, sometimes you forget that other people are human beings."

"Not everyone, Bear. Not everyone."

"I don't think I'm going to do that, Candace," I say.

After I drop the others off, Richard doesn't say anything for a long time. Finally he gives me a strange look and asks, "Is everything okay? With this class and all that?"

"The class is *fine*. I sort of like the class, actually. I don't get why everyone's acting like I need to get back at Lucas, that's all."

"I don't think everyone's saying that. It's possible they think it's a little strange that you're not coming to the game tonight. You're *allowed* to go, you know. The point of doing your punishment is that then you're allowed to stop punishing yourself. Plus there's the homecoming dance."

Because his suspension is over, Lucas will probably go to the dance, too. Even so, I've decided to stay home from all of it. Belinda still hasn't come back to school. No one knows what's going on, or if they do, they won't tell us. She may be gone for good. Though she's older than us— people in her classroom stay in school until they're twenty-two—this is her last year of high school. It doesn't feel right to go through these rituals as if nothing's changed in my life when hers has stopped completely.

"I don't want to go, Richard, but don't worry about me. I'll be fine."

He studies me carefully. "Are you getting together with Chad?"

I haven't had the heart to tell Richard what happened last week in class, which was pretty much nothing. Chad smiled at me a few times but I got nervous and shy and so did he. We worked in separate groups and did no improvs together. At break time, he disappeared outside to make a phone call. At the end of class, he touched my shoulder and said, "See you next week!" I smiled and waved and said nothing at all. I don't even want to think about it.

"No," I say. "I guarantee I won't be doing anything

with Chad this weekend."

As I pull up to his house, Richard seems happy to change the subject. "Okay, then can I tell you something that's happening with me?"

"Yes, of course."

He grins. "I'm thinking about asking someone on a date."

I'm shocked. In the three years that Richard has been my best friend, he's never come close to actually dating someone. "Is it someone I know?"

"Well, it's someone *I* know. Does it matter if you know him?"

Yes, I want to say. *It does matter.* My heart is suddenly hammering in my chest. I want to say: *Don't take risks, Richard. I've tried it and it never turns out well.*

"It's Hugh Weston," he says, beaming.

I remember that name, but only vaguely. I had a class with him freshman year when he was 4'11" and wore different-colored corduroys every day of the week. "Hugh Weston is into guys?"

Richard rolls his eyes and looks away like I've said the wrong thing. "I'm not sure, okay? But we've become friends and I'm starting to think the possibility might be . . . I don't know. In the air. And I want to ask. Barry says I should."

"You talked to *Barry* about this?" I can't believe he's talked to Barry before he's talked to me.

"Yes. He thinks it's a good idea. He reminded me that Weilin asked him out first and nothing would have ever happened if she hadn't because we're all such constitutionally overly cautious people. By the way, that includes you."

Part of me wants to scream, *There's a reason we're overly cautious! Look what happened to Belinda!*

"I want to be brave for once before I leave high school. Is that such a crime?"

"You're brave all the time," I point out. "You're the president of YAC. You stand up and make speeches in the middle of the cafeteria."

He rolls his eyes. "You know what I mean."

I wish I could picture Hugh Weston in my mind as something other than a 4'11" ninth grader. "What class do you have with him?"

"Entrepreneurship."

Now I really don't get it. Richard has done nothing but make fun of the people in his entrepreneurship class all semester, selling chocolate chip cookies every Friday in the cafeteria to raise money for a charity they haven't even picked yet. This group represents the opposite of everything we do for Youth Action Coalition. (Also in our mission statement: "We aren't fundraisers, we're consciousness-raisers. We believe minds are the most undervalued commodity of all.") Has he been ridiculing the whole group so no one will suspect he's got a crush on one of them?

"Is he one of the cookie sellers?" I ask.

"Yes," he says, opening the car door and getting out. "Yes, all right? He's one of the stupid cookie sellers. Now, I'm not telling you any more."

★

The next morning I'm still not sure what I said wrong, but I'm grateful when Richard calls to tell me about the game. "It was *great*," he says, sounding a little breathless. "The team played beautifully. I'm starting to think some of these guys really could play professionally someday. Did you know Ron Moody is getting scouted by Notre Dame?"

"No," I say. By the enthusiastic, happy way he's talking about all this, it sounds like Hugh Weston was at the game.

"The bad part was Lucas Kessler got hurt. I mean, you probably don't care, but everyone else does. Turns out he's an important part of our defense. He played a great game before the injury. If he's out for the season, there's no question—we'll feel it."

He sounds so unlike himself I want to tell him to stop, but I don't. Hugh must be a real football fan. "He might be out for the season?"

"That's what they're saying. They had to carry him off on a stretcher. Everyone said he probably tore his ACL."

I try to imagine this. Suspended for three games, Lucas finally he gets back in to play only to have the rest of the season taken away? It's terrible. It really is.

On Monday at school, I see Lucas in the hallway, standing with crutches and a huge brace Velcroed over thin exercise pants. I wish we'd had more than a handful of conversations—most of them bad—under our belts so I could tell him how sorry I am. I wish he knew me well enough to know that I mean it.

Later that afternoon, I get my chance. I'm standing at

my locker with Richard before calculus, a class we forced each other to sign up for and now we both dread. However good it looks on a college application, it isn't worth the agony we endure slogging through it. Over Richard's shoulder, I see Lucas with one of his teammates. Except for our terse exchanges around the DC meetings, we've never talked in school. Ever. If we pass in the hallway, we pretend we don't see each other. But today feels different.

"Will you wait for me?" I tell Richard.

I realize he's been telling me something and I haven't been listening. My brain is spinning. I'm planning what to say. "Yeah, whatever," Richard says.

I start toward Lucas and call his name. The bell has just rung and the hall is emptying out. "Could I talk to you for a second, Lucas?"

His friends all stop and look at me. "Yeah, sure," Lucas says, nodding for them to go on. One of the boys has two backpacks, meaning one of them must belong to Lucas. "See you there," he says to Lucas.

"I just wanted to say I'm sorry about this." I point to his knee. "Really, really sorry."

"Yeah, thanks."

"If you need a ride to class, I'm happy to give you one."

Leaning on his crutches, Lucas shakes his head. "Oh shit—I forgot about class." I feel bad, like some minion of hell, reminding him of another reason his life sucks right now. "Yeah, I guess I do need a ride."

"If you give me your address, I'll pick you up." He gives me a funny look. "Or maybe not. You shouldn't have to go this week. If anyone has a decent excuse to skip, you do."

"No, that's okay. I'll go. If I skip, it'll just add time at the end, right?" He writes his address on a corner of paper and tears it out.

"I really am sorry," I say, taking the piece of paper. "Everyone says you had a great game before it happened."

One corner of his mouth goes up in a half smirk. "You weren't there?"

"I couldn't make it."

I'm surprised by the way he's looking at me, eyes narrowed as if he's trying to figure out what I'm really saying. "Plus maybe football games suck now?"

I laugh at the surprise of him saying this. "Yeah . . ." I wave my hand.

He looks around the hall like he doesn't want anyone to overhear this. "I had a hard time getting my head in the game. It was shitty."

The bell rings and he steps back. The moment is gone. Whatever we almost admitted to each other—we still feel bad, haunted even, by what happened to Belinda—isn't possible to say.

"I should go," he says, inching forward. "It takes me twenty minutes to get anywhere."

"Sure," I say. "I'll see you Wednesday night."

When I look back up the hall to where I left Richard, he's talking to a tall guy I've smiled at a few times but didn't think I knew until I realize—it's Hugh Weston. He's much taller these days, like over six feet, and dresses better than he used to. Richard is staring at him, wearing an expression I've never seen before, like he's getting ready to laugh hard at whatever Hugh says. It's sweet, actually. Hugh looks nice. I don't want Richard to think I don't support him. I walk over with a friendly hand raised in a wave. "Hi, you guys. Hi, Hugh."

Hugh looks so surprised at my remembering his name, he blushes and looks down at his feet. "Hi," he whispers. He clears his throat. "Emily, right?"

"Right."

"Mr. Hartung, ninth grade?" He smiles.

Even though I remember this, too, I'm surprised he does.

"Yeah," I say and laugh. "So I should get going—I'll see you in calc, okay, Richard?"

"Yeah, okay," he says. Though he could have used this as an excuse to leave his conversation with Hugh, he doesn't. "I'll see you in a few minutes."

When Richard gets to class late—with a teacher who counts tardies—I feel bad enough to write him a note: *Hugh seems really nice. Everything OK?*

Ten minutes later, I get back: *Very OK. We're seeing a movie on Saturday.*

Okay, wait a minute. He and I usually do something on Saturdays.

"So you asked him out?" I ask as soon as we're alone in the hall after class.

"Yes. It's a movie we both want to see. He said great, he'd love to go."

"Does he know it's a date?"

Obviously I've only annoyed Richard all over again. "We didn't use that word specifically, but it's a movie on a Saturday night. It seems self-evident, doesn't it?"

I don't know anymore. Suddenly it seems like everything is changing in ways I don't understand. "Okay," I say.

BELINDA

I THINK MR. FIRTH WANTS me to go back to school. It's a feeling I get during some of the boring scenes with Lizzy traveling to see her friend Charlotte. He's not even on screen and it's like he's whispering in my ear, *You shouldn't stay home forever either.*

Then I hear him actually say it. I really do.

Nan says I have an overactive imagination. She used to worry about me when I played in rooms by myself and used different voices for all the different characters in the stories I was acting out. She and Mom used to fight about it. "She needs to interact with people more!" Nan would say. "She shouldn't be alone all the time!"

And Mom would say, "She is who she is. Why can't we just let her be happy?"

Nan liked to remind Mom that I have a lot of potential. When I was a baby, I had lots of seizures and no one knew how I would turn out. One doctor said I would probably never learn to read. He turned out to be very wrong because I can read. I can also type and alphabetize and sort mail which has been my job for two years at school. I thought this would be my job forever, until Ms. Kretzer told me no, that I'll only do it until the end of this year because she has to give other kids a chance to do it, too.

She didn't even have to tell me, I know which other kids she means. Anthony and Douglas. They are in my class. They both have Down syndrome which is much different than what I have and we are nothing at all alike. It made me so upset to imagine Anthony or Douglas doing my job that I went home that day and cried for a long time. Anthony wears thick glasses and always has food on his face or his shirt. It's hard to imagine how he would sort mail without getting food on it. Douglas is very silly and not at all focused. They'll mix recycling bins or not sort the white paper from the colored. They'll talk while they deliver mail which I never do. I know that people are very busy at work and shouldn't be disturbed.

The night after she told me, I wrote a letter to Ms. Kretzer explaining why I should get to keep my job forever.

Anthony and Douglas canNOT alphabetize. They are also stubborn. If they aren't in the mood to do something, they don't do it. I'm not saying this to be mean but just so you know—they don't strive hard.

I wrote her letters like this every day until finally she told me I had to stop writing her letters. She was sorry, she said, but she had no choice. This was school, not the real world, and even if I could do a better job than them, she had to think about other students, not just me.

"You'll only be in school for the rest of this year, Belinda. They've got three more years," she told me.

That's when I got a little scared. It was the first time I realized that when I don't go to school, I won't have anything else to do either. I have been trying to find a job but everyone says the same thing: it's hard for everyone, not just me. Nan has put my name on waiting lists at three different employment agencies. I tell them I can alphabetize and sort mail and they say they only have a few jobs like that and many applicants for them. They say if I want to wipe tables and sweep a school cafeteria, they might be able to find something like that. Nan says no that's janitorial work and that's beneath me. "She should be in an office doing mail delivery," Nan told the agency lady. "That's what she loves."

The woman looked a little annoyed at Nan. "I have to tell you, for every nice office job like that, we have a wait list of about two hundred people with disabilities who want that job."

I tried to picture two hundred people waiting to do my mail delivery job. I hadn't realized how lucky I was. This summer, Nan didn't give up easily. She kept making calls, trying to get me a summer internship in an office where I wouldn't get paid any money but everyone could see what a good worker I am and how nice I am, too. She never found anything. Eventually she had to give up.

"After you graduate we'll keep our ears and eyes open,"

Nan said over the summer. "We'll find something for you, sweetheart. You're a good worker. You deserve to have a job."

Now she doesn't say this anymore.

Now she thinks I should stay home forever where I can sit on her sofa and be safe and never go back to school or anywhere else. "What was school doing for her anyway?" Nan says to Mom. "All they did was make her work for free at a job she wasn't going to be able to keep."

I don't like hearing Nan say that, but she's also right. I never did get paid.

Now I watch a close-up of Mr. Firth looking out over his moors. His lips don't move, but I hear him say, *You should go back. Finish school and finish your job.*

I'm sure he's saying it. I hear it perfectly.

"NAN!" I scream. "HE'S TALKING TO ME!"

Nan gets scared and runs in, all red in the face. "What is it, baby??"

"Mr. Firth is talking to me!" Right after I say it, I know I shouldn't have. I remember everything she's said about how he can't see me and how he might not even read my letters even though he answered that one. I know I've made a mistake. Nan will get worried. She might say I should go back to the hospital. I don't want to do that, I really don't.

"Nothing," I say, staring at the TV set like it said the thing about Mr. Firth.

"Who was talking to you, Belinda?"

For an old person, Nan's hearing is still pretty good.

"No one was. I don't know why I said that. Let's just forget it, okay?"

Nan squints at me like she's not going to forget it, which I know is true. She's got her eye on me. After she leaves the room, I close my eyes to see if he'll talk to me again. I want to hear him say it again. *You should go back. Finish school and your job.*

I don't hear him say it again but that's okay.

That night for dinner, it's rotisserie chicken, broccoli, and rice. Salt is my favorite spice; I put it on everything. Before I take a bite I tell Nan and Mom that I want to go back to school.

"Really?" Mom says. She looks so surprised that she sits up straighter.

"Absolutely not," Nan says. "We've already decided this." She looks at Mom. "We've had this conversation, Lauren."

"I didn't," I say. "I never had this conversation."

"Your mother and I feel very strongly about this. You were not safe at school; they were not able to protect you."

Mom looks down at her plate. I wish she would say something but she doesn't so I say, "I was safe except for that one time!"

Nan shuts her eyes and breathes through her nose.

"I have to go back. I have a job to do!"

"It's not a *real* job, Belinda. You know that."

"It is too! I know I can't keep it, but it's a real job."

I see Mom peek at me. She wants me to stand up to Nan. Just because she won't do it doesn't mean I can't.

"They need me! Mr. Johnson said so! He said, I don't know what we'll do without you next year, Belinda. He said that!"

"He was being nice, sweetheart. Everyone loves you very much, but that doesn't mean things have changed at school. I'm not just talking about the one incident. They never accommodated you in one of their plays. You were never included in any regular classes. You weren't safe because none of the other kids knew you well enough to be your friend. They couldn't look out for you or protect you. I know that boy isn't there anymore, but the problems still are."

I hate Nan for saying this. It makes me want to cry.

"Nothing will have changed, Belinda. That's all I'm saying."

Maybe she's right, I think. This was my last year to be in a play and I still didn't get cast. Mr. Bergman said he was really sorry this time, that he wanted it to work out before I graduated, but there were more budget cuts and he just didn't have the money. That won't change.

People looking at me in the hallway won't change either. Maybe they'll know what happened with Mitchell Breski and stare at me more. That would be terrible.

I don't have many friends at school. The ones I have are mostly adults. Usually I'm okay if adults are around, but if they're not, I might have a panic attack walking down the hallway. I haven't had one in a long time but I did the first year I got to high school. I had to sit down in the middle of the hallway because I didn't know where I was going.

That was the first time I talked to Mr. Johnson. I thought he was a janitor because he had a walkie-talkie on his belt. Then he asked if I'd like to come to his office with him and it turned out he was the principal.

That could happen again, only this time I'd know Mr. Johnson, of course.

Still, Nan's right. Nothing big will have changed. Mr. Johnson might like me but that doesn't mean I can act in a play. Then I see something surprising: Mom is looking right at me. Her eyes aren't glazed over or red from crying. She's telling me something with them. She's shaking her head. She's trying to say: *Don't listen to Nan.*

Later, after I'm in bed and my lights are out, Mom comes into my room and sits on my bed. When I was little, I couldn't fall asleep unless someone lay down with me in bed. She and Nan used to take turns, but she did it more. "It's the only thing I *can* do," she used to say to Nan.

Now it's been so long that it feels funny at first and then I remember how much I like it. One of her arms lies across my stomach. She nuzzles into my shoulder so I can feel her breath.

"You should go back to school if you want to," she whispers. "Is that what you want?"

"Yes," I say. I squeeze my eyes shut so I don't accidentally cry.

"You're so much braver than I was. I'm so proud of you for that."

"I'm not that brave," I say, because I'm not. I don't feel brave.

96

"Yes, you are. You're braver than I ever was. By the time I got to your age, I was scared of everybody."

I don't know the whole story of what happened to Mom when she had me. I just know it was hard and she never finished high school.

"I'm not brave," I say. "I just don't want to miss my only chance to do a job." I don't open my eyes because there are tears behind them and I don't want Mom to see that. I don't think she knows what the employment agencies said this summer. Sometimes Nan and I don't tell her bad news because we don't want her to feel sadder than she already does.

"I was always so scared of what everyone else might think of me. I was scared of what they'd think when I got pregnant, and then I was scared of what they'd think when my baby had problems. I don't want you to be scared like I was. I want you to go back to school and show everyone how strong you are."

Now that she's said it, I like the idea. Maybe people will look at me and think I'm strong. "Will you come with me?" I say and then I remember I probably shouldn't ask her. Nan says you shouldn't ask people to do things they can't do. Like for years I tried to learn how to make change, but I never could. Dimes don't seem like they're worth more nickels. And nickels look like quarters to me. I always make mistakes. Finally Nan said, "It's okay if you never work a cash register. You shouldn't be asked to do what you can't do. No one should."

Mom doesn't like to leave the house which is why she's

never worked except at home. Nan can't open jars which means Mom and I do it for her. If you can't do something, it's not your fault and no one should force you. That's how it's always been for us, except now I've made a mistake and asked Mom to do something she can't do.

I feel terrible. I don't want Mom to cry or think everything is her fault. It's not her fault what happened with Mitchell Breski. It's not her fault that I can't make change and I have bad eyes. Then she surprises me. She squeezes my hand and sits up in bed.

"Yes," she says. "If you want to go back to school, I'll go with you."

Now she's so nervous and excited she stands up in the dark and walks around my room. "I will," she says again and squeezes my arm. "I'll come with you."

CHAPTER FIVE

EMILY

I SPEND MOST OF SUNDAY wanting to call Richard and find out how his night with Hugh went, but I don't. If it was a disaster, I don't want to force him to talk about it. If it was great, I assume he would have called me early to go over the details, but then I remember we're in new territory. He's never been on a date before so I really don't know what he would do. I don't know if he'll become one of those people who gets into a relationship and drops all his friends. It scares me a little, especially when I go the whole day without hearing from him. Finally, before bed, I send him a text: *So? How was it?*

I get ready for the worst and think about the speech I've planned: "Even if it was a disaster, it's still good that you tried. You were brave, which is the most important part."

Then he answers: *Great. We spent most of today together, too. He needed new dress pants for a band concert coming up. He's a terrible shopper so I went to the mall with him.*

Richard hates shopping. He always says he'd do it more if it didn't involve looking in mirrors or trying on clothes. "I wish we could just walk around with our outfits on hangers dangling from our necks," he usually says.

Where'd you go? I ask.

5 stores. Couldn't find pants but still had a gr8 time. Have done NO hmwrk. I shld go.

I feel like I'm no longer talking to Richard. He doesn't shorten words in texts. We make fun of people who do that, like vowels are such hard work to type out. Plus, Richard is, at heart, a nervous grade grubber. Most Friday afternoons, he goes home and does all his homework so he doesn't have to spend the next two days "worrying" about it. Now he's spent three days without it crossing his mind?

OK. Bye. C U 2morrow.

Hopefully he'll understand what I'm really saying with this text: *You don't sound like yourself. In fact, you sound a little stupid.*

Apparently he doesn't, though, because the next day I don't even talk to him until right before lunch, when he tells me he won't be eating with us today because he's going out with Hugh. "He wants to keep looking for pants. I said I'd go with him. Don't be mad."

"I'm not mad," I say, sounding mad. "So, what, he has a car?" I don't know why this annoys me, but it does. I'm still picturing Hugh being as short as he used to be. I imagine him sitting on phone books to see over the dashboard.

"Yeah, Em. A lot of people have cars."

"Right, I know." I'm just the only one of our friends who does.

Richard loves to point out that he might be gay, but he's not *that* gay. He hates Lady Gaga, for instance, and has never seen a Judy Garland movie except for *The Wizard of Oz*, which doesn't count, according to him. He doesn't worry excessively about his clothes or his hair, he never watches reality TV shows, including *Runway*, which (according to him) was designed to appeal exclusively to gay teens. I'm thinking about all this because it underscores how strange Richard sounds the next day at lunch, describing in elaborate detail the pants they finally bought for Hugh. "They've got a bias cut, which makes them hang beautifully. I almost bought a pair for myself but I don't have occasions for black dress pants. I wish I did."

"Excuse me," I say, unwrapping my sandwich, "but who are you and what have you done with my friend Richard?" This is an old joke Richard used to make the first year we were friends any time I talked about my flag-team days.

Now he sinks a little, like I've just shot him in the chest. "Come on. Don't be like that."

"Like what?"

"Be happy for me."

I tell him I would be happy for him if all this pants shopping meant he found out whether Hugh was gay or not. He's already told me they didn't talk about it. Maybe I'm in an overly negative mood, but it seems entirely possible to me that Hugh is very happy to have Richard as an enthusiastic new friend and Hugh is as straight as I am.

Richard shakes his head. "I mean, maybe you're right, but I don't think so."

"Why don't you *ask* him?"

"We're enjoying getting to know each other. That's all. We're not at the point where we want to talk about who we'd like to kiss or if it should be each other. Why is that bad?"

I want to say: *Because you're going to be heartbroken. You know what you want and becoming better friends isn't it.* Maybe I'm only thinking this because nothing at all has happened with Chad and I haven't had the guts to change that or suggest anything. "You really think you'd be happy just being friends with him if that's all he wants?"

"Of course I would. He's a great guy."

"And what happens a week from now when he tells you all about the girl flute player in orchestra who he wants to ask out?"

"I'll say to myself, 'Oh well, it probably wasn't meant to be.'"

"And you'd be fine?"

"Yes," he says, but I can hear the flicker of doubt in his voice. He wouldn't be fine. He knows it and so do I.

Two days later, Richard meets me at my locker in the morning like he usually does, but instead of talking about the TV shows he watched last night, he's humming. After a few minutes, I finally ask: "Okay, what's going on?"

He looks surprised. "What do you mean?"

"Why are you smiling and humming? What are you not telling me?"

He grins. *"Nothing."*

"Shut up. Just tell me."

"All right, fine. Hugh and I finally had a talk. I found out his gate *does* swing in my direction, and yes, the thought of us going on a date *has* crossed his mind—" He's about to tell more of the conversation and then he just smiles, shakes his head, and stops.

"And what happened?"

"Nothing," he says, smiling.

"Nothing? So why are you so happy?"

"I don't know. Maybe there's something nice about taking it slow. That's all. I like him; he likes me. We'll see what happens."

"So—no kiss yet? No plans for a date? Nothing like that?"

"No. Not yet."

I have to admit—some horrible part of me doesn't want this to work out for Richard. It's like we're in a race for who can be the most mature about a relationship and I'm losing. The longer we walk in silence, the more I think, *I'm definitely losing.* He's suddenly so mature, he's not telling me everything. I can see it on his face: *I want to keep some of this private between Hugh and me. You understand, right? You will when you've met the right person.*

Oh come on, I want to say. *You've known the guy for a week and a half.*

Then I want to say: *Be careful, Richard. He's going to hurt you.*

If that's going to happen, though, it doesn't seem likely in the immediate future. Hugh joins us at the lunch table later that morning and even though I'm wary, he's the right combination of shy and also appreciative. He doesn't say too much but laughs really hard at one of Candace's jokes, which means she'll definitely love him for the rest of her life.

They leave the cafeteria together a few minutes before the bell. Watching Richard and Hugh walk away, I'm struck by a random thought: Hugh looks like the kind of fantasy boyfriend I've imagined in my future. Not that he's so wildly handsome (Chad is better-looking, definitely) but Hugh is closer to who I've pictured myself with. A guy with warm eyes and sweet smile. One who gets the joke but doesn't always have to crack it himself.

And then I realize it's not the *person* I'm crushing on, it's the *idea*. Richard has found someone and I haven't. And I'm jealous.

When they bump shoulders walking up the hallway, I feel such a pang, I turn and look away.

CHAPTER SIX
EMILY

LUCAS LIVES ON A street of small bungalow houses with patchy lawns and chain-link fences and no gardens to speak of. The only color on his lawn is a hand-painted sign the cheerleaders must have made that reads, GET BETTER SOON, #89! WE NEED YOU!

"That's nice," I say, pointing to it. "Does every injured player get that?"

"I don't know. So far there's only two of us out for the season."

I'm surprised he's saying this so easily. "So it's confirmed, then? You're definitely not going back?"

"Yeah," he says as I open the car door for him. Maybe this is obvious, considering it's been five days and he still looks like he's in a lot of pain. It takes him a full minute to get his bad leg in the car and situated in front of him. Of course he's not playing again anytime soon.

"Sorry," I say when I get in the driver's side.

"About what? Why do you keep apologizing?"

Now I feel stupid. "Well, I'm a terrible driver. I'm apologizing for that ahead of time."

He laughs. "Okay." He puts a defensive hand on the dashboard. "I'm ready. Let's see how it goes."

I signal before pulling out onto his empty street. "Maybe I'm not terrible so much as overly cautious to a dangerous degree. I tend to veer when I see a scrap of paper blowing on the sidewalk. I have an overdeveloped fear of hitting pedestrians who are nowhere near me."

"What's your cruising speed on the highway?" Lucas asks.

"About fifty, usually. Sometimes I push it up to fifty-two or fifty-three." I don't take my eyes off the road as I speak.

"And you've probably heard that going too slow causes more accidents than speeding, right?"

"I've heard about some flawed theories with no evidence to support them, yes. The truth is, I *used* to be a terrible driver. I'm a lot better now."

As if to demonstrate the lie of this statement, I accidentally jam on the brakes ten feet from a stop sign. His leg looks like it took a jolt. "Oh God, I'm sorry. I didn't mean to do that."

"No, it's fine. Keep going. I can tell you're much better now."

I ease onto the gas. "I think I'll do better if we change the subject. Can I ask what position you play on the team? I'm probably supposed to know, but I'm sorry, I don't."

"Did play. Defensive end."

"So what does that mean?"

"It's on the D line. Do you know what the D stands for?"

"It stands for downs, right? I'm kidding. I'm a huge football fan. I almost made one of those poster board fences for defense. I didn't actually make it yet but I might. So what does a defensive end *do* exactly? I mean, I *know*, but just remind me."

"We set the edge, keep plays from getting around us and down the sidelines. We keep the QB in the pocket and on our best plays, we sack the QB. We have to be fast, and I know it sounds like I'm just saying this, but we have to be smart about reading other teams and anticipating their plays."

"Are you good at that?"

"Pretty good, yeah."

"Like you're standing on the line, looking at the quarterback, and you can tell he's thinking, I'm going long."

He smiles at me and laughs. "No one thinks that. Have you ever been to a game?"

I have to admit, Lucas's smile is nice. "Sometimes they throw long ones."

"They throw to *receivers*. They need a target. They don't go long and hope for the best."

"I know that. Sort of." I ask if he's ever made any big plays, where the whole game changed because of something he's done. Maybe it's not a question I should ask now that his season is over, but I've always wondered what that would feel like.

"Once I ran a forty-yard touchdown on a strip-sack. That was cool, but that's pretty much it for game changers. One."

"Still, that must have been great. Was everyone in the stands stamping their feet and screaming your name?"

"Kind of. A bunch of girls took off their tops and threw them at me." When I look over, he's laughing. "Okay, not really. I guess the stands were screaming Kessler afterward but for some reason it sounded like MUFF-LER to me. I don't know why."

"That would have been a little random."

"I know, right? I was so used to people sitting in the stands not really following the game or else just watching for Moody and Cartwright to make their plays. It didn't occur to me they might be yelling my name."

I think about the way my friends and I have come to all the football games, less for the football than for the spectacle of it all. The cheerleaders, the band, the social dramas unfolding in the stands around us. It's like a party everyone has been invited to. A party with a show to fill in any awkward gaps in conversation. I think we are reasonably attentive to the game, but Lucas is right, we probably only watch it about a quarter of the time. When we've got the ball. When we're about to make a play. If I was there for it, I don't remember Lucas's interception and touchdown. It must be strange to be the center of so much attention but not really seen. Instead of saying this, I try for a joke. "Maybe they really were yelling Muffler."

He shoots me another look but doesn't laugh.

I try a different strategy and ask a question I've wondered about for a while: "What makes Cartwright and Moody so good? Is it something you're born with or do they train harder than everyone else or what?"

"Do you want to know the fake answer we tell the press or do you want the real answer?"

"Both."

"The official answer is: those guys are natural-born athletes who've raised the bar for each other and the level of play for all of us."

"What's the real answer?"

"The real answer is they're both pretty screwed up." Just saying this seems to make him nervous. "Never mind. I shouldn't have said that. Don't tell anyone I said that."

He looks so nervous now I want to tell him, *You haven't really said anything.* "What do they do? I promise I won't repeat this. Really, Lucas, just tell me." Secretly, I'm thinking, *I'll just tell Richard because he loves this kind of thing.*

"They have this violent streak. Like if you hit someone pretty hard and then help them up afterward, Moody gets really mad. He thinks it shows weakness. They think every game is a battle. If you don't go for the kill, you're a pansy-ass loser."

"That's how he talks?" I don't know Ron Moody at all except that he has a big smile and a lot of freckles. Honestly, it's hard to picture.

"Have you noticed how they don't let him give too many quotes in the paper?"

I shake my head because of course I've never read a whole article about our football team. What would I need to know beyond the headlines?

"He gave these quotes early on promising there'd be blood on the field after we were done with Mansfield. Who *says* something like that? Finally the coaches stopped letting any reporters talk to him."

"Who talks to the reporters now?"

"Cartwright, mostly. Me, a little bit." He looks embarrassed at this. "I mean, not anymore, obviously. But I talked to one reporter." He sounds like he's not sure whether to be proud or embarrassed about this.

"What did you say?"

I look over and he's staring at me, eyebrows raised, as if to say: *You really want to know?* "I said, 'We're just hoping to play our best and have a great time. We love the game and have a lot of respect for the team we're playing. . . .'"

I laugh at the way he's said all this. "Wow, you sound just like . . . a football player."

He smiles. "There should be a class where they teach us quotes like that, but there isn't. I thought it up myself after watching seven thousand players give pregame interviews. I was pretty proud of it."

I ask him if he wants to keep playing in college.

"Yeah, I was hoping for that. Number one in the state, your mind does crazy things. It starts imagining maybe you'll get a scholarship."

"Can't you still get one?"

"Probably not. I haven't played in any of the games the

110

scouts came to. I could send tapes, but getting benched for most of senior year pretty much rules me out."

It's hard to tell how bad he feels about this. Maybe he doesn't even want to go to college. It's a topic my friends can never get off of, but I've always assumed . . . What *have* I assumed? That yes, maybe Lucas will go to college, but he might just as easily not. I've never had a class with him, which means he must be on a different track academically. The one where students get credit for carrying eggs around school. The one we might all be on if we didn't care about having a future that looks different than our present.

Sitting next to Lucas, a strange thought occurs to me: I never picture any of these football players or cheerleaders going to college because why would any of them *want* to? How could their lives get any *better* than high school? Obviously no one can stay in high school forever, but I've always assumed that crowd will stay in some *version* of high school. They'll become dental hygienists or Pilates instructors. They'll marry each other and stay super fit and that will be that. "Do you even *want* to go to college?" I ask.

He gives me a look that I can't read.

"You don't *have* to. It's not like a *requirement*."

Lucas goes quiet. "Right," he says.

"There's lots of other things you can do. Travel. Work." I can see by his face that I'm saying the wrong thing. I wish I could say what I really mean: *At least you've got choices. My friends and I don't.* Or that's what it feels like, anyway. Like we're under a lot of pressure to stuff ourselves into the same chute. If someone said to me, *Hey, don't worry about these applications that feel like a weight on your chest making it hard to breathe*, I'd think: *Great idea! I'd love to!* We're pulling into the parking lot and I can tell he's misunderstood my point. He's opening his door before I've even stopped the car. "Lucas! Wait a minute!"

"Sorry," he says, shutting it again. "I guess not everyone's college-bound or knows when to open doors."

"I didn't mean that. Let me come around and help you."

He lets me help him because he has no choice—I have to pull his crutches out of the backseat—but when he's out of the car, he walks quickly to the building and goes inside without waiting for me.

I know I've made a mistake. I sounded meaner than I meant to, but I don't have time to think about it, because when we walk into class, Mary is already speaking: "Today you're going to talk about what you'd like your ideal boyfriend or girlfriend to look like."

My heart stops for a second because I'm not imagining this: Chad turns around and looks at me after she says that. "Hi," he mouths.

"Hi," I mouth back.

Mary continues, "I don't want you to only think about what this person will look like on the outside. I want you to think about what they'll look like on the *inside*, too."

I'm pretty sure I know what inspired this exercise. Last week, Franklin, who is in his thirties and one of the older members of class, shared his strategy for finding a girlfriend, which seemed to be: ask out every waitress at the restaurant where he works, bussing tables, until one of them finally relents and says yes. "But that might not work, Franklin. They might all say no," Mary pointed out. "No," he said. "Someone will say yes."

Now Mary keeps going, "You want to think about what interests you'd have in common and about things you'd like to do together and share. About finding someone who might have challenges as well so you can share your strategies."

Franklin isn't the only one with deluded hopes. They've all talked about wanting to date celebrities or characters on TV shows. Mary's trying to get them to think realistically, and look around a little closer to home. It's a good idea, though I have to admit the exercise seems challenging. Each person is supposed to make two lists to describe the kind of person they would like to date someday. "On one list, you can describe what their *outside* might look like, and on the other list, you should think about what their *inside* might look like."

This is our first time working one-on-one with the other students since my terrible interview with Harrison and I'm happy to have a chance to redeem myself. I sit down next to Ken, who has his paper in front of him with nothing written on it. "I don't understand this," he says. "How do I know what insides look like?"

"I think she means what would you like their personality to be like?" In an effort to keep him from talking too loud, I whisper and move my chair a little closer.

"You shouldn't sit so close," he says. "I have a girlfriend and she'll get mad."

Two weeks ago, Ken and Annabel announced their breakup to the group. I've never talked to him before so I'm not sure if I should mention this, but I go ahead: "Does that mean you and Annabel are back together?"

"That's right. We use condoms now. Every time."

"Okay! So maybe you want to think of what you like about Annabel's personality."

This question is easy for him to answer. He ticks off a list, using his fingers: she likes baseball, she's funny, she smells nice, she's good at video games, she makes him do things and not be so shy. I write all this down in a list for him and then I look up. "You don't seem shy, Ken." He really doesn't. He's one of the people who talks the most in class.

He nods and adjusts the glasses that have slid down his nose. "Oh, yes. Very shy. I never talk. Ever, usually. Except here. Because of Annabel. She says if we want to get serious and use condoms, I have to start talking more, so I talk now. I talk all the time."

I know he's not trying to be funny, so I work to keep a smile off my face. After Ken is done with his list, I can't help myself—I sneak a look over at Chad, who is smiling at me as if he's just heard something funny, too. Already this feels different from the last few weeks, when Chad and I hardly spoke. After Ken, I move over to Thomas, the one who wears his hat and gloves in class. He hasn't written anything either. "I want her insides to have organs in it, what else am I supposed to say?"

"I think this is a way of describing your ideal personality."

"Why doesn't Mary just *say* that?" He adjusts his hat with his gloved fingers, which is what he does anytime he gets anxious in class. I've gotten used to this quirk of his and have started noticing other things about him. He has nice green eyes. He wears a surprising shell necklace. If you took off the hat and gloves, he'd look like a fairly cute surfer boy, actually.

Once he gets started, Thomas seems to get the idea: he's looking for someone who likes discussing old outboard motorboat engines, the first three seasons of *Doctor Who*, and listening to Iron Maiden. As he writes his list, I try not to fixate on Chad, but it's hard. Every time I glance over, he's looking at me.

At break time, he and I walk outside where it's cooler, which means both of us stick our hands in our pockets. "You're right about this work growing on you," I say. "I'm starting to really like coming to this class."

"And the exercises are things we could all think about, you know? What do you want your girlfriend to look like on the inside? I probably could have used someone asking me that question when I was in high school."

"Yeah, I know," I say, though I wonder if I sound stupid. I still am in high school. "What did your people say they were looking for?" After I ask this, I realize I only saw Chad helping one person, Simon.

"Oh you know. The usual: someone who looks like Angelina Jolie."

I want him to ask me the same question so I can tell him my favorite answer of the night, which wasn't even Ken's. It was Francine's, the bowling gold medalist who interviewed Lucas our first night with this group. "I want to find someone who looks like me on the inside," she said. "I'm a people person and a helper. I want to find someone like that."

I thought it was so sweet, and then I realized: this is how I would describe myself—and what I'm looking for—too. It surprised me because she put it as well (or better) than I could have and made a simple point she didn't even intend: being disabled wasn't the main thing about her. There isn't time to tell Chad this story because Franklin pokes his head out and tells us class is starting again.

"We'll be right there," I tell Franklin because I don't want to go back right away. I keep thinking about Richard saying he wanted to be brave for once in his life. I want this, too. The words are out of my mouth before I've thought much about them: "So, Chad, do you want to have lunch sometime?"

He looks surprised, but in a good way, I think. I fill in quickly. "I want to see your school. I'm thinking about applying there for next year."

"Sure," he smiles. "When?"

I wonder if saying tomorrow would be too soon. I'd like to, though. I'd like to cut my class before and leave Richard alone for a lunch period so we both have our mysteries we're not sharing with each other. "Would tomorrow be okay? That's my freest day at school."

"Tomorrow?" Chad checks his phone, which makes me wonder if he doesn't remember his class schedule this late in the year or if he has so many lunch dates with girls he has to write them down or he'll lose track. "Tomorrow's great!" he says.

I float through the rest of class grinning, until the end, when Mary says, "Emily, would you mind staying behind for a minute?"

"Sure." I turn to Lucas, who's waiting by the door. "I'll meet you at the car."

"I just wanted to talk a little about your work in this class," Mary says when we're alone. "You've been a wonderful addition so far. You've got a light touch and good instincts. Some people are afraid to be themselves around these folks or make any jokes for fear they might say something wrong. You're not like that, which is nice."

"Thanks," I say, though I can tell that she hasn't asked me to stay behind to say this.

"One thing we've discovered about having volunteers in our classes is that we can never predict who will be good with this group. Sometimes we get college students in here who've had a lot of classes in special ed and they just don't have good instincts for engaging our students. They talk to them like they're children, which they aren't. In fact, that's the whole *point* of the class, and they never really get it."

My heart speeds up as I try to imagine where this conversation is headed.

"I'll admit I was a little wary about taking you and Lucas on as volunteers. I thought it was too risky in a class where we explore such sensitive topics, but we were two sessions in and we had no volunteers and the class doesn't work as well without a few. So I said fine, we'd see how you did. If it didn't work, we'd move you over to ballroom dancing or a different class. I watched both of you carefully those first weeks. You, of course, shine doing improv scenes. I love the way you push the other person just enough by adding surprise elements, but you don't take it too far. You intuit how much challenge each person can handle. But here's the thing—"

Suddenly I have a feeling she's about to tell me Lucas isn't working out. This whole class, he was quieter than usual. True, he helped other students with their lists, but twice Mary called on him and he barely responded. I think of what he's been through this week, of the pain he's in with his leg and the effort he made to come even though he could have called in sick. I also think about what I said before he got out of the car. Lucas might not look like he cares, I want to tell her, but he does. More than she might realize. Thinking this makes me feel even worse for what I said earlier in the car, presuming he wouldn't care about college if he couldn't play football. He cares about things besides football. I know that.

"Over the years we've learned a few things about the people who volunteer here. Some do it because they're compulsive do-gooders. Other people—like you and Lucas—are here because you're required by your schools.

118

Others are here, whether they realize it or not, because they're wrestling with some of the same issues our students are. Social skills, anxiety, making connections. Sometimes those people can be great contributors to the group. We let certain people come back because we can see they need this group, too."

I don't understand.

"I'm talking about Chad. He was a volunteer we would not have invited back, but he wanted to come and his mother called and asked if we would agree to take him back and we did. With some hesitation, I should add."

"Why?"

"He can be a little distracted in class. I've noticed you were getting friendlier with him in class and I just thought I'd tell you, we had a few problems last time where he hurt some people's feelings, so I'm trying to have him work less one-on-one with students." She looks at me as if she's waiting for a reaction. "Does this surprise you?"

"Yes," I say. "I thought you were going to say Lucas wasn't working out."

"Lucas? Oh no, he's fine. I think he's doing a pretty good job so far."

"You do?"

"He's got different instincts from yours, but no, his are pretty good, too. He has a nice way of interacting with each person at their own level. You've both surprised me, I have to admit. These are qualities you can't really teach people. With Chad, it hasn't come naturally. That doesn't make him a bad person—I'm sure he's probably a very nice guy—it only means he probably shouldn't be working with this population in the future."

BELINDA

NAN DOESN'T SAY ANYTHING the whole drive over to school. I am wearing one of her prettiest dresses, with a belt and a flower print and a lace collar. It also has a hole in the side that we tried to sew up but Mom couldn't finish in time so I have a safety pin under my armpit. It tickles but I told her it's okay.

Mom is sitting in the front seat next to Nan and I'm in the back. It's nice to see Mom dressed in real clothes with a purse in her lap. She looks pretty. I don't know if she's nervous but she probably is. I wonder if Mr. Johnson, the principal, will remember her from when she was in high school, before she dropped out. Maybe he will and they'll fall in love. I don't know if he's married or if that's even possible but I like imagining other people in love. I picture Mr. Johnson looking up and smiling when he sees Mom in the doorway. I picture him saying, "Lauren, is that you?"

I imagine Mom saying, "Yes, it is. Hello, Mr. Johnson."

That's not what happens, though. Instead everyone in the office is surprised to see me and asks why no one called to let them know I'd be coming in.

The whole ride here Nan didn't say anything because she doesn't think me coming back here is a good idea. Now suddenly Nan is on our side again. "She's still a student at this school, isn't she? Since when do students have to call ahead to let you know they're coming?"

Ms. Swanson, the secretary, gives me a hug and says maybe I should wait in the nurse's office while she makes some calls. First we talk to Ms. Sa-something who is a guidance counselor. Then we talk to another counselor. Then we talk to Mr. Welding, who is dean of students. "We want to make sure this transition back into school is as smooth as possible, that's all," Mr. Welding says. He blinks a lot when he says this, like there's something in his eye.

As we go from office to office, the people I know from delivering their mail a few weeks ago look like they're scared to say hi. Maybe they don't recognize me because I look so different. Maybe they think I'm someone else. I want to wave and say, "Hi! It's me, Belinda," but Nan holds one of my arms and Mom holds the other. Finally they tell me what's been decided: I won't go back to my old classroom or my old schedule because they don't want to put too much pressure on me too soon.

"Let's ease back into things, shall we?" says Mr. Welding. "We know Belinda likes being in our main office here, so why don't we keep her here for the first week or so and see how it goes? She can stay in the nurse's office for the time being."

This sounds exciting, I think. Maybe I can be a nurse's assistant. Then I try to picture what I'll do and I can't. The nurse's office doesn't have any mail to deliver. They have some recycling but not a lot. "What will I do?" I ask.

He doesn't look up from the paper he's reading. "Well, for now, whatever you'd like to do, Belinda. Maybe we can set you up with some books and some paper and pens. Your grandmother has made it clear that she doesn't want you to go back to the Life Skills room, where you had some trouble with a few boys. She wants you in a substantially separate situation, so this is what we can come up with on short notice. It won't be forever, I promise."

Now I know what this is about. I thought maybe Nan forgot, but she hasn't. The last time I was at school, I got in a terrible fight with two boys in my classroom, Anthony and Douglas. Maybe Nan doesn't want me in the same room with them or maybe they think it was my fault and they don't want me back. That's why she's saying no to my old classroom for me.

I say, "What about my job?"

He looks confused. "What job?"

I say, "My *job*." I'm scared I might start to cry. "I deliver the mail at ten every day and I sort recycling on Tuesdays and Thursdays. It's my *job*."

"Hold on just a minute. Let me ask about that." He gets up from behind his desk and steps out of the room.

While he's gone I don't say anything. I also don't look at Mom or Nan. I'm too scared if I do I'll start to cry.

When he comes back in, he claps his hands. "Well, there's some good news and some bad news. The bad news is that we've got some other folks doing Belinda's old job with the mail and all that."

"Who?" I say. My voice sounds shaky. I shouldn't

bother trying not to cry because I know I will.

"I'm not sure exactly." He looks down at a piece of paper. "I think their names are Anthony and Doug, maybe."

"Douglas," I say. Now I'm really crying. I can't help it. Nan's lips go thin. She'll hug me later I know but she doesn't like making scenes in public. She thinks it's important to put on a good face. Mom hugs me and I cry into her shoulder.

"You've been out of school for six weeks, Belinda. That doesn't mean we can't find a different job for you, but it's important for you to know that yes, some things will be different. We're happy to have you back. We can promise that you'll be safe, but you have to understand that some things will be a little different."

I can't stop crying. I don't even know why. I just can't.

He lets me cry for a while and then he asks, "Do you still want to come back?"

Everyone waits for me to say something. I'm embarrassed but I have to wipe my nose on my mother's shirt, I have no choice. "Yes," I say. "I still want to come back."

CHAPTER SEVEN
EMILY

"Isn't this great?" Chad says. Late last night, he texted me to meet him at a Mexican restaurant across from his school. The place is weirdly dirty and full of college students. Everyone seems to be shouting at someone across the room but no one is talking to the person sitting next to them. I don't really get it. A few minutes after we walk in, Chad is doing it, too. "'Ritas on Thursday, man!" he calls to someone across the room who is talking on a phone but gives him a thumbs-up.

"Yeah!" I say a little breathlessly. "It's great!"

They don't really have a menu, it turns out. The counter person has to tell you what kind of tacos they have that day. If you understand what he's saying, you order one of the choices, but I don't, so I say, "That sounds good," to whatever Chad has just ordered.

There are only four small tables, so after we get our food we stand at a counter along the wall with about ten other people. Chad says hi to everyone who squeezes past us, though it's not always clear if he knows them or not. "Do you come here a lot?" I say after we've gotten our food and our salsas and are finally eating.

"Not really," he says, biting into a taco. "Everyone just talks about it a lot. I've only been here once before."

When I ask him to tell me about the classes he's taking, he says, "Here's the thing. I didn't really want to go to college, but my parents said if I didn't, I have to get a job, so that's pretty much why I'm here."

"Oh," I say. "So what made you pick Fairfield?"

He shrugs as if he has no answer for this. "Most of my friends from high school were going, so I figured why not?"

"Is it like high school? Do you still see your old friends a lot?"

"Actually, no. I wish it was more like high school. Mostly we just come here for classes. The parties are still at our parents' houses because no one lives in a dorm. That's the bad part. If I were you, I'd definitely find a college with dorms. That would be way more fun."

I try to imagine what Richard would say if he were here. "What classes are you taking?"

"I guess that's a good thing about Fairfield. It doesn't really matter what classes you take because you don't have to try for a degree. So it's fine to do all art classes or whatever."

"Is that what you take? Art classes?"

"No. I don't know why I said that. I'm taking one web design class because someone said you design video games, but that's not true so I think I might drop that one."

As he keeps going through his classes—each one a random disappointment—I have a strange realization: this must be what conversation at the popular table is like. When I ask him what he does on the weekends, he smiles and says, "Same things I've always done. Whatever. Have fun."

By the end of lunch he seems so casual about everything, I have to ask: "Why did you sign up to volunteer at LLC again?"

"Oh, that. My mom made me. She said she wouldn't pay for my gas anymore if I didn't get a job or at least volunteer for something." He smiles. "So I picked volunteering."

As we finish eating, I decide it's not that Chad is an awful person, he's just not a person I have much in common with. Plus, he's a little bit of an awful person. He does an imitation of Simon from our class that's more mean than funny and then starts talking about how Mary gets on his nerves. "That class could be twice as fun if she wasn't so serious all the time."

"Well, it's kind of a serious subject," I say.

He looks at me like he's not sure what I'm talking about. "Not really."

"You don't think helping these folks learn how to navigate relationships is serious?"

"It's not like any of them are going to really date anyone, right? I mean, they'll make friends, sure. So why not make it a little lighter and friendlier, you know what I'm saying?"

Now he's making me mad. "You don't think these people are capable of having real romantic relationships?"

"Well—I guess I haven't thought about it that much, but no, not really. Do you?"

"Yes," I say more emphatically than I expected. "Look at Ken and Annabel. They got through a rough patch and now they're back together."

"Yeah, I don't really like to think about that too much."

He means sex. He doesn't want to think about them having sex.

We've left the restaurant and are standing in the parking lot now, next to my car. I wish I could tell him how wrong he sounds without seeming shrill and self-righteous, but I can't think of how to say it. Plus, we both need to get going. I have class in a few minutes and so does he, supposedly, though it's hard to tell if he's even planning to go. I thank him for lunch and get in my car before there can be any question of an awkward hug and then I realize something terrible: I left a door ajar and an overhead light on. My battery is dead. I turn the key a few times as if I'm hoping the car might change its mind and flicker on.

Chad takes a few steps away and turns around. "Everything okay?"

Obviously it isn't. I want to tell him I'll be fine, I just have to call one of my parents and wait for them to come, but then I remember—I have to get back for calculus, where I have a quiz starting in twenty-five minutes. "You don't have jumper cables, do you?"

"No," he says.

Of course he doesn't. Chad doesn't know what classes he's taking now, why would he have jumper cables? I have to ask him for a ride back to school. I have no choice. He agrees, but he's a little annoyed, I can tell. If I miss the quiz, my shaky B minus will harden into a C and I'll never pull it back up.

We pull up to the school parking lot and Chad checks his phone for any new texts.

"So thanks again," I say.

"Oh, sure," he says, reading his phone.

"And thanks for the ride. I'm so sorry about my car. That was stupid—"

He still doesn't look up. I'm not sure if I should get out of the car without at least making eye contact, but just as I pull the handle on the door, there's a knock on the window.

"HI, YOU TWO!" It's Lucas, smiling like he thinks it's hilarious that he's caught me in Chad's car, skipping class. "School's not out yet, Em."

I open the door and quickly get out. "I know that, Lucas. He's dropping me off."

When I'm out of the car, Chad pulls away quickly.

"So, wow. That wasn't weird at all," Lucas says after Chad's gone. He's still smiling.

"What are you doing out here?"

"I've got study hall. The proctor let me come out here to get a book I forgot. Remember? I'm a stupid football player so I have a cushy schedule where tutors hold my hand and nothing much is asked of me. Some days I hardly go to class at all." I assume he's talking about the conversation we had in my car. I feel terrible all over again about what I said. We start walking in together. "Kind of like you, Em, by the looks of it."

"I'm sorry for what I said before. I should never have said that."

He stares at me. It's hard to tell if he's kidding anymore.

"I was just trying to say that college isn't the right thing for everyone. I hate when all these teachers assume your life is over if you don't go to college. They don't even acknowledge that a lot of successful people don't go to college. That's all I meant."

"I guess I hate it when everyone assumes that football players are too stupid to understand that college could be about something more than playing football."

"I didn't mean that, but I know it might have sounded that way."

As we walk inside, he holds open the door for me. "So what were you doing out there with Mr. College anyway? Cutting class is kind of an unusual choice for you, right?"

I don't feel quite so embarrassed anymore. It's funny— in some ways, Lucas is starting to feel like an old friend. The way old friends can get prickly sometimes. And also know you a little too well. "I actually cut *two* classes just now," I whisper. "I've never done that before."

"Then you probably haven't heard," he whispers back, in my ear. "If you write a fake note, you won't get in trouble." The bell rings, meaning we've got three minutes to get to class.

"See, I never would have thought of that! Thank you so much, Lucas!"

He smiles in a way that I hardly ever see. "Here to help."

We're staring at each other now and I'm not even sure why. I really need to get to class. I made Chad drive me back because I didn't want to miss calculus, but here I am not moving. "So will you need a ride to class next week?" I say. One of us needs to say something to end this staring/smiling contest.

"Yeah, actually. The doctor says I still can't drive."

"Okay. I'll call you," I say, taking a few steps backward. And then it turns out we're heading up the same hallway. We both laugh a little because now we've got a few more minutes to talk.

"So, what—are you dating Mr. College now?"

"No," I say, though I like the idea of Lucas thinking I might be. "We're just friends."

"Okay, so has he told you why he's still wearing flip-flops even though it's fall and pretty cold out?"

This surprises me. These are the jokes I would expect Richard to make. "Not yet. We haven't gotten to the part where we talk about our shoe choices yet."

"Better hurry up," he says. "Winter's coming."

I don't understand why I'm still blushing two minutes later, after I've walked into calculus and am sitting in front of Richard, who slides a note under my elbow within seconds. *What's up?* it says. *Where were you at lunch?*

Sorry, I write back. *I went out with Chad.*

I'll tell him the truth sooner or later—that getting to

know the flesh-and-blood Chad has definitely ended my crush on the idealized version—but for now I don't say anything. It's enough for him to know he isn't the only person who has lunch dates now.

Then he surprises me. The paper reappears under my elbow. *Okay,* it says. *So what were you doing with Lucas Kessler just now?*

What *was* I doing with Lucas Kessler just now? That little exchange—him getting mad and sticking up for himself, then walking me to class and teasing me about Chad—has stuck in my brain. I can't stop replaying it in my head. I remember once, when I was a freshman, overhearing Charlotte, the prettiest of the senior cheerleaders, complain that anytime she started a dating a boy, others suddenly cropped up and asked her out. "It's like they only notice me *after* they think I'm taken." It was an absurd thing for a gorgeous girl to complain about, but maybe she had a point. As embarrassing as it was to have Lucas knock on the car window, I wonder if it means he's looking at me a in a new way. So what if I don't actually like Chad—it looked like we were sort of on a date. Maybe this explains why Lucas and I stood in the hall staring at each other for so long.

Of course my friends won't see it this way. They see Lucas as someone who not only failed to help Belinda but stopped me from helping her and still felt fine giving me half the blame. I know I have to tell Richard the truth at some point—I have to tell *all* my friends—but now isn't the time, especially when we walk out of class and I see something up the hall that makes my stomach jump.

It's Belinda Montgomery, standing by herself outside of the nurse's office.

She looks so different it's possible it's not even her. She's thinner, and her hair is longer, but I can tell it's her by the way she holds her chin up. I remember this quirk: she always holds her chin up because if she looks down, her glasses fall off. I put my hand on Richard's arm. "Do you see who's up ahead?"

He squints in the direction I point. "No."

"Look again."

Richard has terrible eyesight, but he refuses to wear his glasses outside of the classroom. "I'm having a hard time figuring out what you're pointing at."

"It's Belinda Montgomery," I say. "Only she looks different. She's thinner. And she's wearing a funny dress. It's old-fashioned, like a costume or something." Her dress makes her look like someone's mother. "What should I do?"

We get a little closer and I can see that she looks terrible. She's lost so much weight that her face looks completely different. Even her glasses are too big now. I feel like I've been waiting for this moment for more than a month, planning what I'll say: *I'm sorry, Belinda. I don't know if anyone can make it up to you but I want to try. I'd like to be your friend.*

"What are you doing?" Richard says when I start toward her.

"I'm going to talk to her."

"I'm not so sure about that—"

I cut him off. "I *have* to talk to her."

I leave him behind and walk straight up to her, surprisingly unafraid, as if these weeks of being in Boundaries and Relationships, of improvising as a bolder person, has made me one. "Hi, Belinda," I say. "I'm so glad you're back. We all are."

She turns and studies me, as if it takes her eyes a while to adjust and register who I am. I wonder if I should remind her of my name and the plays we did in Children's Story Theater. Then I think of how she memorized everyone's lines in every play we ever did and I suspect she needs no reminders.

She stares at me for a long time without saying anything. In that terrible moment, I flash on a different memory from my first week of high school back in ninth grade. A memory so awful I've managed to forget it until now. But Belinda hasn't, I know. Her development may be delayed, but her memory is fine.

Here's the awful truth: she remembers exactly who I am because she shakes her head slowly, turns around, and walks away.

BELINDA

I REMEMBER THIS GIRL. SHE played Princess Number Four in *Princess for a Day* and Hunter's Henchman Number Two in *Little Red Riding Hood*. She also played a fox in

Bremen Town Musicians, but that's not the main thing I remember about her. The main thing I remember happened three years ago was when I was a different person. I used to be a person who liked hugging and could sometimes be too friendly when I saw people from Children's Story Theater. Usually I was so happy to see them I hugged them and jumped up and down. Then I saw Emily and hugged her and she got mad. She said, "YOU CAN'T DO THAT! YOU CAN'T JUST HUG PEOPLE LIKE THAT!" That's the first time I learned there are rules around hugging and people should not go around expecting hugs all the time.

Now I don't do that anymore.

In fact, I don't like hugs at all, and if someone in my old classroom like Anthony or Douglas asks for a hug, I say, "No, thank you, you can't do that, you can't just hug people like that." I remember what she said because it sounded like a rule, so I made it one.

I also remember her from the football game which makes my heart speed up. I feel like there's something in my throat because I can't say anything. I don't want to cry in front of her or fall down. I feel like those things could happen. Like I won't be able to breathe unless she walks away which she doesn't.

So I do something smart. I walk away myself.

Once she's not in front of me anymore, I feel better.

Maybe this is a good reason I'm not going back to my old classroom and for now I'll spend my school days sitting in the nurse's office. This way, if I see people who make me have no-breathing panic attacks, I won't have to go to the nurse's office, I'll already be there.

EMILY

IT WAS MY FIRST day of high school and my first realization that friend groups are important and I had none. No one to compare my class schedule with. No one to meet at lunch. No one to help me open my locker, which I'd tried twice with no success. It was almost disorienting, like walking outside your own body, to feel so alone while standing in a crowded hallway. Now I remember it all too well. That whole morning, the only person who'd said hello to me was Belinda Montgomery.

I was terrified. I thought, *Everyone is watching us. They'll remember this forever.*

I was wrong, of course. A month after it took place, even I didn't remember that terrible exchange, when I snapped at her and told her to never do that again.

By the time this horrible exchange is over, Richard has disappeared. Strangely, the first person I see when I walk outside is Lucas again, standing alone beside the parking lot, as if he's waiting for someone to pick him up. Because no one's with him, it feels okay to talk to him. "Belinda's back. Have you seen her?" My voice sounds shaky.

He closes his eyes. It's the first time either one of us has said her name out loud. I don't know if this will feel like a big deal to him. In light of his other problems, maybe it won't. Then he surprises me: "Does she look okay?"

"No, she looks terrible," I say. "Like she's lost a lot of weight."

"Did you talk to her?"

"I tried to but she walked away."

He blows out, like he needs a minute to process all this. "Ms. Sadiq said we can arrange to have a counseling session with Belinda if we want to."

"She *did*? When?"

"I went to talk to her about it. I figured Belinda was going to come back sooner or later, and I wanted to know what to do."

I'm genuinely surprised. This whole time I've assumed Lucas is putting in his time in our Boundaries and Relationships class because the disciplinary committee decreed it. "What else did she say?"

"We should give Belinda the opportunity to accept our apology, but if she doesn't want to talk, we shouldn't push the issue. She wasn't sure, though. She wanted to talk to her mother and grandmother first."

Now I'm really stunned. He's given this possibility way more consideration than I have. He pulls out his phone and checks his messages. "Yep," he says. "Here's a message from her. She says we can stop by her office anytime after sixth period if we want to."

Because neither one of us has anywhere else to be, we walk back into the building and the main office. There's none of that joking around that we were doing two hours ago. In her office, Ms. Sadiq thanks us for coming in and thanks Lucas especially for asking for her help. "I'm very impressed that you came in of your own volition and asked me how to approach this issue. It's a much better idea than going up to Belinda on your own and starting a conversation."

I don't look at Lucas or at her. I wonder if she knows that I *did* go up to Belinda and try to start a conversation.

"So I've talked to her mother and her grandmother. They feel Belinda is still suffering from post-traumatic stress. She's been extremely withdrawn and very fearful and has, until now, refused to go to school. She also hasn't been able to be left alone. Her grandmother brought her to the grocery store once, where she had a panic attack when she saw a boy from school. She's on some medication now that's helping with anxiety, but for the time being, they want to take this as slowly as possible. She's not returning to her old classroom. She'll spend the bulk of her day in the nurse's office, where someone can keep an eye on her."

Wait a minute. In the nurse's office?

I think about Belinda when I knew her from Children's Story Theater. She is three years older than me, which was a lot back then. I was in second grade when I started and didn't even realize she had special needs. Why would I? She played Red Riding Hood and I was one of twelve hunters who ran onstage at the end to cut open the wolf's stomach. She took charge of the prop table and before our big entrance, she stood backstage in her red cape, passing out knives. The next year she played a wizard who cast spells by clapping her hands, loudly, next to someone's face. This was her own invented bit of comedy. She had only two scenes, but everyone agreed, she stole the show.

My last year with the group, our big play was *Charlotte's Web*, and when Belinda got cast as Fern, we wondered if she could handle the pressure. By then we'd figured out that she was different from the rest of us. She might have been able to memorize lines but she had a hard time reading them. She also talked too loudly on our rehearsal breaks, often to herself. When the other girls complained, the director was firm—Belinda was the hardest worker and the most qualified for the role. She'd earned it and it was hers. Then, in the first scene on opening night, we all got confused. The curtain went up and before she said any lines, she started crying. We assumed she was having some terrible meltdown. I imagined an adult going onstage to help her off. And then, in a moment I still remember perfectly, she wiped both sides of her face with the back of her hand and began reciting her lines. That's when we realized: she'd been acting the whole time and was more than good. She was the Meryl Streep of our group.

It's sad to remember all of this now and think about her rushing up and hugging me to welcome me to high school. The Belinda I remember was a social, happy person. She shouldn't be sitting in a nurse's office all day long. "What if someone helps her a little? Maybe if we go with her to class or something like that?"

"Her grandmother thinks it's best if she isn't pushed too hard."

"But—" I want to suggest something else, and then I remember the way she looked at me just now and walked away. How can I suggest anything when I'm so clearly part of the problem?

"Belinda's mother and grandmother want to ease her back into this as gently as possible. She'll just come to school for a few hours a day at first. They feel it's best not to push her into any social situations. For instance, they don't want me to set up a meeting where you two might apologize to Belinda. They appreciate the offer, but for now they feel Belinda is not ready for any discussion about the incident at the football game."

I can't get over this. "They don't want us to say *anything at all*? Even if we see her in the hallway?"

"Yes. That's what they say."

"We should *ignore* her? And not even say we're sorry?"

"Not yet. They appreciate the offer but . . . not yet."

I wonder if I should be honest and say, it's too late, I already *have* talked to her.

"Unfortunately, I have another meeting now, but we should keep in touch over the next couple weeks. We'll check in with each other and I'll let you know how she's doing."

Outside her office, I walk with Lucas back out toward the parking lot.

I flash on another memory of Belinda, one Lucas might share. "Do you remember middle school chorus concerts?" I say. Chorus was a hugely popular class back then. Though we weren't all in class at the same time, about a hundred and fifty kids performed in the concerts. Lucas was probably there—all the popular kids took chorus so they could go on the field trip to Boston at the end of the year.

Lucas looks at me uncertainly. "Yeah?"

"Do you remember Belinda after those concerts?" It's a memory I can't get out of my head—how ecstatic she was; the way she hugged people and said, "I was great!" It made us all laugh and, for a few minutes at least, think about how much we liked her. Then we'd get caught up in who was going out for ice cream with whom. I wonder if it occurred to any of us—even once—to invite Belinda along. I'm guessing no.

"Yeah, I remember," Lucas says. He's not looking at me, he's squinting at something in the distance, but I can tell by his face: he *does* remember.

CHAPTER EIGHT
BELINDA

FROM MY SPECIAL DESK in the corner of the nurse's office, it's easy for me to look out into the main office and see that Anthony and Douglas are not doing a good job with mail delivery. Anthony can't read very well. He knows letters and usually guesses the word by the letter it starts with. In cooking class, any time he sees T in a recipe, he thinks it means tablespoon, even though it might be teaspoon and there's a big difference. He also thinks a half cup in a recipe means anything between one and two cups depending on your mood. We have made some terrible muffins because Anthony was in the mood to use two cups of butter instead of a half cup. That shouldn't have made me cry, I know, but it did the day it happened.

I cry too easily, I know. Especially at school which is where I should be working my hardest not to cry. Holding it together means doing yoga breathing and trying not cry even if you feel like it.

Another thing about Anthony is he likes to hug too much. He hugs people so much the teachers at school have to make rules about hugging and put them up on the wall near Anthony's seat. They're supposed to be for everyone but mostly they're for Anthony:

RULES FOR HUGGING
—No hugs during lesson times.
—Always ask the other person first if you can hug them.
—No full-body hugs
—Only three-second hugs (count one, two, three)

There's a few of us who don't like hugs. I'm one of them. I used to like hugs until Emily Maxwell told me no, people don't like them, and they're not allowed. Now I don't like them because they mess up my clothes. Plus not to be mean but a lot of the time Anthony has food on his shirt and I don't want his breakfast touching my shirt.

I said, "No, thank you," to Anthony's hugs for so long that they put up another list next to the RULES FOR HUGGING list. This one was for me I think.

WAYS TO BE FRIENDLY WITHOUT HUGGING
—Give a high five!
—Bump fists
—Smile and say, "I'm happy to see you, but no hugs, please."
—Say, "Would you like to play a game with me instead?"

This year I got nicer. Before our fight, I didn't always say no when Anthony asked for hugs. Sometimes I said, "If you finish all your work, Anthony, then yes, I'll give you one hug." The teachers liked this because it gave Anthony a motivator to work for. We all have motivators. I earn computer time where I'm allowed to visit Colin Firth websites and read about his life which I can't do at home because we don't have internet. From these sites I have learned that in real life Mr. Firth has three children and is married to a woman who designs green dresses for a living. I don't understand this or why she doesn't pick other colors, too. Anthony's motivators are almost always hugs. He doesn't care about anything else, including food, which is a surprise because that's what all the other boys work for. For Anthony—just hugs.

So this year I didn't mind hugging him too much.

Maybe that started the bigger problem, though. The problem where he started saying he loved me and wanted to marry me. At first I pretended I didn't hear him. Then I told him, "No, Anthony, don't be stupid. You don't love me."

That got me in trouble for saying stupid. So I tried again. "I'm older than you, Anthony. Boys aren't allowed to love a girl who is older. It's against the law."

It turns out that's not true. Cara, one of our teachers, said no, there's no law about that.

"There should be," I said.

"I don't know, Belinda. I don't think I agree with you."

"The girl should never be older than the boy! Never!"

143

She smiled. "Well, sometimes they are. My mom is five years older than my dad and they're very happily married."

I don't like hearing teachers say things like "my mom" and "my dad" because it makes them sound like children, not like teachers, and that's not right. I hate that. It makes me feel flustered. I have to walk away and yoga breathe.

Another reason Anthony shouldn't love me is that Anthony is shorter than me and the boy should never be shorter than the girl. I told him that once and he grew out his curly, puffy hair on top. Now his hair is as tall as I am but I don't know if that counts. I don't know who to ask about that.

Anthony doesn't look handsome like anyone in movies or on TV but he has nice brown eyes that are a little droopy like a basset hound. He also wears braces. I think he'll talk better when he gets his braces off. When he first came to our classroom I could hardly understand anything he said. Now I understand most of what he says, unless he's talking with food in his mouth which he's not supposed to do anyway.

From my desk in the nurse's office, I watch Anthony sort the mail and it seems like he's doing everything wrong. It looks like he's reading the first letter of the last name and putting the mail in the first box he sees with the same letter. In our school there are four teachers whose last name starts with R; six start with S. It's hard for me to think about how many mistakes he's making. Probably ten mistakes. At least.

Douglas can read okay but he is very stubborn and

very lazy. Today he's so lazy he sits down in a chair with a bunch of envelopes in his hand. He flips through them, reading the outside like they're all addressed to him and he's deciding which one to open first. One thing I know for sure—they are NOT addressed to Douglas and he should NOT open them. "Douglas, stand up!" I whisper from the nurse's office, but he doesn't hear me. I tell myself if I see him open one of those envelopes that isn't addressed to him, I'll break the rules and walk out of the nurse's office to stop him.

So far I haven't seen him do that.

The only thing I've seen is both of them doing a terrible job. After they're done mixing up everyone's mail, they push the recycling cart like it's a game to see how many people and desks they can hit with it. "Sorry!" Anthony says every time but I see him smile, like he's earning points for every dent he leaves on a piece of furniture.

"BE CAREFUL!" I scream from my desk in the nurse's office. It's hard for me to watch, but I can't look away.

I guess Anthony didn't know I was here because he looks up and smiles like he's really surprised to see me. "BEMINDA!" he says. "You're back!"

It's like he's forgotten all about the fight we got in before the football game. I can't forget it, but I guess he can. He smiles his big dopey smile at me, then he comes over to stand in the doorway of the nurse's office. "I'm so glad you're back," he says. "You look beautiful."

If Anthony's not careful, Douglas will wander away and fall asleep on a sofa. "Yeah, hi, Anthony," I say. "You should probably get back to work."

Typical Anthony, he doesn't listen. "Why were you gone so long?"

"Just never *mind* that, Anthony. You should do your work."

"But we *missed* you. Cara said Beminda's sick."

"Yeah, I'm not sick anymore."

He looks confused. "Why are you in the nurse's office?"

"I'm here because I can't go back—" I almost say go back to the classroom with you and Douglas, but then I remember people have feelings, even Anthony and Douglas. I might hate them for doing my job but I don't want to hurt their feelings. "I'm trying something new," I say softly, so no one hears. "I'm working here now."

Anthony's eyes get big. "In the nurse office?" He pronounces nurse like "yerse."

I don't tell him that I don't really have a job, just a table in the corner where someone has put paper and a box of colored markers like I'm in preschool. "Yes," I say. "I'm a nurse's assistant." Right away I know this is a mistake. Lying makes me blush. I feel my face go hot.

"What do you do?"

"Never mind that. You should go back and finish your job. If you don't keep after him, Douglas will wander away and fall asleep."

Just thinking about this makes me mad, but Anthony laughs like I've made a good joke. "You're right! He will!"

"That Douglas doesn't *deserve* a job." I sound mean, like Nan talking about one of the neighbors she hates.

"I wish you could do this job with me," Anthony says. "That would be great!"

"Why would I do it with you when I used to do it all by myself?" I don't want to sound mean, so I say, "Nothing against you, Anthony. I'd be happy to do it if they asked me to."

He smiles and claps his hands the way he does, bouncing up and down a little. "Let's ask! They might say yes if we ask!"

This is one of Anthony's big problems. He is nice to everyone and he thinks everyone will be nice back to him. He used to think that if he asked, we could make cupcakes every morning and eat them for lunch every afternoon. Every single morning he clapped his hands and bounced up and down and suggested making cupcakes. Every morning the teachers would say, "Not today, Anthony."

"You go ahead and ask, Anthony. For now I should probably get back to my job here in the nurse's office." I point to my table and hope he doesn't look at what's on there.

"Okay, Beminda! I'm happy you're back! I see you soon!"

"Yeah, okay, Anthony."

He bounces closer to me and asks if he can have a hug. I nod okay because what else can I say? A few minutes ago, I was watching Anthony and Douglas mess up the mail job and I hated them. Now Anthony's hugging me and I'm patting him on the back so he doesn't start to cry or something like that.

EMILY

"**I**S EVERYTHING OKAY?" I ask Lucas.

I'm driving Lucas to class again and he's been quiet for most of the ride. When I picked him up he was standing on the sidewalk in front of his house with his father. He got in the car quickly, even though his father was still talking. After he was in, he rolled down the window. "I don't really have a *choice*, do I, Dad? I have to go."

He rolled the window back up. "Just go. It's fine. I'll talk to him when I get back."

For most of the drive, he's said nothing, though surprisingly it hasn't been too awkward. He turned up a song on one of my mix CDs, which made me feel good. It was one of my favorites, "Long Ride Home" by Patty Griffin, not something I would have expected him to know. I almost asked, *Do you like Patty Griffin?* and then I thought, Stop acting surprised every time he doesn't act like a football player.

"Is everything okay, Lucas?" I ask again.

"Yeah, sure. My dad thinks I shouldn't have to keep coming to this class, because of my leg. I'm supposed to be on restricted movement."

"If you have a doctor's note, you probably *could* skip a class or two."

"But why would I do that? It's not like we move around a lot in class. I'm walking around school okay. I'd just be using it as an excuse. It would feel shitty."

Earlier today, Chad texted me that he was going to miss class tonight. I wasn't sure why he was telling me since we haven't talked once since our lunch date, until he added, *Will you tell Mary*, making it clear: He didn't want to tell her himself.

"He's letting me go to a party this weekend so why shouldn't I do this?"

In these drives together, I've noticed that Lucas hardly ever talks about his friends. If he mentions anyone at school, it's usually his girlfriend, Debbie, and then he says something like, "My girlfriend hates these pants." Or what he says now: "I don't even want to go to the party—my girlfriend says I have to."

He sounds so unenthusiastic about the prospect that I laugh. "She *makes* you go to parties? I thought everyone loves parties."

"Not really." He snorts a laugh. "I'm not a big drinker, I guess."

"Well, technically, if you drink anything, you are a big drinker because, look at you, Lucas. You're huge."

He laughs again. I'm starting to think Lucas might have the same sense of humor as Richard and me. "I know why *I* hate parties."

He peeks at me. "Why?"

"Because the only party I've ever been to I got nervous and drank so much I threw up on myself. After I got cleaned up, my friend Richard had to walk around the party telling everyone to be careful about the sink in the bathroom, it sprays water all over people." Halfway

149

through this story, I'm not sure why I'm telling it to him. "I was so embarrassed to go to school the next week, and then I realized no one even remembered us being there."

"Yeah, they're pretty much all like that. People only notice if you're *not* there."

I don't know if I should correct him: *People notice if you're not there, Lucas. Me, not so much.* I doubt the line, "Wait, where's Emily Maxwell?" has ever been uttered in a party setting. I don't say this, though. Instead, I ask something I've always been curious about: "What do people even *talk* about at those parties?" Maybe I'm thinking about Chad and our terrible non-conversation. It hasn't ever felt like that with Lucas. I'm curious if his friends are different. "Does anyone ever admit they're gay or worried about the environment or something like that?"

"Not really. Mostly we watch TV and if someone gets up from the couch, someone else says, 'Bring me a beer from the kitchen, would you?'"

I think about how my friends and I talk about weightier issues. Usually it's through music and song lyrics that we analyze to death. Richard and Barry will argue about the meaning of some obscure chorus on a Green Day song. "The guy is depressed!" "The guy is psychotic!" "Depression is not psychosis! You're conflating the two!"

Richard has been pretty open about suffering from depression in the past. For him, the worst of it happened before I knew him, when he was in middle school and spent all his time online searching for programs that would make him not gay anymore. He actually used to type in *no more gay thoughts* on the search bar. When he finally told his parents what he was doing, the depression was more of an issue than the homosexuality. He spent a year seeing a psychologist and getting medications adjusted. Even though it gives him dry mouth and hand shakes, he still takes a low dose now because he's so scared of going back to those days.

I wonder if knowing less about your friends makes it easier in a way. Maybe my fears about what will happen with Hugh come from knowing Richard's vulnerabilities. Maybe it's even made me a worse friend.

"What if someone has a real problem—like, I don't know, their mom has cancer—"

He looks at me funny with his eyebrows up again. "What makes you say that?"

"I don't know—it's just a hypothetical. Do your friends rally around and stop by with casseroles and things like that?"

For a long time, he doesn't say anything. Obviously they don't and he doesn't talk about it. We pull into the parking lot. I get out of the car and come around to his side so I can hold Lucas's crutches for him as he gets out of the car. When I turn around, Sheila is standing behind me, holding a Slinky. "Do you guys even know how these things *work*?" she says. "It's supposed to do something but it *doesn't*."

In class, Sheila is the queen of non sequiturs. She'll raise her hand to answer a question about ordering food in a restaurant and then, as if her mouth has a mind of its own, she'll start telling some story about an actress on the cover of *US* magazine. How *weird* she is, and *skinny*, too. With Sheila present, class discussion can veer wildly off topic in under a minute. Because she wants to talk all the time, Mary has instituted a special plan to help her "reach her goal of being a better conversationalist." Now Sheila gets three tickets to use every class period. Whenever she speaks off topic, she has to give the teacher a ticket. When she's used all three, she's "done for the day," and can only talk on the same subject as everyone else. It's probably a good idea; without some system in place, Sheila is a little exhausting to be around. "Not right now, Sheila," I say. "We're trying to help Lucas get inside. You remember how his leg is hurt, right?"

"Yeah, I don't even get why he needs those crutches. It's not like he's got a cast or anything's *broken*."

"It's his knee and he has to be careful. He's not even supposed to be moving around."

Lucas stands up and laughs a little sheepishly. "I'm all right, Sheila. Here, let me see that Slinky. They're not so hard." Instead of taking it, he puts a flat hand beside hers and nudges the Slinky so it snakes off her hand onto his perfectly.

"OH MY GOD!" she screams. "HOW DID YOU DO THAT?"

"Magic," he grins. "No, not really. That's what Slinkies do. Wait till you see one on a set of stairs. If you do it right, that really is magic."

"Will you show me?"

"Sure. We can use the stairs down to the basement. I'm pretty sure we've got time."

This is the most normal conversation I've ever heard Sheila have. Where she's asked a question and actually listened to the answer. Now they're headed inside and she does something equally surprising—she holds the door open for Lucas.

"Many thanks, Sheila," he says as he crutches by her.

Of course she doesn't bother holding it for me. She probably doesn't remember that I'm even here, she's so focused now on Lucas and the prospect of watching her Slinky walk down some stairs. Still, it makes me think about what Mary said   Lucas has good instincts with these students. Different than mine, but good ones.

"This week's exercise is related to what we did last week," Mary says to start class. "This time, I want you to start a new list where you write down one or two things that you are proud of. You might say, I'm very organized and neat. Or, I'm a good listener and friend."

I've noticed Mary uses this trick quite a bit—in presenting an exercise, she gives examples to choose from. Once we get started, most of the class will pick one of these answers.

This time Simon surprises me. "How do you spell badminton player?"

Mary laughs and starts writing a long list of choices on the whiteboard in front. To the ones she already mentioned, she adds: *Hard worker. Good at music, dancing, acting, and/or singing. Nice dresser. Good at drawing/painting/writing stories.* At the end of the list, she spells out *Good badminton player* and puts a smiley face next to it.

Because they have ideas to choose from, the exercise goes faster. I help Annabel write *Good lasagna maker* and I remind Francine of what she said so perfectly last week because it's not one of the choices on the board. "Remember what you told me last time? How you're a people person and you're good at helping others?" A moment earlier she'd been squinting at the board. At this, her whole face brightens. "That's right!" she says. "I am!"

When we move on to the next part of the exercise, Mary asks Lucas and me to take a piece of paper and do the exercise along with everyone else so they can use ours as examples. As she explains what we're doing, I write my name at the top and try to think quickly of two good qualities about myself. I wish I could use Francine's but I can't, so I look up at the board and grab the first two that make sense. *Hard worker* and *Nice friend.*

The next part of the exercise surprises me. The papers are meant to get passed around the room so each person can write their favorite quality about the person whose name is at the top. It's hard because some students have known one another for years and others have only just met. Mary reassures them, "It's okay to write, 'I like the bright colors you wear.' Or, 'I liked a comment you made last week in class.' If you're really stuck, you can pass the paper along without writing anything."

Now I know why she included Lucas and me in this

exercise. This way, presumably everyone will get at least two comments on their sheet.

It's not easy, though. There are some people in the class who have never spoken, meaning it's impossible to comment on anything except their appearance, which doesn't seem right. Luckily, I start with my old pal, Harrison. For him, I write: "You are very smart, plus you have a very cool way of memorizing the Billboard chart." In the second week of class, he told me his secret—that everyone in this group was born within a few years of one another, meaning he hasn't memorized sixty years of Billboard chart toppers, only five years' worth.

"Still," I told him, "that's a lot."

"I suppose," he said. "But five years is a lot less than sixty."

After I finish mine, I lean over to Sheila's desk and see that she has written nothing on hers. "What's your favorite thing about Peter?" I whisper.

"I don't know," she moans. "This is *hard*."

It *is* hard with Peter, who is one of the quiet ones. It's hard to know how much of class Peter follows because he always looks as if he's staring off into space.

"I guess I like his taste in music."

"Good—write that!" I say. "Have you talked about it?"

"I can hear what's playing in his earphones. I like most of it. Not all of it."

I've heard about autistic people having special skills, but can Sheila hear music playing in another person's earbuds this well? I push the paper to my desk and check to see if

Peter needs help. He doesn't. He might not talk much, but he has the smallest, neatest handwriting I've ever seen from a boy. He's also grasped the basic idea of assignment. *Amelia is nice with red hair*, he's written.

"Great job, Peter!" I say and touch his shoulder, which makes him flinch in surprise.

As the papers keep moving around the circle, I help Sheila write something for Amelia ("Her hair is really thick") and for Simon ("I use to be in love with Simon but I'm not anymore"). I write my own notes and eventually, with much cajoling and assistance, every paper makes its way around the circle.

After break, Mary tells us that we're not quite done yet—there's one last step to this exercise. She wants everyone to read over his or her list and make different marks beside the comments that 1) surprised them the most, 2) they agree with the most, 3) they want to work on doing more. A few protests ripple through the crowd. Thomas slumps onto his desk and says he's too tired for anything like this. Simon says he can't read anyone's handwriting.

Mary waits for the talking to stop. "Let me tell you the reason we're doing this. You already know the first thing people notice about you is that you look and act a little different than other people. You can't control that. What you *can* control is the *second* thing they notice about you. You can make sure it's something you like about yourself and something other people like about you, too."

Mary's right about this much: they do look different in one way or another. Simon wears bright, Day-Glo-colored

T-shirts, elastic-waistband pants, and Velcro strap shoes. Francine carries a fuzzy panda-bear backpack. Ken wears a variation of the same outfit every week—a motorcycle decal shirt with sweat pants. Whenever he gets nervous about standing up in front of the class or doing a role-play, he stretches the waistband of his pants out and tucks his T-shirt in. Mary's also right about her second point. Now that we've been coming here for more than a month, that's not the first thing I notice anymore. I know these people well enough now to say that Sheila, with her J. Crew wardrobe, might look the most normal, but is actually the most challenging to have a decent conversation with. And Simon, who looks the strangest, is probably the easiest. Or at least the one most likely to understand a joke and make a funny one himself.

Now I suddenly like this exercise a lot. I look down and reread my own sheets. I have a few surprising ones:

I really like your purse
You're the funniest person I have ever met.
You should be on TV.
You make me laff.

It occurs to me that before coming to this group, I've never thought of myself as a particularly funny person. Funny is reserved for Richard and Barry, who quote long stretches of dialogue from *The Simpsons* or *Anchorman*. Funny people work hard for their title. I wonder if it is a measure of the relatively easy audience this group is that someone has called me "the funniest person I have ever met."

Pretty soon there's no time to think about it because everyone needs help with this assignment. I bend down beside Simon's desk while Lucas pulls a chair over and sits beside Francine. I hear him explain softly to her, "Which one says how you'd *like* people to see you?"

The question is too abstract. Lucas thinks for a second. "How about this? Which one do *you* like the most?" She points to something. *"Really?"* Lucas says. "Your favorite thing about yourself is your pink socks and your barrettes? I think you've got better things on there."

They both read her sheet. She points to a different one and looks at him. He reads it and nods. "Exactly. That's the one I would have picked, too. Now draw a star next to that."

As we move around the room, I can't help imitating the way Lucas helped Francine. Thoughtfully, respectfully. As I circle around the room, I stop by his empty desk and read his list when no one is looking:

You have nice jean pants
You are very big.
Your leg is hurt.
I lik you but I'm also Scared of you. Thats why we ar
    not friends.

Lucas looks like a football player. Everything about him is big—his chest, his neck, his hands. If you don't know him at all, he *is* scary to imagine becoming friends with. If you know him a little, in the context of our school, where football is an obsession and the players all celebrities, it's even scarier. It occurs to me, though—none of these comments say anything about Lucas personally. They're all about his size, his looks, or his injury. If he had to pick his favorite, what could he choose? There's nothing here.

Because we were helping other people, I didn't bother to write anything on his list. Now I pull out my pen to scribble quickly: *You have good instincts and you're a nicer person than I ever expected you'd be.*

I reread it and consider crossing the whole thing out. I don't know if I've said too much or too little because I'm not sure what, exactly, I want to say. I think I want to say: *You've surprised me, in the same way some of our classmates have surprised me. The way Belinda surprised me all those years ago by being so good at theater.* I hope I haven't embarrassed myself or, worse, said something inadvertently unkind: *You don't seem like a nice guy; I'm surprised that you are.*

Once we're back in our seats, I watch Lucas read the new item on his sheet, but he doesn't look at me or around the room to figure out who wrote it. It's pretty obvious. Chad isn't here and Mary hasn't moved from her desk for this exercise. It has to be me, but he doesn't seem to register that.

Even when we walk out of class, he doesn't mention it. Instead we stand in the waiting room for a minute because the class that meets after ours—ballroom dancing—is gathering in front of the main door, creating a blockade. It's a surprisingly big group, twice the size of our class, with about forty participants, an equal mix of men and women. They're required to wear jackets and skirts, though some of them show up in work uniforms they change out of in the bathroom. Lucas and I stand in the lobby and watch the spectacle of them all greeting one another. There are lots of hugs in this crowd. A few of the women are wearing corsages that get pressed and flattened. Because we are standing in the hallway near the bathroom, a man wearing a McDonald's uniform, carrying a brown grocery bag, rushes up and points to our jeans. "Have you two changed yet? Class is about to start."

Lucas holds up a hand. "We're not in this class. The bathroom's all yours."

"Great! Thanks." He hugs his bag and carries it into the bathroom.

As the class starts, we peek into the open door of the gym, where the dancers are already partnering up. "Heads up!" the teacher commands. "Arms raised!"

It isn't a graceful sight. Their raised arms do more colliding than settling onto each other's shoulders. Even the teacher closes her eyes. When she opens them, though, it's happened: they're all in dance position, poised to begin. "Very good," she says softly.

We wait just long enough to see the man we spoke with earlier emerge from the bathroom, still wearing his McDonald's pants, but now he has on a wrinkled button-down shirt and a large, clip-on bow tie.

Lucas flashes him a thumbs-up with a smile. "You look awesome, man."

"Thanks." The man nods seriously and adjusts his tie. "You don't, but that's okay. You're not in the class."

We wait until he's gone to laugh at what he's said. "You don't look awesome either," Lucas says because I'm laughing a little too hard. As I hold the door open for him, he keeps going. "Seriously, where's your tiara? Every week, you show up without it."

In the car, Lucas still doesn't mention my note on his sheet. Apparently we both can't stop thinking about this group we just watched, because after a little silence, he asks: "Do you ever think about what these people do the rest of the time, when they're not at the center?"

I do, actually. I wonder about that a lot. From what I can tell, most of them still live with their parents, though not all: a few talk about group homes, and rules about what chores they must do. No one drives a car, which means they must not see one another much outside of class.

Lucas keeps going. "I know some of them work, but what do they do the rest of the time? Watch TV with their parents?"

"I'm not sure," I say. "Probably."

"It's just kind of *sad*, isn't it?"

Maybe I'm annoyed because he still hasn't mentioned the note I wrote on his sheet, or maybe I'm irritated because he says this with more emotion than I usually hear from him. "Why is that *sad*? Why is staying home with parents on a weekend night so tragic?"

"It's not tragic, it's just—I don't know—don't *you* think it's sad?"

"Not going to parties or being part of the popular crowd isn't sad, Lucas. People can have very nice, happy lives even if they stay home." I realize, as the girl who doesn't go out a lot on weekends, I sound overly defensive saying this, but I want to make the point: happiness looks different to different people.

"That's not what I'm saying."

"What *are* you saying?"

He stares at me like I'm much weirder than he thought. "I'm not sure. Forget it."

I stew over this exchange long after I've dropped Lucas off. What would he think of my life, I wonder, if he knew that most of my social life revolves around going to movies with Richard? I suspect he'd pity me in the same way he pities all our classmates. It's an awful feeling. I don't want his pity. My life is fine.

Even as I think this, though, I wonder if I like doing this class because I feel connected to these people by some intangible loneliness that we all share. Back at home, I pull out my affirmation page to study the handwriting and try to figure out who thinks I'm the funniest person they'll ever meet. Is it Harrison, my first friend, who laughs at my improvs even when I'm not trying to be funny? Or Simon, with whom I now have a few ongoing jokes? It's impossible to tell. All the handwriting is messy and hard to read. Then I notice a little note at the bottom, something I'm certain wasn't there earlier tonight. It's written in red ink—the same color pen Lucas was using to help people star their favorite qualities. It says:

Emily thinks a lot about doing the right thing. It makes me think about it, too.

CHAPTER NINE
BELINDA

IN SCHOOL, WE HAVE to fill out Transition Plans every year where we say what we want our future to look like. Some people write different things every year, like Douglas says he wants to be a farmer one year and professional soccer player the next. This just shows that he is not realistic. He's scared of tractors and lawnmowers but he thinks he can be a farmer.

I always write the same thing: I want to be an actress and get married someday. I try to read magazine articles about being married because in my family no one is married. Any time I see an article with the word marriage in it, I save it so I can learn more things about what to expect. Sometimes that means I have to read about sex which I don't like doing at all. I don't mind thinking about kissing and holding hands, but I don't like thinking about sex. In class whenever Douglas calls a girl a "hot sexy mama" I have to yoga breathe and ask him to please not say things like that.

Once Anthony said, "You're hot and sexy, too, Beminda," but that just made it worse.

That was one thing I said during our big, terrible fight. *You shouldn't copy Douglas because everyone hates Douglas.* It was an awful thing to say. Plus it's not true. I just hate when Douglas calls girls hot and sexy, but I don't really hate him.

I don't like thinking about that fight with Anthony so I don't usually.

I'll just say this: if we hadn't had that fight a few days before the football game, I never would have begged my neighbor Annemarie to give me a ride to the game. I never would have gone to the game at all which makes everything that happened at the game kind of their fault.

I don't think they know this.

That's why I told Nan that I can't look at Anthony or Douglas or sit in the same room with them anymore.

The fight started because Anthony kept saying we should get married someday.

"That's stupid," I said, but we aren't allowed to use that word in class about someone else. If we do, we lose a star toward free choice so I lost a star. That made me mad. I'm always losing stars when Anthony sits next to me. Teachers don't see the way he lets his pencils touch mine and then his leg. Not a lot of touching, just a little, like his leg hairs if he's wearing shorts.

It makes me mad because sometimes I like Anthony. I think he's funny and nice and then I try to imagine waltz dancing with him and I can't. He is not at all a graceful person or a good dancer. Once, at a Best Buddies party, he lay down on the floor and did a dance called the bug that I wish I'd never seen. Just thinking about that makes me mad at Anthony. He looked like he was trying to eat the floor and throw up at the same time.

Another thing about Anthony I don't like is that he'll do things regular kids tell him to do because he thinks everyone will be his friend afterward. It's called being gullible which is a word we learned after he pulled the fire alarm because a bunch of boys told him to. They said they'd buy him pizza in the cafeteria afterward, but they never did because it was a fire alarm and everyone had to leave the building. It turns out they were just trying to get out of a math test. He believed them about the pizza which makes him gullible.

After we learned that word, everyone started calling everyone else gullible no matter what they did. If Douglas talked too loud in the hall, Anthony told him to stop being gullible which goes to show that Anthony doesn't understand the real meaning of a lot of words he uses.

That's one reason I called him stupid for talking about "getting married someday." Anthony probably thinks "get married" means have a big party with bowls of M&Ms (his favorite food) where you kiss in the middle of it. He doesn't understand that it means you have to waltz dance together at the party and afterward you live together.

Anthony says he wants to get married but he also says he wants to live with his mother for the rest of his life. I told him you can't do that unless you marry your mom and he said, "Fine, then I'll marry my mom."

The day we had our fight, he asked me to marry him again and I said, "Don't be stupid, what about your mom?"

He said he asked about it and he's not allowed to marry his mom.

"That's why you want to marry me?" I said.

He smiled like I was joking which I was *not*. "Yes," he said. "Plus I don't want to marry anyone else. I want a girlfriend named Beminda."

Do you see why he upsets me? "I can't be your girlfriend and your wife!" I screamed. "Just forget it, Anthony."

That's when he got very mad at me. He said I didn't listen to him and then he called me gullible. He said that I should stop talking about movies like *Pride and Prejudice* and I should look around and live in the real world like this class which was full of nice people who I ignore.

"That's not true. I don't ignore anybody," I said. Then he asked me if I knew everyone's names and he was right, I didn't.

"You think you're better than everyone," he said. "But you're not."

I wanted to tell him I didn't think I was better than *everyone* in our class but yeah, I was better than some of them. Didn't he think that, too? There are people in our class who can hardly do anything including feed themselves or go to the bathroom alone.

"I'm not better than anyone else," Anthony said.

"Yes, you *are*," I said. "You can walk and talk and eat!"

That's when I looked up and saw Eugene, a boy in

166

our room who uses a motorized wheelchair and a talking computer. He has very bad cerebral palsy but he's also pretty smart, maybe, because he can play computer games like chess and Minecraft.

I don't like thinking about Eugene or even looking at him because he confuses me. Maybe he is smart on the inside and can't show it. Maybe he is nice and smiles at everyone or maybe his face is stuck in a smile. He never talks in class; he just sits there and smiles and drools a little. That's when it got bad. I didn't want Eugene to think I was talking about him so I got nervous and said, really loud, "I *am* better than you at a lot of things, Anthony!"

Anthony got mad and said he didn't want to marry me anymore. He also said that most people in our class don't like me very much and he tries to defend me but he wasn't going to do that anymore. "Then you'll have no friends," he said. "You try and see how it feels."

After that, I started crying so hard even Eugene rolled over and breathed near me for a while to see if I was okay. I cried and cried because I was pretty sure Anthony was right, everyone hated me. That's when I started thinking about Ron again and other people who had been nice to me at the Best Buddies dance last spring. *It's okay,* I thought. *I'll be friends with regular kids.* The nice ones who are friendly, not the mean ones on the bus who steal my food.

The next day at school I found Ron in the cafeteria and I sat down next to him. I sat down with him again in the hallway before school. I went over to him every time I saw him the next few days at school. Usually I couldn't think of anything to say so I said hello and then I just sat there. Mostly it was okay but sometimes I felt uncomfortable. Like maybe his friends were laughing at me. But I never heard them say my name so maybe they weren't laughing at me. Maybe they just laughed a lot. Ron always said hi but he didn't say anything more. He wasn't like Anthony who was always borrowing my pencils and asking me questions and touching my shoulder.

With Ron, I just sat quietly while he talked to other people. I didn't ask him if he wanted to come over to my house and watch *Pride and Prejudice* anymore because I knew he probably couldn't do something like that during football season. He'd already told me how busy he was and I understood. He hardly had enough time to eat and sleep. Which is why, when I overheard a girl saying she would see him later after the game, I said to her, "He can't. He doesn't have time for things like that. He has to eat and sleep."

She looked at me for a long time and then she laughed, really loud. It was a mean laugh, I could tell. It made me think, Good. Now Ron will see that she's mean and he shouldn't be friends with her. The more she laughed at me, the more I smiled, until Ron really surprised me. He took one of her hands and said, "Come on, Janelle. Let's just go."

While he pulled her away, she said to me, "You should probably leave Ron alone. You know that, right?"

Maybe he's pulling her away to tell her he can't be friends with her anymore, I thought. But then he put his arm around her and she put his arm around him and did that thing I don't understand where she slid her hand into the back pocket of his jeans.

I don't understand that.

EMILY

I DON'T KNOW WHICH IS worse: the news itself or how I hear. How I hear is pretty bad. I'm standing in the cafeteria line behind Lucas's girlfriend, Debbie, and a group of her friends. Up close, Debbie is even more beautiful than she is from far away, which is hard to believe but it's true. How are her pores so small and her skin so perfect? I don't get it.

For a while, I don't listen to what they're talking about, but then I hear: "I don't even know if they're really *making* him do it. I think he's just doing it because ever since his mom died, he's looking for reasons to get out of the house and away from his dad."

I know she's talking about Lucas by the way she rolls her eyes like this is one of many things she has to put up with from her boyfriend. Neither Debbie nor any of her friends has looked my direction. She seems so unaware of my presence six inches from their conversation that she must have no idea who I am, which stumps me. I've been driving Lucas to class for two weeks now, but apparently she has never asked him to point me out to her. I can't imagine being so oblivious, but there are a lot of things I can't imagine. Like this horrible fact, made clear by the rest of their conversation: "How did his mom die again?" her friend asks.

"Cancer."

"When was it?"

"Like two years ago, I think."

His mother died of cancer two years ago? I think about my boneheaded questions in the car with Lucas and feel so bad, I step out of line, because I can't even remember what I was going to buy and I'm not hungry anymore. I slink back to my table and sit down across from Richard.

"Everything okay?" he says. Richard and I seem to be in a competition these days to see how long we can go without either one of us mentioning his or her love life. I tried to ask once and he said, "It's kind of private, actually," which made me so mad I decided not to bring it up again. Presumably everything's fine with Hugh, we're just not talking about it, which means everything we say is a little awkward.

Maybe he doesn't see it this way. Maybe his life hasn't changed that radically. He still eats with us every day (Hugh has only made a one-time appearance at our table). He still makes the same jokes. He can still do this—tell I'm upset, even when I say nothing.

"I feel like a jerk," I say softly.

I tell him the whole story and he stares at me. "You didn't know that Lucas's mom died?"

I can't tell if he's kidding. "You *did*?"

"Yeah. I mean—she died of cancer in tenth grade. He was out of school for two weeks."

How does Richard know this? "You knew him in tenth grade?"

"No—I just—" He shrugs. "I don't know. I noticed things like that."

"Big jocks with problems?"

He blushes. "Yeah."

"Does everyone know this except me?"

Everyone nods. "Sure," Weilin says. "It was really sad. I knew his mom a little—she used to volunteer in the library where I went after school in elementary school."

Now I feel even worse. In elementary school, the library had one of the only after-school options for kids whose parents worked. I went three days a week up until fourth grade. "His mom was one of the library ladies?"

"Yeah—her name was Linda. You remember, the one with red hair who did the make-your-own-book projects?"

I feel awful. She was my favorite. She once told me she liked my books so much she was going to put them on the library shelves for a week and see if anyone checked them out. "They're better than some of the other books we have here," she whispered. And then we realized if she did, I might not be able to keep the book and show my parents, so we decided not to. "*That* was his mom?"

Weilin and I must have been there at the same time, but we didn't know each other. She was probably one of the studious kids who did her homework before project time started. Back then I spent most of my time trying to get invited to sleepovers with girls I wasn't really friends with. I wish I could go back and be a different person back

171

then, one who didn't care about the popular-girl crowd, and would have noticed a better friend in the corner quietly doing her homework. Something else occurs to me. "Does that mean Lucas was in that group?"

"I think so," Weilin says. "He wasn't so big back then. Or so noticeable. Plus he was pretty shy. I think he mostly just stayed with his mother and helped her."

I try to remember him and I can't. It's like I noticed all the wrong things back then.

I don't work up the courage to say anything to Lucas until we're back in the car again driving to class. As we pull away from his house, I turn to him. "I'm sorry about those stupid questions I asked you last week. I didn't know about your mom. I felt terrible when I heard."

He's looking away from me, out the window. "It's okay. You're right. My friends are jerks, pretty much."

"I was a bigger jerk. I knew your mom from the library—I had no idea she died and I had no idea she was your mom. I'm really sorry."

He turns and looks at me. "You knew her?"

"She wouldn't remember me, but I remember her. I loved this one project she did with make-your-own books. I kept wanting to make a different one every week and she always let me—she was really nice about it. I remember that."

He smiles a little, like he appreciates this. "She was really nice before she got sick. Then she got breast cancer and it was terrible. She got really moody, but it wasn't really her fault."

"When did she get sick?"

"The first time was when I was in eighth grade. Then it came back in tenth grade."

I wonder if his friends only knew her as the mom with cancer. Maybe none of them has the same picture of the woman that I recall. "I remember she had such a nice laugh."

He smiles now. A real smile. "Yeah."

"And she really laughed at the stupid things kids sometimes say. She liked kids a lot. I remember that."

He seems happy to hear this. And grateful. "Yeah, she did."

There isn't much more to say after this. How is your family doing now? Or what's it like losing a parent? Any option like that feels wrong. I accused his friends of never asking any questions, but the truth is I ask too many sometimes. I sometimes poke and I prod until my friends ask me to please just stop. I don't want to ruin this moment doing that, so for the rest of the ride, we listen to music and say nothing.

This week's class is a potluck dinner party where everyone was supposed to bring a dish they'd cooked themselves or helped to make. At the end of class last week, Mary told Lucas and me not to bring any food. "We always have way too much. We need to do this so everyone can practice socializing around food, but every time, it's the same. People come with three dishes plus a box of Ring Dings." She shakes her head. "It's the horn of plenty, I'm telling you."

173

It turns out she's right. There's a table groaning with food and everyone has taken the "favorite dish" suggestion literally. There's very little in the way of entrées and no salads to speak of. Two people have brought slice-and-bake Christmas sugar cookies. Someone else has brought a large, expensive-looking tin of kettle corn. Mary points to it and asks, "Ken, did you *make* that popcorn?"

"Is okay," Ken says. "I make call to order popcorn. Mom said okay. For party okay. I pay myself."

Mary laughs. "Well, thank you, Ken. That was nice of you."

Before we eat, Mary reminds them of the rules around eating: don't overload your plate, don't take too much of one thing, don't eat all dessert things. When everyone has gotten food and sat back down, Mary has another list of suggestions she's written out ahead of time and taped to the front board:

—Sit *with* someone while you eat.
—In between bites, put down your fork and talk to them.
—Use your napkin!
—If you spill, clean it up!
—If you stand up to get something, ask if someone else needs anything.

We volunteers wait until everyone else has taken food before we start. I haven't seen Chad in the two weeks since we went out to lunch, so I'm surprised when he comes up behind me at the food table and whispers over my shoulder, "So I guess we shouldn't have waited. It looks like all the cotton candy's gone."

I laugh and take a spoonful of something called taco casserole and then, just as I'm stepping away, Chad says, "I see a little spot in the corner where no one's sitting. Should we sneak over there and eat by ourselves?"

I look around the room. In spite of Mary's instructions, about half the group is sitting by themselves. "I don't think so, Chad. I'm pretty sure we're meant to eat with the other students." Do I really need to tell him this?

I walk away and sit down with Simon, who has covered most of his plate with taco casserole. To eat, he bends down to shorten the trip between the plate and his mouth. One glance around the room and I realize Mary's right: they all eat as if they've forgotten they're in a room where other people can see them. Not that they're all so messy; they just approach food passionately, with an embarrassing gusto. Ken sticks his tongue out to place a Dorito flat on it, then snaps his teeth over it and grins like he's tricked the poor chip into getting eaten. Peter sits about six feet away from everyone else, eating one noodle at a time by lowering it into his mouth from a fork held high.

Last week Peter surprised us all by saying there's only one woman he'll ever love, so it doesn't make that much sense for him to learn about meeting other women or starting conversations. In all these weeks, it was the first time he'd ever mentioned a girlfriend. Mary looked just as surprised as the rest of us. "Who is it, Peter?" she said.

"You don't know her," he said. "She used to teach me piano and I love her. That's all. Her voice, her hair, her chest, everything. I love everything about her."

We were all stunned. This was the most Peter had ever said in class.

"What's her name?" Mary asked.

"Mrs. McCarthy."

No one laughed or rolled their eyes at the idea that Peter had a great love of his life but didn't know her first name. Nor did anyone point out that it sounded like Mrs. McCarthy probably had a Mr. McCarthy somewhere. Mary usually walks a fine line with these revelations. She doesn't want to dismiss any feelings but she also doesn't want to perpetuate fantasies. She regularly reminds Sheila that Justin Bieber is not a dating option for her and if she wants to go on dates or make more friends, she'll need to look around closer to home. Over the last month and a half, I've learned that they all have some version of these passionate attachments. Daniel loves tae kwon do and his dojo master so much that Mary allows him to wear his outfit every other week and end class with a short demonstration of some new skill. Usually it involves a roundhouse kick and some chops and a "Heee-yah!" He always gets a round of applause and does a courtly bow at the end. It has nothing to do with the class material we're covering, except maybe it does. Afterward Mary always says, "I love seeing how much you love tae kwon do, Daniel," which is exactly how I feel listening to these folks talk about the things they love. It reminds me of my old self, the girl who loved book-making and acting in plays.

These folks aren't childish; they just haven't lost the enthusiastic attachments I associate with children.

I turn to Simon now. He's nearing the end of his taco casserole, so it seems like a good time to ask him a question. "So where do you work, Simon?" They all talk about jobs vaguely. Cute girls at work. Bad bosses. I've never been sure where these jobs happen.

"No place now," Simon says, lifting his plate so he can tilt what's left on it into his mouth. "I have worked, though. Just a long time ago."

"Oh!" I'm surprised. Simon is one of the class members who seems the most capable. He never misses a *Jeopardy!* question; his class comments are almost always appropriate. "Where would you like to work?"

He pushes his glasses up his nose. "I like restaurants, but every time I try restaurants they let me work a month, then they say no way."

"Why?" It's hard to believe. Simon's quirks—his thick glasses that don't stay up, his enthusiastic fist bumps, his plaintive questions—are almost all endearing. How could he not find a restaurant who appreciates him?

"Food service rules. If you touch your mouth or your nose, you have to wash hands. Every time. You forget, you break the law." Without seeming to realize what he's doing, he wipes the back of his nose with his sleeve pulled over his hand. "Sometimes I forget. I just do." He throws up his hands in an exaggerated shrug. "What can you do? They say I break the law one more time, I have to go. That's the way it is."

"So are you looking for a new job?"

My mind scrambles to think of diners and out-of-the-way lunch counters where cleanliness maybe isn't a top priority. "Have you tried Roosters?" I say. Roosters is a breakfast restaurant that high schoolers go to after a late-night party. I never have, but I hear people talk about it. And I've seen the help wanted sign almost permanently placed in the window. Apparently they have a hard time finding early-rising employees.

"Roosters, no. They say no. No insurance to hire people like me." He runs through a long list of people who say no for reasons like this: McDonald's, no. Wendy's, no. Stop and Shop, no. "Stop and Shop hires people with disabilities, but all full up for now. That's all. No more."

I'm stunned at the number of places he's tried and hasn't succeeded in getting a job.

At break, I ask Mary if she knows how many people in the class have actual jobs. "Not very many," she says. "Most of them go to supervised workshops, or else they have jobs that give them maybe five or eight hours a week. We have about the same number of jobs available for folks with disabilities that we had twenty years ago. The only problem is we have about four times the number of disabled adults now."

I think about the way expectations have shaped us all. How Lucas feels like he has only one shot at college and my friends and I feel like we have no choice *except* college. But what if the world had *no* expectations for you? What if we were leaving school with no prospects at all?

At the end of our meal, I ask Simon what he does with his days. He thinks about it for a while and then he shrugs. "Not too much," he says. "On Wednesdays, I come here."

"Oh, Lucas, it's *terrible*," I say in the car ride home. I'm grateful for this topic to discuss so he doesn't have a chance to tease me about the strangest moment of class—when Chad stood up to leave early and interrupted Mary to make an *I'll call you* hand phone, pointing to me. All the women in class spun around to look at me. After class ended, Sheila asked if Chad and I were getting married. "Of course not," I said, blushing fiercely.

"Why not?" Sheila asked.

I saw Lucas staring, which made me even more nervous. "Well, I'm way too young, for one thing."

"Not *really*," Sheila said. "You're allowed. You should. Just do it. I'd get married if Justin Bieber asked me."

"I would, too," Lucas said. "If it was *Justin*? Totally."

Sheila didn't laugh. She just rolled her eyes. I assumed Lucas would spend the ride home making fun of me about Chad, which made me launch off on this topic with particular zeal. "These people need help finding jobs. There need to be some *changes*."

Lucas smiles and fiddles with his brace. "What—are you going to become a social worker now?"

"No. I'm talking about political activism. Legislative changes. These people need a *voice*." I think about the time I've spent signing people up for their rice-and-bean Oxfam pledges at school. I should have been going into restaurants with Simon pointing out the moral responsibility we have as a society to find a place for him to work in the community. "Doesn't it shock you that most of these folks don't have jobs? They're all capable of working."

"I'm not sure about that."

"Most of them are. With support."

"Right, but how many bosses want to give them that kind of support? Who can afford it?"

"So there should be incentives for businesses who hire workers with disabilities. Like they have for people who hire vets. Something!"

I look over at him and stop. He's smiling at me in a way that's sort of confusing. "Maybe that should be your new slogan," he says. "SOMETHING'S GOTTA BE DONE! You could get people to sign pledges at your lunch table." He's never mentioned my YAC work before. I wouldn't have thought he'd noticed. "Or how about this: I'M GOING TO CHANGE EVERYONE'S LIFE!"

The first comment was funny. This second one seems mean, especially considering what he wrote on my sheet. Theoretically this is what he *likes* about me. "I'm not talking about changing everyone's life. I'm saying this is a vulnerable group that's being ignored right now. No one's helping them get what they really need, which are *jobs*. A sense of productivity. Forget relationships, they need *work*."

"You want to go out and find twenty jobs for those people?"

"Well, someone should! God, Lucas, you know them

as well as I do. They're capable people. You like them."

"I *do* like them."

"Then why aren't you agreeing with me? I'm just saying there should be laws that make it easier for these people to get jobs."

"Okay. I agree. I just don't think screaming about it in a car to me helps anybody. I'd rather think of something I could do."

"Like what?"

"I don't know. I'm still thinking."

"Like volunteering in this class? Do you think that's helped anyone?"

"I don't know." He thinks for a minute and shakes his head. "Not really."

It seems as if we're getting too close to saying what I've really wanted to say, what we've both avoided saying since Belinda came back to school. Our crime involved her and our punishment hasn't done a thing to help her.

I drive in silence for a while until I pull onto Lucas's street. "Let me know if you think of something," I say. It comes off as more sarcastic than I intend it to. I know he does care. He's a more reliable, better volunteer than Chad. It's possible Lucas understands what I don't want to admit: that nothing we're doing will help Belinda. Or—when you get right down to it—anyone else.

That night, it comes to me: an idea so simple I'm not sure why I didn't think of it sooner.

I wait until the next day, after school, to tell Lucas.

I know where he waits by himself for the van that is temporarily driving him home while he's injured. It's in the back parking lot behind school where neither one of us has to worry about being seen talking to each other.

I start by telling him about Belinda back in the Children's Story Theater days. "She was a good actress," I tell him. "She was better than good. She was the best one of all of us. At everything: props, costumes, acting, all of it. She had a real gift, and we've never seen her once in a high school play, right?"

Lucas shrugs. "I wouldn't know."

Of course he wouldn't. Why would a football player have seen every school production the way Richard and I have? "Trust me, she hasn't been in anything. So what if you and I put on a play starring Belinda?"

I can't tell what he's thinking. There's a skeptical expression on his face. "I think we should. If we want to do something that would really help her, this would be it. I'm sure of it."

I look down at his leg brace; hopefully I don't have to point out the obvious: *Your afternoons are pretty free these days. You can't really say you don't have the time.*

"What play would you do?"

"*We.* It would have to be both of us. I don't have enough friends."

He raises his eyebrows. "And I do?"

"Oh, please, Lucas. I have four friends. You have about seventeen times that. Surely there are a few benchwarmers on the cheerleading squad who wouldn't mind staying after school a few extra days a week to help out." He shrugs. I'm right, there probably are.

"What play are you thinking of?"

"She was really great in *Charlotte's Web*."

"Are you kidding?" He laughs as if maybe I am. Then he shakes his head. "Wouldn't someone have to wear a costume and play the pig?"

I've forgotten that ten years have passed since Belinda stole everyone's heart with her phenomenal Fern portrayal. I've forgotten the furry tails and cardboard ears we wore to play barnyard animals. I've forgotten that we're too old now to put on children's plays.

Or maybe not.

"It's a classic, Lucas. Make fun of it all you want, but it's not a terrible idea. It was a great play and she was fantastic. I guarantee if you saw her do the part, you'd be amazed."

He nods as if he's considering it. I'll give him this much: he's not brushing me off or moving away saying, *Yeah, let me get back to you.* Instead he smiles. "Wouldn't someone have to play a spider?"

"We did that with a puppet. Someone stood behind a set piece saying the lines. It was surprisingly effective."

He smiles at me in a funny way, as if he guesses what I'm not telling him. "That was you, wasn't it?"

I glance away because suddenly, looking into his green eyes is confusing. "I'm not telling."

Now he's really smiling. "You played Charlotte the spider."

"All right, fine, I did. It was the high point of my acting career, if you must know."

He really laughs now. "Do you still have the puppet?"

"Of course not. No one's allowed to keep props like that afterward, but we could probably borrow everything from Children's Story Theater if told them what we were doing."

I still can't tell what he thinks. He's not saying yeah, sure, but he's also not saying no. "I don't know," he says. "We're not even supposed to talk to her." He's backing away.

"Right, I know, but if we talk to her grandmother? It's worth a try, isn't it?"

I don't know why this is so important to me or why I feel like I'll cry if Lucas does the easy thing and says, "Yeah, I don't think so."

But he doesn't.

Instead his van pulls up and he crutches over toward it. "Yeah, okay," he says. "Let me think about it."

CHAPTER TEN
BELINDA

THIS SURPRISES ME A lot. I walk into the nurse's office this morning and football player number 89 is sitting on one of the beds with an ice pack on his knee. I don't know number 89's name so I don't say anything and I don't look at him. He was not at the Best Buddies dance and he is not my friend. But sitting here not looking at him makes my heart pound. I feel like I might not be able to breathe pretty soon. I don't understand this. I'm not supposed to be alone in rooms with people who scare me. That's why I'm sitting in the nurse's office, so I don't have to see people like number 89.

My armpits are sweating and so is my face.

I should walk out, but the door is across the room. I'd have to walk past him and I can't.

I can't move at all.

"Hi, Belinda," I hear him say. "I'm sorry to be in your space. I'm supposed to ice my knee for twenty minutes before school, but I could sit somewhere else if you'd rather."

I'm surprised he knows my name because I don't know his. Usually it's the other way around. "It's okay," I get my mouth to say.

"I'm Lucas Kessler," he says. "We've never officially met."

My face goes hot again.

"I know your mom and your grandma didn't want us talking to you but now that we're sitting here by ourselves, I just want to say how sorry Emily and I are about what happened to you. We've been going to this class—"

"Oh my goodness! Belinda, you're here!" Ms. Weintraub, the nurse, is standing in the doorway. She looks nervous because she knows this boy isn't supposed to be here. "We didn't expect you for another half hour. Lucas, why don't you sit out here in the main office."

He gets off the bed and limps into the other room, holding the ice to his knee. I'm glad he's not in the same room anymore but for the rest of the day I wonder what he was about to say when Ms. Weintraub came in. What class are they going to?

The next morning he's there again. I've gotten to school early enough that Ms. Weintraub isn't here again. I made Nan drive me early. I wanted to see if he'd be here and he is. He must have gone to the freezer himself and gotten the ice pack. This time I'm not so scared. I sit two chairs away from him because I've learned about personal space and I never get closer than a Hula Hoop away from people I don't know.

"Hi," he says when I sit down. It looks like he's happy to see me, but I don't know. I've learned from Ron that I shouldn't expect people to be happy to see me.

I don't smile but I keep talking so I can ask him a question. "My name is Belinda. You're Lucas." I know we already know each other's names but I'm nervous so I say this.

"That's right. Hi, Belinda!"

"What were you going to tell me yesterday?"

He looks confused.

"It was something about you and Emily. Taking a class."

"Oh, right! We've been helping out in a class at the Lifelong Learning Center—have you ever heard of it?"

"No," I say.

"It has a lot of different classes like Relationships and ballroom dancing. I think anyone can take them but mostly it's for people with disabilities."

I look at his leg. "Do you have a disability?"

"No. I mean—" He looks down at his leg, too. "Well, sort of."

"Do you take ballroom dancing?"

"No." He laughs like this is a funny question to ask. "I'm not a very good dancer. I don't think I could do it."

"I like waltzes the best."

"*Really?* So you know how to ballroom dance?"

"No." I think of telling him about *Pride and Prejudice* and the dances I've watched them do, but then I remember that I shouldn't be too friendly. People like Lucas don't like it when you're too friendly with them.

Lucas looks at the door. Someone is turning on lights in the main office. "Look—somebody's going to tell me to leave pretty soon so maybe I'll just ask you quickly— Emily had this idea about putting on a play. Only we'd need people to act in it. Is there any chance you might be interested in doing something like that?"

My heart starts to pound. He must know who I am. He must remember my performances at Children's Story Theater. He remembers me from when I was famous and people came up to me in grocery stores and said how good I was. "I might be interested," I say. My stomach has a tingly, exciting feeling. "What play?"

"We're not sure yet. But you might be interested?"

"I don't know. I'm too old for Story Theater. I'm not allowed to do children's plays anymore."

"Oh, okay. Right."

"I'm twenty-one now."

He looks surprised. Maybe he doesn't know that students in my class stay in school longer than other kids. Maybe I sound old to him, I don't know.

"What kind of plays do you like to do these days? We haven't settled on a play yet, so we're open to suggestions."

I can't believe he's asking me this. I close my eyes and breathe through my nose so my body stays calm. "I do have a favorite story," I say.

"You do?"

I'm scared to say it out loud. I think about Ron and

his friends laughing, and then I force myself to stop remembering that. *"Pride and Prejudice,"* I say. It's almost a whisper.

"Really?" he says. "That movie with Keira Knightly?"

"Not that one. The real one starring Colin Firth."

"Oh."

"It's a miniseries. It's eight hours long."

"Huh."

"We probably couldn't do the whole thing."

"No, probably not."

Now that I've said it I feel calmer. I open my eyes and see him looking at me. It's such a strange expression on his face, like he's seeing me for the first time.

"Okay," he says. "That's a great idea. Let's do *Pride and Prejudice.*"

Later that morning, Douglas is either absent or else so lazy he won't help Anthony do their job, so I ask Ms. Weintraub if I can help him.

She says, "That's very nice of you, Belinda. Thank you."

Anthony isn't as friendly with me today as he was a few days ago. Maybe he remembers our fight now. It's hard to tell. Sometimes Anthony never remembers anything and sometimes he does remember things. I say, "I can help you. Ms. Weintraub said so."

"Oh," he says and moves over so I can stand in front of the mailboxes, too. I pull out the mail he's already sorted to see if he he's made any mistakes. I'm surprised. He hasn't.

He says, "Leave that. I do it fine. You do the new ones."

I'm surprised at how annoyed he sounds. He doesn't sound like himself. He sounds like me when I'm annoyed. "Okay," I say.

After we've been working for a while, I ask, "Where's Douglas?"

"Who cares? I'm sick of Douglas. I hate him."

I've never heard Anthony say anything like this. He's two years younger than Douglas but their parents are friends so they've known each other their whole lives. I know they do Boy Scouts together and go camping.

"You don't hate Douglas," I say. "Maybe you just hate how annoying he is sometimes."

Anthony looks confused. "He's not annoying."

Honestly, yes he is. All Douglas cares about is food and saying "She's a really hot mama" anytime anyone mentions the name of a girl who will never in a million years go out with him. "He is, Anthony. He only cares about candy and sexy girls. That's annoying."

"He says you'll never be my girlfriend. He says you'll never come back to our class because you hate me."

A few minutes ago I was so happy about the play and my conversation with Lucas. Now I feel sad. "I don't hate you," I say, because I don't. I hate that he's doing the job I love. I hate that he's in tenth grade and thinks it's okay to ask people who are almost about to graduate to marry him, that's all.

"You don't?" he says.

"No, of course not."

"Why don't you come back to our class?"

Now that he's asked me I'm not sure. I remember our fight and I remember telling Nan I never wanted to see Anthony or Douglas again. Now that I'm seeing them, though, it's fine. Maybe better than fine. I want to tell Anthony all about this play. I've told him about *Pride and Prejudice* before. He watched it last year when I had to have my hernia operation and missed a week of school. When I got back, he said watching it made him miss me less. He said I reminded him exactly of the girl in it, except he couldn't remember which girl or anyone's name.

"I'll come back when I have time, Anthony," I say. "Right now I'm really busy. I have a *Pride and Prejudice* play I'm going to be in."

Anthony blinks like he's confused the way he always is. "What *Pride and Prejudah* play?" Anthony can never pronounce long words but it's okay, I'm used to it.

"We're putting on *Pride and Prejudice* here. You should try out, too, if you want to. I think you'd be a pretty good actor. You just have to pronounce your words carefully so people can understand."

He doesn't say anything for a long time.

Finally he says, "You really think I should be a actor, Beminda?"

"Yes, I do. If you don't get a part, then you can help me keep the props table organized. I usually do that job, plus acting."

Just thinking about all this makes me so happy I want to hug Anthony again. I know he's thinking the same thing because he's looking at me with his arms open.

"Okay," I say. "If you'll audition with me, I'll give you a hug, Anthony."

"Okay," he says and I do. And I'm surprised all over again. It's not bad hugging Anthony. It really isn't.

EMILY

THOUGH OF COURSE THE two things couldn't be connected, it still makes me wonder: the same week that Belinda returned to school, we lost our first football game. Now she's been back for three weeks and last Friday, the unthinkable happened: we lost our division play-offs. We're out of contention for the state championship we all thought we would win.

The Monday after the loss, the posters put up by the student council hang off the wall in pieces that no one has the heart to clean up. At lunch, Weilin wonders if it would have been easier for everyone if we'd lost a few more games along the way. "Then we'd have practice with this." Before this year, by her own admission, Weilin attended *maybe* four sporting events in her entire life. Now she's acting genuinely depressed. "I honestly thought they would *never* lose."

"It's like we're all *mad* at them," Barry says, shaking his head. "Which isn't really fair because we don't actually *know* them."

"Speak for yourself," Richard says. "I've touched arm hairs with Wayne Cartwright. And I don't feel mad at him so much as very disappointed. He missed two plays that could have turned the game around."

"It wasn't all his fault," Weilin says. "His O line wasn't supporting him the way they should have." Suddenly everyone's an armchair quarterback replaying a game they wish they could forget.

By the end of the day, the tough talk turns to pity. Everyone thinks the players won't get offers from the big schools they hoped for. Full scholarships to Michigan and Notre Dame aren't realistic expectations anymore. Everyone says they'll be lucky to get partial rides to state schools. As the rumors mount, a new thought occurs to me. Now that football season is over, Lucas's old teammates will have free afternoons. Maybe it wouldn't be such an outlandish idea to ask three or four of them to help us with a play. We wouldn't need a lot. Just a few nice guys. The point would be getting as many people as possible to go to a staged reading—maybe *Charlotte's Web*, maybe something else—and see that Belinda is an amazingly good actress.

The more I think about it, the better the idea seems. The players are already depressed. Maybe doing a feel-good project like this would make them look big again—or bighearted, at least . to the people who come see the show. Of course we wouldn't get the same crowds as a football game, but football players acting would draw a modest crowd, which is all we'd need to accomplish what I want: for people to see Belinda's talent; for her to feel okay again about being in school; for one memory to replace another. I picture her onstage, doing her curtain calls, bowing and holding hands with the players that we've spent all fall in awe of.

I realize that I might be dreaming here. I haven't forgotten what Lucas said about these guys, but in my fantasy they're nice enough to get the job done and make Belinda feel appreciated by her peers. I'm so convinced about this idea, the first time I see Lucas alone, I walk over and say: "Don't say no right away. Just listen and tell me you'll think about this."

After I've told him, it occurs to me that I've found him in an unusual place: sitting on the floor of the hallway outside the library at lunchtime. He probably doesn't realize that during lunch, this section of linoleum is reserved for the supergeeks who eat out here quickly before disappearing into their book-lined hiding spots. Though I haven't been here in a long time, I know it well. This was my daily lunch spot before I found Richard and joined his crowd. I don't imagine Lucas has ever felt the need to eat a furtive lunch here. I assume he's here for the only reason jocks ever come to the library—he's making up work or in danger of failing a class.

He has a library book—an old one with a red leather binding—open on his lap, which suggests the problem is in his English class. Maybe he's lost whatever paperback copy he was issued and now he's reading the only copy he can find.

"What's that?" I point down.

He covers the book with his hand. "Why don't you tell me your big idea first?"

"Fine. Here it is. I think we should get football players to be in a play with Belinda! And maybe a few cheerleaders while we're at it. They're free in the afternoons now, right? It could be great. People will actually come see it because they love you guys so much and in the process they'll see what a good actress Belinda is."

"Aren't you forgetting something?"

"What?"

"Football players can't act. They'll look like morons."

"Don't they all put on skirts every year to do the powder-puff game?"

"That's totally different."

"What about the cabaret? They all sing karaoke for that, too, right?"

He shrugs. "Yeah, it's true. Some of them do."

"We wouldn't need all of them. Just five or six nice ones. And some of the cheerleaders. They'll do it if you ask them, won't they?"

He squinches up one eye as if he's considering this. "I don't know."

"I still think *Charlotte's Web* is a good idea. Especially if we get one of the littler guys to play Wilbur."

I can't tell by his expression what he's thinking. Finally he says, "Belinda doesn't want to do *Charlotte's Web*."

I stop talking and look at him. "How do you know that?"

He smiles. "I talked to her. Twice. Yesterday and this morning. It was an accident, sort of. Actually, the first time was. I don't think the second time was an accident. I think she wanted to talk to me."

"What did she *say*?"

"I brought up your play idea and I gotta admit, she seemed pretty into it."

"She *did*?" My heart skips a beat—I was right! And if Lucas has gotten this far, it means he wants to do it, too! If he does, it'll happen!

"Here's the thing," he says. "She knows what story she wants to do. She didn't even hesitate when I asked. Are you ready for this?" There's a funny expression on his face. And then he holds up the book he's reading: *Pride and Prejudice*.

"That's not a play."

"Right."

"It's a book."

"Exactly. And a couple of movies, I guess. More than a couple."

"Does she want to stage one of the movie versions?"

"Yeah. I guess the eight-hour version is her favorite."

I laugh out loud. When I keep laughing, he asks me what's so funny. "I'm trying to picture your friends onstage for eight hours."

"Right. That's never going to happen."

"Still—" I say. Suddenly it feels as if disparate pieces are falling together—the football loss, Belinda's return, Lucas's injury. Everything is lining up to make my idea work. "This could be great."

"I'm not promising my teammates will do anything," Lucas says.

It's interesting that he calls them teammates, not friends. "Use your powers of persuasion," I say as he stands up awkwardly, using my shoulder and the wall. A minute later, the bell rings and we both disappear in opposite directions.

That evening, after two hours of typing in Google searches for play versions of *Pride and Prejudice*, I still haven't found much. Then my phone rings. It's Lucas. My heart skips a beat for a second. It's the first time he's called unrelated to getting a ride, I think, and then he says, "I've found something. It's called *First Impressions*. It's a version of *Pride and Prejudice* with a smaller cast. There are twelve parts, but some people could play double parts. Basically, it's *Pride and Prejudice* set in a modern high school. Only the two main characters are dressed in old-fashioned clothes. Everyone else looks like a cheerleader or whatever, but these two are in long skirts and top hats."

I mull this over. *Clueless*—*Emma* set in a contemporary high school—is one of my favorite movies of all time. If it's well-written, it could be fabulous, but we don't have time to put on a full play with costumes and scenery. "We shouldn't try for anything too ambitious, right?"

"Right, but think about the dresses Belinda wears to school now. It's almost like she's already playing the part."

I'm surprised. He's right.

"Okay," I say. "But we'll need to find someone with experience who's willing to direct. There are a lot of pieces involved in putting on a show like this—"

There's a long silence. He's obviously waiting for me to suggest a name. None of his friends direct plays. But my drama phase was a long time ago and none of my friends do either.

Finally he whistles into the phone. "Looks like it'll have to be you."

"*Me?* I can't do it. I've never directed a play." I want to point out that I was a suggesting a low-key, staged reading. He's the one saying we should mount a play with costumes and props.

"You'll be great, Ms. Charlotte the Spider. It'll all come back to you."

"That was sixth grade, Lucas. With puppets. I don't want this to look like—" I pause. What am I suddenly scared of? Looking like I'm trying too hard? Becoming the girl who marched her flag into a bass drum? "Okay, you're right. Let's do it. Let's throw ourselves into it and do costumes and everything."

It only takes twenty-four hours for me to get excited. I read the play and love it so much that I finish all my college essays in a single night so I can turn my attention fully to this. My parents are shocked. Four essays in a night? I've been putting them off for ages thinking I need some inspiration to do them right. I didn't, of course. I needed a reason to want them done.

I can't get over what a good adaptation it is—surprisingly funny and touching. I worry, though, that what works well on the page may be hard to pull off in real life. Especially if Belinda is playing Elizabeth. There are a lot of lines to memorize and a point that isn't subtle, exactly, but needs to be played subtly. These two characters, Darcy and Elizabeth, aren't dressed like anyone else onstage, but they are the only ones who don't see what's obvious to everyone else: they're different than the others and perfect for each other.

Though nothing's been confirmed, Lucas says he'll think about asking his friends.

"We don't have a lot of time," I remind him. In the last four days, I've met with the principal and the director of the drama department. I've talked them into calling this a "student production" and letting us use our school's smaller theater five weeks from now. "We need to get our cast set."

"Right, I know. I'm trying to decide who to ask."

"What about some girls?" I say. Though he never talks about her, I still see Lucas sitting at lunch every day with his girlfriend, Debbie. I assume he'll ask her, and maybe some of her cheerleader friends.

"Right," he says. "I'm warming them up to the idea."

"And what are they saying?" I know I'm being pushy, but we don't have any choice; we need these people to help us out. If we don't get at least four or five of the popular crowd, we'll never get anyone to come to the show.

"What do you *think* they're saying, Em? They're saying it seems like a weird idea and they don't really get it, but yeah, maybe they'll stop by auditions and check it out."

"That's the best you can do? Can't you get them to make a commitment?"

"You don't know these people," he snaps. I'm obviously

pushing him too hard. "They don't like committing to things. What about *your* friends?" he says, which is a valid question.

If I'm forcing him to ask his friends, I should probably ask mine, but that would involve telling them the truth about what happened under the bleachers and I keep putting it off. I decide to wait until our next YAC meeting. I tell Richard ahead of time that I have a proposal without giving him any specifics.

At the meeting, I start with a little preamble: "This idea might require a little more of a time commitment than we've asked of you in the past." I make eye contact with everyone who's showed up—our four core friends and a freshman who looks wide-eyed and surprised, like he's accidentally wandered into the wrong meeting and is too embarrassed to leave. "But it's going to be great and it's going to be worth it, I promise."

A few minutes into my pitch, Candace interrupts me. "Wait, are you talking about putting on a *whole play*?"

"Well, yes," I say. "That's exactly what I'm talking about."

"Have you ever worked on a play at the high school?"

I have to admit, "No, I haven't."

"So maybe you don't realize how many people you need. A backstage crew, people to run the light and sound boards. You also need a stage manager and producers to work the front of house. You're probably talking about thirty people, minimum. And that's not even counting the cast. What kind of cast would you need for this—fifteen? Twenty?"

200

I see our new freshman member glance longingly at the door. Clearly, I've lost him. If I'm lucky, my best friends won't desert me and I'll have a crew of four.

"Look, it doesn't have to be elaborate. The point is, Belinda has gone to our school forever, she loves acting and she's good at it but she's never had a chance to be in a show. Let's give her that. Let's give her a chance to show the world something beyond her disability. Let's let everyone see her *ability*."

I like the sound of this so much I can't believe I made it up on the spot. I smile at Richard, who is usually our slogan genius. He doesn't smile back. "The thing is, Em— none of us are theater people," he says.

"So what?" I say, exasperated. "Aren't we all sick of getting subdivided by labels? Only theater people can put on plays. Only cool people can go to parties. Isn't that the whole problem? Isn't that what we're *fighting*?"

"Yes, but there's also the matter of theater people know what they're doing. Candace has a point. None of us can hang lights or . . . you know, *act*."

Weilin raises her hand. "I hate to say it, Em, but Barry and I have State Youth Orchestra tryouts coming up. We'd like to help but we don't really have the time when we're practicing after school three days a week."

Barry nods. "These tryouts are pretty important for us."

I haven't made it to the end of my pitch and I've lost all of them, I can see. Even Richard has an excuse—suddenly he's mumbling something about taking on a tutoring job. Driving home in the car, he tries to make me feel better.

201

"It's not a bad idea, Em, but you can't take wallflowers and force them to be show people. Some people just hate being onstage."

It's sad to consider the corollary truth: some people—like Belinda—love it.

"Plus, it's not really in line with our mission, if you think about it."

"What do you mean?"

"We're about raising awareness of issues like homelessness or whatever. We're not going out and finding one homeless person and making sure they have a bed for the night. We're making sure everyone looks around and notices—yes, there are homeless people in our town, and gay people, and people with disabilities. . . ."

"But don't you sometimes wonder—what's the point of that? Wouldn't it be better to help one person a lot than to stand around and point out all the people who have problems?"

Richard doesn't say anything.

"I mean—come on. Where do all these stupid ribbon campaigns get anyone? Does it help your life to see people wearing gay pride ribbons?"

I realize, too late, what a horrible question this is. We've spent three years working at this and now I sound like I was doing it all as a favor to him and believed in none of it, which isn't true. I'm just mad no one wants to help me with the play.

For a long time, Richard doesn't say anything. Finally, after I pull up to his house and stop the car, he says, "Sometimes

I wonder if working on behalf of all of humanity has made it hard for us to get to know individual people. Maybe that's your point. Maybe it's time for us to do that."

I suspect he's trying to say something in here about Hugh—that they're two people getting to know each other, not representatives of a gay pride agenda—but I don't want to ask because I don't want to give him the chance to hurt my feelings any more than he already has.

"I should get home," I say. "I have a lot of work."

"Yeah," he says, getting out of the car the minute I pull up to his house. "Me, too."

After the car door is shut, he bends down and knocks on the window for me to open it. "Maybe some of us are wondering what's going on with Lucas and why you're suddenly bending over backward to help this jerk. If he feels guilty about Belinda and wants to put on a play with her, fine. But why does that involve you? You keep telling me I need to have clarity in my relationship, but maybe you should think about that, too."

Before I can answer, he turns around and walks away.

BELINDA

THE FIRST FEW YEARS that I was in high school, I had a hard time figuring out who my friends were. I thought I was friends with anyone I recognized from elementary school or old plays. Even if they didn't say hi, I thought if I

203

hugged them they'd remember me and be my friend. Then I learned from Emily that wasn't true.

That's why I'm teaching Anthony not to hug everyone all the time. Because you have to be careful with hugging. You can make terrible mistakes and hug people who aren't nice.

I never hugged Ron Moody except for once, quickly, after our dance. For a while, I wanted to hug him every time I saw him, but I was careful and I didn't. I thought about how quiet and shy girls have to be in *Pride and Prejudice.* Anytime boys are around, they fold their hands in their laps and look at their knees. That's what I did whenever I saw Ron in school.

Sometimes he said hi, but a lot of times, he didn't, which I thought was because we both felt shy with each other. I thought Ron loved me as much as I loved him. I thought when he talked to other girls, he was only being polite. I never saw him dance with them the way he danced with me. I thought that meant our friendship was different.

After he walked away from me with that girl Janelle, I started to think about him more. I guess maybe I talked about him too much at home because Nan made a rule that I was only allowed to say his name once a day which made me get mad at Nan. That night Mom came into my room and said maybe instead of talking about Ron all the time and getting into fights with each other, we should do some old arts and crafts projects like we used to do.

"You mean make presents for him?" I said, because I was trying not to say his name.

"Sure," Mom said. "Maybe you can give him something

you've made. We'll just work on some projects and we won't tell Nan who they're for."

It was a nice idea because it meant Nan and I could go to Jo-Ann fabric store and Michaels arts and crafts. We love those two stores. This time, we made tissue-paper flowers and letter-bead necklaces and decorated picture frames and two mosaic coasters. They all came out great. I accidentally wrote *Ron* on one of the picture frames I planned to give him, and spelled R-O-N on one of my letter-bead necklaces. Both times, Nan said that counted as my one time that day.

We spent two weeks on our projects and after we were done, I put them in a shoe box. Mom told me to be careful, that I shouldn't give Ron too many things and I definitely shouldn't give him everything at once. I told her I wouldn't, but I couldn't help myself. I was so excited I brought the box to school.

That's what started my worst fight with Anthony. Just having it in my cubby in the classroom made me so excited that I raised my hand at morning meeting and asked if I could do a show-and-tell with all the things I'd made. I wasn't going to tell anyone who they were for, but I forgot that I'd written *Ron* on two of them.

When Anthony saw those, he said, "That's stupid!"

I said, "You're stupid, Anthony!" which got me in more trouble.

After that Anthony and I had to work at separate tables from each other. Except he kept walking near me to use the pencil sharpener. "You think he loves you but he doesn't," he whispered over my shoulder. On his way back, he whispered again, "He's a bad person. He doesn't deserve your presents."

His whispering trick kept getting me in trouble. Teachers didn't hear him. They only heard me shouting, "HE IS NOT!" or "SHUT UP, ANTHONY!"

I didn't listen to anything Anthony said except for one thing that scared me a little. He said, "You give him those presents, he'll laugh at you with his friends. That's what he *does*."

I was never sure exactly why people laughed when I talked to Ron about coming over to my house to watch *Pride and Prejudice*. At first I thought it was because they were all excited about the idea. I didn't want Ron's friends to come over, too, but I also didn't want to be impolite. So I laughed, too, and then I kept thinking Ron would say something like, "What day should I come?" Or, "How about this Friday?"

But he didn't.

I tried a few times. Once I said, "My house is free this whole weekend," and he turned his shoulder away like he didn't hear me. Once Anthony said this, I wasn't so sure.

Anthony made me think maybe Ron didn't love me and maybe him being shy wasn't the reason he didn't talk to me anymore. It made my stomach hurt like I was going to throw up. I started thinking about more things Ron had been doing since we came back to school. Things like he'd see me up the hall and he'd shut his locker and walk away quickly. Or another time I walked up when he was talking to another girl and he said, "Do you mind leaving us alone, Belinda? This is private."

At first I was happy because it had been a long time since he'd said my name out loud, but after Anthony said all his mean things, I started to think about it more. Ron never told anyone else to leave so he could have a private conversation with me. Except for our dance, we never had private conversations. We didn't even have private hellos, or smiles and waves. He mostly looked away when he saw me which I thought was shyness but maybe it was something else. Maybe it was more like he didn't want to see me at all and he hated me.

When I thought of this, I had a hard time breathing. Maybe he was like Mr. Darcy and he was only acting like he hated me or maybe he really hated me. It was terrible not knowing which way he felt.

I kept my present box in my cubby and tried to think of people I could ask about Ron and what they thought his feelings for me might be. Finally I asked Rhonda and she said, "It's probably neither one of those, Belinda. My guess is that he probably thinks about you a lot less than you think about him."

I didn't understand. He had been the main thing I thought about since last spring. Over that whole summer I never saw him, but I imagined being married to him and living in a house that I kept very clean the way I keep Nan's house clean. I pictured him coming home and saying, "What's for dinner?" and I would say "Rice and beans tonight" or maybe "Roast pork."

I thought about those things so much that I got confused and thought some of them had already happened. Like once I imagined us going on a picnic and the next day I thought we really had.

I didn't understand how I could think about him if he wasn't also thinking about me.

"It's a crush," Rhonda told me. "He's the first real person you've had a crush on. It's harder than loving someone on a TV show. It's more complicated. He's right here, doing some things that are nice and some things that are not so nice."

"But does he like me or hate me?"

"I can't answer that, Belinda," she said. "I don't know how somebody else feels. If you really want to know the answer, the only person who can tell you is Ron. But you should be careful. You might hear something that hurts your feelings."

I still wanted to know. Not knowing made it hard for me to eat. I even woke up sometimes in the middle of the night and couldn't fall back asleep because I was thinking so much about Ron.

"It's okay," I told her. "I just want to know."

That whole week, it was impossible to talk to Ron in school. Every time I saw him he was surrounded by other people, mostly girls, who I was starting to not like.

Then I got an idea. I remembered Nan once saying that some people feel pressure to act cool in school and aren't very nice, but away from school they are. This was true of my neighbor Annemarie who talks to me on the walk to the bus stop but never talks to me at school.

Now that Ron had stopped speaking to me at school, I thought maybe he would talk to me away from school. Then we could be nice to each other again. The only problem was I didn't know how to see Ron away from school. The only thing I knew about him was that he played football. I didn't know if he had a job. I didn't know where he lived. I didn't know if he had a big house or a small house or brothers and sisters.

So I would have to go to a football game, I decided.

I would have to see him there and ask him my questions. I typed them out at school on my break time, so I wouldn't forget if I got too nervous. I printed them up privately so no one would see, especially Anthony who I was still in a fight with.

Here were my questions: Do you love me at all? If you don't love me, why did you ask me to dance with you? Why did you stand with me for twenty minutes if you didn't want to be my boyfriend?

I knew if Anthony saw these questions, he would say they were stupid, for a stupid person who is a jerk and doesn't matter. I was starting to think maybe he might be right but I still wanted to know. I wanted to give Ron his box of presents so that at least he would know that if he loved me back, I would make him nice things for the rest of his life. I knew he probably wouldn't, but I still took the box with me.

I asked Annemarie for a ride to the game on our walk to the bus stop, because I know she drives now, not to school but after school.

She was surprised, I could tell. "You want to go to a football game, Belinda? Really?"

"Yes," I said.

"They're super crowded and noisy. Like everyone spends most of the time screaming."

"I know," I said, even though I didn't know that and it made me nervous to hear. I don't like crowded, noisy situations. Sometimes they gave me panic attacks and I have to cover my ears and scream to drown out the noise. It scared me but I still wanted to go.

"I have a friend on the team," I told her. "I want to see him."

"You do?" she said, surprised. "Who?"

I told her and I could tell she was impressed.

"Okay," she said. "I can give you a ride there and home but I can't spend the whole time with you. I'm meeting a guy."

"That's okay." I couldn't tell if she wanted me to ask who the guy was. I've always thought of Annemarie as shy and not that pretty but maybe I'm wrong.

"I'm meeting someone there, too."

"Oh, good! Okay!" she said. So it was fine.

I told Nan and Mom I was going out with Annemarie but I didn't tell them where we were going. I knew if I did, Mom would say "Maybe" and look at Nan, who would say, "No way, Jose," or "Over my dead body."

Nan likes to be crystal clear. Anytime something is risky or loud or happens after dark, that's what she says.

I told them that Annemarie invited me to go to the

movies. I didn't know if they'd believe me. I haven't been to the movies with anyone besides Nan since I was in third grade.

I expected Nan to say, "Why is Annemarie being nice to you after all these years?" If she asked that, I wouldn't know what to say. I've never lied to Nan before. I've never lied to Mom either except when I tell her everything's fine even if it's not, so she doesn't get sad.

This was a big lie and it made me so nervous I waited at the end of our driveway for Annemarie to come. I had my coat on and my hat and my shoe box full of presents. I'd added toilet paper so the presents didn't rattle when I moved. I also taped it shut so nothing fell out.

I didn't know if being on the team meant you were busy the whole time during a football game. I worried about that, but earlier in the day I talked to Ron for the first time in two weeks. "I'm coming tonight," I said and he smiled.

My heart started to pound and he kept smiling. "I'll see you there," he said.

Which meant he must have breaks where he can see people and talk to them.

"What's that?" Annemarie said, looking at my box when I got in the car. I could tell she was nervous about her date. She was wearing lipstick that looked shiny and not very good.

"It's nothing," I said.

"You have to tell me what it is, Belinda. Is it like a gun or a bomb or something?"

"No. It's presents. For my friend on the team."

She looked at me funny. "Okay," she said and started driving.

Before we bought our tickets she told me to meet her next to the ticket booth at ten and not to worry if I couldn't find her during the game. "We may leave for a while. Jacob isn't that into football."

I said okay even though I didn't have any way to tell time and wasn't sure how I would meet her at the right time.

In the beginning, the game was exciting and a little scary. There were a lot of people and everyone was screaming and stamping their feet, but it was happy stamping. No one was mad, they were just excited for the game to start. I had to sit with the marching band because there was no room anywhere else. I asked the boy I sat next to if I could touch one of his gold tassels. He said sure and then, after I touched it for a while, he asked me to stop.

The bad part about sitting with the band was that every time something really good happened in the game they picked up their instruments and played. It was so loud I wanted to change my seat, but I wasn't sure if I was allowed. At school plays you're assigned a seat and you're not allowed to move even if someone very tall sits in front of you. So I kept sitting there.

I couldn't see the game very well but that was okay because there were so many other things to watch, like the cheerleaders and their pyramids! Every time they climbed into another one, my heart started beating and I had to shut my eyes to calm it down. I couldn't look, I was so scared one of them would fall. And then I opened my eyes and they were fine! I felt like I was watching a circus! I've only been to a circus once when I was little and my mom took me. I loved it at first, and then it got confusing. I couldn't figure out where I was supposed to watch. I got so confused I started crying and shaking. "She was a little overwhelmed," my mom told Nan when we got home. Nan had told her the circus was a bad idea for me. "She loved it right up until it was a little too much, Mom."

This time, though, I didn't get overwhelmed. I loved the whole thing! Being there made me laugh and smile so hard my face started to hurt. I wished I was a cheerleader or a band member or a football player or all of them combined! Sometimes what I do when I'm excited like this is close my eyes and imagine I'm the different parts of it. I'm cheerleader and I'm also a tuba player and I'm on the field, too, getting water for the players. I'm part of it all! Everyone is smiling and happy to see me.

That's the part I try to remember now. I wasn't sad or mad when I went to talk to Ron at half time. I was so happy and I wanted him to know that if he didn't want me to, I wasn't going to bother him anymore or be in love with him. I wanted to thank him because he was the reason I came to the game and fell in love with all of it.

I wanted to tell Ron that.

I wanted to tell him he didn't have to worry about me anymore.

CHAPTER ELEVEN
EMILY

"IT LOOKS LIKE CHAD will be taking a few weeks off to concentrate on his college classes," Mary announces at the beginning of class.

Sheila spins around in her seat to look at me. "Did you get in a fight or something?"

"No," I say, wishing—again—that Chad hadn't made that flirty *I'll call you* gesture in front of everyone in class last week.

"They can't be in a fight," Annabel says. "They're supposed to get *married*."

"We're not getting married," I whisper. "We're not even friends, really."

Mary holds her hands up. "Okay, no more conversation about Chad. I wanted you to know he's not going to be with us in class for a while so you'd know what to expect, that's all."

For a fraction of a second, Mary lets her eyes rest on

mine. I never expected Chad to call this week, but it surprises me that he's disappearing so completely on this group. Didn't his mother say he had to do it? Though I won't miss Chad, I have to admit I'll miss the novelty of having a handsome boy pay attention to me. It's vain and stupid, I know, but I'll also miss the fact that everyone in the room assumes we were dating.

Including Lucas, apparently.

Across the room, I see him looking at me. He's not smiling like he can't wait to make a joke about Chad. He looks sympathetic. *I'm sorry,* he mouths. And that's it. He turns back to Mary and the exercise she's introducing at the front of the class.

The truth is: I'm getting more nervous about doing this play. What I originally thought—if Lucas helps, we'll have no problem getting a dozen other people to join us—may not be true. Monday morning he finds me at my locker and asks if it's possible to cut a few characters out of the play.

"We need at least twelve actors," I say. "I've already pared back the story. She only has three sisters now and no aunts and uncles."

Lucas looks confused. I wonder how well he knows this story. He's probably seen the Keira Knightly movie, which was great, but Belinda's right, the Colin Firth one is the best. I've watched both versions with Richard. He thinks the cinematography in the Keira version is pure artistry and Mr. Bingley in that one is gay, not shy. Bookish girls and gay boys who've spent most of high school not dating know *Pride and Prejudice* way too well. Apparently so do girls with special needs and grandmothers who are Masterpiece Theatre fans. There's a logic to the place *Pride and Prejudice* holds in any lonely teen's heart, but what would Lucas know of that?

"What about Wayne Cartwright or Ron Moody?" I say to Lucas. "Could you get either of them to do it?"

"Why are you so interested in those guys? I told you, they're kind of jerks."

Here's the thing—I know they're jerks and I still want them. "If we get one of them, everyone else will think it's a cool thing to do. Plus tons of people will come see it. They might even do an article in the paper. It could be great for them and great for us. And maybe they're not such jerks. Haven't I seen Belinda talking to Ron Moody?"

"There's no way I'm asking that guy."

"Why not?"

"Trust me."

I see his argument—that we need to be careful about who should hang around with Belinda—but I don't think he sees mine: that the whole point of this is to get as many people as possible involved. I still haven't talked to Belinda about the play yet—Lucas has done that because he was the one who first mentioned it to her—but I know she'll want as many people as possible. We've scheduled auditions for this Thursday, which means this whole week I've been lying awake at night imagining how this might go, alternating between a fantasy where throngs of people show up, more than we can handle, and another fantasy of the opposite,

216

where only a handful appear and we sit awkwardly for half an hour waiting for more.

Obviously I'd rather have the former problem than the latter. To me, Ron Moody seems like the easiest of the star players to get. Wayne Cartwright isn't just talented and athletic, he's ridiculously good-looking as well. He walks the halls buffered by two or three pretty girls everywhere he goes. Ron Moody kind of looks like Shrek with red hair and freckles. I assume he'd be a little more available.

"Ron Moody is a dick," Lucas says.

"Fine." I hold up my hands. "Don't ask him."

I don't understand Lucas's hesitation about asking these guys because in every other way, he's working hard to make this happen. He talked to the president of the drama club and got her to let us use costumes from the costume shop. She also promised to get a few light and sound guys on board. The problem is that most of the theater crowd is busy working on *Guys and Dolls*, the spring musical going up on the big stage the weekend after we've booked the small stage. I've tried to make it clear to Lucas, we need to find people *outside* the theater crowd.

"What about some girls?" I ask.

"It turns out they've got a cheerleading competition the same weekend as the performance. They want to, but they can't."

These days it seems like I see Lucas less often with his girlfriend, Debbie. A month ago she was perched beside him every day at lunch. I haven't seen that recently, but I also haven't heard anything about a breakup. She looks perfectly happy. Every time I see her in the cafeteria, she's always in the middle of laughing at something. She has that poker-straight blond hair that's great for flicking when you laugh hard, which she always does.

"They're *all* going to a cheerleading competition? Aren't there a few staying behind?"

"There are a few. A couple girls said they might audition. It just won't be a huge crowd."

"We kind of need a huge crowd, Lucas. That's the point of auditions. You need to get a lot of people so you pick out the best ones."

He leans back on his crutches like he's through talking about it. "I'm trying, okay?"

I know he is and I shouldn't blame him, but I'm getting more nervous.

There's also this: since our one conversation in the hall when she walked away from me, I haven't talked to Belinda at all. Every time I've seen her, she's had other people around and I've gotten too nervous.

The day of auditions, I corner Lucas in the cafeteria beside the dish room. "Tell me you've got at least four guys coming this afternoon." I know I sound curt, but our conversations at school are usually this way. I assume neither one of us wants to be seen talking to the other, so we're always to the point.

"I don't know if I have four. I *might*."

"How many do you have coming for sure?"

He keeps walking but doesn't answer.

"Just tell me, Lucas."

"We'll see when we get there, right?" I wish he didn't sound so casual. "What happened with your friends? What did they say?"

I look away. "They're busy right now. Everyone's got these heavy course loads. . . ."

"Plus they don't want to do it, right?"

I take a deep breath. "Plus they don't want to do it."

We're standing with each other longer than we usually do at school.

Finally he says, "Let's see what happens this afternoon. Maybe we'll be surprised."

BELINDA

THE LONGER THE GAME went on, the more nervous I got about my box. I still wanted to give it to Ron but I wasn't sure how. There was a fence and a track and a row of cheerleaders between the audience and the football team. People couldn't walk over and talk to one of the players. Then I saw one of the coaches running under the bleachers. I asked the boy next to me where he was going and he said, "The locker room."

I waited to see if the team went there, too, after they were done playing, and they did! That's when I made my plan. A locker room for football players was like a dressing room for actors. That meant I could wait for him outside the way people waited for me when I starred in plays. Sometimes they brought me flowers or little kids asked me to sign their programs. I was always polite. I always stopped and talked to anyone who was waiting for me.

Ron will do that, I thought. I know he will.

I said, "That was a great game" to the boy beside me and he said, "It's not over. It's only half time."

I didn't know what that meant but everyone was moving like they were going home so I picked up my box and went down to the bottom of the bleachers. I found a gate that led to the tunnel. It had a latch but it wasn't locked so I opened the gate and walked through it.

I had only done something like that once before, when Nan and Mom and I went to see a singer named Jimmy Martin who Mom used to love when she was a little girl. After the concert, I pretended to accidentally open a gate and walk through to where he was standing so Mom could run after me and shake his hand. It was funny and we all laughed about that for a long time. Sometimes it's okay to walk through gates no one else is using.

Sometimes it means you can shake someone's hand and talk to them for a second.

This time, though, it wasn't the same. The tunnel beyond the gate was really dark. For a while I couldn't see at all. Then my eyes got used to it and I saw that a lot of people don't throw their trash in cans. There were cups and hot dog wrappers and places where it looked like people had spilled a whole box of popcorn.

I started to feel a little bit scared because the sound of

people's footsteps was louder under here than up above. It sounded like elephants were stampeding over my head. I also couldn't tell where the football team had gone. Everything just looked dark and dirty. Then a fence rolled across the tunnel door behind me and clanged shut.

"I'm in here!" I said but no one answered.

That's when I heard something at the other end of the bleachers. It sounded like a laugh. I was so relieved I ran toward it and then there wasn't anyone there. Just the sound of footsteps and the band still playing songs.

I went toward a light at the end of the tunnel. When I got to it and stepped into the light, I heard a voice nearby.

"There you are," it said. "I couldn't see you before."

I hugged my shoe box to my chest. I didn't say anything.

"How'd you get down here? You look a little lost."

I couldn't see the person talking. I could only see a cigarette going up and down.

I heard a door open and the sound of boys cheering, "GO COUGARS!" I was relieved at first. I thought, It's okay. It must be the team coming out. When they get here, I'll be okay. Then I saw a uniform. Not Ron's number which is 47. It was number 89.

"MOVE!" he screamed. I looked around to see who he was yelling at. I couldn't tell. "YOU!" he screamed. "MOVE NOW! BEFORE THEY COME OUT!"

Whoever he was yelling at wouldn't move because he kept yelling until the team came up behind him, a big huge pack of them, running right toward me.

I looked for number 47 so I would know which one was

Ron. I knew he probably wouldn't have time to answer my questions because they were running like it was a race to get back to the field. Which meant the only thing I could do was hold out my box so he'd take it and open it later. Maybe out on the field or after the game. He'd look at what was inside and understand what I was saying. That I thought about him a lot. That if he wanted to get married someday I'd be happy to do that. Hopefully he'd know that I would also understand if he didn't want to get married.

They were running so fast, though, I had a hard time keeping track of Ron.

I held out my box when he got closer. My hands were shaking. I didn't want to drop it or break anything inside. Then I saw 47 again and I saw his hand. I held it out farther and I thought he was reaching for it.

But he wasn't.

He pushed it back at me. Hard. It went into my chest. I fell down and couldn't breathe. I heard him yell over me. "EVERY TIME I TURN AROUND YOU'RE FUCKING RIGHT THERE! I CAN'T STAND IT! I CAN'T FUCKING TAKE IT! LEAVE ME ALONE!"

I lay on the ground trying to breathe but I couldn't.

I heard the rest of the team running. I was in their way, so I covered my head and ears. I got kicked a few times. Someone stepped on my hair which hurt more than the kicking did. Someone said, "What the fuck is this?" I didn't know if he was talking about me. After that, I don't remember much.

I opened my eyes once and feet were still going by.

Someone stepped on a cup and Coke sprayed all over me so I closed my eyes again.

When they were gone, I sat up. My skirt was wet with Coke and my top was dirty. One sleeve of my shirt was torn. I looked around and saw that Ron's box of presents had fallen on the ground and everything had spilled out. His letter-bead necklace, his tissue-paper flowers, and mosaic coaster. The coaster was broken.

I couldn't stand up, so I crawled over to the broken box and started picking things up. I didn't know what else to do.

I was dirty and wet. There was popcorn in my hair.

I had my answer now. Anthony was right. Ron didn't love me.

I knew because he kicked me and spit on me and told me to stay a swear word away from him. That was enough. I didn't start to cry until I saw the pieces of the broken coaster. That was the present that came out the best and now I didn't have it anymore because it was broken. I thought, This is the worst thing that has ever happened to me.

And then I heard a voice and I remembered I wasn't alone.

"Do you need some help?" the voice said.

CHAPTER TWELVE

EMILY

I T'S 3:05 AND NO one is here.

Auditions are happening in the small theater beside the music room where the choir practices after school. Through the wall, I can hear a boy and girl singing a duet with a piano. It sounds like a love song, but they stop so much it's hard to tell. The auditions don't officially start until 3:15, so I spread out the scenes I've xeroxed and the sign-up sheet for people to write their name and contact info. On it, there's room for thirty people to sign up.

There are voices outside in the hallway, but when I look, no one is out there waiting to come in.

By 3:14, I start to panic. Even Lucas hasn't shown up.

I walk out into the hallway to see if he's on his way. Maybe he's bringing a group of his friends in from the parking lot, I think. Then I check the main door that leads out to the parking lot. No one's there. I run quickly to the hallway where his locker is.

Empty.

Now it's 3:19 and I'm not sure what I'm doing except avoiding the room where no one has shown up. Finally, I head back and open the door as quietly as I can. One person is seated in the last row. Lucas.

He doesn't even turn around to see if it's me.

"No one, huh?" he says.

"Not yet," I say, but we both know. The school is empty. Busses left twenty minutes ago. No one is coming.

"What happened to your friends?" I say softly. I know I shouldn't blame him, but I do.

"They're not my friends," he snaps. "I told you that."

"But you asked them, right?" I don't know why I can't let this go. I picture his lunch table with thirty people. Isn't this the point of popularity—so you can get people to *do* things?

"No, I didn't ask most of them. I couldn't."

"What do you mean—you couldn't?"

"I couldn't . . . ask these guys to be around Belinda. It wouldn't have been right."

"Why not? What are you talking about?"

For a long time, he doesn't say anything. Through the wall, we can hear a piano playing while two voices argue about a progression.

For a while now I've wondered if there's more to Lucas's story than he told the disciplinary committee, the way there was more to my story than I could bear to tell anyone. That I knew Belinda once. That the first day of high school I screamed at her and told her never to hug me.

That I can still remember her face, how happy she was to see me, and how I hardened myself to ensure that she didn't mistake us for friends. But what could Lucas have to feel guilty about?

As gently as I can manage, I ask, "Did you know Belinda from before?"

"I knew *of* her. None of us knew her except for Ron and a few guys who went to this Best Buddies dance last spring." He takes a deep breath and turns around, as if he wants to be sure no one is coming in who might hear what he's saying. "Everyone on the team is supposed to do community service every year. Ron and Wayne hadn't done any, so Coach made them go. It pissed the rest of us off because they were getting away with doing this one event and the rest of us have to do twenty hours, but that's how it is. They always get away with things like that."

The music next door has started up again louder. I move over to where Lucas is sitting. His voice has gotten so soft and it's hard to hear.

"Except this time it turned out to be a joke on him. Ron thought he was getting it over with, doing this one hour, but then he met this girl who wouldn't stop following him around. She thought they were going out now because he asked her to dance once. She kept inviting him over to her house in front of other people, which really pissed him off. Finally he complained to Coach about it right before the Mansfield game."

There's a noise outside in the hallway that makes Lucas stop and spin around in his seat. I can tell that he'll be in trouble with his crowd if they find out he's telling me this story. Still, he keeps going: "That game should have been a breeze. We were favored to win by fourteen points but that whole first half, we couldn't get our act together. We weren't connecting; we hadn't even made it on the scoreboard. We were down by seven at half time. In the locker room, everyone was ripshit and blaming each other, which we're never supposed to do. Then someone looked out the window and saw Belinda standing outside the locker room holding a box. It was like in that moment, she brought the whole team together again. Suddenly, everyone was saying *this* was our whole problem this year. People expected too much from us. We were supposed to win games and be fucking Boy Scouts, too. Then it just got worse. They said it was her fault we were losing. They made all these threats about what they were going to do to her when they got out there. They were going to rip her a new one for bothering Ron in the middle of a game. They were going to show a few people what happens when you ask too much of football players."

He stops for a second and shakes his head—as if he's remembering worse threats he doesn't want to tell me. Then he takes a deep breath and starts again. "This is the worst part: I didn't say anything. I could have. A few other guys were trying to say, 'Ignore her, man,' but they were getting drowned out by this tidal wave of trash talk. That's when I realized what assholes these guys are. They're given all this power and they're so insecure they're gonna beat up this poor girl because we're *playing shitty*?"

I'm sitting next to Lucas. Our legs are so close our jeans have touched. I want him to know it's okay he's telling me this story, so I do the boldest thing I've ever done with a boy: I reach over and take his hand. I squeeze it so he understands that I'm his friend and it'll be okay. If he's surprised by the move, I'm even more surprised by what happens next: he cups my hand in both of his and lifts it to his mouth. He kisses it and presses my palm to his cheek.

It's a million things at once and it makes my insides twist. Is it a kiss if it happens on your hand, which is—well, an arm's length away from your mouth?

It feels like it.

We sit for a minute with my hand against his cheek. His eyes are closed, as if he wants to stay in this moment forever. I wouldn't mind doing that, but I have to ask, "What happened after you left the locker room?"

He opens his eyes. There's enough light to see there are tears in them. I can also see that he doesn't want to tell me the rest. But eventually he does. He tried to warn her. He ran out ahead of the rest and told her to run. Then Coach called him back to berate him for breaking huddle early. As the rest of the team headed out, Coach gave him a lecture with a finger stabbing his chest plate. "You keep your mind on the game. You think about your plays and about your teammates. You don't worry about other people. There's a million fucking sad stories out there, you don't think about any of them. You stay right here in this game."

That's when Lucas ran out and saw one thing he expected—Belinda's box and its contents spilled everywhere—and something else he didn't: Mitchell Breski trapping Belinda against a fence.

"My brain froze," he says softly.

It's a feeling I remember too well. He's still holding my hand, only now our fingers are laced and his thumb is rubbing the cuticle around my thumb. "I thought Coach was watching me. I thought this was a test to see what I'd do, if I'd stop and get distracted. Like that makes any sense, but that's what I thought. I jogged past a guy trying to rape a poor girl and the only thing I let myself think was, At least it isn't one of my teammates doing it."

I understand what he's saying. I know the logic of panic makes no sense.

Now that he's told me all this, I want to be honest myself. This will probably be my last chance since after today our play won't happen and we won't be friends anymore. Not the way we have been. I want to tell him I've been cruel to her once myself. Before I can, though, the door opens behind us.

My heart does a somersault. We drop hands and turn around to see two figures standing there.

One is Belinda. "Are these the auditions?" she calls.

Lucas stands up. This morning I was so nervous about who might show up that I had Lucas tell Belinda not to come. "Tell her we already know her acting and we know we want to use her," I said so her feelings wouldn't get hurt.

Now, as if to explain herself, she announces loudly, "I brought someone who wants to audition. This is Anthony."

She points to the thin boy with thick glasses standing beside her. I don't think I've seen him before, which means he's probably an underclassman, one who travels the hallways with his head down, trying to draw as little attention to himself as possible. He still has braces. And pimples. He looks like he hasn't started shaving yet.

Lucas waves to Anthony. "The thing is, we're trying to decide what to do here. We haven't had as many people show up as we hoped."

Try: we haven't had anyone show up. He's trying to carry this off, but we have to tell her the truth.

"It looks like we can't do the play, Belinda," I say. This is the first time I've talked to her since that awful time in the hallway. "We don't have any actors. They're all busy doing *Guys and Dolls*." I gesture toward the room next door with the piano. "We wanted to do it. We really did, Belinda, but all the theater people are busy."

She steps into the light so I can see her face and her furrowed eyebrows. She looks worried but not panicky. "Well, I have Anthony. He wants to audition for a small part, not a big part. Can't we just audition and then we'll see what happens?"

I'm not sure what to say or feel except gratefulness when Lucas leans forward and suggests, "Look, we have one scene with Elizabeth and her father, right, Em? Why don't we have them read from that and see how they do?"

They both nod. I prepared xeroxed scenes to read from, so I hand them each one. I know Belinda can read but her eyesight isn't good. In our old play rehearsals, the director always made large-print copies of her scripts. We weren't expecting Belinda to show up, so I haven't made any of those for her.

"I'm not sure how we should do this, though. I haven't got a script that Belinda can see well enough." I say this softly to Lucas. I don't want to embarrass her in front of Anthony.

Apparently I haven't. "I don't need a script," Belinda says.

Lucas and I look at each other. "You don't?"

She closes her eyes. There's no smile on her lips, but I feel the pride of her accomplishment. Her old gift.

"Have you memorized the lines already?" I ask.

"Not all of them," she says. "But the girl's ones, yes."

Lucas smiles and claps his hands. "Great, then. Why don't we do the first scene with your father?"

Belinda is so serious about acting that sometimes she misses the point—to relax and have fun. Her scene with Anthony is a hand-wringing recitation of Elizabeth imploring her father for help reining in her overly flirtatious younger sisters. Still, there are touching lines delivered too softly by Anthony: "Not everyone can be as book smart as you, dear Lizzie."

It's almost impossible to understand a word he says, but the way he looks at Belinda with so much tenderness and admiration kills me. It also reminds me that I've forgotten one of the main points of the story: Elizabeth is too intellectual for her own good. She overthinks things too much. She doesn't rely on intuition. Maybe it's just as well we'll never put on the show, I think. Instead of proving a point about Belinda's abilities, it might do the opposite.

When they're done, Lucas asks if they'd like to try another scene. Maybe one with Elizabeth and Mr. Darcy. Anthony blushes and puts his hands over his face. "I'm not Mr. Darcy. Not me."

"That's okay," Lucas says. "I could read that part if you'd like to try another scene, Belinda."

This is so kind of him, I wish I could squeeze his hand again. If we can't do the play, he's giving her a chance to play Elizabeth Bennett for an afternoon at least.

"Yes," she says. "I'd like that."

"Why don't we read the first scene at Pemberley? Do you remember this one? When she sees him unexpectedly?"

Belinda nods. She knows the scene, of course.

Lucas hops up onstage, clears his throat, and shakes his head to get into character and then—boom—he is. He doesn't use the affected English accent that Belinda is trying out, but his voice is different than his usual soft monotone. It fills up the room and startles all of us: oddly, even the piano next door goes quiet. "Why are you here, Elizabeth, if it so offends your sensibilities?" he booms.

Belinda sneaks a look at him, smiles, and finds her line. "I had no choice, sir. I came with my aunt and uncle."

"You should know that you're welcome anytime." As they keep going, I'm amazed. Lucas really *gets* this story. He understands that so much of what they say is the opposite of what they mean. It's even possible he's demonstrating how to do it in ways that Belinda picks up on. Because this isn't one of my short xeroxed scenes, they keep going from the script, running the whole scene. Belinda needs prompts on a few lines, but not many. The scene gets better and better as they go along. Anthony steps off the stage and sits down in the front row to watch them.

It's so compelling I don't even hear the door open behind us.

I only realize others have come in when I hear people talking and turn around to see Lucas's girlfriend, Debbie, sitting in the back with two of her friends. One of them has her hand over her mouth, like she can't believe what she's seeing. Debbie's staring at Lucas, not like she's surprised by what a good actor he is, but like she's mad.

More than mad, actually. She's furious.

Which makes me think—wait, didn't he ask her to come and audition? Weren't the cheerleaders meant to be at a competition? And that's when I realize—there isn't any competition.

Lucas hasn't told them anything about this play.

CHAPTER THIRTEEN
BELINDA

Except for the police right afterward, no one has ever asked me what happened with Mitchell Breski. Nan doesn't want his name said in our house, so Mom can't ask. Cynthia and Rhonda, my teachers, haven't asked me either.

I don't think I want to talk about it, but sometimes I would like someone to explain what he was doing. I thought at first he was trying to help me. He knew I was crying and embarrassed and he kept saying, "Shh, shh . . . it's okay. I'll help you pick up your things."

I said, "Thank you," because I needed help. Everything was broken and there were a lot of pieces. Then he started rubbing my arm, which didn't make sense because my arm wasn't hurt. He said those guys were a swear word and I shouldn't pay any attention to them.

He was touching me more which I didn't like so I tried crawling away, but he grabbed my sweater and said, "Hey, girly, not so fast—you can't walk back out there like that, all covered in dirt. Let me wipe you off first."

I stood up near the gate to the field. It was very dark where I stood and bright up ahead. I thought maybe he was right—if I walked out everyone would know what just happened and would laugh at me. I knew I couldn't go back and sit with the band, with Coke on my skirt and popcorn in my hair.

"Let me help you," he said again.

And then he was so close in the dark, I could smell his breath which was terrible, like he'd been eating metal. He touched my hair and put his mouth on my neck. It felt like when a dog licks you. You want to push the dog away but Nan always says you have to be nice to dogs, they're just dogs, so you shouldn't push them away. I tried to push him away, but he kept doing something with his mouth like he wanted to eat my neck.

"You have pretty yellow hair," he said.

"I have to go," I said. I definitely didn't want him to put his mouth on me anymore but he was holding my shoe box. "Can I have that back, please?"

He held it away like he wanted to make it a game, where I grabbed for it and he kept holding it back farther. I didn't want to play that game but the rest of him was trapping me against the fence. He kept leaning so I had to grab the fence to lean away from him. My hair got caught on the fence and hurt when I pulled. I started to cry it hurt so much and I was so scared.

He said, "Shh, don't cry."

Then he started touching my chest but I don't think he

235

liked what he was doing. His face was red and sweaty and he made noises like it was hurting him.

Then he said, "Don't look," and he unzipped his pants.

I *did* look even though he told me not to. I looked and that's when I screamed so loud that a janitor came.

I knew what it was called but I had never seen anything like that before. It scared me because it was ugly and his face was red and ugly when he pulled it out. In school we learned about personal space and good touch/bad touch. Good touch is things like hugs from your family. Bad touch is people who hug you when you don't want to be hugged or touch your private parts. Private parts are any places on your body that a bathing suit hides.

When we talk about it in class, everyone asks, "Is a belly button private?" "Is your neck private?" When Anthony said this, I told him to please think before he asked questions like that. "Is your neck underneath your bathing suit? I don't think so."

I got mad at Anthony because I didn't think boys and girls should all be in the same room learning this stuff. I thought it would only give the boys ideas and they were already too girl crazy to start with. All Douglas wants to talk about is girls, girls, girls. I think sometimes you should not talk about certain things, the way they do in *Pride and Prejudice* when no one wants to say what a bad singer Mary is or how Lydia is flirting too much. They are polite and don't say anything. That's how I think we should all be about sex. We should just not say anything.

When I told Rhonda this she said it was not a good

idea. She said that sooner or later we will all have feelings about wanting to touch somebody else and sooner or later someone will want to touch us and we have to learn how to say no if we don't want it.

We practiced that a lot in class. We took turns saying, "No, you're in my personal space. I don't want you to stand so close."

It worked fine in class where the other kids knew they had to step away if you said it. Mitchell Breski didn't step away, though. Now I think maybe Rhonda was right—that it's okay to talk about some of these things because I would like to understand what happened and what I did wrong.

Anthony did a good job at the audition, but he was very nervous, especially around the armpits. When he asked if I could tell they were sweaty I said yes because I don't like to lie to anyone, especially not to Anthony. "It's okay, though, because other people didn't see it," I said, which wasn't true. His face was sweaty and everyone could see that, too.

For me, auditions are fun. They don't make me nervous anymore because I've had lots of practice doing them. For Anthony it was different. He sounded like he was saying his lines with food in his mouth. It was very hard to understand him. I still told him he was great afterward, though, because I thought he was.

Then I get home that night and I start to worry: What if I get a part and Anthony doesn't? I'll feel terrible if that happens. Maybe I'll find Lucas or Emily tomorrow and

237

tell them that Anthony works very hard and gets much better at things with practice. When he first got to high school, he couldn't open his locker which didn't surprise me because no one in our class uses the lockers we got in ninth grade. We all tried to open them once and we couldn't so we left our things in our classroom and forgot about our lockers, but Anthony kept trying and trying. Every morning he went back and finally in November he opened it by himself. Then he offered private classes called How to Open Your Locker. We each took turns being his student. He taught me in three days which made me his best student, he said.

Maybe that's when I first knew Anthony liked me but I couldn't like him back because he was in ninth grade and I was in eleventh.

Now he says age doesn't matter if you're in love.

I tell him, "We're not in love, Anthony!" which we aren't.

Except I'm so worried about him getting a part in this play that it's almost like I care more about him being in it than me. Which doesn't make sense except I can't help it.

EMILY

I CAN'T BELIEVE HOW MUCH time I've wasted sitting on my bed, staring at my phone. I'm waiting for Lucas to call so we can decide what to do about our failed play project, but really I want him to tell me what happened with Debbie after the audition. By the time she interrupted us, it was already 4:15, just enough time to end our auditions and get Belinda and Anthony onto the late bus. Packing up our things, I tried not to be obvious, but I watched Lucas talk to Debbie in the corner. He didn't look embarrassed so much as tired of whatever conversation they were having. She did most of the talking. He listened and nodded.

If he'd never told her what we were doing—which seemed pretty obvious by the expression on her face—how much of a couple could they really be, I thought, but maybe I've got this wrong.

When I first saw Debbie in the back of the theater, I thought I knew what was going on. The reason no one had shown up to our audition was that Lucas hadn't told any of his friends—including his girlfriend—what we were doing. Earlier today that would have made me mad. I thought I wanted popular people to show up so we could prove to Belinda that lots of people will help her even if we didn't that one time. Now I understand the story is more complicated. Lucas has ostracized himself from this group because they aren't the people to demonstrate anything to Belinda, least of all kindness.

His teammates were terrible to Belinda. Ron was the worst, but every one of them had run by her without stopping to help her up. Lucas was right. None of these people should have been part of our show. He understood that and I didn't.

Now I see all the ways Lucas has distanced himself

239

from his teammates. He not only agreed to be in a play, he found just the right one. When no one showed up, he felt as bad as I did and something happened—something real—in that moment when he held my hand. I'm sure of that. Which is why I assume he'll call me the minute he gets done breaking up with Debbie.

Except he doesn't.

Fine, I think. He doesn't have to call me, but he *can't* keep going out with her. He just can't. He's too kind, he's too decent; he's too smart to waste himself on a girl like her. That's all I want to tell him. *You don't have to date me, just don't date her. Please, as your friend, I'm begging you not to date someone who doesn't appreciate you.*

I *am* his friend, I think, staring at the phone. And good friends talk like this. They say *You're too smart for that person.* Richard says it to me all the time even when it's not true. He always tells me I'm too good for every boy I've ever liked who didn't like me back. In my case it wasn't true, but in Lucas's case, it's so true it's almost hard for me to breathe. He isn't a football-playing, cheerleader-dating idiot. He's so different from the rest of that crowd that I don't want him to ever waste his time with them again. He should be hanging out with me and my friends. He should be laughing with us and being himself. He should get to know them so they can get to know him and see what I see: how unexpected and amazing and sweet he is.

Of course I also realize why this is making me so nervous. I think about the way he kissed the back of my hand and then held it to his cheek. I don't just want to be friends, I want more than that. I want to kiss him. I want to walk down the hallway with one finger hooked around a belt loop on his pants. I want everything Debbie has and doesn't appreciate. I want things I can't have because the laws of social stratification in high school might allow us to be friends for a while, but would never permit any more than that. I'm not blind; I know this much. He couldn't sit comfortably at my lunch table any more than I could sit comfortably at his.

I think about watching him up onstage playing Mr. Darcy with tiny perfect gestures: his folded lips, his one raised finger. I think about him looking at Belinda, then at me, then back to Belinda. He feels it, too. I know he does. My heart races stupidly at the thought. At least I think he does. To me it was so obvious by the end of his scene with Belinda that I half expected him to look out into the audience and break up with Debbie right then. After the day we'd just spent, how could he *not*? But now four hours have gone by and nothing has happened. He hasn't called. He hasn't texted or emailed. I feel the knot of expectation in my stomach loosen to make room for the story I'll have to tell myself tomorrow and the next day and the day after that when we see each other and talk about everything except this.

I can already imagine it and I can't stand the picture. We'll talk about the play and agree we can't do it. It was a nice idea, we'll say, but you can't put on a show if you have no actors. We'll shrug and walk away from this thing we've been working on for weeks because we have no other choice.

All these thoughts are confirmed the next day when I see Lucas once in the morning, talking to a boy I don't recognize but who, judging by his size, must be a football player. Lucas holds up a finger in my direction but I can't tell if he's trying to say *Wait, I want to talk to you* or if it's a simple, one-finger hi.

He doesn't stop talking, so I keep walking with a laugh that sounds fake because it is.

At lunch I see him again but he doesn't see me or look in my direction. I realize that he's making a choice, not looking over. For two weeks we dropped all self-consciousness with each other. We talked easily in the hallway and in the cafeteria. We had a purpose that made us unshy with each other. As if, because we were talking about a play few people would ever see, we didn't think anyone would notice us talking.

Now even looking over in his direction, at the table full of his friends, feels loaded and dangerous. As if a thousand eyes will notice what an idiot I've been. As if they'll see what I'm thinking because it's written on my face: Why did we do all that if we're just going to give up? Didn't we hold hands for three minutes because Belinda's story wasn't the only thing that made us sad, the idea of not doing this play did, too?

I keep thinking that we can't go this whole day without saying anything, but apparently we can because we do.

CHAPTER FOURTEEN
EMILY

I SPEND MOST OF THE weekend by myself at home. In three days, Lucas hasn't called or messaged me once. The only explanation I can think of now is that what happened before Belinda and Anthony walked in wasn't about me at all, it was about the story he told. He hates these guys. Telling me was a relief. Holding my hand was a courtesy. Kissing it was a thank-you. That's all, I decide. Now that our time in the Boundaries and Relationships class is almost over—we have three more classes—we won't even share that anymore. Next semester we might say hi when we pass in the hall, but it's possible we won't even do that. It's possible this whole time will be something neither one of us ever understands well enough to talk about.

We felt bad about what happened to Belinda. Really bad. Then we moved on.

As if Lucas is trying to prove my theory right, we don't talk the next week in school. He doesn't ask for a ride and on Wednesday night, he doesn't show up to Boundaries and Relationships.

But here's a surprise: Chad does.

"Hey! How're you doing?" Chad says, smiling at me and spinning around in his chair when I walk past him to get to an empty seat. "I was just thinking about you the other day."

I whisper, "Hi," and then point up to the front. "I think Mary's about to start."

Mary claps her hands and says, "We've got a new topic, everyone! Today we're going to talk about expectations."

I look over at the empty chair where Lucas usually sits. Even Mary pauses when she registers the fact that Lucas isn't here. This whole time—even with his injury—he's never missed a class.

"Who can tell us what that word—expectations—means?" Two hands go up. "Yes, Thomas?"

"It's when you expect something like a package in the mail."

"Good!" Mary says. "It's something that you hope will happen but you also think it probably will happen. Like a package coming. That's a good example, Thomas. Thank you. What are some expectations that people might have when they get in a relationship?"

The question is confusing for this group. She's jumped too quickly—from packages to relationships. No one says anything. They blink up at her and then around at one another.

"Sheila, when you imagine having a boyfriend, what

are some of the things you picture doing with that person?"

Sheila doesn't have to think about this for long. She makes a list on her fingers. "Go shopping at the mall, but not for candles. I hate candles. Go to movies. Eat tacos in restaurants. Maybe roller-skating, maybe not. Probably not."

"Great!" Mary claps her hands. "That's perfect."

Sheila grins. "If it's Justin Bieber, I might pick different things."

"That's right. With different people, you might pick different things. Okay, Simon, how about you—when you imagine having a girlfriend, what do you picture doing with her?"

"I don't understand the question."

"If you had a girlfriend, what would you do with her?"

"Touch her butt."

Chad laughs and gives Simon a thumbs-up. Mary gives him a warning look, though I'm not sure he sees it. "Okay, what else?"

Simon screws up his lips to think. "Touch her tummy?"

"Okay. Do you picture doing things together, like going to the movies or out to dinner?"

Simon shakes his head. "Movie theaters smell like poo. I don't go to movies anymore."

"Do they always smell like that, Simon, or did that just happen once?"

"It just happened once, but it was *bad*."

"Okay, fine. Thank you, Simon. Let's look at the difference between what Sheila expects to do with a boyfriend and what Simon expects to do with a girlfriend."

She goes to the whiteboard and gets help from the group making two lists. I have to admit it's a pretty good exercise: the woman wants to go out, the man wants to stay home and touch things that aren't technically private parts but have obviously been driving Simon crazy for years. By the time the list is complete (now it includes "touch her shoulder, hug, smell her hair") he's red in the face.

Mary asks, "Does anyone look at these lists and see any problems that might come up?"

Not at first, they don't. They squint to read the board. A few play with shirt threads or stare out the window. For them, the conversation got too hard with the first part of the first sentence, "When you imagine . . ." But slowly they seem to get the point she's trying to make: men and woman expect different things out of relationships. Women are more public; they want to do things together and "show off their boyfriend." Men are more private. They'd rather stay home together and not bring other people into the equation.

I think about Lucas and me, sitting in the dark of the empty auditorium, saying something with our hands that neither one of us was brave enough to say out loud. Whatever was happening between us these last two weeks felt scary and unfamiliar because it also felt real. It wasn't the head rush of a college boy asking for my phone number. With Lucas, it was completely different. We talked; we plotted; we disagreed. Up until the day of the audition, I had no expectations. I marveled at how much I liked

Lucas but my brain made no time-warp leaps ahead. I didn't imagine anything except putting on a decent show starring Belinda. Which he wanted, too. Our expectations were the same. Maybe we surprised each other with our inexplicable intensity. Without talking about why, we egged each other into caring more about this idea. We imagined the whole school would come and see Belinda. They'd be awed by her talent and her life would change forever. We both believed our classmates would think the same way we did, that they'd show up to audition for a play to be nice to a girl we all felt bad for. Now when I think about everyone's busy schedules—the sports practices, the college apps, the AP exams—I don't feel mad that no one came. I feel mystified that I ever thought they would.

Lucas and I both wanted it to happen so much that we convinced ourselves it would.

Expectations are sad and complicated things.

At break, I do something I've been promising to do for weeks now: I sit with Sheila and look through a Justin Bieber scrapbook she has brought from home. She has many of these, apparently, but is only allowed to bring in one at a time that she can share with one person each class session. This is Mary's way of reminding her that certain conversation topics have to be limited. At an early meeting with Lucas and me, Mary explained it this way: "She should get to have one good Justin Bieber conversation a class. That way, she can learn it's a fine topic in *small* doses."

Though Sheila is explaining every picture she points to, Chad pulls a chair over to my other side and starts talking.

"Do you want to go to the vending machines," he whispers, "and I'll tell you about a cool party I'm having this weekend?"

Even Sheila looks confused at his interruption.

"Not right now, Chad," I say. "I'm finally getting my chance to see Sheila's Justin Bieber scrapbook." What I'm doing is important, though Chad either never got that talk from Mary or else he didn't hear it. He leans over and whispers, "I'm trying to *rescue you*. It's our break time."

"No, thanks," I say.

After he has left the room, Sheila turns to me. "He's rude," she pronounces.

Suddenly it occurs to me: these students understood this about Chad long before I did. That was the reason no one volunteered to act with him the first class. That was why he so often asked me to be his partner. No one else would do it.

At the end of class, Chad disappears quickly and Mary walks out with me to ask if everything is okay with Lucas. I almost tell her, "I'm not sure—we had a fight," which makes no sense because we didn't. It just feels that way. Not talking in school. Not saying hello.

"Well, tell him he'll need to add a class at the end because he's missed this one."

"I will," I say. I notice she's not asking Chad to add any classes for the ones he's skipped.

"We missed him today," Mary says. "Tell him that, too."

Somehow what Mary has said, combined with the class activity about expectations, has made me think differently

248

about all this. Instead of being mad at Lucas for ignoring me in school and skipping class, I call him when I get home and tell him I'm sorry that our plan didn't work.

"Yeah," he sighs, like it's been an hour since we talked, not six days. "I'm sorry, too."

It's a little awkward, but I'm surprised—it isn't nearly as awkward as I imagined it would be. After we've talked for a while, we agree that we don't really have a choice. We have to cancel the show. From the sadness in his voice, it's pretty clear—the reason we haven't talked is that neither one of us wanted to have to say this.

"What should we say to Belinda and Anthony?" he says. "I don't want her to think it's her fault. You were right. She's a really good actress. I was surprised."

After all this, it feels so easy talking to him that I surprise myself. "So were you, Lucas. Who would have guessed you've got a little Mr. Darcy in you. . . ."

"What—I'm arrogant? Pretentious?"

I pause and then just say it. "No—more the smoldering, sensitive stuff. You were almost as good as Keira Knightly's Mr. Darcy."

"I *could* be as good as him. I just need the cape and the hair that looks like brown straw."

I laugh. "Watching you guys, I kept thinking, I wish we could pare this play down to three actors, or even two."

This time he laughs. "Anthony was pretty bad, wasn't he?"

"But he was so sweet." We both laugh together, at the memory of him screaming lines that were impossible to

249

understand. "Maybe we could find a different job for him."

There's a pause. "I don't think we should try to put on a two-person play, Em."

My stomach flutters every time he calls me Em. "Yeah, you're right."

"So how was class today?"

"It was good. We missed you. Where were you?"

"My dad and I had a fight and he grounded me. He says if I can't get a football scholarship, I have to join ROTC. I guess I overreacted a little and told him to fuck off."

"What's ROTC?" I've heard of it, I just don't remember what it is.

For a moment, he doesn't answer. "Do you really not know?" he says softly.

I have to admit, I don't.

"The army," he says. "If I want to go to college, I have to join the army."

He explains that his older brother lost his football scholarship after an injury his freshman year and had to get a scholarship through ROTC to keep going. After he graduated, he spent eighteen months in Afghanistan. When he came home, he never talked about what it was like or what he'd done over there, but he was different.

"Where is he now?" I ask.

"He went back. He didn't have any choice. If they pay for college, you have to sign on for four years afterward," he explains.

We're silent for a little while because all of this is sad and there's not much either one of us can say. I wonder if he told Debbie about this fight. I wonder what she said. I can't ask, of course. For now I'm just glad I called him—that we can talk and be normal again, like the real friends we've become. "It's good you said no. Even if he got mad, I admire that."

"You do? Why?"

"You're not afraid of saying what you think. You're braver than I expected." My heart is beating. I'm treading into dangerous territory here, but I can't help myself. Even if he's been too chicken to talk to me for the last week, I still admire other things he's done: caring about Belinda, and doing the right thing. I can't imagine anyone else on the football team trying as hard as he has.

"So, listen, about that thing with Debbie walking into our auditions."

As much as I wanted to talk about this last week, I'm now terrified at what he might say.

"I guess she came into the auditorium earlier, before Belinda and Anthony. She saw what we were doing. That holding hands thing."

She did? I don't say anything. I'm shocked that he's saying it straight out like this.

"She wasn't very happy about it."

"What did you say?" I steel myself for the worst: *I told her it didn't mean anything. We were upset because no one showed up.* Even if he says this, I tell myself it will be okay. I like him so much I can understand the bind he's in: we're connected in ways that make us feel older, but the reality remains that we are still in high school, at opposite ends of the social hierarchy.

And then he says, "I told her the truth. That I like you."

He stops there. I wonder if he can hear my heart beating wildly over the phone. "And then what?"

"She didn't say much. Well, yes, she did. She said I was a jerk. And then we broke up."

"You *did*?"

"Pretty much."

Now I *really* don't understand. Why didn't he *call* me, then? "What was your plan? Were we going to not talk about this for the rest of the year?"

"I don't know. I kept getting nervous every time I saw you, so, yeah, I guess that was my plan. Just to be really awkward whenever you were around."

"Okay. Should we just go with that plan or should we think of something else? Like maybe going out for coffee some time and getting to know each other. Except I hate coffee, so whatever. Hot chocolate."

"See, this is why you worry me."

"Why?"

"Because with Debbie, it was easy. Debbie never wanted to go out and talk."

I think of telling him about class today, about Sheila and Simon and their list of expectations. "What did Debbie want?"

"She wanted to eat lunch at our table and have a boyfriend to sit next to. Plus she doesn't have a car so she needs rides to parties."

Is he serious? Was that their *whole* relationship? "I'm weird because I'm saying let's go out and talk? That's not that weird, Lucas."

"No, it's just harder. You already know stuff I never talk to girls about. Like, ever."

"You've never been friends with a girl before?"

"No. I mean—not really. Have you?"

How could I tell him I've *only* been friends with every boy I've ever known? If he is bad at talking—and he isn't, I assure him, he really isn't—I'm bad at everything else. Finally I just say it. "Listen, I'm terrible at dating people. I've been on maybe five dates my whole life, and that's counting lunch with lame Chad."

He laughs at that. "So College Boy is lame?"

"Very. I mean, I'm sorry, but yeah." I feel some need to explain my confession. "I haven't dated a lot because my friend Richard and I were planning to fall in love when we get to college."

"Huh. Not with each other?"

"No, he's gay so not with each other. Then he started dating someone and changed the plan, I guess." I wonder how this sounds to him. "That's how people like us get through high school. We expect to have a much better time when we get out." Maybe I sound like a snob. Or even more of a loser than he already thinks.

We're quiet for a while and then he surprises me. "But you're so pretty."

I feel like I might die. "Well, thanks, Lucas, but I'm not high-school pretty. I don't wear a pound of makeup or walk around in a string-bikini top. My charms are more subtle."

"Don't worry about the makeup. You shouldn't wear makeup. Guys don't really like that. The bikini top's not a bad idea, though."

"Shut up."

"I'm just saying, don't close all the doors. Explore your options."

"Fine, I'll wear a bikini top if you'll wear a Speedo around all day. How about that?"

"Yeah, probably not."

"So should we just skip the coffee idea? Since I don't like coffee and you don't like talking, it seems like maybe it won't go well."

"Here's the thing, though. I should probably grow up and learn how to talk to someone over coffee, and you should definitely grow up and learn how to drink coffee. So I'm coming around. I think we should do it."

I smile. "Okay."

"You want to try next Wednesday after school? Then I could give you a ride to class."

Suggesting a week from now seems strange, like maybe he's not as excited about this as I am. *You want to wait a week?* I feel like saying but don't. All this flirting has taken it out of me. I'm covered in sweat and exhausted.

"Sure, that sounds great," I say.

CHAPTER FIFTEEN
BELINDA

NOW THAT WE'VE GOTTEN through the audition, Anthony is very excited but also very nervous about being in this play. At school the next day he walks around our classroom saying, "Yes! I'm a very good actor!" Then he gets scared and changes his mind. On Tuesday afternoon, he doesn't come back from lunch on time. I ask if I can go look for him and I find him standing next to his locker shaking his head. "I'm not an actor, Beminda. I can't do a play. I'm too scared."

I tell him, "Anthony, you've been scared before, but you have never let that stop you. We were all scared of our lockers. We were all scared of the cafeteria, but you were the bravest one of all of us. Do you remember that?"

I tell him this to make him feel better. Also because I remember how good it felt when Mom called me the bravest person she knew before I came back to school. Brave is what you want to feel when you are very scared of something.

"I'm not an actor," he says again.

"You're not an actor *yet*," I tell him. "You have to practice and work hard, that's all."

"No lines! I can't remember lines."

"You don't have to worry about that. I'll remember your lines. If you forget, I'll say them. I did that in my old plays and it worked out great. Everyone said I was great."

"You *are* great."

"I'm not that great. I need your help."

He looks confused. "You do?"

"I need your help keeping track of everything backstage. It can be a real mess if people aren't neat."

"I'm neat."

No, he's not, but I don't say that. "That's why I need you. We're a team now."

"A tea?"

"A team. M. Say M."

"Emmm!" He's smiling now. It makes me feel better.

"But I can't do this if you don't do it."

Anthony looks surprised. "You can't?"

"No. I can't, Anthony. I need you."

It makes me feel a little dizzy saying this. I look at Anthony's face. I can tell it makes him happy. He's smiling big, showing all his braces and some of the food he ate for lunch.

"I won't let you down. I'll never let Beminda down. No down."

I remember something funny. The first day Anthony came to our classroom everyone had to say their name and something about themselves. Most people said they had a pet or what their favorite food was, but Anthony said, "I sometimes have Down syndrome."

Rhonda, our teacher, said, "Only sometimes?"

"That's right," he said. Then he smiled. "Mostly I'm UP!"

"It's okay," I say. "You won't let me down. I know that. You're not down, you're up!"

We're both smiling now. "Sometimes I'm down! Mostly I'm up!" He points up with his finger and we both laugh hard. I don't even notice when he hugs me without asking first. He just does. We hug each other. It doesn't bother me or hurt or knock my glasses off. It's easy.

Besides opening his locker, the other thing Anthony does that rest of us don't is eat in the cafeteria. We all tried it when we first got to high school because it has french fries and a salad bar with choose-your-own dressing every day. Then we all had problems because the cafeteria is crowded and confusing and sooner or later you make a mistake like drop your tray or touch things in the salad bar with your hands. Then people get very mean and it's easier just to eat lunch in the classroom. If you order in the morning, one of the teachers will go pick up food for you which makes it even easier.

Except for Anthony.

Anthony likes going to the cafeteria. He never has any problems with his tray or the salad bar. He eats there every single day, even if he's brought a lunch from home.

Sometimes Doug will go with him or one of our teachers but sometimes he'll go by himself and just eat. A few times I went to my office job early just so I could walk by the cafeteria and see if he was really sitting there by himself. He always was. He's not scared of anything which is another reason why I think he'll be good in the play. He got nervous and sweaty before the audition but he never said, "I'm too scared to do this." I like Anthony for that. I also like him for eating lunch in the cafeteria even when no one will go with him.

That's why I said okay, yes, I'll eat lunch with Anthony today. I can tell everyone is surprised when I say this. Because I have a little bit of a bad history in the cafeteria. In ninth grade I dropped my tray and my food went everywhere including my chocolate pudding and I cried for so long they had to get the nurse to come and help me stop crying. I don't want to talk about that, though.

On the way to the cafeteria we look at the drama department bulletin board. It's a week after we auditioned, and there is still no cast list.

"No list," Anthony says. "It's okay."

"It's *not* okay!" I say. "We need to know! We don't have much practice time. We have to get organized! Plays don't work unless you're organized."

"Beminda is organdized."

"That's right, I am. I think maybe they need my help."

"You help. I help, too."

"We may end up doing a lot of things, Anthony. That's what happens sometimes. You paint your own sets and you make your costumes. That's how it is sometimes in theater."

"O-kay."

"You can't expect other people to do all the jobs. You see a job, you say, I'll do it."

"I do it."

"That's right."

"The backstage crew is just as important as the people onstage."

"O-kay."

I say this because I'm pretty sure Anthony is the reason there isn't any cast list up. They don't want to make him feel bad but they don't think he can do a big part. I think I'll talk to them. I'll tell them he *can* do a part. I'll tell them he *has* to. I can't imagine doing the play without him, so maybe he'll have to work backstage. That will be okay, too. I'll show him what to do and help him. We're a team that way now. Like friends, only maybe we're more than friends. Like we're best friends now.

I've never had a best friend before except for Nan and Mom of course. But I think this is what having a best friend feels like. Where you care about them being happy as much as you care about yourself being happy. Maybe even more.

It scares me a little because I maybe care about Anthony more than I care about being in this play, which isn't like me. I wonder if I don't just look different since I went to that football game. I think maybe I am different. I don't know whether that's good or bad.

Sometimes all this makes me laugh for no reason and then sometimes it makes me cry for no reason, too.

EMILY

FIRST THING THE NEXT morning, I find Lucas at his locker and tell him what I've been thinking about since we got off the phone the night before. "Don't worry, I'm not going to eat lunch with all your friends and I'm not going to make you eat with the nerd brigade. Let's keep things separate at school, okay?"

He looks over his shoulder like he's not sure where this is coming from. "Good morning, Emily. Nice talking to you last night." He shuts his locker. "Well, I enjoyed it, anyway. Maybe you lost sleep thinking about all the ramifications."

I feel terrible because he's right. I did lose sleep partly from excitement, partly from stewing over ramifications. "I just don't want to push it. I don't want you to think you have to change your life at school because of me. I keep thinking it'd be easier if we didn't go to the same school. Then we could get to know each other without all this school stuff."

Just being near him makes me nervous. I can't stop thinking about holding his hand. I want to touch it now but the hallway around us has started to fill up with people.

"That's kind of like saying the easiest thing would be if we never *met*."

"I'm not saying that. You know what I'm saying." Now that everything has changed between us, his eyes look ridiculously beautiful to me—green with little golden flecks. I want to stand here and stare at them all day and I can't let myself. "All I'm saying is that I don't think anything has to change at school."

As I see it, I *have* to be the one to say this. Even though I don't care about his kind of popularity, the fact remains: he has far more power than I do in this situation. I can't stand the idea of waiting to see if he'll talk to me at lunch.

"Fine," he says, and I catch him right there—the eyes I've just been staring into wander up the hallway, looking over my shoulder nervously at one of his friends. It was fine for us to talk in a school hallway before when we had to, but now things have changed, and I can see he's different. More self-conscious. More nervous about what others might think.

"So I'll see you next Wednesday for coffee!" I say a little too loud. "Okay?"

"Yeah, okay."

I spin around and walk away before I see him look around for any more of his friends.

That day at lunch, Hugh joins us for his second time at our lunch table, which should make us more comfortable, but unfortunately it doesn't. I study the way Richard watches him eat and try to decide what's happening with them as a couple. Surely they've kissed by now, but Richard hasn't told me, nor have I asked. Judging by how nervous Richard still looks—as if he doesn't want to eat too much or end up with food on his face—I'm guessing they haven't done much more than kiss.

Of course, what do I know about how couples should progress?

So far, we've learned that Hugh is a clarinet player in the marching band, which is why we haven't had any classes with him in the last three years. (Band members usually have a slightly different schedule.) Barry and Weilin joke with Hugh about some marching band hijinks they heard a rumor about. Even though I don't really get the joke, I laugh along with them in case Lucas is watching and wondering what my group of friends is like. I want him to think we are hilarious and fun but then, in the middle of my fake laugh, I look up and see something that stops me: Belinda and Anthony eating lunch in the cafeteria.

I'm not sure where they usually eat, but I know I've never seen her here before. I sit up straighter and watch them. They don't seem to be talking; they're just eating their lunch and looking around.

I want to do something. Go over and say hi. Ask them to join us. If this is Belinda's first time in the cafeteria, it's an event that should be acknowledged. Or even celebrated. Then I look over at Lucas and my heart melts a little. He's noticed the same thing. He's looking at me and then over at them. He raises his hands in a question: *What should we do?*

I point to myself: *Let me go over and say something. With me, it will draw less attention.* I hate to suggest this, but it's true. If Lucas got up and crossed the room, everyone would notice. With me, my friends will notice, but no one else.

I'm nervous enough that I stop at the water fountain before I go to their table. "Hi, you guys!" I say like I'm surprised when I walk by them.

Anthony grins and waves with his whole hand when he sees me. "Hi! Look, Beminda! It's the girl from the play!"

Belinda rolls her eyes in my direction but doesn't smile or speak. She's obviously upset.

"You guys were both great in that audition," I say.

Belinda huffs and folds her arms on the table. "But the cast list isn't up. We keep looking on the board and there's no list!"

"Oh my gosh," I pull out a chair and sit down at the otherwise empty table. "We really wanted to do the show, but the theater crowd is already busy doing *Guys and Dolls*. We didn't get enough people to show up for auditions, so we had to cancel the show."

Belinda looks like her brain can't register this information. "What do you *mean*? We have to rehearse is all. Then we put it on. Anthony can learn his lines. I've learned mine. I know them all."

I look over at Lucas, helpless. He's standing with his tray so I wave him over. "Belinda's already learned all her lines," I say when he walks up.

"I know I might not get Elizabeth, but I can help whoever plays her with lines."

Lucas pulls out a chair and sits down. "Oh, believe me, you'd get that part. Hands down. No one was as good as you were, Belinda."

She blushes such a deep crimson red, it's clear that no matter how many times we've told her, she never heard us saying *no one else auditioned*. "The problem isn't either one of you. It's that we don't have enough actors or crew. We'd need a few people on lights and a few people backstage and we don't have anyone."

Belinda flops down so her face is buried in her arms. I can't tell if she's crying or not.

"Beminda?" Anthony says. "Are you crying?"

She nods her head but she doesn't lift it up.

A bad taste fills my mouth. I can't look at Lucas. I have the terrible feeling that Richard was right—we never should have started this without being sure we could follow through. Maybe what we've done is worse than never raising the possibility at all.

"Beminda?" Anthony says, patting the back of her head. "Why are you crying?"

She lifts her head up. "I'm happy crying."

Lucas and I look at each other. *Happy crying?* I'm not sure what it means.

"I got the part!!" She sits up straight, smiling. Before we know it, she's hugging herself, then hugging Anthony. Anthony's so happy for the hug, he won't let go. "Did Anthony get a part, too?" she says from the crush of his embrace. "He doesn't need a big part. He's not a very good actor yet. Just something little."

"Yes," I hear Lucas say. He's not thinking, obviously, but I don't stop him or say anything either. "Anthony

264

definitely has a part. We couldn't do it without him."

One of Anthony's fists goes in the air. "Yes!" he screams. "I got a part!"

BELINDA

THAT AFTERNOON, MS. SADIQ stops by the nurse's office to see how I'm doing.

"Great!" I say. "I'm going to play Elizabeth in *Pride and Prejudice*."

Her eyebrows go up like she's surprised to hear this. "You are?"

"Yes! With my friends Lucas and Emily! They said yes, I definitely got the part!"

"I'm not sure about this Belinda. I'm going to have to look into it. You'd need your grandmother's permission to do anything like this," Ms. Sadiq says. She's looking at me like she knows Nan probably won't say yes. "You remember that, right?"

I say, "Yes, I remember that, but could I ask my mom instead?"

"You could, but I'd want to make sure everyone agrees it's a good idea."

"Oh, it's a good idea. It's a very good idea."

"Right, you might think so, Belinda, but will your grandmother and mom say that, too?"

I don't say anything because I don't know what they'll

say. They used to love it when I was in Children's Story Theater shows. Nan and I always made a special trip to Jo-Ann fabric so I could pick out the prettiest colors and she could make me the best costume of all. I think if I tell Nan, "Let's make me a pretty dress to play Lizzie," she'll say, "Okay, yes, Belinda. That sounds exciting."

In my mind, I picture her saying this. I imagine looking at materials and her saying, "No, that one is too hard to work with." Or, "That won't make a skirt that falls nicely." Nan can just look at material and know what kind of dress it will make. I can't do that and neither can Mom. I think most people are like me and reach for material that is the sparkliest.

I've pictured it all so much, I forget to go slow when I ask them that night at dinner. We are eating our pork chops and rice and green beans and I say it all too quickly. "Guess-what-we're-doing-a-play-at-school-it's-*Pride-and-Prejudice*-and-I-got-cast-I'm-Elizabeth!"

They blink at me. I remember that I never told them about auditioning because Nan said she never wanted me to audition for anything again if that director was never going to put me in a play. "You're too good for him!" she said. "We have our pride! We don't beg for things around here if people don't want us."

Now she looks at me with squinty eyes and I know she's probably thinking I didn't have pride. I begged for a part and they finally gave me one. I start over and go slowly so I can explain. "It's not with the drama teacher. It's a student show. That means students are doing the whole thing. We're directing it and getting props and all of it."

Mom smiles but her forehead looks a little funny. "That sounds wonderful. Imagine them picking your favorite story—"

"Which students?" Nan says. Her mouth looks like a line with no lips. She's also sweating even though it's not hot.

"My friend Anthony and a boy named Lucas and a girl named Emily."

Nan looks at Mom. "Absolutely not. You know who those two are, right?"

"Yes, Mother, of course. But it sounds like they're trying to do something nice for her."

Nan's sweating more now and shaking her head. "It's a little late for that, don't you think? They weren't very nice to her at the football game, were they?"

I'm surprised she's saying this because it breaks her rule that we don't talk about the football game. "Right, but maybe—" Mom puts down her fork. "Mother, are you okay?"

"Yes—" Nan says, pushing herself away from the table like she's going to stand up but she doesn't stand up. For a long time, we wait for her to say something but she doesn't say anything. Instead she bends over and, just like that, she throws up on the floor.

Mom stands up so fast her chair tips over which scares me and I scream. Nan is still bent over so I can only see the top of her head where her hair is thin and the pink skin shows through it.

"NAN?" Mom says, really loud now. "CAN YOU ANSWER ME?"

Nan is breathing a lot but not answering. A little string of throw-up is hanging from her mouth which is gross and not like Nan.

"GET THE PHONE, BELINDA!" Mom screams. "RIGHT NOW!"

I get the phone but I don't understand why she's making a phone call when Nan looks so sick. Then I hear her say, "Hello, yes. We have an emergency. My mother is having a heart attack."

When the ambulance drivers come in, they don't say much except for questions that are hard for Mom to answer. What medications is she on? What chronic conditions does she have? Mom is so upset she keeps shaking her head. She answers some of the questions but not all of them. I go and get Nan's pill bottles because I clean and organize her bathroom once a week and I know where they are. I put her pills on a little tray. I bring the tray down while they're putting Nan on a stretcher. I've been careful not to knock any of them over but the ambulance driver opens a bag and pushes them all in. He is not careful which is rude and makes me mad.

When I tell Mom this, she says it's not their fault, they have to get Nan to the hospital as quickly as possible. When I ask why, she looks at me like she doesn't understand the question. "Because she might die," she says. "People *die* from heart attacks."

I didn't know this.

I thought she was having an episode like Mrs. Bennett's in *Pride and Prejudice*, only with throw-up. I didn't know she might die.

We drive to the hospital as fast as we can. Right before we leave the house, Mom says, "Don't start crying now, Belinda. Please. I mean it." We don't say anything in the car because I don't know what to say and I'm trying to concentrate on not crying.

The whole drive I keep swallowing because I feel like maybe I'm having a heart attack and I need to throw up. My chest really hurts and I can't breathe. When we get inside I tell Mom, "I think maybe I'm dying, too."

"Oh, stop, Belinda," she says. "Not now."

If I die, she'll feel bad, but I don't tell her that.

Sitting in the hospital waiting room is scary. There are a lot of people here, but no one looks at each other. Everyone has their own person they're worried about. Some people are talking on the phone loudly like they don't realize we can all hear what they're saying.

Some people are saying personal, private things that we should not be hearing, like, "He drank too much. I told him this would happen if he did it again."

There is a sign saying No Cell Phones in the Hospital. Please Have Your Conversation Outside which apparently I can read but other people can't.

Mom looks very worried. I don't know if she's worried about Nan or worried that maybe she went to high school with some of these people. I am worried about Nan and I am also worried that if Nan had a heart attack I really won't be able to do the play. I'll have to call Emily on the phone and tell her except I don't have her phone number and I can't look it up because the print in the phone book is too small for me to read. I will have to tell her on Monday that my nan almost died, that's how much she doesn't want me to be in the play.

I think maybe Nan doesn't want me to do the play because she's still mad at Emily and Lucas about the football game.

I am still not sure what I think about that. Sometimes it makes me very mad to remember and sometimes I think, people make mistakes, including me. I'm not sure why we haven't ever talked about it. I thought maybe they'd say something at the audition, but then Anthony was there and I was glad they didn't. Now when I see them, Anthony is always there, so we keep not saying anything. But when I tell them I can't do the play, I'll probably say something like, "Plays are nice but people shouldn't have to scream for custodians to get help when they need it. That was not OK."

Just thinking about this makes me want to cry about not doing the play when I should be crying about Nan. I shouldn't be thinking about the play at all but I can't help it, I do and my throat gets tight and my eyes start to cry.

Mom has found a pocket pack of Kleenexes in her purse, which is lucky for me, but after a while they run out and I have to reuse the balled-up ones sitting in my lap. We've been here for a while now. We've talked to one doctor. He says she's stabilized for now but they're going to run more tests before they admit her. Even though we know she's going to be okay now, I still can't stop crying.

It makes Mom start crying, too. "She's going to be okay, Bee. I think we should try to get ahold of ourselves here."

"I'm not crying about Nan," I say. I blow my nose.

"You're not?" She looks surprised.

"No. I'm crying because I can't be in the play if it gives Nan a heart attack."

Mom makes a funny sound. Like a laugh cry. "I thought you were upset because if Nan's going to be in the hospital for a while, I'll be the only one home to take care of you. I thought you didn't want to be home alone with me."

"No." I laugh because that sounds silly. Mom and I have fun. We do different things than I do with Nan but it's still fun. Mom and I used to play Guess Who a lot, and Payday, and Who Will Be My Date? Mom likes board games and so do I. Usually I win which means I collect the highest salary on Payday and have the handsomest boy as my date. Mom always says, "Oh well," and laughs when she loses which is called being a good sport. I'm almost never a good sport. I usually cry when I lose games or get mad at the person who wins because it doesn't seem fair to have to lose. Mom tells me that everyone has to lose sometimes. That's how it is.

"We can play games and I'll let you win sometimes," I say because Mom is still crying and I want her to stop.

271

It's not nice being around a crying person especially if you love them.

"That would make me happy. I'm sorry I'm crying. I know how close you are to Nan and sometimes it makes me jealous and I know I shouldn't feel that way. We all love each other equally but you're my baby, not hers. I wish I could tell her that. I wish I could tell her that I'd like to make some decisions—it shouldn't always be the two of you deciding everything."

I think about this. It makes sense, except for the part about me being a baby because I'm definitely not a baby. "What do you want to decide?" I ask. If Nan is going to be in the hospital for a while, Mom could decide what to eat for dinner. Usually Nan does all the dinner cooking so mostly we eat what Nan likes—pork chops maybe, or chicken and green beans. Even though noodles are my favorite food, she never makes them for dinner. She says pasta is Italian and she can't cook foreign food.

"You could be in charge of dinner," I say. "That would probably be good."

"Yeah, that would be good, wouldn't it?" Mom laughs which is better than crying. "Maybe we could take a pork chop break."

"You could make spaghetti or something like that."

She laughs again. "How did I know you would suggest that?"

I shrug. "It's your decision."

"Maybe it can be *our* decision. If I decide on dinner, you can decide some other things. How about that?"

"Like lunch?" For lunch, Nan usually heats up a can of soup with toast or sometimes crackers.

"Like being in your play."

"I can't be in the play," I remind her. "Being in the play gave Nan a heart attack."

"No, it didn't," Mom says. Now she looks serious. "Nan has always had a heart condition and she doesn't always do what the doctor tells her to. That's what gave her a heart attack."

"Does that mean I can be in the play?"

"I think it should be *your* decision. I think you need to talk to those kids about what happened. I never agreed with Nan that no one should talk about it around you. I don't think that helps."

My throat goes hot and tight like I might start crying again. I don't know if I want to talk about what happened but I know I want to be in the play.

EMILY

"So I have a few ideas," Lucas says. "One is probably terrible, one might not be so bad."

It's finally Wednesday, we're finally on our coffee date, and I know it's not ideas for *us* that Lucas is talking about. It's Belinda and Anthony. It's this play they're so ecstatic to be part of that Ms. Sadiq scolded Lucas for talking to Belinda about it and then, in the same breath, thanked him for finding something that made her so happy.

We've been messaging every night this week, unsure what to do. In that heady moment after we told them they'd both been cast, their euphoria was so overwhelming neither one of us could bear to clarify what we were saying: *Yes, you're both in the show, but unfortunately it will never take place.* In the days since then, we've been swapping ideas, most of them not very good. His idea: we wait until *Guys and Dolls* is over, then rehearse for a week and a half with whoever will do it. My idea: the four of us—meaning Belinda and Anthony, Lucas and me—perform it on the street in our costumes, like a flash mob without the mob.

"Ah, no," Lucas said to that. "I'm sorry but no."

We've gone through a bunch of stabs like this. Some funny, some not. I was worried this might be the only thing we talk about. Since the one phone conversation where we set up this date, we haven't talked about us, or Debbie, or alluded, even passingly, to the hand-holding episode. We haven't even flirted much. We've just talked about this play and whether we made a terrible mistake getting Belinda and Anthony's hopes up for something that will never happen.

Haunting us both are Belinda's words after she and Anthony finished celebrating. "I've never been cast in a play since *Charlotte's Web*! Mr. Bergman lets me try out for all of them but he always says, You know I can't cast you, Belinda, I wish I could."

I couldn't believe it. "He *says* that to you? The drama teacher?"

"He doesn't have extra staff so I can't be in a play. I'm not allowed. I'm only allowed to audition. That's what he says."

Lucas looked as shocked as I was. "That doesn't sound right, Belinda."

Belinda shook her head. "I'm allowed to try out. I just can't be in a play. That's the rule. No after-school clubs. No activities."

"Wait a second," I say. I want to make sure I'm clear about this. "The school made this rule or your mom?"

"Mr. Bergman told me, sorry, that's the rule."

"See, Belinda, he shouldn't say that. He can't say you can never be in a play because we don't have staff for it. That's illegal." I hoped I was right about this.

"Oh." Belinda looked confused. "And is Anthony allowed, too?"

"Of course. You guys should be able to do any after-school clubs that you want."

As I got more emphatic, I also got more nervous that maybe I was wrong. But that night I looked it up and I was right—all special ed students have a right to access an equal education, including access to all sports, clubs, and after-school activities, according to the site I read. If a student with a disability wants to play a sport or join a club, accommodations have to be made. They can't be denied a spot because of their disability.

They've been doing this to Belinda for four years, I wrote Lucas that night. *She's been going to approximately two auditions a year—every play, and every musical—and they've told her she's*

275

welcome to audition but they can't give her a part because of staffing issue. That's about fifteen violations of federal law!

He writes back. *Are you sure you're in AP calculus?*

Twelve violations, whatever. I'm serious. This is a big deal. They weren't even cagey about it, saying you're not right for this part. They just said no, because of your disability, you'll never be in a play. When I figured all this out, I was so mad I wrote an email to the free legal aid to victims of IDEA violations.

Now we sit across from each other both drinking hot chocolate. The issue has made us both less nervous about the "date" aspects of this date.

"Here's the thing," he says. "The point is giving Belinda a chance to act in her favorite story, not to right every wrong that's ever been committed against special ed kids in the school."

He has a good point. "Okay," I say.

"So here's my idea. What if we do the play with four people? You and Belinda will be Lizzie and Jane, Anthony and I will be Darcy and Bingley."

"Anthony as Mr. Darcy?" I don't want to be mean, but we also have to be realistic. "It's almost impossible to understand anything Anthony says."

"No, I'll be Darcy. I mean . . . don't you think that's better?"

I think of the story he told about Ron. How all the problems started when he asked Belinda to dance once. "I do think that's better, but what if she gets a crush on you? Or switches whatever feelings she had for Ron over to you? We have to be careful about that."

"Actually, I don't think that will happen." He smiles as he says this. "I think she and Anthony are becoming an item. I talked to him about it the other day. He told me he's loved her since seventh grade and apparently she's finally coming around. She's agreed not to date anyone else until the play is over. So they've cleared that up."

I wonder if Lucas is thinking the same thing I am: *They've cleared it up better than you and I have.*

He keeps going: "We rehearse the show after school for the next two weeks, just a few scenes with the costumes, then we put it on at LLC for the last day of class. Maybe we could invite the ballroom dance class to join us so we have a bigger audience. We'll see Mary tonight and ask her. After all, *Pride and Prejudice* is a story about boundaries and relationships, right? I don't know—" He shakes his head and smiles. "That sounded better in my head when I thought of it. Saying it out loud it sounds stupid."

"It doesn't sound stupid," I slide one had across the table and put a finger on his wrist. "It's a *great* idea."

He looks at the finger and up at me. "It is?"

I don't know how to flirt. I hate the idea of being obvious and coy at the same time. For years I've watched cheerleaders play flirty games to get the attention of every boy in the room, asking a whole math class if anyone can see her bra under her shirt or if anyone could do the homework last night because she sure couldn't. Flirting makes you feel stupid. It forces you to slip outside your own body and watch yourself flirt. Flirting makes you think: *Oh my God. I look and sound like every girl I hate.* At the same time, it's hard to hold myself back. I love this idea; I love that he's given this so much thought. "It's a great idea because it's doable. We don't have a lot of options. This way Belinda can be in a play and we'll have a guaranteed audience of, what? About forty, maybe? But would we just put on one performance for the class?"

"For now, yes. Maybe—I don't know—we could find other venues. We'll see how it goes. I know we talked about getting kids at school to see what Belinda and Anthony can do, but maybe that's not the most important thing for them. Maybe it would be nice for Belinda to check out the center. After she's finished with high school, she'll be able to take classes there. Maybe she could sign up for ballroom dance classes."

He's absolutely right and it kills me that he's thought of this, not me. However scared we are about the unknowns of next year, surely Belinda, with no job and nowhere to go, is more scared. My mind races ahead a little—I picture introducing Belinda and Anthony to Mary, telling them a little bit about Mary's class. How it helps people who want to start dating. It teaches you about communicating and managing expectations. It's helped me a lot, I'll have to admit, because it's sort of true. Not even sort of. Just true.

"It's a great idea, Lucas," I say, grinning. "I wish I'd thought of it."

He smiles at me in a way that says a lot of things without saying them: he hasn't forgotten this is meant to be a date.

When we get outside, he asks me how I think it went.

"You mean me learning to drink coffee? Unfortunately I think you have to order coffee before you can learn how to like it."

"Not that," he says. "The other part. The conversation thing."

"I never thought you were bad at that, Lucas. You're better than you think."

"I remember some of our conversations not going so well. Maybe in the beginning there when you were dating Joe College."

"Yeah . . ." I think about it for a minute. "It's remotely possible some of that was my fault. I think maybe I misjudged you."

"What? You assumed I was stupid and insensitive just because I play football?" He steps closer as he says this. It makes me nervous but I don't step away. He smells like soap and coffee, a surprisingly intoxicating combination.

"Sort of."

"Just because 85 percent of the team is doesn't mean we all are." He takes another step. He's done all this before. He knows how to reach over and play with someone's sleeve. I don't. I'm terrified that he'll kiss me and I'll get so nervous I'll do something I don't mean to, like start laughing. Or stomp on his foot. My nerves are all jangly and unpredictable.

"We're not all jerks," he says. "Just like your crowd isn't all National Merit snobs."

Now he's got both sleeves of my shirt pinched between his fingers and he's really leaning in. I keep being sure we're going to kiss and then we don't. "Just to be clear, I'm not a National Merit anything. That's Candace. Plus Barry and Weilin were finalists."

"Both?" He leans back, surprised. "That's kind of intense because they're dating too—they must have cheated, right?"

Before we started driving together, he didn't know any of my friends' names. This didn't surprise me, of course, even though I knew most of his friends. What surprises me now—catches my breath, really—is that even though he's still never been introduced, he knows them well enough to make a joke. "I know, right? They're both super smart and they're a couple. I totally think they cheated. It's too coincidental otherwise."

He laughs and then, suddenly, we're kissing. Only our lips touch at first, not our bodies. It's not a crazy kiss. Just a lovely slow gentle one.

"That was nice," he says after it's over. "Maybe we should try this again some time."

I want to say, *How about now? Let's kiss again now.*

"Maybe we could get together and iron out play details this weekend," I say. Then I realize it's Wednesday and I probably sound too eager. No, I definitely sound too eager. Kiss the girl on Wednesday and suddenly her Friday and Saturday calendar are cleared of any plans.

"I'd like to but I can't," he says. "I have to work all weekend for my dad."

I can't tell if this is an excuse or not. He's never mentioned working for his dad before. He's only talked about fighting with him. "You *do*? I didn't know you had a job."

"It's a little embarrassing. I guess I don't talk about it too much."

"What is it?" I try to imagine embarrassing jobs and I can't.

"He's a stonemason."

I study his face but it's impossible to read. "Why is that embarrassing?"

"Do you know any stonemasons?"

"No. I mean, maybe. I don't know what it is exactly."

"Our best work is building and repairing stone walls. That's kind of cool, but we don't do too much of that. Most of our jobs are mixing cement and laying brick. That's less cool. That's working with a lot of guys who are in between prison terms, if you know what I mean."

"Really?" I'm not even sure what to say. "I've never met anyone who's been in prison."

"Yeah, generally speaking they're not a barrel of laughs. If it was possible to go to college and *not* do this forever, I'd pick that."

Now I understand what he's really saying. I understand why he got so mad that time that I said he was lucky to have choices, and didn't *have* to go to college. He doesn't have more choices than me; he has fewer. If he doesn't go to school next year, this will be his job. And maybe the fact that he's never once mentioned it in all this time is a measure of how much he doesn't want to do it.

BELINDA

ONE THING ABOUT NAN is she never throws anything away. Like newspapers or coupons for things she might want to buy someday. Even my grandfather's clothes she's never thrown away. Whenever I ask, she says, "You never know when another man might come into our life who needs them."

I want to say, "But wouldn't he already have his own clothes?"

I don't because sometimes Nan gets mad if you ask her questions like that. Now that Nan's been in the hospital for a few days, Mom does something surprising. She picks up a stack of old magazines and puts it in the paper-recycling container. Then she goes back, picks up the rest of the stack, and puts it all in recycling. Just watching her do this makes me nervous. Nan doesn't like people moving things around. Then she can't find anything when she goes to look.

I watch Mom put more piles in the container. She doesn't even look at what she's throwing away. There could be mail in there, or coupons that are still good. "Why are you doing that?" I say. "Nan'll get mad."

"We have to do this sooner or later or we're going to start living like hoarders. If I do it now, she'll be so mad at me when she gets home she won't have time to think about you and your play."

She smiles as she says this like we have a secret between

us. It's nice of Mom but it means she's also worried about what Nan will say about me being in the play.

Maybe it doesn't matter because all day at school I'm happy about going to my first rehearsal in the afternoon which is going to be in the little theater where we auditioned. Lucas came to the nurse's office and gave me a note about it which me so happy I burst out laughing. I've been imagining the party scenes where someone will bow and ask me to dance. Where there will be music and other dancers and everyone will be wearing pretty dresses but mine will be the prettiest.

That's why I can't believe it when I get to rehearsal and only four people are there.

"Where's everyone else?" I say.

Emily says, "Remember, we explained this, Belinda—it's only going to be us. No one else auditioned."

She keeps going. She says we're not doing the whole play either, only scenes from the play because there's only four of us. It's hard for me to hear what she's saying because my heart is beating fast and my hands start to sweat. I want to tell her, "But every scene is important!" I forget my yoga breathing which makes me a little dizzy. I keep thinking, you can't do part of a play or scenes from a play. You have to do the *whole* play, that's the rule.

"We don't have a choice on this, Belinda," Emily says. "We have to do it this way, but let me finish—we're doing it for a special audience. Lucas and I have been working at a place for adults with disabilities called the Lifelong Learning Center. We're part of a class called Boundaries and Relationships, where they act out scenes of people who are trying to start relationships and then we talk about the scene afterward. We've asked the teacher about this idea and she thinks it's a good one. She says we can also invite the people from a ballroom dance class next door to come watch, too. It will be very interactive, Belinda. It won't be like a regular play. We'll get a chance to talk about each scene in between and what is happening between Elizabeth and Mr. Darcy."

"Did you say ballroom dancing?" I say. I once asked Nan if I could take a class like this. She said she wished I could, but no one does ballroom dancing anymore.

"That's right," Emily says. "There's a ballroom dance class that meets next door."

This makes my heart calm down a little. "Do they waltz dance?"

"I don't know, actually." She looks at Lucas. "Do you know? I assume so. Waltzing is sort of a basic one, right?"

Anthony raises his hand even though there are only four of us and he doesn't need to raise his hand to say something. "I'm a very good dancer," he says.

"That's great," Emily says. "Maybe we could try one of the dance scenes."

I have a different idea. I raise my hand to be polite. "Yes, Belinda?"

"Maybe we could do our play and they could give us a lesson on waltz dancing."

Emily claps her hands. "That's a great idea! Lucas, what do you think?"

Lucas doesn't say anything. He's smiling at Emily and shaking his head like maybe he wants a chance to dance with her but is nervous about it. Like I am nervous about dancing with Anthony. If he is such a good dancer maybe he will know right away that I have only danced one time before and that was with Ron Moody.

"It's a good idea," Lucas says. "It might mean we do a shorter show but then we work harder on those scenes and make them really good."

I see Anthony shake his head. I can tell he's starting to get nervous again. He's making weird noises like he might start to cry which has happened in class a couple of times. I thought I'd talked him out of all that, but I guess I didn't. "I don't know, you guys," he says. "I'm not a good actor. You do the play without me."

"No, Anthony!" I say. My voice is so loud I surprise myself. "Don't start that now!"

"Please, Anthony," Emily says. "We really need you."

Lucas surprises me. We are sitting in desk chairs in a circle so we are all close. He reaches over and puts his hand on Anthony's shoulder. "Anthony, my friend," he says, "don't leave me high and dry as the only guy in this very girl-centric play."

Anthony doesn't know what girl-centric means. I don't know what girl-centric means either, but it sounds like a funny word and it makes Anthony smile. Suddenly he's in a much better mood. He opens his arms and leans over to Lucas and I think, oh no, Anthony needs another sheet of hugging rules:

—Don't hug football players.

—Don't hug football players' girlfriends.

—No hugging anyone while we're performing the play.

—No hugging audience members you don't know afterward.

I'm surprised, though. Lucas doesn't mind the hug. He hugs Anthony back and says, "Seriously, man, this could be great, but we really can't do it without you."

"Okay, yeah. Okay, I'll do it. I'll do it, Beminda, don't worry."

CHAPTER SIXTEEN
EMILY

I TOLD LUCAS THAT IF I was going to direct, he would have to be my producer.

"Sure," he smiled. "Except I don't know what that means."

"It means you'll do all the administrative work. You'll reserve the space for after-school rehearsals, you'll do the xeroxing, things like that."

For three years, this has been my job for YAC. Richard thinks up the bigger ideas and I take care of the administrative details—table reservations, xeroxing petitions. It means he's out front putting himself on the line a little more, but I'm the one making sure things happen.

Once I gave Lucas this role, I worried right away that it was asking too much. What would he know about the bureaucratic nightmare of filling out room-usage forms with the main office? So far, though, he's done a great job with everything I asked. He reserved the room, made up a rehearsal schedule and now, two days later, he's here with xeroxed play scripts in hand. Belinda and Anthony are here as well—looking up at me, ready for my instructions.

The only person who's not prepared, apparently, is me. I panic a little. I didn't expect everyone to be so ready, right away. I have no ideas; I don't know where to start.

And then it comes. At our first rehearsal, we do a read-through. At our second, we block the four scenes we've chosen to concentrate on. The blocking is a little messy. Neither Belinda nor Anthony can reliably tell the difference between their left and their right, so Lucas cues them with a tip of his head. At our first break, Belinda seems upset about something. I hear Anthony beside her. "Is okay, Beminda. We're very good."

"I don't know," Belinda says. She's obviously unhappy. "Just doing one show for this one class seems like not very many people will see it. We're doing all this work—I just wish it could be on TV or something."

I remember something else about Belinda back in our Children's Story Theater days. When she made up her mind, she could be very stubborn and have fits at the most inopportune times—like once during final dress rehearsal, she wouldn't come out of the bathroom because her costume wasn't right.

"No, Belinda," I say, so forcefully I surprise myself. "Acting isn't about getting on TV and being a big star."

Belinda looks up at me and straightens her glasses. "Yes, it is. When I was Red Riding Hood, I was famous. People stopped me in the store and told me how good I was."

"That's nice, but that's not what it's about."

I can tell both Belinda and Anthony are mystified by this. "It's not?" Belinda says.

"No. It's about telling a story for this particular audience who can learn something from it. These people don't know *Pride and Prejudice* at all. We're acting it out so you can *show* them why you love it so much and the lessons they can learn from it. What do you think the main lesson from *Pride and Prejudice* is?"

Belinda thinks about her answer for a long time before she says it. "They love each other and get married?"

"Sort of. But what happens *before* they fall in love with each other?"

I've lost Anthony, I fear. He looks like he's stopped listening and is staring up at the ceiling.

"Mr. Darcy goes swimming with all his clothes on?"

I'm afraid if I let her, she'll keep guessing all day. "Yes, but do you remember the main thing—how they misjudged each other based on their appearances?" I've said this the wrong way. "They decided they could never like each other based on how they looked. And then *they got to know each other* and they fell in love."

It turns out Anthony *has* been listening because he grins right at me and then at Belinda. "I always loved Beminda. First time I saw her, I loved her."

Belinda turns and snaps at him: "That's *not* true, Anthony. You were too young and too short and I said, 'No, you can't love me, you're only in ninth grade.' "

I can't do anything but look at Lucas and smile. It's hard not to laugh at how well this epitomizes the point of the story. Plus the surprise that fills me with reassurance: Belinda *is* loved, by this boy who she must care about, too, because she's brought him into this project that was intended only for her.

Lucas has his hand over his mouth but I can tell he's smiling behind it.

"And now you've changed your mind a little bit, right, Belinda?" It's tempting to say her name the sweet way Anthony says it: Beminda. "You've become good friends with Anthony now that you've gotten to know him."

She sits up straighter and turns to look at him. "Yes," she nods. "He's my best friend."

He grins and laughs and rocks back and forth clapping his hands. "See!" he says. "I told my mom, she'll love me someday! She doesn't know it yet, but she will!"

Beside him, Belinda doesn't laugh or even smile, which I think I understand. For her, this hasn't been easy. There's the complication of Mitchell Breski and the terrible fear she must have of standing too close to a boy's fierce desires. There's also the countless times she's watched *Pride and Prejudice*. She's learned about love by watching people who don't act or look like anyone we know. Maybe we all have in a way. It's an adjustment for everyone, I think, looking over at Lucas. Every time I do this, I'm surprised all over again, sometimes by how cute he is, other times by something I haven't noticed before—look at his shoulders! They're so wide! Or his hands! They've got freckles! Sometimes it's a completely different feeling, though. It's like: *Wait, him? Is this really who I've been awake at night obsessing over?* Suddenly

Lucas will look ordinary to me again, like a regular person. It's almost like I need to get away from him to overinflate him again in my mind. But it's interesting—the more time I spend with him, the less I want to do that. I want to stay here with him and keep being surprised. Which is what I really am when he takes his hand away from his mouth and leans forward on the seat in front of him. "Actually, Em, there is a way we can get on TV if we want to." He whispers this, like he doesn't mean to undermine my great point.

Belinda spins around. *"How?"* she says. She's definitely interested.

"My mother used to work for the local access public TV station. I could call them up and see if someone could come film this."

Suddenly Belinda is rocking and clapping and wreathed in smiles.

Sheesh, I think. She sits stony-faced beside Anthony's sweet declaration of true love but turns cartwheels at the prospect of a movie camera filming her. "Yes!" she says. "Call them now! Then my mom can see it and my nan, too. And my cousins. And Anthony's two sisters." She keeps going, naming all the people who will be able to see them now. She's obviously thrilled; Anthony's happy because she's happy.

Lucas looks to me apologetically. "Is that okay?"

I sort of wish I hadn't made him producer. "Fine," I say. Obviously everyone has missed my larger message that we're not doing this for ourselves, but for the folks in the audience.

Oh well, I think. Maybe we are doing this for ourselves.

BELINDA

AFTER OUR SECOND REHEARSAL, Anthony and I walk to the city bus stop together. That means we aren't taking a late school bus home, we're taking a regular bus. We've both taken travel training courses so we know how, sort of. Anthony had to take the course twice because he kept getting confused about transfers. For me, the hardest part is getting exact change and seeing the sign that says where the bus is going. As long as you ask the driver where you need to get off and then sit right behind him so he doesn't forget to tell you, transfers are easy. Then, even if you can't see the street signs, you're okay. Sometimes I tell the bus driver I'm almost blind which isn't true. I'm not almost blind, I just have cloudy spots that move and sometimes I can't read street signs.

I tell Anthony this while we're standing at the bus stop. "You have to sit behind the driver, Anthony. That's how you know where to get off. He tells you."

"I'm sitting next to you, Beminda."

"Well, I'm sitting behind him."

Anthony does what most people do which is look up the street the whole time to watch for the bus coming. Sometimes people even step into the street to see if it's coming, but that is against travel training rules so I never do it. It also doesn't make it come any faster, my travel training teacher told me. Anthony doesn't want to look for the bus, he wants to ask me questions he's always wondered about like why do I like

Pride and Prejudice so much and how come he's never met my dad at any of the family potlucks.

"Douglas thinks maybe he's probably dead so I said I'm going to ask her," he says.

"He's not dead, Anthony."

"That's good!"

"It's not that good either because the last time I saw him was seven years ago, maybe, I forget." I don't really forget, I just pretend to forget.

"Oh!" Anthony says. "Why don't you see him if he's your dad?"

"That's a personal private question, Anthony. You're not allowed to ask people personal private questions."

"Okay, sorry," he says. Then I guess he thinks about it. "But if you're my girlfriend, I'm allowed to, I think."

"No, I don't think so."

"I'm pretty sure I am."

"Okay, fine. I don't see my dad because I don't know why I don't see him. He's not a very responsible person and plus he doesn't like me, I guess."

"That's impossible, Beminda. He likes you very much, I know he does."

"That's nice of you to say but no he doesn't. Sometimes it's better to just face facts, that's what my nan says. So that's one of my facts."

"Okay."

It's weird. I feel sort of glad we're talking like this. Like maybe it would be okay to tell Anthony other things, like what happened at the football game. I don't know, though.

Maybe it wouldn't. So instead I ask him, "Do you have anything personal private I should know?"

He does, of course. He tells me all of them with a big smile on his face. How he sometimes doesn't shake after he pees and gets wet spots on his underwear. And sometimes he pretends to read stuff he can't read. And once he accidentally crossed the street right in front of a car and almost died.

"Okay," I say. "That's enough."

He smiles at me. "O-kay," he says.

When our bus comes we get on and show the driver our passes that mean we can ride for free during the day but not at night because people like us should never ride at night. Then we both sit down where I told Anthony we should sit, right behind the bus driver.

Even though he got his travel training certificate, I don't think Anthony's ever ridden the bus like this without a teacher because we've never been in a club before or had any reason to stay after school. It's exciting that we have a reason now. It's exciting to ride a city bus home like everybody else. I know Anthony's happy because he holds my hand which he's never done before.

A woman across the aisle looks at us. At first I'm embarrassed like maybe holding hands isn't allowed on buses. But I've seen other people do it, so I know that's not true. I don't pull my hand away or tell Anthony no. We're like anyone else now. We're allowed to ride this bus and we're allowed to hold hands.

It feels good except we probably shouldn't make loud

noises like Anthony does when we get to our stop and he stands up and screams, "YAHOO, BEMINDA! WE DID IT!"

The next day I tell Emily I can't go to rehearsal number three because I have an IEP meeting. IEP stands for Individualized Education Program, I think. These used to be meetings where Nan and Mom talked to the teachers about what I should be learning in school. Since I turned sixteen, though, I've been going to my own IEP meetings once a year. Now we talk mostly about what my future plans should be. My favorite part of IEP meetings is the beginning when all the teachers say nice things about me. Rhonda will say, "Belinda is the best typist in our classroom." Or: "I love how Belinda keeps her desk area and her space so neat and tidy. She's a good role model for other students."

The nice things are supposed to help us think of what I should do after I leave school which is called MY FUTURE VISION. We used to say I should be an office secretary. Now we don't say that since we found out there aren't any jobs like that for people like me.

This is the first time Nan hasn't come to one of my IEP meetings, which is strange but maybe it's okay because this time Mom talks more and makes suggestions. "Maybe she could do data entry like I do," she says.

The teachers say, with my eyesight issues, it's not a practical possibility.

"How about mail sorting? Or a job at a post office?"

It's a good idea, they say, but the post office has been

laying off employees lately. To be a mail carrier, I'd have to be able to drive which I can't.

I like seeing my mom here, dressed up in regular clothes and talking, but I can tell she might be getting a little sad. "You're not giving us any options for after Belinda leaves here. She's spent the last eighteen years in school working hard, improving her capabilities, and you're telling us there's *nothing* out there for her?"

"Oh, no," they all say. "There are day programs. Nice, well-run day programs where she'll have a range of activities to choose from."

"But haven't we been working all this time to get her a job? Wasn't that the *whole point*?"

No one says anything. They all look at each other. I don't want my mom to cry in front of all these people. They hardly know her and I want them to see the mom I love.

"I do have a job," I say.

I talk so little at these meetings that everyone is surprised.

"Of course, dear. Your school office job, that's right," Rhonda says.

"Not that job," I say because maybe she's forgotten, I don't have that one anymore, Anthony and Douglas do. "I have a different job now. I have the job of acting in a play and putting it on for people like me, except they don't know *Price and Prejudice*."

I look at Mom sitting across the table. She looks proud of me. She's happy I'm doing this even though Nan told me not to. She's crying a little but it's happy crying so it's okay.

This is how we explain it to Nan when we go back to the hospital that night and tell her what's going on.

"Belinda has been offered a job, Mom!" my mom says. Nan opens her eyes wide like she's excited and then, real quick, Mom tells her. "A job acting in a play that she'll put on for other disabled young adults. It's a teaching tool. She'll be like a teacher. An actress-teacher."

Nan's eyes go to slits. "That's not a job."

I can't believe it. Mom takes a deep yoga breath—in through the nose and out through her mouth. "Yes, it is, Nan. True, she might not be getting a paycheck for it, but it's an important job and she'll be connecting with other people she needs to connect with."

Nan shakes her head. "It's a mistake, Lauren. She's not like those other people." She whispers this like she doesn't want me to hear it, but I do anyway. I'm standing right here.

"Yes, she is, Mom. She *is* like those other people. It doesn't help if we isolate her. It doesn't give her a better life—it gives her less of a life."

I'm surprised by Mom saying all this. She hardly ever disagrees with Nan.

Nan can't say too much. She has her oxygen nose tube and her IV in her hand so she can't sit up or get mad at Mom. Instead she shakes her head and looks like she's going to cry. "It just makes me sad," Nan says.

"It's not sad, Nan. I'm happy she's doing this. So is she."

Even though she's talking about being happy, no one smiles.

CHAPTER SEVENTEEN
EMILY

BY OUR FIFTH REHEARSAL, a few things have emerged: Belinda and Anthony are both pretty good, but with similar weaknesses. Belinda is hard to understand and Anthony is almost impossible. Belinda tries to help by repeating Anthony's lines: "Did you just say . . ." and then she'll repeat his line word for word. At first it's funny and then I realize it will slow our show down by an extra forty minutes. Plus, Belinda's articulation isn't as good as it used to be when we were kids. She mumbles too much and says too many of her lines staring at the floor.

"Look up! We want to see your face, Belinda!" I call from the director's spot in the front row of the small theater we're rehearsing in. "Your face is beautiful, Belinda, but it's always in shadows. We need your head up, chest lifted. We need to hear your old booming voice."

She adjusts for a line or two and then goes back to mumbling.

A little later, when I interrupt her to repeat, "Louder! Both of you!" she flounces down on the floor. "I can't do it," she says. "It's too hard. Anthony and me quit."

"No, Belinda!" I jump up. "That was my fault. I shouldn't have interrupted you. You were doing fine. You were great."

Anthony shakes his head. "You can't quit, Beminda. This show is important."

Unfortunately, this hasn't been Belinda's only meltdown. She had another one yesterday when I mentioned wearing makeup. "NO MAKEUP!" she screamed. I thought makeup would help her look and feel like a real actress when we didn't have a stage or any special lights hung. "Makeup gets in my mouth and hurts my eyes," she insisted.

So far, I've conceded to her on virtually everything. Fine, no makeup. Okay, wear the straw sun hat with plastic flowers that were certainly not around in Jane Austen's time. Ditto to the Japanese fan she wants to hold in the first scene where she meets Mr. Darcy. "But it's got a geisha lady on it," Lucas gently pointed out.

"So?" she spat. "I don't care!"

It's like Belinda has no idea how hard we've worked to make this happen or how spoiled she sometimes seems in light of those efforts. When she sits down on the floor for this final hissy fit, I feel like saying, *Fine, Belinda, you're right. Let's not do the show.*

I'm grateful that Lucas has a doctor's appointment the next day, which means we have to cancel rehearsal. I'm even more grateful when I head out to my car after school and find Richard standing beside the passenger door. Ever since my friends refused to help on this play, I've told them very little about what we're doing. I also haven't seen them much because I haven't given anyone a ride lately.

"Is this okay?" Richard says. "I wasn't sure about your—whatever. Schedule."

"Yeah, of course!" I say. I'm stupidly happy to see him. I want to ask him about Hugh, which I never can at lunch because it feels like too many people are listening. I want to hear what's going on. It feels like we've been in a fight, though we haven't exactly. Or the fight never happened, only the bad-feelings aftermath. I haven't asked him about Hugh in over two weeks.

"You don't have rehearsal? Or someone else you're giving a ride to?" His voice is a little wobbly. Like he's nervous, too.

"No, Richard. Come on. Get in the car."

I haven't said anything to Richard (or anyone) about Lucas. I don't know if he's noticed Lucas and me talking in the hallway, but we do it so infrequently, it doesn't seem likely. For a week now, I've thought about how I might tell him what's going on, but I haven't been able to find the right words: *You remember the boy I was so mad at earlier this year? The one I blamed for not helping Belinda? It turns out he's a nice guy! It also turns out I like him!* It's hard to imagine conveying what I really want to say: Lucas was never the problem, I was. I may be cofounder of the Youth Action Coalition but I have a little problem taking action when I need to.

Before I can even bring up this subject or ask about Hugh, Richard asks how the show is going. I say, "Fine. I mean, it's terrible, but fine. I'm hoping to keep it as short as possible. How bad can any thirty-minute performance be, right?"

Even saying this much feels wrong. I'm being mean about something I care a lot about and I don't know why. It's hard to care and be the caustic, witty person your friends know you as at the same time.

"You're doing *Pride and Prejudice* in thirty minutes?"

"Scenes from *Pride and Prejudice*. It's like a mash-up montage of Colin Firth GIFs done live with dialogue you can't really understand."

He laughs. Maybe it's okay for me to be a little mean, I think. Richard is my old friend and this is the way we talk to each other. Just as I'm thinking this, though, I look over at Richard in the seat beside me and realize he isn't laughing, he's crying.

"Oh my God, what's wrong?" I press the brake even though we're not anywhere near a stop sign. I've never seen Richard cry before.

"It turns out Hugh is kind of a dick," he says, wiping his face. "A nice dick. But a dick."

"What's going on? What did he do?"

"It's more like everything he hasn't done." He closes his eyes, trying to get himself to stop crying, but it doesn't work. When he opens them, his lashes are all wet. "Like introduce me to any of his friends."

"Okay, tell me *exactly* what's happened."

"I wasn't even talking about introducing me as his boyfriend or whatever. I just told him I wanted to meet his friends." He stops his story to fish through his backpack for a Kleenex. "And he said, 'I'm sorry, it's not a good idea.'"

"That's what he *said*?"

He nods miserably and blows his nose. "Plus he's not out to his family so I can't call him at home. His mother reads his texts so I can't text him. I understand taking it slow but this feels like not moving. Anywhere. Ever. We're kind of paralyzed."

"This is Hugh's problem. It's not you, you know that, right?"

"I know. It's just frustrating. When we're by ourselves, we're good together. We really are. But how often has that happened? It's like that first week shopping for his pants was our high point. We never ran into anyone from school. It was heaven."

I want to comfort him and tell him Hugh is being a jerk, but even as I think this, I know I'm being a hypocrite: Hugh is too nervous to tell his friends about Richard and I'm too nervous to tell mine about Lucas. I wish I could tell Richard, *It's not you he's insecure about, it's himself.* "Being with you probably makes him feel like a different person and he doesn't know how to be that person and still hang out with his friends," I try.

"That's nice of you to say, but we're not talking about seventy-year-old grandparents here. These are teenagers acquainted with the idea of gay people."

"It's just awkward for some people. You probably aren't

the person they expected Hugh to end up with. It takes a little time to adjust, that's all."

We drive for a while in silence. Is it so wrong to be scared of what your friends might think? I want to tell Richard about Lucas but every time I almost do it, I have a strange mini panic attack where I can't catch my breath. With every day that goes by, I like Lucas more. Even when I hardly talk to him, I can't help it: I see Lucas in the hallway, we smile at each other, and I'm breathless for a few seconds. I don't know how to explain this to my friends— how freeing this feels, how new, how it's like being on vacation from my old self—so I don't.

By the time we get to his house, Richard seems better. Or at least okay enough to make a joke: "I'm starting to wonder if maybe we were right before. Maybe helping groups is a better idea than getting to know individuals."

I think about Belinda and all her complaints. "Real people are harder, it's true."

He smiles sadly. "I think I'd rather fight to hold a gay prom than figure out if my real boyfriend would go to one with me."

BELINDA

On Tuesday, something surprising happens. Rhonda, my teacher, comes to the nurse's office and asks me if I think I'm ready to come back to the classroom and see my old friends. At first I say, "I don't know," and then I think about Eugene rolling around in his chair.

I hardly know Eugene and this is my last year in school so it's my last chance to get to know him. I think, Maybe I should go back for a little while. To tell him I'm sorry about saying I thought I was better than other people in our class. I don't think that anymore.

This whole fall, when I loved Ron so much and couldn't stop thinking about him, I acted mean toward other people. I know that now. I wanted Ron to think I belonged with him and his friends more than I belonged with any of the people in my classroom. But now I know what Ron is really like. No one in our classroom was ever mean like that. Sometimes they were annoying, like Douglas, but that's different than mean.

Annoying you can ignore. Annoying you can say, "That's enough, Douglas."

With meanness, you can't say anything because you can't breathe.

I tell Rhonda I would like to come back for morning activities and see how it goes. I don't know if anyone besides Anthony will be happy to see me. They probably remember the mean things I said.

Maybe they've planned some mean things to say back.

Of course Eugene would have to type it with the pointer stick attached to his head, but he's had plenty of time to type a few mean things. He could say, "You're not better than me," because it's true, I'm not. He could say, "You should try and get to know me," because he'd be right, I haven't. His wheelchair makes me nervous. So do his shoes that always look new because he never walks on them. He could say a lot of things but he doesn't. When I walk in the room, he holds up his one hand that sort of works and says, "Huuh," which is his version of hi.

He does his version of a smile which isn't so much a smile as opening his mouth wider and leaving it open. When Rhonda tells everyone I'm back, one person claps and Eugene opens his mouth wider.

They all want to show me things they've been working on. I guess they made place mats while I was gone because mostly people show me place mats that all look the same except in different colors. I tell everyone I like the colors they chose since there isn't too much else to say.

Anthony says, "I'm giving mine to you! I made mine for Beminda."

Before everything that happened with Ron, I would have been embarrassed at Anthony making presents for me and giving them to me in front of everyone. I might have even said, "No, you can't *do* that, Anthony. You're not *allowed*." I don't do that, though. I say, "Thank you, Anthony. Are you sure your mom doesn't want it?"

"Yeah, I'm sure."

Behind him, Eugene is staring at us. His mouth is wide open. I think he's happy for us. I feel so relieved, I start crying a little.

Then Douglas comes over and says, "You can't have my place mat, so don't try to steal it." Then I don't feel like crying anymore, I feel like telling Douglas he might get a girlfriend someday if he watched Anthony and took some lessons on being nice to girls.

That afternoon, during social skills class, Rhonda asks if Anthony and I would like to tell the rest of the group about the play we're doing. Before we can say anything, Douglas says, "It's a kissy-kissy play."

"It is NOT!" I say, maybe a little too loud. "You have to stop being so immature, Douglas."

I'm pretty sure I don't lose stars for calling people immature, except Rhonda looks at me like she wants to make a new rule. I shut my mouth because I can't lose stars this week. This week Anthony and I are working to earn practice time in the OT room. If I lose a star, Anthony will be in there by himself, and he really needs me to help him practice.

"I'M SORRY, DOUGLAS," I say really loud even though I don't mean it. "If you don't like plays, you don't have to come see this one. In fact you probably shouldn't. None of you should come because you probably won't understand it."

Rhonda folds her arms over her chest. "Belinda, was that a nice thing to say?"

"They won't. You have to be mature to understand Jane Austen. No one here is."

"Belinda!"

"What?"

She looks at me like I've already lost some stars. "You have to learn to treat your friends better than this. Being in a play is exciting and it's something you'd like to share with other people, I'm guessing. It doesn't make much sense to put on plays that no one comes to, does it? That wouldn't be much fun, would it?"

I don't want to talk about it anymore. I don't want these people to come because I'm starting to get scared that doing this play is a big mistake. It's possible that Anthony won't be the only person who is bad in this play. Lucas and Emily are trying hard, but they're not very good either. The worst person, though, might be me.

I don't understand why this is happening. Sometimes I'm fine and sometimes I open my mouth to say a line and no sound comes out. I move my lips but nothing happens. Then I can't breathe and I get dizzy and I have to sit down. This week it's happened two times in rehearsals. The first time, Anthony thought I was dying and started to cry and hug me like he was doing a Heinz maneuver. Afterward I told him he didn't have to worry, I wasn't dying, I was panicking. "You should probably stay calm if it happens again," I said.

And then it happened again, the next day.

And he did stay calm. He held my hand and said, "Yoga breathe, Beminda. Yoga breathe."

I think my body is afraid Mitchell Breski will be in the audience watching me, even though I know that's impossible because he's not allowed out of the place where he lives now which is called juvenile detention. Still I remember standing in the light near the locker room and how I couldn't see him because he was in the dark. It was like being onstage. That was the first thing I thought when he called me sweetheart and stepped out of the dark. I thought, He's been standing there, watching me.

And I didn't understand why, but at first I liked it.

Except now I remember, he didn't call my name. He said, "Hey, you," like we knew each other but we didn't. He didn't know me.

I know what happened to me with Mitchell Breski isn't supposed to happen. It wasn't love or even like. It wasn't romance.

A couple of times Nan has said I could talk to the nice doctor I met at the hospital about what happened if I want to. Every time she says this, I say, "No, thank you." I'm scared if I talk about Mitchell Breski, it'll feel like it's happening all over again. Sometimes words can do that. They can make something happen again in your mind. That's why I didn't talk about anything for a long time after it happened. I was scared if I did, I'd say his name accidentally and then it would feel like he was there in the same room with me. That's what happened when I said his name to the police. It was like he was there with his hand over my mouth.

Afterward the policewoman who'd been asking me questions said, "Just keep the box of Kleenex if you need it for the ride home."

She was very nice and said she didn't think she'd ever forget talking to me. That surprised me because I assumed she spent every day talking to people who had terrible things happen to them. When I asked her why, she said, "You're so brave," she said and started to cry, too.

"You didn't get any help from those cretins who saw what was happening, but you stopped it anyway. You got help yourself. And now you've identified the perpetrator. You're a star, Belinda. You really are."

That made me feel good. I still cried on the way home which made Nan drive even worse than she usually does, but her calling me a star made it easier to breathe again.

I loved being a star every time I was one. Linda who ran Children's Story Theater said everyone was a star whether they had a big part or not, but that's not really true. Townsperson Number Three isn't a star. Neither is the clownfish in *Little Mermaid*. When I played Fern and Little Red Riding Hood I *was* a star. I felt like it and everyone said so afterward.

Driving home from the police station with Nan, I was still sad and scared, but I couldn't stop thinking about what that policewoman said. It made me feel better. Like what had just happened wasn't real. Like I was an actress in a scary movie and I'd done a good job playing my part. But now it's confusing. It's like now that I'm acting again, I keep being scared of the same thing happening. Like if I stand in the light, someone will step out of the dark and do something terrible.

Sometimes I have dreams about it that make me sweat so much I think maybe I wet the bed. Once I *did* wet the bed but I didn't tell Nan or Mom. I washed the sheets myself so it was like it hadn't happened. I'm allowed to pretend things never happened if I clean up myself and if it doesn't show anymore. Like Anthony doesn't need to know what happened with Mitchell Breski. If I don't want to tell him, I don't have to.

And I definitely don't want to tell him. If he knows, he will look at me different. I also think he will probably stop saying he loves me and wants to marry me all the time. I used to hate when he said that, but I don't hate it anymore. Now I understand he doesn't mean we should get married right *now*. He means he wants to be my friend and help each other on things like plays. I can help him be brave and be an actor and he can help me be brave and eat lunch in the cafeteria. It's good that we're a team now because he worries a lot.

One time he got so worried I thought he might cry and I hugged him even though he hadn't asked for it. He started to laugh and rock and asked me if I would be his girlfriend now.

I didn't say my usual answer, which is, "No, Anthony. I'm too old to be your girlfriend."

Instead, I said, "Maybe." Then I said, "I promise I won't be anyone *else's* girlfriend, but we're busy with this play right now. Let's get through this play and *then* maybe I'll be your girlfriend."

I could tell he thought this meant yes. He was laughing and blushing and covering his face with his hands.

"It's a big decision, Anthony. Being someone's girlfriend means your life changes a lot."

He stopped laughing and looked at me. "It does?"

I explained some of the things that have to happen if we're boyfriend and girlfriend. We'll have to share food and watch TV together and sometimes we'll have to watch shows we don't like. "For instance, you like wrestling and I don't," I said. "But if I was your girlfriend, I'd have to say, okay, I'll watch a little bit of wrestling."

"We have to kiss, too, Beminda."

I looked away because that was the part I was hoping maybe he didn't know about. Part of me doesn't mind the idea of kissing Anthony and part of me is very scared to do anything at all like that. I think if he knew what happened with Mitchell Breski, he would say no, thank you to being my boyfriend. He would think I was dirty for being on the ground like that with Coke on my skirt and popcorn in my hair.

He would hate me very much like I hate myself when I think about it.

I wish I could take a pill and not think about it. I told Anthony some people are couples but they never kiss at all. That's just how they are. They don't like kissing, so they don't.

He said, "Nuh-uh. You love someone, you kiss them."

This makes me even more nervous. It's like Anthony seems to know a few things already.

At our next rehearsal, I start to think maybe Emily and Lucas like each other. He looks at her a lot when she's giving us directions, then he writes down everything she says so he won't forget. Once Emily says, "You don't have to write this all down, Lucas. It's just something to think about."

I think he felt stupid, like I sometimes feel when someone says, "You don't have to try so hard, Belinda. Just relax."

I wanted to tell Emily, "It's hard to relax when a lot of things are happening at once. He should write down whatever he wants to write down." She doesn't know that she makes him nervous. One time she said, "This is like that scene in *Sense and Sensibility*," and he said, "What's *Sense and Sensibility*?" I started to say, "A movie starring Emma Thompson and Hugh Grant," but she said, "Jane Austen's second most famous book, Lucas? Does that not ring a bell?"

I don't think she meant to sound mean because she reached over and patted his shoulder, but I knew he was embarrassed. Thinking about Lucas and Emily helps me not think too much about Anthony and Mitchell Breski or the things that I am trying not to think about.

When the cable access people come to meet with Emily and Lucas about filming the show, Emily hugs Lucas afterward and thanks him with a smile. Hugging Lucas is hard because he's so big. She has to get up on her tiptoes to put her arms around his shoulders. Afterward he holds her hand for a little while. It looks like his hand has swallowed hers up. I think we aren't supposed to see them holding hands because when Anthony says, "What did they say?" really loud, they remember us and stop.

"They're going to film the whole thing with lights and sound equipment and they're going to air it three times the week afterward!" Emily smiles and looks at Lucas.

Even though I thought I wanted them to film our play, I'm not so sure anymore. I wanted Mom and Nan to be able to see it but now I keep thinking if it's on TV, that means Mitchell Breski or Ron or the rest of the football team can see it. Just thinking this makes me feel like I have to tell Emily and Lucas I'm sorry, I was wrong, I don't want to be on TV. I'll have to say, "I *thought* I wanted that but now I know I definitely don't."

They'll probably say I'm being too demanding. I can hear Nan saying, "No one wants to be your friend when you act so bossy, Belinda."

I want Lucas and Emily to be my friends. I want to be Anthony's girlfriend when this is over. I don't want them to think I'm a bossy person who changes her mind all the time.

I can do this, I tell myself, except I'm not sure if that's true.

There are a lot of things I can't control like panic attacks and crying and not being able to breathe. I can't control hearing Mitchell Breski's voice sometimes in my head.

I can't control seeing his face when I close my eyes at night.

EMILY

HERE'S A SURPRISE: BEING around each other more, every day after school for an hour and a half, seems to make Lucas and me more shy with each other. If we get to the theater before Belinda and Anthony, we laugh at the surprise of being alone and whisper like we're scared of getting caught any minute. I told him that I didn't want Belinda and Anthony to know there was anything going on between us. "It would be *terrible* if she found out," I said. This isn't the general in-school self-consciousness we feel around each other. *Your friends aren't like my friends* is entirely different than *We met while you were being attacked and now we're going out.* "We have to be completely focused on the play. This is about Belinda first and foremost. That's it. Period."

Lucas understands this. He never pushes it or flirts the way Chad did in class. He never refers to things we've done or said outside of rehearsal when we're in rehearsal. Not that we've done a lot beyond message each other and talk on the phone at night. I have to admit, I like the way circumstances have forced us to get to know each other slowly. At rehearsals I watch him out of the corner of my eye and I notice a million little things: He's not on his phone so much these days, thumbing through texts. He reads more and even keeps a book tucked in the back pocket of his jeans. When Belinda asked him what it was, he held it up so all of us could see the title: *All Quiet on the Western Front.* "My mom always wanted me to read this," he said.

"Why?" I asked softly. Rehearsal hadn't started. Belinda and Anthony were talking to each other.

He smiled, though his face looked sad. "So I wouldn't join the army, I think."

I couldn't say any more. It was too private a conversation, considering the fight he'd told me about with his dad, but I noticed all of it. I noticed that he was reading to figure out options for himself. I noticed that he mentioned his mother more often. Once during rehearsal, he brought her name up, and Belinda asked if she was coming to the show.

"No," he said. "She died a few years ago."

Hearing this again, I understood why he hardly ever brings it up. Nothing stops a conversation quite like this information. What can anyone say when every option— *I'm so sorry! That's so sad for you!*—feels wrong? Or at least it seems so to most people. But not Belinda and Anthony, who both perked up with lots of questions. They started with how she died and then they kept going.

"Did she lose all her hair and wear a wig?" Belinda asked.

"Yeah," Lucas said. "I think everyone who has chemotherapy loses their hair."

Belinda nodded. Anthony's turn: "Were her eyes open when she died?"

"No," Lucas said. "She was asleep so they were closed."

"Did she make a sound when it happened? Or say anything?"

Even though it was the middle of our rehearsal time, I let them keep going because Lucas didn't seem to mind and I was curious, too. He even smiled as he answered. "No, no sounds. She was at home so that was good."

Belinda asked, "Was she alone when she died?" and Lucas said no. "My dad and I took turns sleeping on the floor next to her bed so she wouldn't be."

I imagined huge Lucas, on the floor beside his mother, his hand raised to hold hers. It's so completely the opposite of my first impression of him: seated outside the guidance counselor's office, arms folded across his chest, legs stuck out in front of him. I wondered how long it would have taken me to hear these stories if Belinda and Anthony hadn't asked their questions. Maybe I never would have. Maybe I'd never have the picture in my mind of Lucas on the floor holding his dying mother's hand.

Those are the moments when I appreciate Belinda.

As we get closer, though, there are fewer of those. Belinda's anxiety escalates until we are spending a good part of every rehearsal reassuring her that nothing horrible will happen while we're putting on the show.

"This will be a very friendly audience," I tell her. "You'll see. They'll probably give us a standing ovation."

"They can't whistle," she says. She's biting her fingernails now, a habit I don't remember seeing before. "Whistling hurts my ears. You have to say no whistling."

"Fine, Belinda. We'll tell them no whistling, but you shouldn't worry about that."

She nods, but she's worried, I can tell. Her eyebrows are furrowed and her gaze is clouded like she's waiting to get on some terrifying roller coaster other people are forcing her to ride. I don't know what to do about this or if I should even acknowledge it.

In our second-to-last rehearsal—our "wet tech," as we call it, because Belinda loves her theater lingo—she seems a little better. She is focused and in character and helps

Anthony when he skips a whole scene and starts saying lines that are ten pages ahead in the story. "Not yet, good sir," Belinda says, staying in character. "We must talk about the ball first."

In editing the play, I've boiled the story down to eight scenes. Gone are all the fun, contemporary high school parts. That would be way too confusing for this crowd. Instead, it's two couples wearing old-fashioned clothes who meet in every other scene and spend the in-between scenes discussing their misconceptions about each other.

As I've edited it, some of the scenes make almost no sense. We don't know why he's asked her to marry him and we don't have the Wickham backstory to explain why she turns him down so angrily. With this crowd, my guess is it won't matter. I know this audience and their attention span. They don't need plot details that they won't be able to follow anyway. They'll enjoy the drama of the fight without understanding the reasons behind it.

Then I'm surprised: driving to our last Boundaries and Relationships class before we put on the show next week, Lucas tells me he's asked Mary if he can talk to the group about the story ahead of time. "Just to prep them a little about the story. Fill in some of the holes."

"What holes?" I snap. I've gotten too sensitive lately. Today at rehearsal he suggested making a change in the blocking and I couldn't help feeling annoyed. "Why don't we just have one director here, okay, Lucas?"

"Fine," he said, holding up his hands in surrender. "You're in charge."

Afterward I apologized. I told him I was feeling nervous and I didn't want to confuse Belinda and Anthony with last-minute changes. "They're finally getting better, but we're not out of the woods yet. There's still the possibility this will be a disaster of fairly epic proportions."

"Exactly," he said. Now he tells me, "That's why I asked Mary if we could talk to group about what to expect."

It seems like a risky idea to me. A boring plot summary may turn them off completely. When I tell him this, he says, "Yeah, I may do it a little differently if that's okay."

I look over at him and wonder what he has in mind.

"It won't be anything long. Just five minutes, I promise."

"Okay, fine," I say. "Go ahead."

Thirty seconds into Lucas's summary in front of the group, it feels like a big mistake. He starts by saying he wants to talk about the "show" we're putting on next week, which confuses everyone. They think it's going to be a TV show starring actors they've heard of. Sheila is hoping Justin Bieber will be in it.

"No, Sheila, sorry," Lucas says. "We couldn't get the J-Man for this."

"But did you even *ask*?" she says.

"It's not that kind of show, guys," Lucas says, holding up one hand to stop the interruptions. "It's a *play*, okay? We're the actors—Emily and I—along with two of our friends from school. They're not famous either, so don't get your hopes up."

He flashes me a smile and I smile back. It's nice that he's called them friends and hasn't mentioned their disabilities. There's also this: the room is silent now, listening to Lucas.

"It's an old-fashioned story by this woman named Jane Austen who wrote some books a long time ago about all the rules around people trying to start relationships. Back then the rules were different. They were mostly about how rich your parents were, but there's one thing that's still the same. Everyone judges each other based on the way they look. They meet each other at a party and they all think certain things, like he's really stuck up, or she's kind of silly. They don't take time to ask a few questions and get to know each other."

It's hard to tell how many people understand what he's saying.

"Has anyone here ever done that? Where you thought a person was one way and then you got to know them and they were completely different?"

I'm surprised. Three people raise their hands. "Oh, I have! I have!" Annabel says. "I hated Subway chicken salad and then I tried it and it wasn't so bad except for the chicken tasted funny and it had apples in it."

"That's sort of what this story is about that, Annabel. Only it's not about chicken salad, it's about people taking a little time and getting to know each other before they make judgments. Can anyone think of any other examples?"

Sheila raises her hand. I can tell Lucas is hesitating. With Sheila, there's a pretty good chance she'll respond to a question like this by complaining about her bus driver today or announcing that she's bought new shoes. Unfortunately, hers is the only hand still raised. "Yes, Sheila?" he says.

"I didn't like you when you first came to class."

He laughs at the surprise of this. "Perfect example! Why not?"

"I thought you were too big to be a normal person and you might beat me up."

He smiles. "And now?"

"I think you're nice and you probably won't beat anyone up."

He walks over to Sheila and shakes her hand, and does a funny, courtly bow. "That was perfectly on topic."

He's right, I think. It was. Of course, the nice moment doesn't last too long. When he asks if there are any other questions, there are.

"Will refreshments be served?"

"Can we talk while the play is going on?"

"Will people have to pay attention or can they leave if they don't like it?"

I'm surprised at how well Lucas fields these without any help from Mary. "No, Ken, it's a play, which means people will be right here, acting it out. We've worked hard on it and practiced a lot, so do you think it would be nice to walk out if you're bored?"

Ken looks stumped for a minute, then shakes his head. "No!" he says.

"That's right. That wouldn't be a nice thing to do."

Afterward in the car, I gush a little. "That was so well done, Lucas. Seriously. Whatever happens next week, I think we'll be okay. They'll be polite and patient. They'll understand the main point we're trying to make. And afterward we'll dance and eat snacks and it won't matter if the show is terrible or not. I'm so glad you did that."

He looks over at me. "Listen to you."

"What?"

"The dumb ox had a decent idea."

I'm flabbergasted he'd say this. "I *don't* think of you as a dumb ox, Lucas. My God . . ."

"Right, okay."

I look at him. "I *don't*."

"Okay." He's smiling, which I hope means he believes me, but I'm not sure. These car rides have become our only time to be together without other people hovering on the periphery, and even here, we're shy with each other, as if there are issues we're afraid to talk about. Is he *really* worried that I think he's dumb? I like him so much I don't understand. I don't know what I could say that would reassure him, except something that would make me sound dumb myself: *I really like you. I really really do.*

BELINDA

Right in the middle of getting my costume made, we get a surprise. The doctor calls and says Nan is well enough to come home from the hospital.

In the car ride over, Mom says she's nervous that Nan'll be mad about her cleaning the house and throwing things

321

away. I tell her I'm nervous Nan'll still be mad about the play.

We're both surprised, though. It turns out the only thing Nan criticizes after she's been home for an hour is the bonnet Mom is making for my costume. "You don't have any decorative elements. There's no fringe and there's nothing to that bow."

"You're probably right, Nan." Mom smiles. It's nice to hear Nan sound like her old self especially since she looks so different now. She's very thin and hunched over and it looks like her skin got too big. Even her hands look different. In the car ride home she told us she wished she'd died when she had the heart attack. Now she has to change everything she eats. No salt anymore. Nothing from cans. "I just don't know if I see any point," she said. It sounded like how I felt after the football game. I was never hungry and I thought there was no point in eating because nothing tasted good.

Now Mom says, "Would you mind helping me with it, Nan? You've always been a better seamstress than I am."

Later, while they're both working, I tell them Emily has no bonnet at all, and Mom says, "Well, Nan'll have to make that one, I don't have time. I've got the rest of your skirt to finish."

Mom stays up almost all night to finish my dress and the two bonnets in time for the dress rehearsal. The next morning she drives me to school with Nan in the car. Each of us carries a different thing into my classroom. I carry the dress. Mom carries one bonnet, Nan carries the other.

Nan walks so slowly that it's hard to stay with her. Finally we tell her to sit on a bench and we'll take the bonnet the rest of the way. I can tell she doesn't want to do that, though. She wants people to see her bonnets and say they look great.

That's when Emily walks up and says, "Oh my gosh, it's your costume!"

I haven't told her about the bonnet we made for her because that's my big surprise. Now I say, "This one's for you," and I point to the one Nan is holding.

I want her to be extra happy, so I'm giving her the one with more frills.

"Oh, that's so nice!" she says and even though Nan doesn't like hugs that much, she gives her a big one. "It's beautiful! I love it!" She puts it on for a second which makes her look silly because the rest of her clothes are a T-shirt and jeans. "Thank you both so much for doing this and for letting Belinda be in the play. She's amazing. Wait until you see her."

I'm happy she says this looking at Nan and Mom. It makes me think maybe everything will be all right. Nan will see that doing the play was a good idea and she'll forgive Mom for saying yes I could do it. I don't know for sure that this will happen but it seems like it might.

After school, at our last rehearsal, Anthony and I both wear our costumes which are so much better than Emily and Lucas's costumes, it's like we're acting in different plays, one with good costumes, one with bad costumes.

"You guys look so good," Emily says. She's wearing a

long skirt that she tied around her waist like an apron. She looks like a pioneer, not like a lady. The bonnet helps a little but not that much.

"You should have a real dress," I say to Emily. And then I tell Lucas, "And you shouldn't wear that outfit at all." He has on tan pants and a blue suit jacket. He looks like a big teenager going to church, not like a man in the 1700s.

Then I remember something else I have to do and I get nervous again. This whole week, I've had a hard time sleeping. Last night I couldn't sleep at all so finally I got up and typed a letter:

Dear Mr. Firth,

I hope that you are well and that your wife and children are well, too. I wanted to write and tell you that I have some news. I'm going to play Elizabeth Bennett in a short play version of Pride and Prejudice. I am very excited but I'm also very nervous. I have not acted in eight years. I used to be a very good actress. Some things have happened to me that I still don't want to tell you about. I don't know if bad things happening to a person can change them forever. I'm very nervous and I used to never get nervous at all. Sometimes other kids would get terrible stage fright and I'd have to go on for them or do their job. Now I'm worried that might happen to me. Do you ever feel this way? Like you might throw up or maybe have a heart attack? I asked my mom and she said twenty-one-year-old people usually don't get heart attacks, so I think maybe I have stage fright.

I am worried that I may ruin the whole show because

of a panic attack. My mom has panic attacks and they are
terrible to watch. If you have time, you can either write me a
letter or just think about me. That might help.

    Your friend,
    Belinda

Writing to Mr. Firth helped a little but I still couldn't sleep after I go back to bed. Every time I closed my eyes, I kept thinking about Ron and Mitchell Breski.

I've decided maybe Nan is wrong. There are some things you try to forget and you can't. Since that one time in the cafeteria, I keep thinking about everything terrible that happened at the football game, and how I have never talked to Emily and Lucas about it. I don't know if they remember it the way I do, but I don't think I can do the play until I ask them a few questions. I'd like to ask them: What happened? Why didn't you help me? He was hurting me and I was crying and you both ran away. That is not okay.

I hope if I talk about it, I will stop thinking about it so much. I don't know if it will work, but I'm going to try.

This morning I told Mom what I'm going to do. She said I was brave and she thought my instincts were probably better than hers. This made me feel good except I don't know what instincts are.

When I asked her she said, "Your common-sense feelings about people."

"Yes," I said. "Except for Ron. I was wrong about him. He didn't deserve to get any presents from me."

"That's true," Mom said.

And even though it's sad to think about this, I wasn't sad for too long because I've got a new idea. Something I can do with my box of presents. It's a good idea but I'm not going to say anything about it because I want it to be a surprise.

For now, we still haven't started rehearsal and I know I have to say something, but I also know I don't want to say it in front of Anthony. While Emily and Lucas are talking, I ask if Anthony would mind leaving the room for a few minutes.

"Where should I go?" he says.

"I don't know," I whisper. "I need to talk to Emily and Lucas about something private that doesn't involve you, so it doesn't matter where you go. You just shouldn't be here."

"I don't understand. Why do you have something private that doesn't involve me?"

"It just *is*," I say. "Trust me."

"Is it a secret?"

"Sort of. Yes, it's a secret." Anthony looks like he might cry. I should have remembered he hates secrets. "It's not a *secret* secret. It's an unpleasant topic. I don't like talking about it so I don't want to do it in front of you." I'm trying to whisper but my whisper voice isn't very good. I'm pretty sure Emily and Lucas can hear what we're saying.

Anthony looks up at me like all of the sudden he's thought of something. "Is it about what happened to you at the football game?"

I feel like an invisible hand just punched me in the

stomach. *"No,"* I say.

Anthony isn't supposed to know anything about this. But he keeps going: "With that boy under the bleachers?"

For a long time I don't know what to say. I have no idea how Anthony knows about this or who could have told him. I think it must be Douglas and I want to kill Douglas or whoever else it was. I want to say, *No, it is not about that because that never happened. Whoever told you that is a terrible liar and shouldn't be your friend.*

But I can't say it because it isn't true.

Anthony knows what happened with Mitchell Breski. I thought it was my secret but it's not. I thought only Lucas and Emily knew and they hadn't said anything because they were being polite. Now I don't know what to think.

I wonder if everyone knows.

I can't help it, I start crying.

"Don't cry, Belinda," Anthony says. He scoots his chair closer and puts his arm around me. "It wasn't your fault."

"Yes it *was.* It was my fault because I thought I was like everyone else and could go to a football game but I'm not and I can't. That's why I can't do this play either. Because bad things happen when I think I'm like everyone else."

I can't look up, but I hear Emily and Lucas scrape their chairs closer. "No," Emily says. "Bad things happen when people don't help each other. That's what really happened, Belinda. Lucas and I were there and we didn't help you."

Lucas has both hands over his face. He's shaking his head.

Emily keeps going: "Ms. Sadiq told us we could do this play with you but we weren't supposed to bring it up. She said your grandmother didn't want anyone talking to you about it."

"That's because she doesn't like talking about sad things. Sometimes my mom gets too sad, so we make rules about it."

"Do you want to talk about it now?"

Now I'm confused. I don't know what I want to talk about.

Lucas takes his hands down from his face and stops shaking his head. "It's okay, Belinda. You brought it up so I think we *should* talk about it." His voice is low but it isn't scary. Sometimes low voices scare me, but his doesn't. "Emily and I have wanted to tell you how sorry we are. That's why we suggested doing this play. We wanted to do something you would like, so people could get to know you. So *we* could get to know you."

Now I'm really confused. "You don't like *Pride and Prejudice*?"

"Yes, of course we do, but maybe we wouldn't have chosen it as a play. We wanted to do something you'd like."

Anthony is rocking back and forth in his chair. I can tell Anthony wants to have this conversation be over. "They did it for you, Beminda! That's nice!"

It is nice but I still don't understand. "Why didn't you help me back then? That would have been easier than putting on a play."

They're both quiet. Emily answers first. "Sometimes

people get scared of things like speaking up, Belinda. I'm not sure why. I wish I could explain it better and I can't."

I don't understand what she's saying.

Lucas says, "We were both having bad days and we were both thinking about ourselves. Sometimes that happens. I don't think either one of us realized what was really going on."

I understand this better. I've had bad days, too. "Okay," I say.

I don't know if this will help me sleep better or not, but I'm glad we talked about it. "Maybe we should just rehearse now," I say.

Anthony claps and hugs me and even though I didn't want him to know any of this, now that I know he does, I'm happy it's over and I don't have to worry about him finding out.

CHAPTER EIGHTEEN
EMILY

THOUGH I'VE BEEN SITTING across from him talking for about ten minutes, it's not clear how much Mr. Johnson, our principal, is hearing.

"We're asking for a policy change to ensure that all students with disabilities are allowed to participate in any after-school activities they want to."

He shuffles through some papers on his desk that have nothing to do with what I'm saying because I haven't given him anything to read.

"The law states that students with disabilities must have equal access to the same education as their peers. After-school activities are part of that education. If they need help doing it, Richard and I and the Youth Action Coalition are willing to organize a peer helper program."

I'm grateful to have Richard sitting next to me. Last night I showed him my research and told him what I wanted to say. He helped me shape my argument and offered to do the talking, but I told him I knew the points I wanted to make and the examples I wanted to use. It's the first time I've ever taken the lead and done the talking. Since Mr. Johnson still hasn't said anything, I keep going: "We believe that if Belinda Montgomery had been allowed to participate in theater throughout her high school career, she wouldn't have been as vulnerable as she was at the football game."

Saying her name gets Mr. Johnson to stop shuffling his papers and look up.

"I think she would have developed more skills interacting with the wider school population, which would have made her safer. She would have known not to follow the team under the bleachers; she wouldn't have tried to talk to them in the middle of a game."

This is a speculative argument, Richard pointed out last night, but it's also a pretty reasonable one. I can see Mr. Johnson is listening now.

"These aren't students who need *protection* from the real world, they need *experience* in it. Clubs and activities will offer them a chance to get that experience. When Belinda went to that football game, it was the first nighttime school activity she'd ever been to. She was overwhelmed and unsafe because she had no practice being in a situation like that and protecting herself. She needs that exposure. They all do. Let's give them the chance."

I look over at Richard and can tell by his expression that I'm doing okay. Maybe even better than okay.

Finally Mr. Johnson says, "I have to admit I haven't

thought about the issue quite this way. You know we all love Belinda and the other kids in her classroom. We want to do the right thing for them but we also have a responsibility to protect them. The more you put them out in the general school population, the more chance there is that they'll get bullied or hurt. That's what I have to consider. Do you want me to be taking that kind of risk?"

"If you're worried about their safety and you don't think peer helpers can ensure that, you could always hire more staff to stay after school." Richard has a way of saying things nicely, even when it's clear what he really means: *Just do it, buddy. Part with the money and pay staff to stay.*

"I'd like to, of course." Now Mr. Johnson seems nervous. He starts the paper-shuffling again. "The problem is, I hear a lot of good ideas. I have people from every after-school activity coming to me every week, telling me what I should pay for with a very small allocation of funds I have. I have to say no to a lot of people with a lot of good ideas."

"The thing is, sir—" I lean forward as I speak to make my point perfectly clear. "This isn't just a good idea. It's actually the law."

By lunchtime, four periods later, I'm still soaring from our success. Mr. Johnson agreed with the bulk of our request and we've already scheduled another meeting to make sure there's follow-through: a policy change written into the handbook, communication with teachers so everyone knows. "We'd like to make sure this is an enforceable change," Richard said at the end. I loved that he said "we."

That because he's my friend, this has become his issue, too.

When I get to our lunch table, Richard is already there, telling everyone the story about our meeting with Mr. Johnson, which is nice to hear, but it makes me think there's something else I haven't done. I keep thinking about the way Belinda finally brought up the football game at our last rehearsal. She might have thought she didn't want Anthony to know about what happened, but the relief on her face when she realized he did made it clear: love isn't about looking perfect to the other person. It's about being able to show your imperfections. Belinda was brave in a way that prompted me to set up this meeting with Mr. Johnson, but it also reminded me: I've never been honest with my friends about my failure at the football game. I've also never told them about Lucas.

I've told myself it's because I like Lucas so much I don't want to jinx it. We're not an obvious couple to anyone who knows me well. I'm worried they'll make jokes and I won't be able to laugh. I'll stammer my explanations, which will involve telling them who I really I am and what really happened at the game.

Belinda didn't want to do it and I don't either.

And then I watched her afterward and the way Anthony hugged her around the neck and kissed the top of her head and patted her shoulders. They didn't look like two children playing at being "in love." They looked like two people who'd taken a big step toward knowing each other better. That's what I want from my friends, but who knows if I'll get it. I imagine all the things they might say if I tell them Lucas and I might start dating soon: Candace rolling her eyes and asking, "Does his girlfriend know?" Barry and Weilin screwing up their faces in worry: "Is this a phase like your flag-team days?" Richard shaking his head: "I just don't see it, Em. I'm sorry but I don't."

I wish I could explain it to them in a way that doesn't sound defensive. Instead I sit down at our lunch table and start the conversation with this: "I want you all to come see this show we're doing tomorrow night. It will be the strangest, least coherent rendition of *Pride and Prejudice* you've ever seen and I still want you to come."

Everyone stares at me.

"Do you mean tomorrow like the same night *Walking Dead* is on?" Candace says. She's serious. She never misses an episode. She's even written papers in AP English analyzing the complexity of the zombie apocalypse, which she always gets As on.

"Yes, Candace. It directly conflicts but I still want you to come. It'll be worth it. Actually, I can't absolutely guarantee it'll be worth it, but I think it will."

Weilin sets down her fork. "But you're doing it at the center for disabled people, right?" I nod. "So why would you want us there?"

I know what she's trying not to say: *Won't it be a little embarrassing?*

The answer is, yes, it might be. The other answer is, "I want people at our school to see Belinda the way Lucas and I have started to see her. She's different, but she's also brave in ways that I wish I was. That I wish all of us were.

Including Hugh." I add this at the end because Richard hasn't said anything so far.

Now he looks up. *"Lucas and I?"* Richard says. "That's kind of interesting."

"He's a nice person, Richard. I'm sorry about the mean things I said before about him. He didn't deserve it. I wasn't—" I hesitate because now I've got everyone's attention. "I wasn't completely honest about what happened at that football game. Lucas and I were equally to blame for not helping Belinda."

Though I'm not looking at anyone and can't see their response, it feels good to say this. Almost instantly, I feel my chest lighten up.

And then Candace slaps her hand on the table. *"Hello?* Except that he weighs a hundred pounds more than you and should have taken that guy *out."*

Weilin leans toward me. "Candace is right, Em. You shouldn't take blame for something just because he turned out to be an okay guy."

I shake my head and close my eyes. "That's not what happened. I was there first. I should have called someone right away and I didn't. I panicked and I froze. I can't explain it any better. Lucas came out after I ran away. He assumed I was running to get help."

I open my eyes. Everyone is staring at me.

"That's kind of a different story than you told us," Richard says.

"I know. That's why I'm telling you the truth now. You guys are my best friends and I lied about what happened because I couldn't admit it to you. I failed. I freaked out."

For a long time, no one says anything.

Finally Weilin says, "I wish I could come, Emily. If you'd told us earlier, maybe we could have arranged it, but Barry and I have a rehearsal tomorrow night."

"That's right," Barry says.

I turn to Candace. "All right, I'm not just saying this because it's *Walking Dead* tomorrow night—I seriously can't. I have a lab due that I'm way behind on."

I steel myself and turn to Richard—my oldest, truest friend. The only boy I've ever said I love you to. He'll look at me and understand what I'm saying, I think. He'll see how important this is to me.

But he doesn't. "You should have told us earlier, Em. I have plans with Hugh."

I gather all my courage and plead, "You could bring him along."

Why do I care so much? Why do I feel like I'm going to cry if my friends won't do this for me?

"Yeah, I don't think so," Richard says. "We're having a hard enough time communicating these days. I don't want to ask him for a favor on top of it."

I know I shouldn't feel as hurt as I do. I shouldn't have made this a test, because we're already too stressed about tests in every other area of our lives.

Still, I can't help feeling, if this *had* been a test, they all failed.

BELINDA

IT'S FUNNY, EVER SINCE my talk about what happened at the football game, I'm not so nervous about the play anymore. I'm more nervous about what will happen afterward. I told Anthony I'll be his girlfriend after the play is over, which means tonight I'll have to start being his girlfriend. I don't know exactly how we do this, but I'm pretty sure he'll say we have to kiss.

One thing I'm glad about: Mitchell Breski never kissed me. Or he kissed my neck which doesn't count, so I don't have to remember that when I kiss Anthony. Also, Anthony won't smell bad and not know my name.

It won't be the same but I'm still nervous because I don't know how to kiss.

I've seen people do it in *Pride and Prejudice* and other movies, but watching it isn't the same thing as doing it. There might be rules everyone knows but I don't. Like what do you do with your hands when you kiss? And do you keep breathing or do you hold your breath the whole time? I think you hold your breath, but I'm not sure.

I can't ask Anthony because I don't want him to know I'm nervous about all this. I want him to think I'll still be a good girlfriend for him even though I don't know. If I can do this, I don't think I'll worry about Mitchell Breski and Ron and those other boys so much because I'll have other things to keep me busy like being Anthony's girlfriend which will take up a lot of time.

In the afternoon before the show, while I'm at home putting on my costume, I start to get more nervous. Mom comes into my room and reminds me that they aren't going to come see the play because Nan gets out of breath if she takes more than ten steps. Mom is going to drive me there and pick me up afterward. She isn't going to stay because she's worried about leaving Nan home alone for that much time. They will watch it on cable, she says, which means it has to be on TV. I don't have a choice, even if it scares me.

The whole car ride there I don't say anything. I'm glad for my bonnet because my face is sweating and I don't want Mom to see. I don't know if I'm more nervous about the play or about kissing Anthony. I think it's both.

"Are you going to be okay?" Mom says when we get there.

The Lifelong Learning Center looks big and brightly lit inside. There are glass doors with a sign that spells out WELCOME so big even I can read it from the parking lot.

We are here an hour early but I can see through the glass windows that there are people in the lobby. Some of them look dressed up like maybe they're going to be in another play I haven't heard about. Then I remember the ballroom dance class.

When Emily told us about the ballroom dance class coming to our show, the first thing I thought was, *I wonder if I can take that class.* Ballroom dance school used to be called cotillion which I know because that's where Nan met my grandfather. He didn't like dance classes, but he liked her so he kept going. The rule was the boys had to bow every time they asked a girl to dance. "I loved it!" Nan said when she told me about it. "After a while I was the only girl he asked and he bowed every single time!"

Mom always says she's sorry I didn't know her dad because he was a nice man. I would have loved him and he would have loved me. Nan says they waltz danced once a year on their anniversary every year they were married. She says she never looked for another man after he died because there was only one man for her and she'd already married him. That was that.

I think if I ever waltz dance with someone I will feel that way. That will be that.

The problem is I'm scared to go inside now because I am wearing my costume which makes me look like Elizabeth Bennett, but also makes me look silly if I am standing in a lobby full of people who don't know I'm wearing a costume. Suddenly I get so nervous I want to hide like I felt when I had Coke on my skirt and popcorn in my hair. It's the same feeling.

Like I can't breathe and there's a voice in my head screaming very loud.

"I can't go in," I say. My body starts rocking to calm itself down but it doesn't calm down. My bonnet is too tight. I can't breathe and I feel like I'm choking. Mom is talking but I only hear a little. "Don't do this now . . . You promised these people . . . You have to go in . . ."

I rock so hard the car starts to move. "BE QUIET!" I scream.

I don't know how to calm myself down. I hum and keep rocking until I hear a knock on the window. It's Anthony, wearing his costume, only he's wearing a new hat that makes me stop rocking. It's tall like the hat that Abe Lincoln wears. I don't remember seeing any hat like that on Colin Firth. It's also too small so he has to hold it on his head with one hand. I start to breathe again. I roll down the window. "What's that hat?" I say.

"It's okay! I look good!"

"Not if you have to hold on to your hat the whole time."

"It's okay!" He doesn't take his hand off. "I'll hold it, that's all. It's good!"

This hat thing has made me forget my panic. "You can't hold a hat on your head for the whole show, Anthony. That's not a good idea."

"Yes I can, Beminda. You can't all the time boss me around." He's smiling like he thinks it's funny to not listen to what I'm saying.

I open the car door. "I'm not bossing you around, I'm worried. Let me see your hat!"

EMILY

WITH EVERY DISASTER SCENARIO I've imagined for this play, I never pictured this one: Lucas, who once mentioned a slight history with fear of public speaking, is sitting across from me experiencing what I can only describe as an all-out flop sweat. His face is red as a tomato, puffy and wet.

"I'm *sorry* about this," he says, sitting in a back room fanning himself with a copy of our script. "I have no control over it."

"Is your shirt too tight?" I try.

"No, I'm just hyperventilating or something. This used to happen before games sometimes and I'd duck in the shower."

"Lucas, there's no shower here."

"Right, I know. That's what sucks."

It's sweet and endearing and also fairly worrying. He looks like he needs medical attention. I leave him in the back office because I have no choice—the cable access people are setting up in the classroom, with lights that make me worry Lucas won't last five minutes. Mary has set up forty or so chairs for the audience along with a potluck buffet of food in the back for the party afterward.

"Don't worry," Mary says when she sees my face. "This will be fine. I'll admit I didn't expect the TV cameras to be quite so imposing, but I'm sure it'll go fine."

Standing in front of one of their lights, I feel my own flop sweat start. I can't let Belinda or Anthony see these cameras and lights before the show starts. If they do, they'll fall apart more than Lucas has.

Then I see something that *really* surprises me: Chad is here. He sees me and smiles and walks over. "So you're putting on a play, Mary says. Like with costumes and actors. Pretty intense." He laughs like this should be the start of a joke.

I wish he wasn't here. I wish I didn't have to worry about looking more stupid than we already will. I don't want to even care what he thinks. "Yes," I say. "I should go, though. We're getting ready back there."

BELINDA

BEFORE I KNOW IT, I've followed Anthony inside, right past the lobby full of people who are all here to see our play and afterward ballroom dance. Anthony is still holding the hat on his head when he shows me our dressing room which isn't really a dressing room because it doesn't have mirrors. It looks more like someone's office.

I say, "How about this, Anthony? I'll let you wear that hat for the whole play if you'll take it off afterward and waltz dance with me."

He turns around and smiles at me for a long time, like maybe he's thinking about this kissing thing, too. "Okay," he says. "I'll waltz dance with you. What's waltz dance?"

That's when I look over and see a surprise. Lucas is sitting in the corner of our dressing room. He looks sweaty and not very good. He looks like maybe he's having a heart attack.

"Are you having a heart attack?" I say.

He shakes his head. "I have a little problem when I

get nervous. I sweat a little."

"But you're sweating a *lot*," I say because he is. His neck is sweaty and his shirt, too.

"I'll be okay, I think. Emily's getting me some water."

I don't want Lucas to have a heart attack. I hate heart attacks. "Why don't you do some yoga breathing. I can show you how. Maybe we should all do it but we have to stand up."

Anthony stands up but not Lucas.

"You have to stand up, Lucas. We're going to yoga calm ourselves so you can stop sweating."

"Oh. Okay." He stands up. Even his pants look wet, but not like pee. More like his knees are sweating.

"Let's start with tree of life, but you don't have to stand on one foot. That's too hard in our costumes. You can just close your eyes and bring your hands together."

I used to do a yoga tape every day at school so I didn't have to go to any PE classes. I remember all the moves so well I can do them with my eyes closed. "Feel your breath," I say. "In through your nose, out through your mouth."

I peek my eyes open and I'm surprised. He's doing what I'm saying. So is Anthony.

We keep going for a little bit and then I say, "Okay, that's enough."

Lucas looks a little better, I think, but it's hard to tell.

I look at Anthony's costume that his mother put together. It's a purple velour jacket with shiny gold piping around the edges. I don't remember seeing a jacket like that in any of the movies, but I still love it. I especially love his shoes which are green and left over from a Halloween costume when he was Peter Pan.

I take a deep breath. "You look good, Anthony," I say. I don't want to mention how Lucas looks because it's still not very good.

"I know, thank you," Anthony says. "You look beautiful, too, Beminda!" The way he says it, it sounds like *bootiful*.

EMILY

I F LUCAS FREAKING OUT is my first surprise of the night and Chad is the second, here is my third: I walk into the lobby to get Lucas some water and there's Richard in the corner, standing by himself.

"Hugh dropped me off, so I need a ride home," he says. "Is that okay?"

I'm so happy to see him I put my water down and give him a hug. "Of course," I say. "Thank you for coming. Hugh couldn't stay?" I step away and look at him.

"Too much homework, but he was happy to drive me here. That way he can be nice and a dick at the same time. That's sort of his specialty. He's an almost-great boyfriend."

He's smiling enough for me to see—it's not terrible. He's almost great. I want to say, maybe for now this is okay. My almost boyfriend looks like he's gone swimming in his clothes so neither one of us is exactly living the dream. But we're living something and it's more than either one of us expected this year.

"Why don't you come back to the dressing room? Maybe you can help calm everyone down. We're having a little issue with stage fright." I roll my eyes a little. "And they haven't even seen the TV cameras yet."

"Excuse me, Emily?" I turn around to see Belinda, in her costume—homemade but resplendent, with yards of puffy material in a lavender color that flatters her beautifully.

"You look great, Belinda!" I say.

Her lips are pinched. "We have a problem," she says. "Not with me, but with Lucas. Anthony and I don't think he should do his part plus narrate."

I'd forgotten this last-minute addition I made, based on the wonderful job he did last week talking to the class about the story. I suggested having Lucas narrate some of the plot holes I had to leave out in editing. We hadn't gotten too specific or written any lines because I thought he'd be fine ad-libbing it.

"We can skip the narration, Belinda. That'll be okay," I say, wondering if Lucas is all right in my absence. "This is my friend Richard, Belinda. Maybe he can help us out."

"Hi, Belinda. It's nice to meet you. I'd be happy to narrate a little. I think I've watched *Pride and Prejudice* enough times . . ."

Belinda's eyes widen. "How many?"

"I don't know. Maybe five."

She nods. "I've watched it a lot more than that."

"Would *you* like to narrate, Belinda?" I suggest. Maybe having more responsibility is the secret for calming her nerves.

She thinks about this for a minute. "No, thank you. I need to concentrate on my part. Why don't we let Richard do it."

Richard shoots me a look that's almost a laugh but not quite. Hopefully this won't be a disaster. He'll see— up close—why I wanted him here, why this feels different than the other work we've done.

Thankfully there isn't time to get any more nervous than we are. Back in the dressing room, Richard ties an ascot scarf around his neck and borrows Anthony's hat to open the show. I explain the most important part with the audience. "Make it short and simple. Don't include too many details."

Richard looks through the scripts quickly and points out a few of the gaping holes I'm missing in the plot. "Never mind that," I say. "Just fill in the story and emphasize the main emotions coming up. That's what they'll be watching for."

On this score, he's perfect. We miraculously get through our first scene by starting quickly before Belinda and the others have had a chance to see how big the camera lights are. After that, Richard steps onstage, welcomes everyone, and explains, "What you are watching is a love story, though it might take a while for you to figure that out, because this is what happens with the best love stories sometimes. No one realizes they're happening in the beginning." He smiles at me and then cues the audience for what's coming up. "It's going to be a party scene, but watch for this, everyone. He sees her and thinks he might like her, but he can't bring himself to be nice to her."

For this scene, Lucas pulls it together beautifully. He might be acting in clothes that are 80 percent damp, but he's every bit as good as he was the first time he read this scene with Belinda in auditions. Subtle, complicated, wildly effective. When he finishes the scene and steps "offstage" behind the curtain we've set up, I squeeze his hand and say, "You should be an actor, Lucas."

He opens his jacket so I remember why he shouldn't.

I want to kiss him right there, but I resist.

He's even better in his third scene, the marriage proposal, which has killed me every time we rehearse it: the way he hesitates and grapples and swallows right before he spits out the words. There *is* a bit of Mr. Darcy in Lucas. Even Belinda, who has a hard time noticing anyone else onstage, seems to love it. Her fan flutters wildly all through the scene, which prompts Anthony to overact in our next dance-party scene where he's playing Bingley and I'm playing Jane. We're supposed to be pretending we're too shy to say how we feel, but Anthony gets so carried away that our scene culminates in a kiss we have certainly not planned.

"Sorry," he says right afterward, smiling at me. His hat is skewed and his ascot rumpled by the spontaneous moment.

"It's okay," I whisper, and the audience applauds, as they do for virtually everything we've done tonight, including walk onstage.

There are plenty of mistakes, like a terrible moment where Belinda falls over her dress, which is too long, and delivers her line from the ground as if she's hoping no one will notice. But for me, the biggest surprise of the night is the way I can see and feel the whole class on the edge of their seats, following the story. Francine nods her head wildly anytime a character talks about love, and Simon shakes his head if any character speaks disparagingly of anyone else. I can hear him in the audience saying, "That's not *right*."

Halfway through the show, we break for "questions and suggestions," and everyone has something to say: "She should just give him a *chance*."

"He shouldn't listen to his friend all the time."

"I just want everyone to fall in love!"

The last comment surprises me most of all because it's from Harrison, my first partner in the group, who, in all these weeks, has never once said he wants to go on a date or fall in love. Now I watch him zeroing in on Richard and I understand why he's hesitant about all this. Apparently it's possible to be legally blind, autistic, and gay.

I don't know if Richard sees this, too, but he and Lucas seem comfortable enough at our "intermission discussion" for me to leave them fielding questions while I take Belinda and Anthony for a quick trip to the bathroom. This is another quirk I've learned working with these two.

They can seem so high-functioning—memorizing their lines and discussing Jane Austen—but would definitely get lost if I told them, "The bathroom is three doors down on the left."

Alone in the hallway, I tell them they're both doing a great job. Belinda is grinning ear to ear, happy in a way I haven't seen her be in ages.

"I was great, wasn't I!" she says, clapping her hands.

Anthony can't take his eyes off her. "Very great, Beminda."

"So were you, Anthony! That was so good when you kissed her." I laugh at this. I wasn't sure how Belinda would react to Anthony's spontaneous stage moment, but she's right not to be jealous. It was a great, actorly flourish.

"I have to say, I think it really worked, Anthony," I tell him. "It took people by surprise and grabbed their attention."

"I was great, Beminda. Did you hear that?"

I remind them that we're not done yet, we still have the second half—two scenes—to go, and Belinda turns to me: "If this is shown on TV, do you think the football team will watch it?"

Her question takes me by surprise and then I think of the scene Lucas described to me: Ron Moody screaming at her, the rest of the team running over her. In three weeks of working together, she's never once mentioned the football team, but how could they ever be far from her thoughts? I don't want to dismiss the fear I see flashing in her eyes. "It's not on TV *yet*," I explain slowly. "They're making a recording that *could* be on TV, but it doesn't have to be." Lucas had already told me they sometimes film events they don't put on the air. He meant this to be a comfort. *If we flame out completely, we can cancel.*

Belinda considers this for a minute and says that she wants *some* people to see this—her mother and grandmother, her teachers and friends from school—but she definitely doesn't want the football boys to see it.

I think about my original impulse a month ago—let's get the football team to act with Belinda! Let them see how talented she is! She's demonstrating something I am only just learning myself: *Choose carefully the people whose approval you seek.* This whole performance, my eyes have been flicking nervously to Chad sitting in the front row with two conspicuously empty seats beside him. Why do I even care what he thinks?

Lucas was right to keep the football team away from Belinda. Instead of saying any of this, I stay with the question she's asked. "If it's shown on cable access TV, it isn't likely they'd see it, but they *could*. If you don't want that, we could arrange something else."

"Like what?"

"Like—" I think quickly. "We could arrange a private screening at school. For your classmates and teachers." Suddenly the idea doesn't seem bad. "We could do the same thing we're doing here—talk about the issues the story raises . . ."

She nods, still thinking. "Maybe that's better. Maybe that's what we should do."

CHAPTER NINETEEN
BELINDA

I AM HAPPY WHEN IT'S over.

It wasn't a perfect play but that was okay. Anthony got a little too enthusiastic and I fell down but I don't know if people noticed those things. It seems like everyone followed the story and liked how all the characters ended up with someone else at the end.

So that was good.

And I was happy when Emily said it doesn't have to be on TV, maybe we can do a special showing for just the people we want to see it. That means I can sit with Mom and Nan and watch it with them. Plus, we can explain it to our school friends so they understand it.

Now it's over which means I'm relieved and also nervous again. It's time for the party and the ballroom dance class to set up. They have to move all the chairs they were just sitting in to watch our show. Some people move their chair a few feet, then sit down to rest. It makes me want to shout,

"LET'S GO, PEOPLE, OR THERE WON'T BE ANY TIME TO DANCE!" If Nan were here, she would tell me it's rude to yell at people, especially when we're all wearing fancy dresses and getting ready to ballroom dance. "You can't just look like a lady," Nan says. "You have to act like one, too!"

Nan is right.

There are lots of girls here looking and acting like ladies. There is one with long red hair and a pretty tiara. There is another wearing a sparkly purple dress that I love. If I ever get to sign up for this class, I will ask Nan to make me a special dress out of the sparkliest material we can find. If she says, "No, it's too sparkly," I'll say, "Please, just this once."

Because I see it's going to take a long time before we start dancing, I leave the main room to look for Anthony who I haven't seen since we took our bows.

One bad thing about Anthony is that he falls asleep very easily, especially if we've had a lot of excitement to tire us out. This always happens any time our classroom takes a field trip which isn't very often so maybe we get over-excited, but every time, on the van ride home, Anthony falls asleep. That's why I'm not surprised after the play when I look in the dressing room and there he is, asleep in a desk chair.

I don't want to wake him, so I sit down quietly next to him with a plate of food I know he'll like.

Then I cough so he'll wake up which he does. "Here, Anthony," I say. "I brought you some food. You should rest for now but when you're done resting, you should think about maybe coming out to the party and dancing with me." I thought it would be hard or maybe embarrassing to ask him this, but it's not. He smiles.

"O-kay. I'll dance with you. Now?"

"Not now. First they have to show us how to ballroom dance, then we have to do it."

He's smiling but he still looks sleepy, like his eyes are about to close.

"You can sleep for now, it's okay. I'll wake you up when it's time."

"I don't want to sleep anymore, Beminda," he says and smiles at me in this new way he has.

Uh-oh, I think. Here it comes. I can tell he's going to ask about kissing. Then it's funny. He doesn't say anything, I do. "Do you want to kiss now, Anthony? Because the play is over and we can if you want to."

He doesn't do anything silly like clap his hands which makes me glad. "Yes," he says. "I want to very much."

I move my chair closer and he moves his chair closer, too. "I haven't done this before." I didn't mean to tell him this but now I have.

"I know," he says. "It's okay. It'll be okay."

"I don't know a lot of things like whether you keep breathing or not." I forgot that I didn't want to tell him this either and now it's too late.

"You should keep breathing, I think." When he says it, it sounds like "briefing."

"Okay."

Then he says I should stop talking because he thinks you can breathe and kiss at the same time but you can't talk and kiss.

I say, "Okay, that makes sense."

And then we kiss and I'm surprised because I like it a lot more than I thought I would. It's not scary or like we're different people. It's Anthony and me and it's so nice we start laughing a little. He wants us to push our chairs even closer which we do. Then he says, "Or you could sit on my lap."

I don't know what to do. I've never seen that in a movie but I want to say, "Okay." So I do. I stand up and move so I can sit in his lap and we can keep kissing with our arms all the way around each other. It feels different but good. It feels like something I never thought I'd feel. Like maybe I'm on TV or else I'm part of something I only thought I'd ever see on TV. I'm not sure, but it's nice.

A few minutes later, we go into the big room where the chairs are cleared away and food is set up and I find Emily and Lucas sitting together. I'm holding my shoe box of presents I made for Ron. Mom has been helping me put them back together so I can give them tonight as cast presents for my new friends. This time I can see Emily and Lucas are definitely holding hands. I walk over to them with my box and ask, "Are you boyfriend and girlfriend now?"

He looks at her and turns red again which makes me remember this is a personal private question and I shouldn't have asked it.

Then, even though he's red, he says, "We're thinking about it, Belinda. We've liked getting to know each other, working on this. So . . . maybe yes—we're headed in that direction."

"I've decided Anthony is definitely my boyfriend and I'm going to be his girlfriend, too."

"That's great!" Emily says, smiling like she means it. "We really like Anthony a lot."

She looks like she wants to hold Lucas's hand again.

"It's okay with me if you hold hands," I say. "I don't mind."

She laughs even though I'm not trying to be funny. Then she takes his hand.

"I have presents I want to give you guys and then I think you should ballroom dance with me and Anthony. But first Lucas has to bow and ask you to dance. That's the rule."

I open my box. I want to save the best present for Anthony but I have plenty in here to choose from. My mom and I found some old things we never gave anyone before. There's a Christmas tree ornament and a candlestick holder with dried flowers glued to it. I give Emily the candleholder and Lucas the ornament. "These are presents to say thank you for putting on my show. I made them myself because it made me very happy to be in it."

I'm surprised at how I almost start to cry saying this. I don't know why, because the play is over and I don't need to be nervous anymore. I'm not sad about anything. I'm happy, but maybe happy is a little like sad because I do start to cry.

They love their presents and hug me.

I say, "Okay, that's enough. I don't like hugs that much."

A few minutes later, the music starts and I panic for a second. I don't know what to do. The other couples are holding up their arms and getting into position. I don't know how we do this or where we put our arms. Anthony is standing beside me. All I know is this: "First you have to ask me to dance and bow."

"Okay." He bows nicely. "You wanna dance, Beminda?"

"Yes, thank you," I say. We walk out to the dance floor and suddenly I feel different. I look like Elizabeth Bennett and I feel like her, too. I have my Mr. Darcy and we're about to dance.

"Dancing is the first step toward falling in love," Nan used to say about being in dance class and meeting my grandpa. It's a line from *Pride and Prejudice* so it must be true.

We look at the other couples to figure out where to put our hands. It doesn't feel like hugging which is nice. There's space between us except we're connected and we have to move together so we need to be quiet and pay attention to the music. It's easier for me to do this if I close my eyes so I do that and it works. We move perfectly without crashing into each other or anyone else. At the end, I'm so happy I start crying again.

I look over and see Emily and Lucas. They're still sitting in their chairs not dancing. Maybe they're scared or maybe they don't know how either.

Then I'm surprised. Lucas stands up next to Emily. He says something and bows really low. It makes me think maybe they don't know any more than Anthony and I do. So he's doing what I told him to which is bow when he asks her to dance. She smiles and holds out her hand so he can lead her back out to the dance floor. Pretty soon they're dancing, too. They still don't look quite as good as Anthony and I do, but they're close.

That makes me feel good.

EMILY

AFTER IT'S ALL OVER, Richard and I stand outside while Lucas helps the cable access TV people load their equipment into their truck.

"Lucas will just be a minute," I say. "We're giving him a ride, too."

"So speaking of Lucas." Richard smiles. "Some of us have a little bet that you and he are maybe more than just fellow felons doing your community service—would you care to comment on that?"

I look up at him and laugh. "Which way did you bet?"

"I'm not going to say until you answer."

"You bet yes, didn't you, because you think you know me so well."

"I do know you better than you know yourself, which is why I bet yes. Candace doesn't believe it's possible;

neither does Barry. But Weilin and I know better. We've seen the evidence."

"What evidence?"

"You never look at his table at lunch. You also never mention him, even in passing. Plus the passenger seat in your car is about six inches back from where it usually is."

I think about watching Belinda and Anthony tonight and the way they took care of each other. With everything that's happened to her, I don't know how she's remained fearless in a way that I've never been, and have never seen in my friends. We've tiptoed through high school, expecting nothing good to happen. Afraid of the worst, we've limited ourselves, and here is Belinda, who saw the worst and didn't do the same. I want to follow her lead. I don't want to be afraid of everything I don't know about the future.

"Okay, fine, you're right, but not that much has happened," I say, blushing. "He broke up with Debbie and I guess we like each other, but we decided not to go out or do anything officially until after the play is over."

He's really smiling now. "So I guess you're really happy the play is over."

"I am," I say, and we both laugh.

"It's great, Em. I'm happy for you. I'm not sure I understood it until I came tonight, but now I do. This was great. All of it. I like these people."

"I'm so happy you were here."

In truth I don't know what part of this night to be

happiest about—making it through the play, or Richard being here.

In the car driving home, Richard is chattier than usual. "You want to know what song was number one on the Billboard charts the week I was born?"

I smile. Apparently he got the chance to talk to Harrison.

"'It's Raining Men.' Can you believe that? I'm interpreting this as an extremely positive sign for the future."

I don't believe it, actually. In class a few weeks ago, Harrison admitted that it's impossible for him to remember all the Billboard number-one hits, so he fudges the ones he isn't sure of.

"It's a *great* sign for the future," I say, smiling at him.

"Watch the road there, Em," Lucas says. "Shoulders aren't lanes you're meant to drive in."

"Sorry," I say, adjusting the wheel. "I'm just happy."

Lucas smiles and reaches over to adjust the wheel himself. "So am I," he says. "Just aim it straight, though. I'll do the wheel, you do the pedal stuff."

After we drop Richard off, Lucas asks me to pull over to the side of the road so he can drive. "This isn't about your driving, I swear," he says.

He gets out of the car and we meet in the front, in the dark triangle between the two headlights. "I just wanted to do this," he says and pulls me into a kiss.

It's warm and delicious and more of a real kiss than anything we've let ourselves have until now. "You were great tonight," I whisper.

"No, I wasn't," he says. "But here's why I'm happy. I knew I'd have that panic thing, and then I got through it! I wasn't awesome, but that part was awesome! I did it!"

"And you met my friend."

"I like him. He's nice."

"He likes you, too. Maybe you could—I don't know—eat lunch with us sometime?"

"You mean leave the table full of assholes? Yeah, I don't think I'd mind that too much."

"You wouldn't?"

"I really wouldn't."

He kisses me again. Strangely, considering how much sweating he was doing earlier, he doesn't smell bad. In fact, he smells clean. When I tell him this, he says, "Belinda gave me some powder. She said I should use it before I dance with you."

"And you did?"

"I was desperate. This was our big night and I looked like I'd just run a marathon wearing a suit."

I laugh. "So it was a good idea. She's full of good relationship advice, it turns out."

When we're back in the car, I ask Lucas if he remembers where the gas pedal is, and the brake pedal and all that. He gives me a funny look. "I probably shouldn't tell you this, but I've been driving for a while now."

"Are you telling me you didn't need rides this whole time?"

Now he's blushing. "Not really."

He turns on the radio and pulls out slowly. After a few minutes, I realize he drives even more cautiously than I do. "Is thirty-five about the speed you always go?"

He squeezes my hand. "Didn't your list of qualities in a perfect boyfriend say, 'Sweats a lot when he gets nervous' and 'Drives like an old lady'? I thought I read those two things."

I laugh pretty hard. "I wrote them lightly in pencil because I didn't dare hope I could find them."

"That's what I thought."

"Once we get on the highway do you think you'll drive a little bit faster?" I ask.

"I don't know," he says. "Probably not. Is that a problem?"

ACKNOWLEDGMENTS

THIS BOOK WOULD NOT exist if I hadn't befriended an extraordinary group of women fourteen years ago, all mothers of young children with special needs, to start an organization called Whole Children. In the beginning our mission was to create a few after-school classes where our children could work on the skills they were so deficient in—gross motor, fine motor, and speech—in the company of other kids. In truth, I don't think we expected it to last much beyond those early years and our own desperate need for a little company. Then, slowly but surely, we watched our children surprise us on a regular basis—with the skills they were learning, the odds they were defying, and the friendships they were making. This book was written as Whole Children celebrated its amazing tenth anniversary with the over seven hundred children, young adults, and families we've served. I thank everyone who has joined us on this journey—as a teacher, a participant, or a cheerleader from the sidelines willing to donate your time and/or money. I have learned more about resilience, joy, happiness, and community sitting in that lobby than I have anywhere else, and you are all part of it.

This book would also not exist if I hadn't been allowed to watch the exceptional work of teachers Brian Melanson and Meghan Carroll, who pioneered a class called "Boundaries and Relationships" at the newly developed Milestones program—designed for the young adults our Whole Children constituents were becoming—to help them navigate their way toward more meaningful friendships. It would *definitely* not exist without the countless young adults I've befriended at Whole Children/Milestones, but especially the incomparable Molly Ciszewski, with her bright smiling face, her big romantic heart, and her wonderful mother, Lee.

I thank all my early readers who have given me more help than you will ever know: Mike Floquet, Carrie McGee, Valle Dwight, Melinda Reid, Katie McGovern, Bill McGovern, Monty McGovern, and Charlie Floquet.

Margaret Riley King has been a perfect agent match for this second half of my career with young adult and children's books. I am so grateful to have you on this journey with me. It's hard for me to imagine a better editor than Tara Weikum, who asks all the right questions and then trusts my instincts when I raise a few questions of my own. And Christopher Hernandez deserves a special nod because, apparently, I may be able to write books, but I certainly can't write titles. He thought of not only this title but—with his characteristic quiet modesty—also the title for my next book as well. A huge thanks to the rest of the Harper team, who are all so smart about books, in addition to being so good at what they do—Christina Colangelo, Gina Rizzo, Ann Shen, Sarah Creech, and Alison Donalty.

This story is partly about the extraordinary power of theater and being on stage for teens and young adults with disabilities. I want to thank John Bechtold at Amherst Regional High School, who in no way reflects the drama teacher in this book, for the opportunity he's given my son and others like him to fully participate in their school musicals.

And last but not least, no one was luckier than I with the family I married into. I want to thank *all* the Floquets and Pentzes, especially Joanne, for filling my summers with so much happiness and the most peaceful place on earth to write. And Mike, Ethan, Charlie, and Henry, who give me more joy than they will ever know.